The Italian's Love-Child

Three hot-blooded, arrogant Mediterranean millionaires… Three women with very special secrets!

Three passionate, sensual romances from three favourite Mills & Boon authors!

In April 2009 Mills & Boon bring you
two classic collections, each
featuring three favourite romances
by our bestselling authors…

THE ITALIAN'S LOVE-CHILD

The Italian's Stolen Bride by Emma Darcy
The Marchese's Love-Child
by Sara Craven
The Italian's Marriage Demand
by Diana Hamilton

RECLAIMING HIS WIFE

The Ruthless Marriage Bid
by Elizabeth Power
Back in Her Husband's Bed
by Melanie Milburne
The Prodigal Wife by Susan Fox

The Italian's Love-Child

THE ITALIAN'S STOLEN BRIDE
by
Emma Darcy

THE MARCHESE'S LOVE-CHILD
by
Sara Craven

THE ITALIAN'S MARRIAGE DEMAND
by
Diana Hamilton

MILLS & BOON
Pure reading pleasure

*Harlequin Mills & Boon Limited,
Eton House, 18-24 Paradise Road, Richmond, Surrey TW9 1SR*

THE ITALIAN'S LOVE-CHILD
© by Harlequin Enterprises II B.V./S.à.r.l 2009

The Italian's Stolen Bride, The Marchese's Love-Child and *The
Italian's Marriage Demand* were first published in Great Britain
by Harlequin Mills & Boon Limited in separate, single volumes.

The Italian's Stolen Bride © Emma Darcy 2005
The Marchese's Love-Child © Sara Craven 2004
The Italian's Marriage Demand © Diana Hamilton 2005

ISBN: 978 0 263 87128 9

05-0409

*Printed and bound in Spain
by Litografia Rosés S.A., Barcelona*

THE ITALIAN'S STOLEN BRIDE

by

Emma Darcy

Initially a French/English teacher, **Emma Darcy** changed careers to computer programming before the happy demands of marriage and motherhood. Very much a people person, and always interested in relationships, she finds the world of romance fiction a thrilling one and the challenge of creating her own cast of characters very addictive.

**Don't miss Emma Darcy's exciting new novel,
Ruthless Billionaire, Forbidden Baby, available in
July 2009 from Mills & Boon® Modern™.**

CHAPTER ONE

'REMEMBER Skye... Skye Sumner...'

It was a shock to hear the name, falling from his brother's lips in a laboured whisper. Luciano Peretti frowned at the dark anguish in Roberto's eyes. Why speak of *her* now? Why waste any time at all on *her* when time was so precious?

In a few minutes Roberto would be wheeled out of this intensive care cubicle for the surgery that might or might not save his life. A fifty-fifty chance, the doctors had told the family. Their parents were out in the waiting room with the priest and Roberto's wife because of his brother's request to speak to him alone, and it seemed crazy to bring up Skye Sumner—an old wound between them that Luc had long since set aside for the sake of family harmony.

'Water under the bridge,' he muttered, wanting to dismiss whatever lingering guilt Roberto felt over the betrayal involved. 'Forgiven and forgotten,' he added for extra assurance.

'No, Luc.' It obviously pained him to speak but the determination to get out what he wanted to say demanded respect for the effort. 'I lied. It wasn't Skye...in the photos. She was never with me...like that. I set it up...to get her out of your life.'

Not Skye?

Luc's whole body clenched in denial. It couldn't be true. It was too...monstrous! Yet why would

5

Roberto make such a statement, a confession of such destructive deceit, unless he wanted—needed—to clear his conscience?

And if what he said was true... Horror swept through Luc's mind, unlocking a sealed compartment of memories, letting loose the ghosts of intense hurt and fury, images of the damning photos that had driven him to cut Skye Sumner out of his life. Roberto having sex with her, the raspberry birthmark on her thigh, the long blonde hair streaming across the pillow, the distinctive bracelet—three circles of white, rose and yellow-gold—around her wrist.

Her face—the incredibly appealing face with joy always sparkling in vivid blue eyes, the sexy full-lipped mouth that had so many different smiles, the fascinating dimples that came and went—had been hidden by Roberto's head, bent low as though he was whispering something in her ear, but Luc had not doubted it was Skye. The hair, the long lissome legs, the birthmark, the bracelet...

Apart from which, Roberto had backed up the evidence, admitting to a *playboy dalliance* with her, belligerently stating he'd seen Skye first, and why shouldn't he have her when she was willing?

Willing to laugh with Roberto, flirt with him... Luc had dismissed it as just light-hearted fun between them, glad that Skye had felt comfortable with at least one member of his family. He'd actually felt grateful to his brother...until the photos had blasted him into a different reality.

Blinded by the unbearable images, he'd seen no reason to suspect a set-up, no reason to accept Skye's wild denials, no reason to believe her explanation that she'd mislaid the bracelet, then miraculously found it, no reason to think anything but she was a two-timing slut who'd enjoyed having both brothers.

'Why?' The word croaked from his throat—a throat that had tightened from a wild melee of surging emotions. 'I *loved* her, Roberto.'

He rose to his feet, hands clenched, barely able to contain the violence erupting in him. If his brother wasn't half-dead already, lying in front of him as white as the sheet covering his broken body...

'Why?' he cried again, struggling to understand such—such malignance. From his own brother whom he'd trusted...trusted ahead of Skye...because he was family and family honour meant his word was his bond. 'What satisfaction could it have given you? Destroying my love for her...'

Stabbing me so deeply in the heart, I've never let any other woman into it.

'Dad wanted her out.'

A judgement Luc had flouted.

'Not suitable.'

A ruling made.

A sad irony glittered through the pain in Roberto's eyes as he struggled to spell out the rest. 'He had Gaia...picked out for you.'

Gaia Luzzani, who had never sparked one bit of sexual interest in Luc. Gaia, whom Roberto had married, earning their father's approval and placing himself to eventually take over the Luzzani multi-million dollar construction business—a business that complemented the Peretti property development company. The irony was that the grandchildren so eagerly anticipated by both Italian families had not been born.

Gaia had suffered two miscarriages so far, and if Roberto died...

'I was...jealous of you, Luc. The oldest son. The favoured son. I wanted Dad...to turn to me...have confidence in me...'

Luc shook his head, not knowing what to answer. His mind was spinning, trying to put the pieces together. 'Doesn't matter,' he growled, dropping back onto the chair under the weight of crushing despair.

Life had moved on. Six years had passed and there'd be no getting back with Skye. She wouldn't have a bar of him after the way he'd brutally dismissed everything she'd said, rejecting everything she was.

And facing him was his brother who might die in the next few hours. What good would it do to rail against him when his thinking had been dominated by their father...their conniving, determined to get his own way father!

Luc brought his own will to bear on what had to be done now—let his brother be at peace with himself before the operation. He took a deep breath and spoke soothing words. 'I'm sorry if I made life difficult for you, Roberto...being the first son.'

'Not your fault.'

The struggle for more breath was dreadful to watch. Smashed ribs, so much internal damage from the car accident...it was a wonder Roberto was still alive. And conscious.

'Got to tell you—'

'You've said enough,' Luc cut in tersely, wanting to block out thoughts of Skye and determined to save his brother any more extreme distress. 'It's okay. I'll deal with it.'

'Listen...' His eyes begged patience.

Luc waited, hating having to watch Roberto dragging up the effort to say more.

'Skye...was pregnant...'

'What?' Luc's mind reeled again. His memory of her denied any sign of pregnancy and she certainly hadn't told him there was any chance of one. She'd been on the pill. Yet the certainty in his brother's eyes made Luc question, 'How do you know?'

'Her stepfather came to Dad...with proof.'

'Why not to me?'

'He was...after money.'

'Did he get it?'

'Yes. I don't know if Skye...had the child...but you might have one...somewhere, Luc.' Tears filmed the pain and his eyelids closed over them as he heaved for more breath and choked out, 'I leave none.'

'Don't give up, Roberto!' Luc commanded. 'Don't you dare give up! You're my brother, dammit, and I don't care what you've done or not done!'

A faint smile tilted his mouth. 'I liked it...when we were kids...and you were the leader, Luc.'

'We had a lot of fun,' he gruffly agreed.

'Sorry...the fun...got lost.'

'We can have more together, Roberto,' Luc promised, fighting the finality he felt coming from his younger brother. He reached out and grasped his hand, willing his own strong life-force into the broken body on the bed. 'You'll make it through the operation. I won't let you die on me.'

The faint smile lingered.

The hospital orderlies came to take Roberto to the operating theatre. Luc had to let go, get out of the way. He found himself hopelessly tongue-tied, wanting to say more, yet floundering in the face of imminent separation...possibly final separation. It was Roberto who spoke the last words between them.

'Find...Skye.'

CHAPTER TWO

SKYE enjoyed walking her five-year-old son home from school. Matt was always bubbling over with news of what he'd done: the activities in the class-room, praise he'd received from the teacher, games he'd played with his new friends. Today he was burst-ing with pride at having shown off his reading skills, having been asked to read a story to the whole kin-dergarten class.

'What was the story about?' she inquired.

'A rabbit. His name was Jack and…'

Skye smiled as he recounted every detail of the story for her. Matt was so bright, so advanced for his age. She had worried about him fitting in with other five-year-olds who had yet to learn what he had some-how absorbed just through her reading bed-time stories to him every night. But he was still very much a little boy at heart and loved having play-mates.

It was now a month since he'd started school—no tears from him at having to leave his mother for most of the day. Excitement had sparkled from his lively blue eyes as he'd waved her goodbye, more than ready to charge straight into the new adventure of a bigger world for him. So far it was proving a very happy one.

Much to her relief.

It wasn't easy being a single mother with no-one

close to advise her or simply listen to her concerns. Matt seemed well adjusted to their situation. In fact, he'd coped extremely well with it, rarely pestering her when she was working with clients. Though now he was at school with children from normal families…what was she going to say when he asked about *his* father? As he inevitably would.

For so long there had just been the two of them. Matt didn't remember his grandmother, who'd died only eighteen months after he'd been born. And Skye herself had been the only child of an only child—no aunts or uncles or cousins. Her pregnancy, having the baby, caring for her mother through the bouts of chemotherapy that had proved useless in the end…the friendships she'd made at university had just dwindled away. Then setting up her massage business…no time for making social contacts.

If she'd gone out to work…but she hadn't wanted to leave Matt to a baby-sitter or put him in day-care. He was *her* child. Best to work at home, she'd thought. However, it had been a very closeted life these past few years. A lonely life.

Now that it was opening up for Matt, she should start re-thinking her own situation, look at other options for her future, maybe complete the physiotherapy course she'd had to drop, put herself in the way of meeting a possible husband, a father for Matt.

They turned the corner into the street where they lived and Matt instantly broke off his school chatter, pointing excitedly as he cried, 'Wow! Look at that red car, Mummy!'

Her gaze had already jerked to it. A red Ferrari— instantly recognisable to her, having been driven around in one by Luc Peretti. It was like a stab to her heart seeing it here, opening up painful memories, especially as she'd just been thinking about a father for Matt.

'Could we get a car like that?' he asked, clearly awe-struck by its brilliant colour and racy style, as she'd once been.

'We don't need a car, Matt.'

Nor could she afford one. Paying the rental on their small, two-bedroom cottage, plus living expenses, ate up most of her income. What she saved was emergency money. In fact, given that this neighbourhood was very modest real estate, and relatively cheap because of being under the flight-path to Mascot Airport, she wondered why such a classy and extravagant car was parked in their street.

'Other Mummies pick up their kids from school in cars,' Matt argued.

Skye grimaced at the all-too-true comment. The comparisons were starting. She tried emphasising the positive side of their own situation. 'I guess those kids don't live so close to school, Matt. We're lucky, being able to walk and enjoy the sunshine.'

'It's not so good when it rains,' he pointed out.

'I thought you liked wearing your yellow rain boots.'

'Yes, I do.'

She smiled at him. 'And splashing in puddles.'

'Mmm...' His gaze darted across the street to the red Ferrari. 'But I like that car, too.'

Skye rolled her eyes to the seductive object of little boys' dreams and shock ripped through her, thumping her heart, halting her feet, making her stomach contract with tension. The driver's door was open and the man emerging from the car...it couldn't be, her mind reasoned frantically.

Then he turned his head, looking directly at her, and it was. It was Luc Peretti! No mistaking those distinctively carved features, the hard handsome maleness of that face, the riveting, heavily lashed, dark eyes, the thick black hair dipping with a wave at his right temple, just as Matt's did.

Matt!

A wave of panic churned through the shock. Had Luc somehow found out she'd kept her baby—the money given to her not used for an abortion? But why look for a child who—in Luc's mind, she thought savagely—might not even be his? Not Roberto's, either, given he believed she was a bed-hopping slut.

He half-turned to close and lock the car door. Maybe she was panicking for nothing. One look... She and Matt were the only people walking nearby. He could have been checking them out before leaving his high-class car—harmless people, just a young mother escorting her son home from school.

She didn't look eye-catching with all her hair drawn into a single plait down her back, no make-up apart from a touch of pink lipstick, unremarkable clothes—just white cotton slacks and T-shirt, which she wore to work in. He might not have recognised her at all, might have parked in this street for some other reason entirely, not because *she* lived here.

'Mummy?'

She tore her gaze from Luc Peretti to look down at her son. 'Yes?'

'Why are we stopped?'

Because I'm frozen with fright.

Skye quickly drew in a quick breath and came up with, 'I've just remembered I've forgotten something.'

'What?'

'Something... I meant to do for a client. I'll do it tomorrow,' she said, desperately temporising as she frantically willed Luc Peretti to be walking away from them, setting her free from this dreadful inner angst.

'Better put it on your list,' Matt advised, grinning at her habit of making careful lists for everything. 'Then you won't forget.'

'I'll do that as soon as we get home.'

'Well, come on.' He grabbed her hand to urge her forward again.

Skye forced her feet to move. She had to look, to see where Luc Peretti was now. The jolt to her heart was worse this time. He was crossing the road to *their* sidewalk, watching them, his face set in grimly determined purpose. If Matt hadn't been tugging on her hand, Skye might have stopped dead again. As it was, she felt weirdly disembodied from her legs which kept pumping forward, matching her son's steps.

There was no avoiding a confrontation now, she told herself. Luc Peretti was clearly intent on one. Having reached the sidewalk, he moved straight to the front gate of their house and stood there waiting for them, his gaze trained on Matt as they walked towards them.

Looking for some likeness to himself, Skye thought, the panic rising again, making her dizzy with turbulent fears. The Peretti family was so wealthy. If Luc decided to make a claim on Matt...and God knew she'd had experience of them playing dirty, getting some woman to look like her in the photos, stealing her bracelet and returning it so she'd be wearing it when Luc came to accuse her...accuse her and dump her for an infidelity she'd never committed.

Ruthless people.

Cruel people.

Callous people, uncaring of the lives of others.

She fiercely told herself Luc couldn't be sure Matt was his child. Yes, he had olive skin, very dark hair and long thick eyelashes, but he also had her blue eyes, her mouth, and certainly her more sunny personality. Luc would have to get a DNA test to be sure. Could she refuse it, fight it?

'Do you know that man at our gate, Mummy?'

No point in denying it. Luc was bound to address her by name. 'Yes. Yes, I do, Matt.'

'Can I ask him for a ride in his red car?'

'No!' The word exploded from the volcano of fear inside her. She instantly halted and dropped into a crouch, turning Matt for an urgent face-to-face talk. 'You must never get in his car. Never go with him anywhere. Do you hear me, Matt?'

Her vehemence frightened him. She could see him trying to understand and her heart ached for the simplicity of their life which was being so terribly threatened.

'Is he a bad man?' His voice quavered, reflecting her alarm.

Was Luc bad? She had loved him once, loved him with an all-consuming intensity that had made his disbelief in her integrity totally devastating. Even now she couldn't bring herself to say he was bad, though he'd let himself be deceived by his family, making himself one of them, against her.

'You just mustn't go with anyone unless I say it's all right. No matter how much you want to, Matt.' Her hands squeezed his anxiously. 'Promise me?'

'Promise,' he repeated, troubled by her intensity.

'I'm going to give you the door-key now. When we get to the front gate, you go straight inside and wait for me. Have your milk and cookies. Okay?'

'Are you going to talk to the man?'

'Yes. I'll have to. He won't go away until I do.'

Matt shot a frowning look at Luc. 'He's big. I can call the 'mergency number for help, Mummy.'

She'd taught him that—a necessary precaution since she was the only adult in the house and if something happened to her... Skye tried to calm herself, realising Matt was picking up on her fear, wanting to fix what he sensed was a bad situation.

'No, there's no need for that,' she assured him. 'I'll only be a few minutes.' She took the door-keys out of her pants pocket and pressed them into his hand. 'Just do as I say, Matt. Okay?'

He nodded gravely.

She straightened up and they resumed their walk, hands tightly linked, mother and son solidly together. And let no one try to separate them, Skye thought on a savage wave of determination.

Luc had shifted his gaze to her, a dark burning gaze that made her pulse race and her inner muscles quiver. She lifted her chin high in a proud defiance of his power to affect her in any way whatsoever. The time had long gone when she had giddily welcomed him into her life, when she had so completely succumbed to his many seductive attractions.

He was big in Matt's eyes but in Skye's, that translated to powerful...tall, broad-shouldered, slim-hipped, a strong muscular physique with not an ounce of flab anywhere. He had the kind of perfect masculinity that automatically drew a woman's attention, looking strikingly sexy in any clothes, especially none at all.

He was wearing black jeans, no doubt with a designer label. A black sports shirt showed off the impressive width of his chest and the bared strength of his forearms. One hand was gripping the top of her gate, as though ready to block any escape from him.

He had no right to. No rights at all where she was concerned. And he still had to prove he had any paternal right to Matt. She glared furious independence at him, shifted her gaze pointedly to the trespassing hand, then back to him with a belligerent challenge. He dropped his hold on her property, moving the offending hand into a gesture of appeal.

'Could I have a word with you, Skye?'

The deep timbre of his voice struck more painful memories, how he'd used it to make her believe he loved her, intimate murmurs in bed, reinforced by how he'd touched her, kissed her. A flood of heat raced up her neck and scorched her cheeks—shame at having let him remind her of how it had once been between them.

She kept a safe distance, halting a metre away from him, a blazing demand in her eyes. 'Please move aside from the gate. I'll stay and have a word with you but my son needs to go inside.'

He opened it before stepping back, giving Matt free passage. 'I'd like you to introduce us,' he said, smiling down at the boy that might be his, pouring out all his Italian charm in case it was.

Steel shot up Skye's backbone. 'He's *my* child. That's all you need to know.' She released Matt's hand and nudged his shoulder forward. 'Go on now. Do as I told you.'

He obeyed, at least to moving past the opened gate. Then he stopped and turned, delivering his own childish challenge to Luc Peretti. 'Don't you hurt my Mummy!'

Luc shook his head, a surprisingly pained look on his face. 'I didn't come to hurt her. Just to talk,' he answered gently.

Matt glared at him a moment longer, then glanced uncertainly at Skye who gestured for him to leave them. Much to her relief, he did, running up the front path to the door. She watched him unlock it and close it behind him before she looked back at the man who had no right to be here. No moral right. And he had to know it!

'What do you want to say?' she clipped out, hating him for what he'd put her through, was putting her through now with this intrusion on their lives.

'He's my child, too, Skye,' he stated with not the slightest flicker of uncertainty in the darkly burning eyes.

'No, he's not,' she retorted vehemently, needing to sow doubt, to make him leave them alone.

'I've seen a copy of his birth certificate,' he started to argue. 'The date alone...'

'No father was named on it,' she whipped back. 'I

wrote *unknown*. After all, I was a bed-hopping slut, remember?'

He flinched at the hit. 'I was wrong about that.'

She raised a derisive eyebrow. 'A bit late to revise your opinion, isn't it?'

'I'm sorry. I should have believed you, Skye. You weren't the woman in the photos. I know that now.'

She wrenched her gaze away from the glittering apology in his. It didn't change anything. Nothing could change the deep, bitter hurts of the past, the grief, the hardships, the loss of all he'd taken from her on that one life-shattering night. And she would not let him soften her up with a facile apology.

Regathering her defences against the insidious attraction that could still tug at her, Skye swung her gaze back, hard and straight. 'How do you know it?' she mocked. 'Your brother was a starring player in those photos. Who better to believe?'

His jaw tightened. The expression in his eyes clouded, taking on a bleak distance. 'My brother... died...a month ago.'

Roberto dead?

So young?

The shock of Luc's flat statement completely smashed Skye's concentration on rejecting him as fast and as effectively as she could. An image of Roberto Peretti flew into her mind—a head of riotous black curls, wickedly flirtatious eyes, teasing smiles backing up his playboy charm, not as tall nor as solidly built as Luc, not as strikingly dynamic, but with a quick-silver energy that had instant appeal. She had liked him, laughed with him, but as far as serious attraction went, he'd always faded into insignificance beside Luc.

Roberto had been fun.

Until she'd seen him in the damning photos.

That reminder swiftly brought Skye back to her current crisis. 'I'm sorry for your loss, Luc,' she said stiffly. 'But it has nothing to do with me.'

'You were on his conscience just before he died. His last words were about you, Skye,' he said quietly.

So Roberto had confessed the truth, removing the totally undeserved stain on her character. And, of course, Luc would believe his brother's deathbed confession. 'It makes no difference,' she muttered.

'It does to me,' he shot at her.

'You don't count,' she flung back. 'You ceased to count for anything in my life a long time ago.'

He grimaced, sucked in a deep breath, then slowly nodded. 'Fair enough.' The concession was swiftly followed by more resolute purpose. 'But the fact of your pregnancy was kept from me until Roberto revealed it. And I now know there is a child to consider. *Our* child, Skye.'

'No. Mine!'

Everything within her revolted at any claim of possession from him. His ignorance of her pregnancy had no bearing on Matt's life—the life *she* had given Matt—the life the Peretti family had wanted to snuff out, along with all involvement with her.

Luc gestured an appeal for reason. 'DNA tests can prove—'

'Have you spoken to your father about this?' she cut in, needing to know if Luc was acting alone, without the backing of the very powerful and wealthy

Maurizio Peretti. The threat he embodied was bad enough, but if he had his father's approval to make this approach...

'It's none of his business,' came the terse reply.

'He made it his business,' Skye corrected him, relieved to be able to use her last piece of ammunition against any claim on Matt. 'Your father paid out a thousand dollars for an abortion. He killed *your* child, Luc.'

'No!' He shook his head, appalled at the accusation. 'He wouldn't do that. He'd *never* do that.'

'He did. So don't think you can resurrect a paternity issue six years down the track. My son is *my* son. I chose to have him.'

'Skye—' an anguished appeal in his eyes '—I had nothing to do with any of this.'

She hardened her heart against him. 'Yes, you did, Luc. You didn't believe me. You accepted what your family told you. Go back to them and the life they planned for you. You're not wanted here.'

The gate was still open.

He was clearly in shock over what she had revealed.

Skye took the chance he wouldn't try to stop her. With bristling dignity she stepped past him, closed the gate behind her without so much as a glance at him and proceeded up the path to the front door, her ears alert to any sound that might indicate pursuit, her heart pounding hard with the fear of not making good her escape.

Matt had left the key in the door for her.

Good boy! she thought in fierce relief.

Her whole body was tense, expecting a call or some

preventative action from Luc, but it didn't come. She unlocked the door, moved into the protective shelter of the house and closed out the man who should never have re-entered her life.

It wasn't fair.

It wasn't right.

Luc Peretti could only bring her more grief.

CHAPTER THREE

LUC barely controlled a burning rage as he drove up the grand carriage loop to the neo-Gothic mansion his father had bought at Bellevue Hill. Twenty million dollars he'd paid for it five years ago, and he could probably sell it for thirty now, given its heritage listing and commanding views of the Sydney Opera House and Harbour Bridge.

Twenty million for a piece of personal property.

Next to nothing for a grandson!

Paid off, Roberto had said. That hadn't added up to Luc when the private investigator had found Skye and her son living in a cheap rental at Brighton-Le-Sands. She hadn't even completed her physiotherapy course, working as a masseur to make ends meet. No car. No credit rating. No evidence of a nest-egg account anywhere.

He'd wondered if she'd torn up his father's cheque, scorning to take anything from a family who'd made her out to be little better than a whore. Her whole demeanour this afternoon had been stamped with steely pride, determined on rejecting anything he offered. Their child was *her* son. Hers alone. Sold to her for a thousand dollars—a measly thousand dollars!

Luc still could not bring himself to believe his father had paid her that sum for an abortion. Such an act was totally against Italian culture and Maurizio

Peretti was nothing if not traditionally Italian. He might want an unwanted bastard child to disappear, especially if it could become a glitch in the Peretti-Luzzani master plan, but demanding its life be ended? No.

Nevertheless, Luc was determined on confronting his father with the accusation, given Skye's belief in it.

He'd lost her—lost five years of his son's life—because he hadn't believed her. He was not about to repeat that mistake. Let his father answer for what had been done. And not done. Maybe then the truth could be pieced together.

He brought the Ferrari to a crunching halt at the front entrance to the huge sandstone home. Forty-five rooms, he thought derisively, more than enough to house a large extended family in the grandeur his father's ambition demanded. Roberto would have obliged with the desired grandchildren, but Roberto was dead and his childless widow had returned to the bosom of the Luzzani family for comfort. The nursery rooms were empty. So many rooms empty.

Luc felt the emptiness echoing all around him as he walked down the great hall to the sitting room his mother favoured. She was occupying her usual armchair, dressed in mourning black, drowning her sorrows with Bristol Cream Sherry as she watched the early evening news on television.

'Where's Dad, Mamma?' he asked from the doorway.

She didn't turn her head. In the dull flat tone that characterised her every utterance since Roberto's death, she answered, 'In the library.'

No interest in him. No interest in anything. Luc doubted she even heard or saw the news being reported. None of it impinged on her very protected life. But great wealth could not protect against miscarriages nor accidental death. Nor could it provide solace for the loss of her beloved younger son and all his life had promised.

He left her and moved on, bent on pursuing his own needs which were far more imperative right now. Besides, he remembered only too well his mother had not approved of Skye. If she had been in on the conspiracy, too... Luc gritted his teeth against the wave of violence that churned through him.

The machinations that had taken place behind his back were a dark ferment in his mind—a ferment he had to contain while he listened and observed, weighing whether he could even keep on being involved with his parents. Certainly, in Skye's mind, his family was *the enemy* to any future he might forge with his son. And she had no reason to think otherwise.

He entered the library without giving a courtesy knock on the door. His father sat at a magnificent mahogany antique desk, tapping at a pocketbook computer he carried with him everywhere, probably checking up on any movement in his investments. His agile brain kept track of an incredible array of figures which he could rattle out at any pertinent moment.

Luc had always admired his father—a formidable go-getter who knew what he wanted and went after it, using every resource he could pull into play. Maurizio Peretti had friends in politics, friends in the church, friends in many high places, all of them impressed by what he could do for them, and, of course, the occasional favour was asked and given in return.

But it wasn't just his accumulated wealth that impressed them. It was his business acumen and a charismatic presence that shouted leadership quality; the tall, powerful physique, the almost mesmerising intelligence in the commanding dark eyes, the thick thatch of wavy iron-grey hair, the hawkish nose, and the mouth that never spoke rubbish.

He looked up from his notebook, surprise and pleasure instantly lightening the air of deeply focused concentration. 'Luciano! Glad you came by! Have you spoken to your mother?'

Family first... Luc's mouth curled in black irony. He'd give his father *family!* He crossed the room in a few quick strides and tossed the large envelope he carried onto the desk. 'Something requiring your immediate attention, Dad,' he drawled.

His father frowned at the disrespect implicit in Luc's manner. 'What is this?' he demanded curtly.

'Photos. Remember the photos you presented to me six years ago?'

The frown deepened. 'Why would you keep them?'

'I didn't. These are new photos, Dad.'

'I don't understand.'

'You will. Since you seem reluctant to look at them, let me help.' Luc snatched back the envelope, ripped it open, removed its contents and slapped the photos one by one, face up, across his father's desk. 'Skye Sumner with my son,' he declared in bitter fury. 'My son who is now a schoolboy. My son whose first five years of life I have missed because I did not know of his existence. Look at him, Dad!'

The passionate outburst drew no more than a shuttered glance at the photos and a stoney-faced defence. 'How do you know it is your son?'

Luc's arm flew out in a fiercely dismissive gesture. 'Don't come at me with that.' He drew himself up in towering contempt. 'Roberto confessed to your indecent conspiracy against Skye on his deathbed. He told me about the pregnancy, told me you'd paid her off. Don't even start denying it!'

His father's mouth compressed into a thin line of distaste. He sat back in his antique studded leather chair and viewed Luc through narrowed eyes, eyes that were weighing options for dealing with this crisis. 'Surely, in hindsight, you realise she was an unsuitable wife for you,' he stated unequivocally.

'Don't go there, Dad,' Luc warned, hard ruthless steel in his own eyes. 'You've lost one son. You're very close to losing another.'

'I did what I thought was best for you, Luciano,' he said, attempting a tone of appeasement. 'You were blindly infatuated—'

'I'm here to give you one chance—' Luc held up his index finger for pointed emphasis '—one chance to answer Skye's accusation that you paid her off with a thousand dollars to have an abortion.'

'That's a lie!' He exploded up from his chair, hurling his hands out in furious counter-challenge. 'You see what a scheming little bitch she is, trying to turn you against me? I paid out one hundred thousand dollars, with more to come when it was needed!'

'Then why doesn't she have any money?' Luc bored in. 'Why is she living in borderline poverty?'

'She must be hiding it.'

'No, she's not. Trust me on this. A thorough investigation has been done. There is...*no money!* In fact, she has no support whatsoever. Her stepfather did a flit while she was still pregnant. Her mother died of cancer when the baby was only eighteen months old. She was left with nothing but old furniture and she has survived—*with my son*—by building up a modest massage business.'

'Massage,' his father jeered, his eyes flashing a filthy interpretation of that profession.

Luc's hands clenched. He barely held back the urge to smash his father's face in. 'Remedial massage,' he bit out. 'A natural offshoot from the physiotherapy course she was doing at university when I knew her— a course she didn't—couldn't—complete with neither the money nor support needed to go the distance. So the evidence—*the evidence, Dad!*—is all against your having paid her off with anything more than the thousand dollars Skye claims.'

His father bristled with offended dignity. 'You doubt my word?'

'I have every reason to doubt your word where Skye Sumner is concerned,' Luc fired at him point-blank, not giving a millimetre.

His father's chin lifted aggressively. 'I can prove the money was given. And more to come.'

'Then start proving it!'

'The papers are at my solicitor's office.'

'Call your solicitor. Get him to bring the papers here. Show them to me...before you have the chance to cook up more lies behind my back.'

For several tense moments the air between them was charged with Maurizio Peretti's fierce pride and

Luc's explosive mistrust—a mistrust that Maurizio finally realised could destroy everything between them. He reached for the telephone and began dialling.

Needing to put a cooling distance between himself and his father, Luc moved over to one of the tall, narrow, lancet windows which gave a limited view of the east garden. Limited views was not only a problem with the old-fashioned architecture of this house. The limited view his father had of Skye Sumner was deeply offensive to him, especially since she'd been innocent of the damning sins manufactured against her. He wasn't sure he could ever forgive his father for that. If the solicitor couldn't bring proof of some caring…

'John, I'm sorry to break in on your evening but this is an emergency. I need the Skye Sumner file and I need it now.'

Silence while the other man spoke.

'Yes,' his father replied tersely. 'I'm at home. Bring it here as soon as you can.'

End of conversation.

Luc didn't turn around. He had nothing more to say to his father at this point and the tension inside him needed some calming. Seeing Skye in the flesh today, being in touchable distance of her…it wasn't only his son he wanted. Had he ever stopped wanting her?

It had driven him mad, seeing her with Roberto in the photos, thinking of her giving his brother what he'd believed was all his, only his, the gift of herself in loving abandonment. Somehow he had to persuade her she could trust him with that gift again. Somehow…

'A trust fund was set up for the child's support and education,' his father stated, the leather of his chair creaking as he resumed his seat behind the desk to wait for the solicitor's arrival.

If that was true, there could not have been an instruction to abort the child. Not from his father. Yet Luc would not disbelieve Skye. So where had the instruction come from? Had one of his father's underlings decided that cutting corners would be the best result for his boss?

'All she had to do was apply in writing for funds to become available,' his father went on tersely, hating being in a defensive position.

'Then why didn't she?' Luc challenged, not bothering to even glance over his shoulder.

No answer to that.

Luc deduced the solicitor had told his father the file had not been re-opened since it had first been set up. It was the only answer that made sense of what he knew about Skye's life. Certainly *she* was not aware of any trust fund.

There was a drumming of fingertips on the highly polished desk. Then came the first line of counter-attack to the accusation of irredeemable guilt where caring for a grandchild was concerned.

'I dealt with the stepfather. Everything was worked through him. You said he did a flit before she had the child. If what you say about her circumstances is true, he must have scammed the money and never told her about the trust fund.'

The stepfather...neatly removing all responsibility from himself. But not blame, Luc thought viciously.

None of this would have happened without his father's controlling hand behind it.

'Then you made a huge mistake of judgement in trusting him, didn't you?' he mocked. 'As well as not caring enough to check up on what was happening to *my child.*'

'Luc...' It was a brusque appeal, looking for some foothold on a meeting ground where he could twist around to regain some credibility.

'Let's wait for the file to arrive. That might...' He half-turned to stare long and hard at the man who had interfered so intolerably with what should have been. '...might...' he bit out warningly, '...go some little way to restoring a viable relationship between us.'

'You're my son. What was done was done for—'

'Don't say *for me.* You weren't thinking of me. Nor Skye. Nor our child. You were thinking of what *you* wanted. When you stop thinking of what *you* want and start respecting what I want, perhaps we'll have something to talk about.'

'I'm giving you what you want. I called John to bring you the proof...'

'Step One.'

His chin came up aggressively. 'What is Step Two?'

'You will immediately start revising your attitude towards Skye Sumner. If you speak once more of her in any kind of deprecatory manner, I will walk out and I won't come back.'

He grimaced but didn't argue. 'Is there a Step Three?'

'Step Three is full acceptance of her and our son in my life. That means no undermining act behind my back. And believe me, I'll know about it if you so much as raise a finger to interfere between us again.'

A giving gesture was waved. 'If you want to take an interest in the boy...'

'Not just the boy. I intend to do everything within my power to persuade Skye Sumner to marry me.'

Shock cracked the facade of appeasement. 'Surely there's no need for that.' The words whipped out of him. 'I can understand about the boy...'

The violence Luc had held in check erupted, his body jerking into action, his legs closing the distance between them so fast, everything was a blur except the need to punch home his point. His fist crashed down on the desk, making his father flinch back in his chair.

'Understand *me!*' His eyes blazed unshakeable resolution as he reinforced it with all the turbulent passion stirred by the situation. 'Skye Sumner should have been my wife. I want her as my wife. And I will have her as my wife.'

CHAPTER FOUR

NOTHING felt safe anymore.

Skye told herself that was another reason why she had to meet Luc Peretti this morning. Ever since the solicitor had come, showing her all the legal documents and the private investigator's report on her stepfather, she had been feeling the power of the Peretti family closing around her, squeezing for a claim on Matt. She had to find out what their aim was—the end goal.

Right from her first encounter with Luc two weeks ago, she'd been afraid he wouldn't just walk away. Now she knew he'd confronted his father and moved relentlessly to demonstrate how terribly deceived she'd been by her stepfather. But that didn't make the Peretti family right in what they'd done, she argued to herself.

Her pulse kicked in shock as she glanced at the clock and saw it was already nine-thirty.

She had to get moving.

A last check in the door mirror of her bedroom showed she had eaten off some of her lipstick, probably from nervously chewing at her lips. Her hand was shaking as she quickly replenished it. Stupid to worry about her appearance, she thought. It didn't make any difference to what would happen.

Luc's mother would probably sniff her disapproval of the cheap cotton sundress she wore, but she wasn't meeting Luc's mother and never would again. It had been the hottest summer on record in Australia and even though it was now mid-March, the weather still hadn't cooled. She had a half-hour walk ahead of her and the sundress should keep her from feeling over-heated and sticky at the meeting with Luc.

She'd pulled her long hair into a clip at the back of her neck and she quickly jammed the wide-brimmed straw hat on her head, slid her feet into com-fortable sandals, grabbed her sunglasses and handbag, and left the house, her heart fluttering uncontrollably over having to deal with the man who knew he was Matt's father.

At least, he hadn't asked for Matt to accompany her. In fact, there had been no threatening pressure attached to his request for a meeting, as relayed by the solicitor. The choice of time and place had been hers and it was to be just the two of them.

The request had seemed reasonable, the meeting necessary, given the dreadful fraud her stepfather had perpetrated, including forging her signature on some papers, using her pregnancy to extort the awesome sum of money from the Peretti family.

One hundred thousand dollars!

Her mind still boggled over it.

And the cheque Luc had written to cover the loss of it was burning a hole in her handbag. It had been attached to all the other papers the solicitor had left with her, but she couldn't keep it. Firstly, the money had been stolen by her stepfather, not by Luc. Just because it was irrecoverable didn't make it right for her to accept full replacement of it.

Besides, if she was to stick to her independent

stance, she had to return the cheque, and meeting Luc was the most direct, most telling way to accomplish it. She had to make it clear to him that *she* hadn't asked for money and didn't want it now. None of it. No way could she use the trust fund. It would tie Matt to the Peretti family, and she didn't believe that was a good connection for him at all.

Tainted money.

Better not to owe the Peretti family anything.

She could manage to bring up Matt by herself.

Skye bolstered this determination with every step she took towards the meeting place—the waterfront park, directly across from the Brighton-Le-Sands Novotel Hotel, a public area which she could check out before showing up. It was just on ten o'clock— her stipulated time—when she reached the hotel and hurried up to the first floor to take the overhead walk-way spanning the busy coast road to the park. From there the whole area could be scanned.

She spotted Luc instantly, seated on a park bench under the shade of one of the Norfolk pines that skirted the shoreline. His head was turned towards the long runway at Mascot Airport where big jets were constantly landing or taking off. One arm was casually hooked over the back rest of the bench, making him look relaxed.

Skye certainly wasn't. The tension gripping her nerves was so bad, she paused to take several deep breaths, trying to calm herself. It was important to appear cool and confident, not get rattled. It was totally irrelevant that he was still the most attractive man she'd ever met, still able to tug at her physically. Luc Peretti and everything related to him had to be

ejected from her life. With this resolution firmly fixed
in her mind, she forced herself to walk on.

His gaze swung to her as she descended the steps
on the park side of the walkway. Although her thighs
started quivering, her legs kept carrying her down,
driven by sheer willpower. He stood up, waiting by
the park bench, watching her approach, his dark brilliant eyes keenly observing everything about her.

She was glad she'd armoured herself with sunglasses. Not only did they hide her thoughts and feelings, but they allowed her to return his scrutiny without being obvious about it. Again he was wearing
casual clothes; beige cotton slacks, a loose cotton knit
top in white and beige, V-necked, short sleeves—very
smart, undoubtedly expensive, but not intimidating.

Skye surmised he hadn't come to throw his weight
around. Or were the clothes another deception, meant
to put her off-guard while he set up the big guns to
attack her position?

His mouth twitched into a sensual little smile, making her acutely conscious that her sundress left a lot
of flesh bare.

Was it possible he still found her desirable?

Her stomach curled at the thought.

Worse—her pulse-rate zoomed into overdrive as
his smile widened and his eyes warmed with pleasure.

'Good to see you again, Skye,' he said with what
seemed genuine sincerity.

Her mind jammed for a moment, then spun with
wild speculation. Was this manner aimed at winning
her compliance with whatever he wanted? Did he
think she could forget how he'd spurned her? Casting

her out of his life on the very night she'd meant to tell him she was pregnant with his child!

A surge of anger spilled into a bitter outpouring. 'I can't say it's good to see you, Luc. I only came to return your cheque. To place it in your hands personally so it *can't* get mislaid or misappropriated or mis...anything else.'

She started fumbling with her handbag, desperately eager to get the zippered compartment open, extract the cheque, get rid of the burden of Peretti money.

'Skye, you're owed child support for the past five years,' he argued in a gentle, soothing tone. 'The law courts would award it to you.'

'I don't want it. I didn't ask for it,' she gabbled. The wretched zipper had stuck. 'I didn't know my stepfather had gone to your family for money until he handed me the thousand dollars for...for...'

'Yes, that was very clever of him, handing over enough money to convince you it was meant for an abortion. Which, of course, neatly tied off the scam for him. No child. No more interest from the Peretti family. No comeback for him to worry about.'

Luc rolled off his interpretation of the situation so fast, Skye was distracted by how closely it matched her own anguished reasoning. She stopped struggling with the zipper to stare at him. 'You believe me?'

'Without a doubt,' he assured her.

Which instantly played havoc with her heart. If only he had believed her against his brother and those terrible photos...

'It's abundantly clear that your stepfather saw the opportunity to milk the situation for all he could get, intending to feather his own nest,' Luc went on, reminding Skye he was working off evidence this time, as well.

His belief in her word meant nothing!

Easy enough to deduce the truth from the investigator's report, which had supplied the date when her stepfather had left Sydney, flitting off to the Gold Coast in Queensland. It had also stated the money had been gambled away and her stepfather's current credit rating was not only nil, but criminal charges were pending over embezzlement at the used car yard where he'd worked as a salesman.

Her stepfather!

Skye burned over the rotten deception he'd played.

'At least he isn't my real father,' she flashed at Luc. 'I don't have to live with him like you do yours.'

Maurizio Peretti had also played a rotten deception, keeping the news of her pregnancy from Luc, intent on feathering his nest with the *right* kind of woman for his precious son.

Skye resumed tugging at the zipper, telling herself it was stupid to be affected by anything Luc said. He had probably moved on to relationships with women who were far more compatible with his family. Which would make his father's judgement ultimately right.

'My father has been made very aware of my feelings about his past actions on my behalf,' Luc answered grimly. 'He knows not to interfere between us again.'

'I just don't want him or you or anybody employed by your family to interfere with *me*,' Skye said fiercely, finally getting the zipper open, removing the cheque and thrusting it at Luc. 'Take back your blood money. It won't buy me or Matt.'

He shook his head, leaving the cheque hanging from her hand. 'It wasn't meant to buy you, Skye. It was meant to contribute what a father should, at least in financial support, towards his child's upbringing.'

'I've managed without it all these years and I much prefer to keep it that way.'

'It wasn't right that you had to manage alone,' he strongly demurred.

'Do you think this makes anything *right*, Luc?' she mocked savagely.

'It can help.'

'No. We occupy different worlds and Matt belongs in mine. It won't be good for him to have that line blurred by your money. I won't have it. Please…take it back.'

Again he shook his head.

Frustrated by his refusal and hating even the feel of the paper representing an obscene amount of money, she ripped it into pieces, marched over to a nearby litter bin and dropped the fragments into it, determined on making the point that he couldn't buy into his son's life.

'Money corrupts,' she flung at him as she wiped her hands of its touch. 'We both have firsthand knowledge of that, don't we, Luc?'

'It can, but it doesn't have to,' he argued. 'It can be used to good effect. Which was what it was meant for.'

Maybe…maybe not. Skye knew she wasn't prepared to risk finding out how good the intentions were behind so much money. She walked back from the litter bin, feeling lighter and more self-assured. 'I can manage without it,' she said with confidence. 'I've proved that already. Matt is a happy, well-adjusted little boy. He doesn't need—'

'You're not thinking of him,' Luc sliced in, an aggressive note of accusation warning her he was going on the attack now that she had destroyed the money link he'd tried to forge. No more soothing. 'You've made this choice because it's what *you* want,' he threw at her.

'I'm his mother,' she retorted, ramming home the close relationship he'd never had with their child. 'I know what's best for him.'

'Like my father knew what was best for me?' he shot back, bleak mockery in his eyes.

The challenge and the expression behind it gave Skye pause for thought. It was true she was reacting to her previous experience with the Peretti family, not wanting anything to do with them, not wanting Matt to have anything to do with them, either. But was she doing right by...their son?

Her gut feeling was *yes*.

Or was that fear talking—fear of becoming involved in something she might not be able to control.

Controlling the path of his son's life was what Maurizio Peretti had been about in breaking up her relationship with Luc. Was she heading the same way herself with Matt, making decisions for him she had no right to make?

'Can you honestly say, six years down the track, that your father didn't know what was best for you?' she asked.

'Yes, I can,' Luc replied without hesitation. His eyes bored into hers with searing intensity as he softly added, 'I lost you. And I lost five years of my son's life.'

The different tone, and the mountain of feeling behind it, shook Skye into protesting, 'But you must have met other women who were more...more compatible with your family.'

'Oh, yes.' His mouth curled cynically. 'I've had many *suitable* women paraded in front of me. Not one did I want to take as my wife.'

'Why not?'

'Because I couldn't feel with them what I'd felt with you, Skye.'

'That's gone,' she said defensively, frightened of him sensing her vulnerability to the strong attraction that *should* have died...but hadn't.

He didn't reply. He simply looked at her, making her skin crawl over the lie she had spoken. But she would not take it back, couldn't afford to take it back. How could she ever trust him again with her heart?

'Yes, what we once had is gone,' he finally agreed, the regret in his voice hitting her hard as he added, 'And the fault was mine in not believing your word against Roberto's. It's true we've occupied different worlds and that, too, was part of it. You might have come after me to pursue the truth if I'd been more accessible to you.'

No. She'd been too crushed to attempt a fighting pursuit. The memory of how he'd looked at her, how he'd spoken to her, how he'd rejected her so utterly...even now, everything within her cringed from it. And knowing his family was behind the deception had added immeasurably to her sense of absolute defeat. Luc was right about that.

He cocked his head consideringly. 'I wonder how you would have reacted, shown photos of your sister—if you had one—on top of a man who looked like me, a man who was wearing a distinctive watch which you'd given me, and had a very personal identification mark—a man your sister swore was me. Would you have believed my denial, Skye?'

It was difficult to think herself into the turn-around scenario but in fairness to him, she tried to focus on it. Would she have believed a denial, knowing how attractive he was—rich, handsome, any woman's dream? Would she have believed he was hers and hers alone, given a sister's sworn word—and photographic evidence—that he'd been intimate with her, too? Wouldn't her insecurities about his family background have whispered to her that he was arrogantly having fun with both sisters?

'The difference is... I would have fought the accusation, far beyond what you did,' Luc said quietly, a wry sadness in his eyes. 'Though I certainly don't blame you for not trying. The simple truth is I had the resources to fight and you didn't. Which was what my family counted on. You didn't have the power or the money to find the photographer or the woman who looked like you, to prove your innocence. So my family won. And we lost something very special. I lost most of all. What we had together...and my child.'

Regardless of the heat in the air around them, her skin broke out in goose-bumps...as though ghosts of what might have been were wafting over the graveyard of their love. The poignant sense of loss squeezed her heart unbearably. She wrenched her gaze from his and stared out at Botany Bay, fiercely telling herself this was all water under the bridge. They couldn't go back. They couldn't change anything. And what they once had *was* gone. They were different people now. Time and experience had moved them even further apart.

'Is it fair for you to insist I keep losing, Skye?' he appealed.

'You made a choice,' she cried, fighting not to be drawn into making emotional concessions. Steeling herself to maintain a shield around the vulnerability he could still touch, she swung her gaze back to his. 'Do you think I'm ever going to forget your choice, Luc?'

'No.' He heaved a rueful sigh. 'I was hoping you might understand it.'

'I do. I always did.'

'And possibly…forgive it?'

'That, too.'

'Then…?'

'It's an issue of trust. I don't want you or your family anywhere near my son. I don't trust any of you to be fair. If you'd been fair to me, Luc, you would have investigated Roberto's claims. You admit you had the resources to do so.'

'Yes, in hindsight, I wish I'd done that. It makes me even more conscious of the need to be fair now. What good purpose would it serve to alienate you…the only parent my son has known? And clearly loves.'

Her chin lifted in pride. 'Matt and I do have a very special closeness. Why can't you just leave us alone, Luc? You walked away from me. Walk away from him, too. Go and forget we even exist. We'll all be happier that way.'

'No.' His chin lifted in hard aggression and the sudden gleam of ruthlessness in his eyes sent a shiver down her spine. 'I will not remain the loser where he is concerned. I'll fight for visitation rights if I have to. I'll drag this whole business through the lawcourts if I have to, and I will spare no one along the way. I don't care what it takes. I will be part of my son's life.'

The waves of relentless purpose coming from him were warning enough that her worst fears could come true. Her chest felt so tight, it was as though Luc had just wrapped steel bands around it. No room to breathe. Nowhere to move.

'You can choose to make this a hostile battleground and put us all through hell,' he went on, making a flippant gesture towards the park bench. 'Or you can choose to sit down with me and discuss how Matt could benefit by having his father in his life.'

There was no choice and he knew it. The kind of fight he was threatening would be terribly damaging to Matt.

'What will it be, Skye?'

He was demanding a trust she couldn't give, but maybe he would earn it if he truly had Matt's best interests at heart.

'Of one thing you can be absolutely certain,' he said, mocking the turmoil of doubts in her mind. 'This time...this time...nothing on earth will make me walk away!'

CHAPTER FIVE

SATURDAY... Matt's first day with his father.

Luc instantly made the most of his arrival, turning up in a red Alfa hatchback, presenting Skye with the car keys and announcing, much to Matt's delight, that the car was for his Mummy, so she could drive him to soccer training during the week and matches on the weekend.

An expensive Italian car, not a cheap runaround which would have been far more suitable. The house they lived in did not have a garage attached. The car had to be left parked in the street and a red Alfa would stick out like a sore thumb in this neighbourhood. But did a Peretti think like that? No. And she hadn't thought to advise Luc sensibly when he'd insisted she needed her own transport for the activities *his son* would want to pursue.

Like soccer. Matt's friends at school were signing up for soccer today. Skye hadn't driven a car since her mother had died and the Alfa made her nervous, not to mention having Luc sitting beside her in the front passenger seat. Somehow she managed to get them to the football oval without doing anything stupid.

Luc took care of the signing up. Skye gritted her teeth over the pride in Matt's voice as he announced to his play-mates, "This is my father."

So far he'd been quite shy with Luc, wary of what

this new intrusion in his life might mean, not quite understanding the background and sensing Skye's fearful reservations. But even a little boy could see that the other boys' fathers did not match up to Luc Peretti, certainly not in looks, and not in authoritative and charismatic presence.

They were exchanging smiles now.

With a sinking heart, Skye realised there'd be no stopping an attachment forming. Luc was intent on it and Matt was responding.

He'd better not walk away, she thought fiercely. If he ever hurt Matt as he'd hurt her... Skye took a deep breath and unclenched her hands. It was impossible to fight this. All she could do was watch over it, which *she* had insisted upon. No way would she agree to Luc taking Matt anywhere without her, and nowhere that didn't have her approval. To her intense relief he had made those concessions.

For now, she added to herself.

She didn't trust him to keep to them for long.

Next stop was a shopping mall where Luc had Matt fitted with a proper pair of soccer boots, which he paid for. They proceeded to a toy shop where he also bought for Matt a soccer ball and a goal structure complete with netting so *his son* could practise shooting goals—which could have been done with simply setting up two sticks in the backyard.

Skye could feel herself bristling at the money being spent without a second thought. They ate lunch in a restaurant—another expensive exercise—with Matt full of excitement at being treated to his favourite chicken nuggets and a banana smoothie. He ate and drank with gusto, while Skye could barely swallow the chicken Caesar salad Luc had ordered for her, remembering it had been one of her favourite meals when they'd been going out together.

She didn't want those memories revived. It was hard enough, having to be with Luc all day, having to be agreeable for Matt's sake, feeling forced to accept the Peretti largesse which was bound to have an insidious influence on Matt.

At least the buying stopped with lunch. She drove them home and Luc spent the afternoon in the backyard with Matt, setting up the goal, showing how to kick the soccer ball with the side of the foot, not the toe, practising dribbling the ball and demonstrating other skills that fascinated Matt into trying to copy them.

It hurt to watch them—father and son—having fun together, chatting, laughing, cheering and clapping achievements. Matt was having a great time, completely relaxed now with his new Dad, liking him and loving the different kind of attention he was getting. *Male* attention. *Male* understanding. *Male* activity.

It brought home to Skye that no single parent could supply everything a child needed, no matter how well-balanced one tried to be. Better to have the input from both parents, *if* it could be given in harmony. And it had to be conceded Luc was delivering on his promises. So far.

At last the day was over, with Matt bathed, fed, put to bed and enjoying the novelty of reading his father a story before lights out. Luc was astonished that his five-year-old son could actually read, and when they left Matt's bedroom, having kissed him goodnight, Skye found herself being forcibly steered back to the kitchen instead of carrying out her intention to see Luc out the front door.

'Let go of me!' she growled, resenting being denied a ready escape from the prolonged tension of his company.

'I just want to say thank you, Skye,' he said reasonably, releasing her arm once he'd accomplished his purpose of regaining territorial advantage.

She stepped away quickly, moving to put the small kitchen table between them, instinctively rubbing at the heat he'd left on her skin. He frowned at the action but she'd didn't care if he found it offensive. He had no right to touch her, to use his dominant strength to get his own way.

'I don't want you frightened of me,' he said in sharp concern.

'Then please leave. You've had your day. You've said thank you. There's no reason for you to stay any longer.'

He shook his head, still frowning. 'Did I do something wrong with Matt?'

'No. He had a happy first day with you.'

He raised his hands in a gesture of appeal. 'So why can't we talk about it?'

'What do you want? My stamp of approval?' she snapped, screaming inside for him to go because any more of him today was unbearable. She'd had to hold in so much for Matt's sake, pretending she was pleased for him to have his father, giving Luc the freedom to court his son, while all the time feeling that the little world she had constructed was under terrible attack.

Instead of answering, Luc eyed her with searching

intensity, looking for the reason behind her hostile stance. 'Is it really so hard to share him with me, Skye?' he asked in the soft tone that stripped her of defences.

She gripped the back of a chair, trying to hold herself together. Tears were welling—tears of emotional exhaustion—and the lump in her throat made it difficult to speak. 'You've won him over,' she pushed out. 'It's done. Please...just go now. Let yourself out.'

Her eyes blurred and she swung blindly around, stepping over to the sink, frantically turning on the taps so as to look busy, though there was nothing to wash, only a glass that had already been rinsed. She didn't hear Luc move, didn't even sense him closing in on her. Her whole concentration was aimed at not breaking up before he went.

It shocked her when his hand reached out and turned off the taps. Her fingers didn't have the strength to resist when the glass was taken from them and placed on the draining rack. Her mind was completely seized up, incapable of directing any action. Her body could have been that of a rag doll's as Luc turned her towards him, wrapping her in a supportive embrace, holding her, pressing her head onto his shoulder, rubbing his cheek against her hair with a tenderness that broke open the floodgates to the tears she'd tried so hard to contain.

The storm of weeping was draining, reducing her to such a helpless state, she couldn't find the pride that might have dragged her away from him. His broad shoulder was there to lean on. His warmth and strength was like a blanket of comfort. And it had been a long, long time since anyone had held her, emitting a sense of caring.

That it was Luc didn't seem to matter. In fact, the familiarity of past intimacy between them somehow made it easy to sag against his body. It didn't feel strange or wrong. There was a sense of belonging that she simply didn't have the will to fight, however false it might be.

Eventually the tears dried up, leaving her aching from the emotional upheaval and limp from all the energy spent. She became conscious of Luc's fingers gently raking through her hair and realised he must have removed the clip at the back of her neck, re-leasing and loosening the long flow of it—a liberty— but she didn't mind. It felt good.

'Skye—' her name gravelled from his throat as though scraping over painful barriers '—I'm not try-ing to win Matt from you. Please believe that.'

She closed her eyes and dragged in a deep breath, needing to fill her lungs with air, ease the ache in her chest. She felt too tired to speak. Her mind didn't want to take up the fight over trust. It was too hard.

'You're his mother,' Luc went on, a deeper, strong throb in his voice—a throb that somehow moved into her sluggish bloodstream and revived all the maternal feelings in her heart.

'You've done a wonderful job of bringing up our son. You can be very proud of the boy he is…the boy you've shaped him to be…'

The warmth of his approval flooded through her.

'I don't know how to thank you…doing it all alone. He's amazing. A happy child, well-mannered, eager to have a go at everything, and reading at his young age...'

He sounded so awed, a smile tugged at the corners of Skye's mouth. She was proud of Matt. Justly proud. And she was glad Luc felt she had done a good job of bringing up their son.

'If you've been thinking I might take him away from you, I swear to you I won't, Skye. That was never my intention. And seeing how he is to-day...why would I want to? Matt couldn't have a better mother. So please...don't be afraid of me.'

She didn't want to be. But even if he truly meant what he said now...she stirred herself to raise her head, open her eyes, look straight at him, speak her fears. 'Today...Matt was a novelty to you and you were a novelty to Matt. It won't stay that way. You won't want to give him so much quality time and if Matt feels let down by you...'

'I'll do my best not to let him down.'

'Things change, Luc. Other people can interfere...'

'Not this time.' The resolute gleam in his eyes suddenly burned into something else entirely. 'And some things don't change.'

Her heart kicked in alarm as he whipped his hands up to cup her face, his thumbs slowly fanning the line of her lower lip, making it tingle. 'Remember how it was, Skye?'

Raw desire was blazing at her, furring his voice, stunning her into mesmerised passivity. Her hands were pressed against his chest but she didn't think to push away. Some magnetic force kept them glued there. She didn't think to move her head aside, either, though his was bending closer and closer, his intention unmistakable. She was conscious only of a thundering need to let it happen...to know, to feel, to match the memory.

His mouth covered hers, instantly triggering an electric sensitivity. She hadn't been kissed since he had last kissed her and her mind filled with wonder that it could be so fascinating, so seductive, the soft sensuality of having her lips tasted, the exciting slick of his tongue opening them further, teasing and tantalising as it slid into her mouth to entice hers into play.

The temptation to respond was irresistible. The desire to feel again what she'd once felt with him surged out of the sense of having been cheated of it, cut off as though she was dead, through no fault of her own.

But she wasn't dead. It was as if every cell in her body was springing into vibrant life, screaming out for what had been lost. She wanted it back—the all-consuming passion they'd shared. He owed it to her. He owed her so much...

A torrent of feelings pumped through her, driving her out of passivity, long-buried needs rising, demanding at least some satisfaction. Her tongue sprang into an erotic tango with his. Her hands clawed their way up his chest, over his shoulders, fingers thrusting through the thick matt of his hair, curling around his head, fiercely denying any end to the kiss which turned into a wild battleground for possession—invasion, assault, frenzied passion, no retreat, ragged pauses only to regather breath enough to engage again.

He no longer held her face. His hands clutched her bottom, fingers digging into the soft rounded flesh as he dragged her closer, lifting her into more intimate contact with him, and a mad exultation fizzed through her brain as she felt his arousal. She rubbed against it, wantonly provocative, deliberately stirring the desire he'd turned his back on, building the heat he had doused with ice, not believing it had only been for him.

No ice now.

He wrenched his mouth from hers, scooped her off her feet, and carried her out of the kitchen, down the central hallway, into her bedroom at the front of the house, his chest heaving but there was not one falter in the long, strong strides that were driven by the compulsion to get her to a bed.

Skye didn't protest, didn't struggle to assert herself in any way. It was wildly exhilarating to be swept off by Luc, knowing he wasn't thinking of anything but having her—the woman he'd cast out of his life. He wasn't about to walk away now. Oh, no! And Skye's whole body tingled with a sense of power—a deep, primitive power that clamoured to be used, claiming this man as hers, so completely hers all the more *suitable* women would never get a chance with him.

It was twilight outside, almost dark in the bedroom, though she could see Luc clearly enough, see the strained look on his face as he put her down and worked at speed to strip them both. No finesse in the undressing. No stopping to touch, kiss or caress. Urgent need.

She didn't try to help or hinder, didn't care about her own nakedness. She watched him, secretly revelling in the desire that couldn't wait, that was raging out of Luc's control, his eyes hungrily feasting on her

femininity as he moved onto the bed, knees intent on
parting her legs, his own magnificent physique right
in her face now, smooth shiny olive skin stretched
over tight muscles, his whole body yearning for hers,
craving the union he'd put behind him.

And for a moment she hated him for it, a fierce
flash of hatred for the contempt he'd dealt out, making all she'd given of herself negligible, dirty…yet
everything within her sighed a sweet welcome as he
entered her, plunging deep, filling the emptiness she'd
known for far too long.

He paused there, sighing himself, and Skye savagely hoped it signalled the feeling of having come
home—home to where his heart was. Except she
couldn't really believe it because he would never have
left her if that was true.

She closed her eyes and focused on feeling him
inside her, no longer caring what it meant for him,
wanting to recapture all the sensations she had forgotten, the rippling pleasures of the rhythm, the build-
up of intense physical excitement. And Luc delivered.
He always had delivered. Not usually as roughly as
this. But that had its exciting edge, too, knowing control had been sabotaged by need, adding to the power
of his wanting her.

He was breathing hard.

She was, too, her body instinctively accommodat-
ing the wild pounding, exulting in it, her legs wound
around his taut buttocks urging him on, her back
arched, her hands raking the bunched muscles of his
shoulders, the tips of her breasts brushing his chest
as he rocked back and forth in a frenzy of driven

possession, the tension of it becoming more and more explosive.

The shattering started, the ecstatic meltdown she had only ever known with him, and even as she started floating with it, she felt the release of his climax, the jerking spurts of heat spilling from him, mingling with her own contentment, increasing the sweet pleasure of it, the sense of fulfilment that matched the memories.

He collapsed on top of her, his face buried in the stream of her hair across the pillow, and she hugged him tightly to her, clutching the intimacy of the moment before it went away. For this little time, at least, he was hers, and she consciously shut out the realities of the worlds they occupied, feeling only their togetherness—a dream that had been lost—a dream that couldn't last.

CHAPTER SIX

HER beautiful hair, soft, silky, incredibly sensual...the feel of it, the feel of her, had started this, propelling him down a path he hadn't meant to take yet, and certainly not with the frenzied need that had driven his every action. He had to start thinking now, seize advantage of the knowledge that the need had been mutual.

She was clasping him tightly to her. Was it reaction to the physical upheaval of climaxing, or a desire to hold onto him? He had to move, take his weight off her before she became too conscious of it, too conscious of what she had allowed to happen, regretting it, spurning him as he'd once spurned her.

He rolled onto his back, carrying her with him, keeping one of her legs trapped by his to retain an intimate entanglement, using his hands to travel up and down the curve of her spine, over the soft roundness of her bottom, wanting her to feel him loving her, everything about her.

The sex had been too crude, too fast. He'd meant to woo her, win back her trust. Her fear of him had been intolerable, a barrier he'd had to break, though he'd lost sight of that aim as her tension had collapsed into tears. Holding her in his arms again—impossible not to remember how it had once been with her, stirring the urge to make her remember, too.

Show her, kiss her...

He hadn't anticipated the fierce response.

Given Skye's hostility—justified hostility—what was behind *her* burst of passion? He couldn't believe it was a raging desire for him. Though there was no doubting she had wanted the sexual connection, responding to it all the way. That certainly hadn't changed. But was it enough to build on?

It had to be because there was no going back to a more careful courtship. Besides, it would be better for Matt to have both parents as a constant in his life. And it would prove his own commitment to fatherhood to Skye, removing her fear of a transient and possibly damaging dalliance with his son. So best that he speak now, before her mind got active against him again.

Her head was resting over his heart. He wound a long tress of her hair around his hand to hold her there. He told himself she could not be more vulnerable to the idea than she was at this moment with both of them naked and intimately entwined, reinforcing what they could and did share.

It would come out baldly, he knew, but dressing it up with feelings she might scorn could very well tip the scales in a very negative fashion. She wouldn't trust emotions. Working from her reaction seemed the most viable option. He had to use reason and do it convincingly.

Trying to keep the enormous tension he felt out of his voice, Luc simply announced what he was aiming for.

'I want you to marry me.'

*   *   *

Marry him...

The shock of the proposal rolled through Skye's sluggish mind, setting off alarm signals. She hadn't wanted to think of what she'd done with Luc. Much easier to just drift in a haze of feeling, blocking realities out until they had to be faced. But a proposal of *marriage*...it was so off the wall, Skye struggled to get her head around what it meant.

She started to shift, acutely aware of his heart drumming under her ear—a soothing sound just a few moments ago—a disturbing one now.

'No. Stay with me.'

The brusque command unsettled her further. He had no right to force her compliance to his will, not over anything so personal as this. She'd conceded his right to involve himself with Matt, but what happened between her and Luc was most certainly a matter of choice. Just because she'd had sex with him didn't mean he could do anything he liked with her.

'Don't make this a fight, Luc,' she warned, trying to gather wits enough to understand what had motivated his proposal. 'Let me move.'

'Why do you want to?'

'I've just remembered who you are,' she answered, not caring if it hurt him, instinctively using shock to give herself room for retreat to a less vulnerable position so she could think straight, not be influenced by the strong sexual connection he was pressing.

'Don't give me that!' He whipped her over onto her back and propped himself up, one arm on either side of her so that she was looking directly into his eyes—eyes blazing with a certainty that poured into passionate words. 'You knew who was kissing you... knew who brought you to this bed...knew who was—'

'Screwing me again?' she fired at him, angered by the physical domination he was exerting when she had made a clear request to be released.

His face tightened, his mouth compressing into a thin line. 'You wanted this, too, Skye,' he bit out, shaking his head over her accusation.

He was using it against her—the far too short-sighted surrender to what had probably always been a fantasy—her and Luc together, their love so strong it could ride through anything. It hadn't. And he'd moved on to other women while she had struggled on by herself. He'd still be moving on, but for Matt.

'Was it good for you, Luc?' she asked, resenting all his infidelities.

'Yes. And you wouldn't have responded as you did if it wasn't good for you,' he retorted, determined on making her admit it.

'So you think you can capitalise on it, move straight in and take over my life.'

'We're good together. We always were,' he argued.

'A pity you didn't remember that when it counted.'

'It counts now,' he snapped back, ignoring the past, accentuating the present. 'We have a son. We should be a family.'

Matt. She was right about what Luc really wanted. 'There's more to marriage than having a child. I don't want you as my husband.'

'You came to bed with me.'

She couldn't leave him with that weapon to use against her. 'I wanted you to remember what you gave up, Luc,' she said mockingly.

His brows beetled down into a deep frown.

'How many women have there been since me?' she asked, hating him for moving on, leaving her behind, then thinking he could turn around and take her as his wife when it suited him.

'They're irrelevant.' It was a fierce mutter, wanting her to forget them.

'When you shared a bed with them, did you remember me?'

'Yes, I did. Nothing was ever like what we had together.'

For a moment, his vehement reply rocked Skye out of her bitter train of thought. There had only ever been Luc for her. No one else. If he felt the same way... But he couldn't. He'd put his brother's word ahead of hers, his family's view of her ahead of his own.

'I don't believe you!' she cried, and with all her strength, slammed her hands against his shoulders and thrust him far enough away for her to scramble off the bed, out of reach.

'It's true!' he hurled after her.

'Be quiet! Matt's in the next room,' she hissed at him as she grabbed her houserobe from the one chair in her bedroom, putting it on as fast as she could, determined on shutting out any resumption of intimacy with him.

'Our son, Skye,' he swiftly reminded her, his voice lowered but still emphatic in delivery. 'Don't you think it would be better for him to have a full-time father as well as mother?'

She wrapped the robe around her and tied the belt savagely as she swung to face him again. 'That's what you're after, isn't it? Matt. Not me. Get the mother, get the boy.'

'Wrong! I want both of you.'

He was still stretched out on the bed, propped up on one arm, looking moody and magnificent, every part of him male perfection. No wonder she hadn't wanted any other man. And maybe never would. Which gave her pause for thought. She could have him. All she had to do was say yes to his marriage proposal.

But could she live with him—live with his family—and be happy? How could she trust any of them to really care about her, given how they'd treated her in the past?

She had to finish this—get him out of her bedroom, out of her house—not let him play on the desires he could so easily tap into. Treacherous feelings! The sense of intimacy still swirling in this darkened room drove her over to the light-switch by the door. She flicked it on, telling herself she would see more clearly now, think more clearly.

But it didn't help. Luc's nakedness gathered even more power in the light, vividly reminding her of how every part of him had felt. And his claim of wanting her burned from his eyes, heating her skin all over again, making her toes curl, making her stomach contract, making her breasts ache, her nipples tighten into tell-tale prominence.

Panicking over his effect on her, she folded her arms across the wildly fluttering beat of her heart and rushed into defensive speech. 'Don't think having sex with you means anything, Luc.'

'You can't make me believe you'd have sex indiscriminately, Skye.' His mouth curled in bitter irony. 'I believed it once and made the biggest mistake of my life. No one can sell it to me a second time.'

'This is different,' she hotly argued.

'How is it different?' he mocked.

She frantically sought a convincing explanation. 'Being pregnant hardly makes you desirable to other men. And having a baby takes up all your time, not to mention nursing your mother through chemotherapy, losing her, then trying to establish a life while being a single parent. I haven't had sex since I was with you six years ago and you caught me at a weak moment. That's all it was.'

'Because it *was* me,' he pointed out with arrogant certainty.

She glared at him, unable to deny a truth which was only too self-evident, anyway.

He stretched out an inviting arm. 'Come back to bed. Let me show you...'

'No!' The physical pleasure she knew he would give could not be allowed to cloud her mind again. 'I want you to get dressed and go, Luc.'

'Let me answer your needs, Skye,' he promised temptingly.

'You can't answer all of them,' she retorted. 'And please do as I ask. This wasn't in our agreement. If you have any integrity at all...'

He moved, swinging his legs off the bed. Fear of him coming at her choked off any further speech and drove her into instant recoil. She shrank back against the doorjamb, hugging herself even more tightly.

Luc sat on the edge of the bed, absolutely still, frowning at her. Every nerve in her body screeched with tension as she waited for his next action. The silence was electric with barely contained emotions and challenges she was too frightened to acknowledge, yet the strong sense of them pinned her to the wall, draining her of any further initiative.

'Integrity...' The word fell from his lips, heavy with guilt and regret. 'I lost faith in yours so you have no belief in mine.' He lifted deeply pained eyes, probing her soul with searing intensity. 'Did it ever occur to you that I cared too much about integrity, Skye? That seeing you...in bed with my brother...was such a killing blow...'

'I was never in bed with your brother!'

'Goddammit!' He rose to his feet, towering up to his full height, pumping out waves of violent energy as he hurled out his truth. 'It wasn't just the photos! You were charmed with Roberto's wit and you didn't stop him from flirting with you. Every time the three of us were together, Roberto would claim your attention and you gave it to him. Willingly!'

'He was nice to me, Luc. Your parents looked at me as though I was trash, treated me with icy politeness. Why wouldn't I warm to your brother?' she flung back at him.

'Warm...' His hands lifted, fingers outstretched like upturned talons, left empty and frustrated because what he'd wanted to hold on to had been ripped away. 'Where does warmth turn into heat? Roberto swore it was so...swore I was making a fool of myself for loving you...and there were the photos to prove it, to prove there was no integrity in your love for me...'

'It wasn't true,' Skye cried, deeply agitated by the

pain pouring from him and the artful lies that had been woven around her behaviour.

'He was my brother! We'd shared all our lives together! Why would he confess to such a divisive and destructive truth if it wasn't the truth?'

A *killing blow*...she could see it now, feel how it was for him.

'You were the light of my life and he tore it out of me and left me in darkness. A darkness so black I couldn't see you any more. Not the person you were.' His hands dropped in a helpless fashion as the raw anguish on his face fell into a terrible bleakness. 'All in the name of integrity...which he sacrificed...to please my father.'

He shook his head and slowly bent down to pick up his clothes as though there was nothing left to do and there was certainly no joy to be had from any more exposure. On any level.

A poignant sense of loss permeated the sudden silence and Skye's heart felt as though it was being wrung by merciless hands. The hurt was too great— his hurt and hers—what had been done to both of them! Her mind was a chaos of confusion. Was it wrong of her to keep blaming him for turning traitor to their love when he had suffered the devastation of a double treachery? The woman he loved...the brother he loved...

'Don't be frightened of me, Skye,' he said softly, looking at her with an expression of rueful appeal. He was putting on his shirt, doing up the buttons. 'This time around...it's not about taking from you. It's about giving.'

She couldn't bring herself to speak. She wasn't so

sure of her ground any more. All she could think of was how much she had loved this man and maybe she could love him again if…but weren't there too many *ifs?* And Matt was in the middle of them. Her precious son whom she had to protect against the Peretti family. She mustn't forget Matt, just because Luc could still get to her, twisting her around, making her feel…

Watching him pull on his underpants and jeans, everything within her quivered, not from fear but from the freshly awakened sexual memory of how it had been with him…the intimacy they'd shared on the very bed she had to sleep in tonight. Alone…as she'd been alone all these years. She had Matt but a child's love—her love for him—was different. Being a mother did not fulfil everything she wanted as a woman.

Luc tucked his shirt in, did up his zipper, shot her a look that mocked the security she'd wanted from him being clothed again. 'It won't go away—the chemistry between us, Skye. No matter what you're telling yourself, it will still be there next week, next month, next year, and all the years to follow.'

The relentless beat of his prediction struck chords of truth that twanged through her entire body. Her mind could produce no answer to it. She simply stared back at him, silently demanding the distance she needed right now, telling herself not to concede anything more at this point.

He sat on the bed to put on his socks and Reeboks, doing it with commendable alacrity, not dragging out his time with her. He stood up and she stiffened her backbone, determined on an air of self-containment as he walked over to the doorway, emanating a dynamic energy that would not acknowledge defeat.

He paused beside her, his dark brilliant eyes engaging hers in an intense battle of wills. 'I can't give you back the years that were taken from us but we can make a future together,' he said quietly.

They had to...around Matt. But she now knew Luc was intent on pushing for more, and even as she thought it, he laid it out to her again.

'I doubt any marriage is perfect, but I promise you this. I'll work damned hard at making it as good as I can for you. Think about it, Skye. I'll be back next Saturday...as agreed.'

He walked on into the hallway. She heard the front door click open, then shut behind him.

Gone.

Air whooshed out of her lungs on a huge sigh of relief. She sagged against the wall, staring at the bed where she had wantonly surrendered her independence. Was it possible to claw it back? Did she want to? Did she have to?

She needed to know the answers before Luc came again.

Next Saturday.

As agreed.

Because he was Matt's father.

CHAPTER SEVEN

'DADDY'S here!' Matt yelled from the front porch. 'And he's come in *his* red car!'

The Ferrari! The excitement in her son's voice shot Skye out of dallying in the kitchen. He'd been outside, waiting and watching for his father in a fever of impatience, and the double attraction of the Ferrari spelled danger! She raced down the hallway to the opened front door in time to see Matt unlatching the gate and Luc emerging from his car on the other side of the street.

'Don't run onto the road, Matt!' she called.

It alerted Luc, who instantly spotted him and held up a hand. 'Wait on the sidewalk.' Commanding authority.

Matt obeyed, but he literally jiggled with pleasure as Luc strode across the road towards him, smiling his own pleasure in this obvious welcome from his son. He swooped down, picked him up and hoisted him up against his shoulder, laughing as Matt laughed—the sound of mutual happiness. 'So how did it go at soccer training?' he asked.

And Matt bubbled over with news of the two afterschool sessions he'd attended during the week. No shyness. A quick and easy rapport with his father, plus unadulterated delight in his interest and company.

Which put a little hollow in Skye's heart. It was

68

hard, realising she couldn't supply all her son's needs. Not even years of loving him, doing everything she could for him, was enough. He wanted his father.

She waited on the porch, watching them bonding as Luc carried Matt back to her. They *were* alike, though maybe she was seeing the similarities more acutely now that it was impossible to deny them with Luc right in front of her again. And he wasn't going to go away.

The only question was...how far should she let him into their lives?

All week she had been weighing it up in her mind and was no closer to an answer. It was no use even trying to think of him as the much younger Luc she had loved. He was different, just as she was different. He'd spoken of darkness and she sensed it ran very deeply, married to a steely resolve that encompassed her because of what had been done to him.

She wasn't sure love had any part in it...yet watching him with Matt, seeing him drink in the innocence of his child's natural response to him...his heart was surely being touched. It wasn't just ownership.

So maybe he was still capable of loving. Whether that could extend to her...if she was his wife...but there was still the Peretti family in the background, a powerful father who would hate having his will thwarted.

Then Luc turned his gaze from Matt to her, a direct blaze of power that thumped into her heart and burned into her brain the unequivocal fact that he wasn't about to have his will thwarted, either.

'Daddy said I had to ask you if I can have a ride in his car,' Matt piped up. 'Can I, Mummy? Can I?'

'May I,' Skye corrected automatically, wrenching her gaze away from Luc's, 'We can't all fit in that car, Matt. If we're going to Darling Harbour...' The outing agreed upon.

'Perhaps a quick spin around the block?' Luc suggested.

'He's not a stranger any more, Mummy. It can't be a bad thing to do.'

Skye flushed at the reminder of the argument she'd used in a protective need to keep Luc a stranger to Matt. 'Just a short ride then,' she muttered, feeling hamstrung by her own dictate.

'Five minutes at most,' Luc promised, undoubtedly realising it was stretching her trust to let him go off alone with their son. It was against their agreement.

'Okay, five minutes,' she conceded, shooting him a warning look. One transgression didn't mean he could trample anywhere he liked.

He grinned at her, triumph dancing in his eyes. Matt whooped with joy and they were off, leaving Skye to fret over the feeling that control was slipping away from her.

In fact, it had been slipping away ever since Luc had re-entered her life. Her independent stance was gone. Any peace of mind was gone. The future directions she had been considering were hopelessly blurred by the now prime consideration of whether or not she should entertain the idea of marrying Luc Peretti.

With a helpless sigh, Skye retreated into the house, checked that everything needed for their day out had been put in the backpack before zipping it shut, slung it over one arm, grabbed both her hat and Matt's, and went back out to the porch, locking the front door behind her.

The Ferrari came vrooming down the street as she walked towards the Alfa. Luc had kept his word. He didn't want her to be frightened of him. The problem was it was difficult not to be when her knees went weak at the sight of him.

She unlocked the Alfa and waited beside it, wondering how she was going to cope in his company all day long—a morning visit to the aquarium, lunch in one of the many restaurants overlooking Darling Harbour, idling the afternoon away at the children's playground or the Japanese Gardens.

Father and son emerged from the Ferrari, holding hands to cross the road, both of them wearing jeans and T-shirts, just as she was. The three of them were dressed like a family, going on a holiday tour together, and Matt was skipping with excited anticipation. He'd had his ride in his father's flash car and now he was going to see all the fish from his favourite movie, *Finding Nemo*.

Skye handed the Alfa's key to Luc. 'You drive. I haven't been near inner-city traffic for so long, it would make me nervous.'

'Then this should be a practice run for you,' he argued.

'I'd rather do that alone.'

'I could help you avoid mistakes.'

'Just let me be a passenger, Luc. It's your day with Matt.' *Not with me.*

He instantly picked up the implication not to assume too much and gave her an ironic little smile as he took the key. 'Keeping your distance, Skye?'

'Keeping out of trouble,' she answered.

She had trouble enough, sitting so closely beside him in the car on their way to Darling Harbour. His physical presence in such a small space dominated her consciousness, even though she kept her gaze fixed on the traffic, trying her utmost to ignore how acutely all her other senses were attuned to him.

Nor could she stop her body from feeling all keyed up—whether to repel any touch from him or welcome it, she didn't know. Just being near him aroused the fresh sexual memories from last week, but she couldn't let that happen again, couldn't risk any kind of intimate contact while she was still trying to sort through the situation between them.

Matt was full of chatter, keeping Luc engaged in conversation, for which Skye was intensely grateful. She listened to their voices. No strain in either of them—happy, cheerful, having fun. Would Luc be a good father in the long run? Discovering a son was still very new to him. He wanted to indulge Matt, but there was more to parenting than indulgence.

Still, Skye couldn't quarrel with the indulgence when they finally reached the aquarium and walked into a new entrancing world for Matt. The touching pond and the showcases of fish were fantastic. Seeing sharks swimming overhead was positively awesome. She could not have afforded to give Matt this experience and he was loving every minute of it.

The tropical fish, of course, were a very special attraction, and he told Luc the names of those he recognised from having watched *Finding Nemo* many times since Skye had bought him the video for Christmas. Naturally the clownfish was his favourite.

Eventually they'd exhausted every attraction and Skye suggested a toilet visit before going on to lunch. She automatically took Matt's hand to lead him into the Ladies' Room, only to be halted by Luc.

'He should come with me, Skye.'

'But he's a little boy,' she objected.

'I'll look after him.' Hard challenge in his eyes.

It was *his* day with Matt.

Rather than make a fight of it, Skye reluctantly let them go together. She was waiting for them when they came out and Matt rushed over to her to whisper proudly, 'I peed in the urinal with Daddy.'

Skye grimaced over this highly basic piece of male bonding and rolled her eyes at Luc who was totally unabashed about it. 'About time I had a first in my son's upbringing,' he said pointedly, reminding her of all the *firsts* he'd missed—first word, first step, first day at school...

Matt skipped on ahead of them as they walked towards the aquarium exit and Luc seized the chance for some private talk between them, stunning her with his opening line. 'Any chance you might have conceived another child last week?'

'No,' she answered quickly, a wave of heat whooshing up her neck at the abrupt reference to their intimacy.

'I didn't use protection, Skye, and your own long drought from any sex suggests you didn't, either.'

'It was a safe time.' A fact she'd only figured out—frantically—when the possible consequence of pregnancy had occurred to her after he'd gone.

'Sure about that?'

'Yes,' she bit out grimly, remembering the churning panic while she had checked dates.

'I was rather hoping it wasn't,' he drawled.

'What?' She threw an appalled look at him.

'I'm here to take care of you this time.' His eyes glittered ruthless determination. 'And I'd like us to have a child we both shared from the very beginning.'

She felt his strongly embittered sense of having been cheated of years with Matt and kept her mouth shut. This was not something she could argue against. Yet a revulsion against the ruthlessness she saw in him forced her to ask, 'Were you thinking of getting me pregnant when you carried me off to bed?'

'No.' He sliced her a sardonic little smile. 'I just wanted you, Skye. So much that protection didn't enter my head. And it didn't enter yours, either.' He paused before softly adding, 'What do you think that says about our need for each other?'

She didn't answer.

Luc called out to Matt, bringing him back in line with them, taking his hand—a hand that was readily given, unlike hers. Skye wondered if Luc would stoop to seriously playing Matt as a persuasive force in getting her to accept his proposal of marriage. Or was he simply counting on her own vulnerability to a connection with him?

She couldn't block out the powerful attraction he exerted on her, yet marriage was something else entirely. No way was she going to rush into a decision. Six years was a huge gap to bridge and she was far too conscious of the murky waters that flowed all around them, making a foundation on which to build seem very rocky.

They proceeded to a harbourside restaurant where Luc had booked a table out on the open terrace so they could watch the colourful passing parade of people and the boats in the water—lots of boats on show this weekend, reminding Skye of how she had first met Luc and his brother.

It was at the end of her second year of university and she'd got a casual summer job in the supply shop at the big Cronulla marina. The Peretti family had owned a huge waterfront home nearby in those days. Probably still did. She and her mother had moved from the adjoining suburb of Caringbah after her step-father had deserted them.

But that summer, the Peretti brothers had sailed every weekend. She had met Roberto first, serving him in the shop. He'd flirted with her and she'd thought him a rather gorgeous playboy until Luc had appeared, completely knocking out the attraction of his younger brother. It wasn't so much he was better looking, more that he somehow made Roberto seem lightweight in comparison, instantly relegated to the sidelines.

He still had that power.

Skye glanced around the men seated at other tables, the men walking by…all of them paled in comparison to Luc. He commanded attention, compelled attention, and she knew she was in a hopeless position, trying to hold him at a distance when he was intent on reclaiming her.

After lunch they strolled down to the playground area where Luc directed that he and Skye sit on a grassy bank, watching how brave Matt was at using the slippery dip by himself. Encouraged to show off,

Matt was only too eager to demonstrate to his father how capable he was of using all the playground equipment, which neatly took him out of earshot.

Skye resigned herself to another private conversation with Luc, knowing there was no ultimate way of avoiding it. One way or another, he'd make the opportunity. Besides, her nerves were so on edge waiting for it, she might as well get it over with. They sat side by side, their knees hitched up, arms resting on them, no doubt looking very relaxed together to Matt, and at least Luc made no move to get closer.

'Let's discuss marriage,' he started without any preamble.

Skye plucked a blade of grass and began slowly shredding it as she struggled to put her thoughts into some kind of sensible framework.

'You've had time to think about it,' Luc pressed.

'I don't know the man you are now,' Skye said truthfully, keeping her focus on the strips of grass.

'You want more time.'

'Yes.'

'Then you *are* considering it.'

The satisfaction in his voice stirred rebellion against the pressure he was laying on her. 'There's a hell of a lot to consider, Luc.'

He came straight back with, 'Tell me what's on your mind.'

More pressure.

She slanted him a curious look. 'Have you run the idea of marrying me past your parents, Luc?'

'I didn't discuss it with them, no. I told them flatly that they either accept you as my wife or lose me.

And having just lost one son, I don't think they'll be inclined to buck my ultimatum.'

It shocked her speechless. She stared at him, stunned by the starkly drawn stand he had made, the sheer ruthlessness of his planning, and the assumption that they would marry, all laid out as though it was already decided.

'When...' Her mouth had gone so dry she had to work some moisture in it before managing to choke out the question skating through her dazed mind. 'When did you tell them?'

'After I faced my father with your accusation that he'd paid for an abortion,' he said matter-of-factly. 'And the whole truth of what had happened six years ago was finally disclosed.'

Not this past week...much, much before...after coming face to face with her and Matt for the first time. He'd decided *then!* Was it to spite his father for keeping all knowledge of Matt from him—a vengeful act on his whole family for having sabotaged his right to choose whatever woman he wanted in his life?

'Your parents won't want me as your wife,' she stated with utter certainty.

A hard relentless pride looked back at her. 'They don't have a choice.'

'I do, Luc,' she pointedly reminded him.

'They will accept you, Skye. They have too much to lose if they don't.'

'I don't want to be involved in your fight with them. I don't want Matt to be a pawn in your game. He'll feel it. He'll know he's not what they want. You can't force approval from people when they don't feel it inside.'

'This is no game, Skye. Believe me, I'm deadly serious.'

Deadly was right, she thought.

'My parents will love Matt. Unreservedly,' he pushed on, laying out cogent arguments. 'He's their only grandchild and the only one they'll have if you don't marry me. Roberto is dead and his marriage produced no children. The whole future of the Peretti family is now narrowed down to *our* son.' His smile held a dark wealth of satisfaction as he added, 'That makes Matt very precious to them.'

A convulsive little shiver ran down Skye's spine. 'Don't put that weight on me. Or Matt,' she cried. 'It's not fair!'

'I think it balances the scales very nicely. You should feel it does, too, Skye.'

She shook her head. 'You're taking advantage of your brother's death. For all the wrong he did to me and to you, it doesn't make this right. Nothing can make this right.' It was incredibly painful to say it but she truly felt the alternative would cause even more pain. 'You should marry someone else...leave Matt and me out of it.'

'But I won't, Skye.' In a soft, insidiously invasive voice that curled around her heart, demanding entry, he added, 'You're the only woman I've ever loved...or will love.'

She jerked her head away, frightened of showing how deeply it touched her when she hadn't realised herself how much it would mean.

He must have interpreted it as a negative reaction. With barely a pause he spoke in a much harder tone, determined possession underlining every word.

'And Matt is my son.'

CHAPTER EIGHT

'THEY'RE grading all the kids for the soccer teams tomorrow,' Matt announced on the way home from Darling Harbour. 'Can you come, Daddy?'

'Your father has other things to do tomorrow,' Skye quickly inserted, panicking at the thought of having to withstand Luc's pursuit of marriage with her a second day in a row. Besides, a Sunday visit was not part of their agreement. Her hands clenched, the need to fight against any pressure racing through her mind.

'I bet all the other fathers will be there,' Matt grumbled.

Luc's hands tightened around the steering wheel. Skye's heart sank. She knew what Luc was thinking—robbed of five years of fatherhood and still being blocked from taking part in his son's life. It violated *his* sense of justice and threw Skye into confusion over what was fair and what wasn't.

Was she being selfish, limiting his access to Matt? Did she have to protect them both from the Peretti family when Luc had placed himself so unequivocally beside them, prepared to ward off any harmful interference in their lives?

'It's not until four o'clock,' Matt informed, his voice brightening with the hope the late time might make a difference. 'You can have all day to do other things.'

Skye closed her eyes despairingly. It wasn't Luc using Matt to pressure her into doing what *he* wanted. Their son was doing a good job of it all by himself. She heard Luc's swift intake of breath hissing between his teeth. He was hating this, and God help her, she hated it, too. It wasn't how it should be for Matt.

Luc spoke, determinedly testing her resistance to the idea. 'Perhaps I could come by the soccer park...'

Words left hanging for her to pick up on, words carefully strained of any forceful persuasion, words that begged this concession from her.

And she heard herself say, 'Matt would like that.'

Luc's relief was palpable.

The thin edge of the wedge, Skye thought, but it was difficult to regret it, listening to Matt's bubbling pleasure in the possibility his father would come to watch him.

Not possibility.

Certainty.

Skye had no doubt about that. Luc confirmed it before he left that evening, pausing on the front porch to thank her for stretching their agreement and thankfully not pressing her for anything else.

Though his eyes did. His eyes bored into hers, intent on smashing every barrier between them. She knew he wouldn't be content until there were no limitations on their relationship. But she wasn't sure what was the driving force behind the burning intent.

Love...possession...revenge?

All of them powerful feelings.

Long into the night Skye lay awake, feeling her own way through Luc's current conflict with his parents. He'd thrown down the gauntlet to them—lose him or accept her as his wife and Matt as his son. He expected to win the challenge, but would he?

The method used to separate them last time had been an extreme act, demonstrating the depth of his family's opposition to a relationship which didn't fit into their world. To Skye's mind, their grief over losing their younger son, was highly unlikely to change their attitude towards her. They would want Luc to fulfil their plans for him even more now—their one son left to uphold all they stood for.

Luc thought Matt would be a swaying factor—their one grandchild—but Skye doubted *her* son had the power to pull them into acceptance. The trust fund proved how much they would pay to keep the unwanted by-blow out of their lives. He wasn't wanted any more than she was.

They probably saw Luc's reaction to Roberto's deathbed confession as a rebellion against having been manipulated into giving up a woman he'd wanted—shock at discovering he had a child. His knowledge might stay their hand from any further interference with her life or Matt's, but there would surely be mounting pressure on Luc to drop them from his life.

It could become a very bitter battle.

Luc had spoken of his parents losing but Skye couldn't see them rolling over to oblige what might be considered as only wounded pride on his part. Yet it wasn't pride she felt pulsing from him when he was with her and Matt. It was need. And it kept stirring need in her, as well. Even more unsettling...need in Matt.

Where would it all end?

Roberto's deathbed revelations had set in motion a train of action she had no way of stopping. Luc was the engine driver and she and Matt were captive passengers. All she could hope for was they didn't crash against an immovable force which would break them apart with worse wounds to carry into the future.

Eventually Skye fell into a fretful sleep. She was wakened the next morning by an overexcited Matt who declared he was going to practice playing soccer all day. No prizes for working out why, Skye thought wryly. 'Daddy' featured in practically everything he said.

Luc was already at the playing field when they arrived. Matt, of course, had spotted the red Ferrari in the parking lot, so there was absolutely no sense of disappointment to suffer through. The only suffering was done by Skye, continually torn by Luc's and Matt's pleasure in each other and the fear that she had made a big mistake in not enforcing the limits she had imposed on their relationship.

Yet could the damage be limited, if damage there was going to be? Did time limits mean anything when emotions were involved—emotions that were probably heightened because there wasn't constant contact. Wasn't it said, absence made the heart grow fonder?

Watching Matt adoring his father for the caring interest and the soccer advice Luc was giving him as they watched other boys play their games, Skye could barely contain surges of heightened emotion herself. It was all too easy to fall in love with Luc Peretti. Hard experience could bolster her will to fight her feelings, but Matt didn't know how, wouldn't understand why there was any necessity to shield himself from possible hurt. She found herself violently thinking she would kill Luc if he ever let Matt down.

There were a hundred and sixty five-year-olds to be graded into teams. Short games were organised for the coaches to view and judge levels of talent. When Matt's rostered game came up, he ran onto the field with eager anticipation, determined to show how good he was at running after and kicking the soccer ball.

Luc grinned at her as they were left standing on the sidelines. 'Keen, isn't he?'

'Very,' she dryly agreed. And to stop Luc from assuming too much from the relaxation of rules today, she added, 'Once they start playing in earnest the soccer matches will be on Saturday.'

His day.

The grin faded into an ironic little smile. 'My Sundays are not full of other things, Skye. I'd much prefer to spend them with you.'

'That would be cutting yourself off from the life you've led these past six years,' she said, trying desperately for a matter-of-fact tone.

'I'm far more interested in a life with you and Matt,' he returned without the slightest hesitation for second thoughts.

Her eyes begged him to be honest. 'We don't belong in your world, Luc.'

'Are you saying I must give up everything else to have you and Matt?'

Her heart skipped at the intense purpose he loaded into his question. Would he do it? But surely he would regret it if he did, regret it and blame her for forcing such a decision in years to come.

She sucked in a quick breath and answered, 'No.

I'm just saying we're prisoners of our different back-grounds and it's foolish not to recognise that reality.'

His mouth quirked into a mocking smile. 'You'd be surprised how little my background means to me. You hit the nail on the head in calling it a prison— an oppressive prison I wish to be free of.'

She shook her head. 'It's not how you're acting, Luc. The bonds are very tight. You're pressuring your parents to accept us and they won't.'

'I'm simply giving them the chance, Skye.'

'You're using force.'

'No. Just telling them I've made my choice. Whether they want to live with it or not is up to them.'

'You're prepared to walk away from everything you've known?' She couldn't believe it.

He looked back at her with a searing blaze of un-wavering resolution. 'If I have to, yes.'

Her heart turned over. All her resistance to him melted under the heat of wildly hopeful desires, sud-denly let loose from the restrictions she had placed on them. He reached out and took her hand, interlac-ing her fingers with his, gripping hard, and it felt as though he was providing an anchor that would hold her from breaking adrift in any storm.

'Don't doubt my commitment to you and Matt, Skye,' he said, his voice a low throb that drummed on and on in her head. 'Don't doubt it for a second.'

The referee's whistle blew, alerting them to the start of Matt's game. The soccer ball was kicked from the centre line and then there was a blur of boys rac-ing after it. Skye was far too conscious of Luc's grip on her to concentrate on picking Matt out of the melee.

She could not stop herself from wanting this link with him. It felt good—warm, firm, secure. Maybe it was because she'd been alone for too long and Luc was Matt's father. He was also the only man she had ever loved and he was here for her, here for the child they'd made together, too. They should be together.

'Go for it, Matt!'

Luc's yell snapped Skye out of her thoughts. She saw Matt streaking ahead of the other boys, chasing down the ball which had been kicked towards the goal-posts. He reached it first, dribbled it away from the reach of the goalie who had run out to pick it up, then shot it into the net.

'Goal!' Luc yelled, releasing Skye's hand to throw his arms up in accolade to Matt's triumph—a triumph that beamed from his little boy face as he turned to see if they'd been watching and he instantly copied Luc's action, the shared joy of it making the triumph even better.

Skye clapped so hard her hands hurt. 'Well done, Matt!' she called and he trotted back proudly to the centre of the field to start play again.

'That's our son!' Luc said just as proudly, throwing one of his lowered arms around Skye's shoulders and hugging her close. 'Fastest boy on the field and proving he's a striker.'

What if he'd been the slowest and a dud at soccer, Skye thought. But he wasn't so there was no point in thinking it. She doubted Matt was going to be a dud at anything. He was Luc's son.

And hers.

Parents together.

Luc rubbed his cheek over her hair and murmured, 'Marry me, Skye. This is how it should be.'

She wanted to say yes. Being held so close to him, her whole body yearned for the intimacy that could bind them much closer. But the fears she had of consequences could not be banished.

'Give it time, Luc,' she muttered, ducking her head to break the yearning she felt coming from the caress of his cheek.

'Well, at least that's not a no,' he said on a sigh of satisfaction, and dropped his arm from her shoulder to take her hand again, squeezing it possessively. 'I'm here to stay, Skye. The sooner you realise that, the sooner we can become a family.'

That might be true.

But Skye couldn't bring herself to risk making any commitment to him when they'd only spent a couple of days together.

There was a long future ahead of them.

Let Luc prove what he said.

CHAPTER NINE

LUC rolled up the designs for the new apartment complex he'd been working on and set about clearing his desk. Today was the last day of Matt's first school term. Tomorrow was Good Friday. Soccer on Saturday. And on Monday...an elated grin broke out on his face at the thought of it...on Monday he was flying Skye and Matt up to the Gold Coast in Queensland for a family vacation.

Skye's lack of trust in him had been his trump card in breaking down her resistance to the plan. As a *separated* parent, he was entitled to have his son for a week of any school vacation. A family law court would certainly grant it to him. It was an argument that couldn't be refuted but she was afraid of how he might use the time with Matt.

The power of the Peretti family weighed on her mind and he couldn't blame her for worrying about what might happen if he introduced Matt to them behind her back. Not that he would, and the fear wasn't spoken, but her tension over letting Matt out of her sight for so long and the very negative emphasis she'd previously laid on his family background, left Luc in no doubt about how she thought and felt.

It also assured him she would be tempted by his invitation to supervise every moment Matt was with him. He'd produced an internet printout on the *three*-bedroom penthouse apartment he'd booked, plus printouts on the major tourist attractions they could take Matt to—Sea World, Warner Bros. Movie World, Dream World...a family fun vacation all laid out to both of them so Matt's eagerness for his mother to accompany them, and the lure of sharing in her son's new adventures, added to the winning package.

'*Three* bedrooms,' she'd said pointedly, denying the other temptation he had very much on his mind.

'Definitely three,' he assured her, though he privately wanted only two to be used.

He intended a very deliberate seduction this time—no driven quickness about any of the lovemaking. Once he had Skye contentedly sharing his bed, feeling thoroughly loved, the step to marriage should not be such a difficult one for her to take. He wanted her as his wife. And Matt was not the only child he wanted to have.

He fiercely resented having missed out on his son's birth, his babyhood, the toddler years. After he and Skye were married... Luc checked his own eagerness as he realised he knew nothing about how Matt's birth had been for her, whether she would be keen to have more children.

They'd had such little private time to talk—mostly small snatches he'd deliberately manoeuvred. Skye avoided being alone with him whenever she could. Avoidance, however, would be much more difficult for her while staying in the same apartment for a week. After Matt went to bed...

Luc's train of thought was abruptly broken by his father's unheralded arrival—no call from his secretary, the office door swept open, and in he stepped with all the arrogant hauteur of a man who took authority as though it was his right.

Luc felt himself bristling into attack mode and deliberately adopted a relaxed air, leaning back in the chair behind his desk and viewing his father with whimsical curiosity. 'To what do I owe the honour of this visit?' he drawled.

Since their confrontation over Skye at the Bellevue Hill mansion two months ago, they had only met in boardroom meetings with nothing but business on the agenda. Only current and future property development projects were discussed between them, across a table with all other heads of departments present.

His father viewed him now with barely contained impatience, obviously frustrated by Luc's stubborn and rebellious stand against conforming to expectations. 'We will be celebrating Easter Sunday as usual this year,' he stated tersely.

Which meant a big gathering of Italian families for a highly festive lunch. 'I'm glad Mamma feels up to it,' Luc answered dryly.

His father's mouth tightened in anger. 'I'm amazed you have any consideration for her feelings since you haven't seen fit to give her the comfort of a visit or a call.'

'I've been too long on a one-way street with consideration of feelings, Dad. When it starts to go two ways...'

'She is still grieving over Roberto.'

'Then I'm not the son she wants with her, am I?'

'You are the only son she has now.'

'Don't expect me to dance to that tune. Especially not on Roberto's grave.'

'He was your brother.' The emphatic reminder was meant to sting and it did.

'More your son than my brother,' Luc flared back, losing his cool. 'His allegiance was to you, not to me. He sold me out for your approval.'

'He saved you from folly,' his father thundered.

Luc sucked in a quick breath and forced himself to contain the violent emotions surging through him. There was no point in arguing against entrenched prejudice. Waste of time and breath. 'Have you said all you want to say?' he asked in a calmer tone.

He watched his father fight an inner war before coming to the conclusion that it was time to shift ground before bad blood was irrevocably spilled. 'Your mother expects you to lunch on Sunday,' he tossed out as though he himself disdained any need for his surviving son's presence at the family table.

'Are Skye and Matt invited?'

'They are not,' he snapped, refusing to give a moment's consideration to the challenge.

Which was just as well, Luc thought, because he doubted he could persuade Skye into any meeting with his parents at this early juncture. 'Then I won't be there,' he stated unequivocally.

It earned a furious glare. 'Your mother will be disappointed.'

'I'm sorry for her disappointment but it is of your making, Dad. Let's get this in precise perspective.'

'Perspective!' His father snorted in disgust. 'I can only hope your blindness soon passes.'

With the satisfaction of having the last word, he walked out, slamming the door shut behind him.

Luc was somewhat surprised to find he didn't care

how his parents viewed his absence. All his life he had attended their parties, been a focus of their pride and pleasure. He'd actually fed their expectations of him. And been liberally rewarded for it.

But taking Skye from him...taking Matt from him...it had killed any consideration he might have had for their feelings. He didn't want to be with them. He wasn't sure he ever wanted to be with them again...certainly not without Skye and Matt at his side, and both of them being welcomed into their company.

Easter Sunday...

No doubt he would be missed and his absence commented upon by family friends, much to the chagrin of his parents, but for Luc, Easter Sunday was simply the day he had to live through before he could take Skye and Matt away with him for a whole week together. He would quite happily stay in his Bondi Beach apartment; planning, anticipating, gearing himself up to win what he wanted to win.

He stared at the door his father had shut and felt the world he had belonged to receding from him, losing its influence, losing its importance. He suspected the longer he stayed away from it, the less it would mean to him. In fact, it hadn't meant much for a long time—just old familiar connections that had floated through the emptiness of his life after his family had got rid of Skye. He'd given them his courtesy and attention but would he really miss them?

He didn't need them.

He needed Skye.

And their son.

Though he couldn't deny there was also a bitterly burning need in him to have the injustice done to them acknowledged by his parents—acknowledged and redressed!

CHAPTER TEN

ANOTHER day of guilty pleasures, Skye thought as she stood under the shower in her ensuite bathroom, using the expensive perfumed soap which came supplied with all the other luxury items in the penthouse apartment. Luc was paying for everything—absolutely everything—and she shouldn't really be riding along on his vacation with Matt, taking all he was giving.

First class seats on the flight—Matt's first ride in an aeroplane.

More than first class accommodation—every possible comfort, plus wonderful ocean views and the big screen television set in the living room was connected to pay TV, luxury indeed for Matt who was fascinated by the huge variety of shows he could watch.

Yesterday they'd had a marvellous time at Sea World—seeing the awesome Polar bears, watching the fun-loving seals and actually having shallow water encounters with dolphins. And Matt had had enormous fun today, playing with the Looney Tunes characters in the Splash Zone at Warner Bros. Movie World.

She, too, was enjoying herself—couldn't deny it—yet she had the uncomfortable sense of being put in Luc's debt, despite his insistence that he owed her far more than he could ever repay. Worse than that was the secret pleasure of simply being with him. It wasn't just sharing the joy of watching their son have the time of his life. The more time she spent with Luc, the more he reminded her of everything she had loved about him.

It was extremely difficult to keep her focus on Matt. Not difficult...impossible! she ruefully corrected herself. Even here, in the shower, just running the soap over her naked body was stirring sensual memories of how Luc had once caressed her, making her feel how much she missed having that kind of intimacy with him.

He certainly wanted it. There was no mistaking the simmering desire in his eyes whenever he looked at her, whether they were sharing some mutual pleasure in Matt or having a practical discussion on what they were to eat for their next meal. No direct reference was made to it, not by her, not by him. However, the simmering did keep her on edge, trying to ensure nothing she said or did turned up the heat.

The mental cage she'd put around her own feelings for Luc was being continually rattled. The physical attraction was reinforced every time he touched her— a protective arm around her waist in a crowd, a courteous taking of her arm when entering a restaurant, holding her hand—and Matt's—as they walked along together. There was nothing overtly sexual about any of it, yet it subtly made her acutely aware of wanting more from him.

Marry me...

Skye wished it could be as simple as that. She couldn't bring herself to believe it, not with her past experience of the Peretti family. Luc might think he was in control of all the complex factors that would come into play if a marriage between them did take place, but she could feel their shadows in the background, waiting to grow more and more substance, threatening to strangle whatever happiness they might have together.

Besides which, she couldn't help having doubts about Luc's motivation for a marriage with her. It wasn't a clear-cut case of loving her, loving Matt, wanting them to be together. She felt the payback element very strongly—people being manipulated, including herself, which made her very uneasy about accepting anything at face value.

Sexual chemistry was something else.

Luc was certainly right about its not going away.

With a wistful sigh, Skye finished washing herself, turned off the shower, and reached for the lovely soft bath towel—another luxury to revel in—another guilt, wrapping herself in what Luc's wealth provided. This kind of living where cost was no object to every material pleasure was horribly seductive. And could very easily become addictive.

Did Luc mean it to be?

Was it another form of manipulation to get his own way?

A one-week family vacation, showing her a bed of roses...

No vacation was real life, Skye firmly told herself, more like a dream...time out of time. She had to keep remembering that, not let it influence her into glossing over the thorns in the situation with Luc's family.

Although it was mid-April, the days were still hot and the evenings balmy on the Gold Coast. Skye chose to slip into her white and brown sundress, wanting to feel cool and relaxed after wearing rather sticky jeans all day. It was also a relief to brush out her hair from the pinned top-knot and she left it loose. Luc had gone out to get takeaway for dinner tonight so she didn't bother with sandals, padding out to the living-room barefoot to check on Matt.

Having already supervised his bath and put him in pyjamas, she'd left him esconced in front of the television, happily watching a channel which only showed cartoons. He was still there, although now there was a pizza box beside him, and he was eating a big slice dripping with melted cheese and a tomato base.

'Not waiting for us?' she asked in surprise. Luc had made a big thing of having meals together.

'I'm hungry and Daddy said I could have it here,' Matt informed her between bites. 'He's just gone to have a shower. There's a whole lot of stuff in the kitchen,' he added in case she was hungry, too, and couldn't wait.

'I'll check it out.'

Matt's attention was already glued to the screen again, happily engrossed in watching more antics from the Looney Tunes characters.

Skye moved into the kitchen, expecting to find other pizza boxes. All the ingredients for a very tasty salad were sitting on the sink—lettuce, tomato, capsicum, avocado, cucumber, a bottle of Italian dressing. A loaf of twisted bread, made with cheese and spinach, sat on an oven tray ready to be heated up. Slabs of rump steak were being marinaded on a meat plate, and a covered plastic dish containing ten little chat potatoes with butter and parsley was waiting to be put into the microwave oven. Pizza was clearly not on their menu tonight.

'Thought we'd have a proper meal instead,' Luc said, breezing into the kitchen, barefoot like herself, and wearing a fresh pair of white shorts with a brightly coloured Hawaiian shirt he hadn't bothered to button up.

The air was sucked straight out of Skye's lungs. The mental cage flew open and the wild beast of desire flexed its muscles and ran riot through her entire body. Muscles quivered or contracted. Her pulse-rate hopped, skipped and jumped. Heat zoomed through her bloodstream. Her skin tingled. Even her scalp tingled. And her breasts tightened and strained against the cups of cotton that kept them contained.

The blast of virile masculinity was so strong it took an act of will to stop staring, turn her back on it and find enough presence of mind to say, 'I'll wash the lettuce.'

'I'll go set the table out on the balcony,' Luc said cheerfully, busying himself collecting plates and cutlery. 'Best to eat there where we can chat over dinner without the noise and distraction of Matt's cartoons.'

Chat... Skye clung to that word as her hands automatically went to work, tearing off lettuce leaves, running the water in the sink.

Luc had stopped her from retreating into her bedroom the first evening they were here, pleading that he knew nothing of the years he'd missed with Matt and asking her to fill him in on them—such a reasonable request it was only fair to oblige him.

Last night he had drawn her out about her own life since they'd been parted—her mother's death, the move from Caringbah to Brighton-Le-Sands, building up a clientele for her massage business. Only when he'd asked about future plans had she felt it was time to excuse herself and retire, conscious that he now dominated any thinking about the future, making it too slippery a subject. She didn't want to fall into the dangerous trap of discussing marriage with him.

What did Luc have planned for tonight?

Should she plead a headache and escape?

The brief breathing space while he was out on the balcony was not long enough to get the panic at her own vulnerability to him under control. On returning, he headed straight to the refrigerator, just as she was lifting a salad bowl out of the kitchen cupboard next to it, and it felt like a whirlwind coming at her, intent on catching her up in it.

But he didn't touch her. He grinned as he opened the refrigerator door, tossing nothing but companionable words at her. 'Managed to buy a fine bottle of Chardonnay as well, already chilled. Might as well pour us a drink now. It won't take me long to grill the steaks.'

Wine!

Adding an intoxicant to the chaos in her head was not a good idea, but Skye had accepted a glass of wine on the flight up here, and at the restaurants where they'd dined the past two evenings. Refusing one now might alert Luc to a difference in her mood—one she didn't want to explain. Besides, she could sip sparingly. Better not to make an issue of it.

'Thanks,' she said, forcing a smile.

'I remembered how you liked cheesecake, too,' he went on, his eyes dancing with pleasure in his planning. 'Bought two slices with a mango topping and a jar of cream to have for sweets.'

He was remembering more than cheesecake, Skye thought, and making her remember, too. 'You have been busy,' she said dryly, moving back to the sink with the bowl, ready to attack the other vegetables to put in the salad. 'I thought you were getting us pizzas.'

'Impulsive change of mind,' he excused.

With a lot more impulses involved!

'Hope you approve,' he added, his voice loaded with persuasive appeal.

'It's fine, Luc,' she obliged, recognising there was no reasonable argument against what he'd done. Normal politeness forced her to say, 'And special thanks for the cheesecake. I'll enjoy it.'

He set her glass of wine on the bench beside the sink. Still no attempt at touching. There was absolutely nothing Skye could object to in his behaviour. Nor in his dress which she had to admit was as appropriate as her own for an evening at home on the Gold Coast—cool, casual, relaxed.

And Luc did appear to be completely relaxed as he went about cooking what had to be cooked, meat under the griller, bread in the oven, potatoes in the microwave, chatting to her about the day they'd just spent together, acting like a happy father who'd given his son a special treat, *acting like a happy husband sharing it all with his wife...before they shared a lot more in bed.*

Skye couldn't get that last thought out of her head.

The buzz of anticipation *was* in the air, charged with so much sexual electricity she was amazed to find she had actually prepared the salad and tossed the dressing through it, which gave her the chance to escape from the highly charged intimacy of working in the kitchen with Luc. She carried the bowl out to the balcony and paused there long enough to take several deep breaths of fresh sea air.

Nothing was going to happen unless she let it happen.

Skye fixed this maxim firmly in her mind in a desperate effort to counteract the rampant desires that were clamouring to sneak right past it, whispering their tempting promises of pleasure, insidiously urging her to satisfy more than a weakness for cheesecake, demanding to know why shouldn't she take what was on offer? It didn't commit her to marriage.

'Lovely evening, isn't it?'

Her heart jolted at the realisation Luc was just behind her. She whipped around from the balcony railing, gearing up to fight off any move on her, only to find him standing on the other side of the table, setting down an ice bucket containing the bottle of wine.

'Yes, it is,' she choked out, hoping she didn't look alarmed.

Was it all in *her* mind?

He smiled, watching the light sea breeze gently lifting the silky fan of her hair around her shoulders.

No, it wasn't just her.

The smile was very sensual. And satisfaction glinted in his eyes as he said, 'Matt's fallen asleep on the floor. Shall I carry him in to bed?'

Out of the way. No possible distraction from a little boy who was totally worn out from the day's excitement, too exhausted to care where he slept. Had that been planned, too?

'I'll do it while you finish up in the kitchen,' Skye answered, wanting the activity, anything to put space between her and Luc.

'Okay.' He shrugged and retreated.

Skye followed him inside. Matt had simply toppled over beside the pizza box, not even a cushion under his head. He didn't stir when she gathered him up in her arms and remained a dead weight as he was carried into his bedroom, head lolling on her shoulder, arms and legs limp. She laid him down on the pillow, manouevred his body in between the sheets, tucked him in and dropped a kiss on his forehead.

There was not so much as a flutter of consciousness from Matt. He was completely at peace, leaving it up to his parents to take care of his future.

Skye wished she had a crystal ball to look into and see the consequences of all the futures that could radiate out from this point in her life. Right now she was just meeting each day as it came, trying to evade any decisions which might commit her to a course that would put Matt and herself in a bad place. It would be so easy to shift all the responsibility on to Luc, to surrender them both into his keeping, for better or for worse, but she'd come too far on her own to give up all control.

Somehow she had to see her way more clearly. Luc had been asking about Matt's life and hers. Since she had to get through the next hour or two with him, why not ask about his life? Up until now she had shied away from showing any personal interest in him, sensing he would seize some advantage from it, draw her into knowing more than she would feel comfortable with.

Her mouth curved in black irony as she turned away from Matt and caught sight of her reflection in the mirrors covering the doors of the built-in cupboard. It was not the reflection of a woman who felt comfortable with anything.

Her eyes were wide and anxious. Her shoulders were stiff, carrying too many burdens. Her hair looked undisciplined, floating free. And while it might not be discernible to other eyes, the ache in her body—screaming to be soothed—seemed to be telegraphed from every taut curve outlined by the too skimpy dress.

Bad choice!

She should have worn a less *inviting* outfit. Though her reaction to Luc would have been the same. It was too late to change now—too obvious a move, telling Luc how deeply disturbed she was by him. Better to concentrate on using tonight to find out where he was coming from, where he might take her to if she weakened.

She forced her legs to take her out of the shelter of Matt's bedroom. The stark truth was…there was no hiding place from Luc Peretti. If he wasn't present physically, he was certainly in her mind. Everything he represented had to be faced, sooner or later. Postponing the evil hour wouldn't help one bit.

The television was still playing cartoons. She found the remote control panel and turned it off. The abrupt fall of silence prompted her to wryly imagine a drumroll, heralding curtain up. The stage had definitely been set. The waft of warm bread was enough to tease an appetite. No doubt Luc would set the ball rolling on action. What she had to do was catch the ball and direct some action herself.

'Ready, Skye?' he called from the kitchen.

'Yes,' she replied. 'Do you need a hand with anything?'

'No. I'm serving now. Go on out to the table and I'll be with you in a minute.'

She did as he directed since it suited her, as well. The table was round, big enough to seat six, not so wide that sitting opposite each other was an awkward distance but wide enough to prevent any easy physical touching. As long as she sat down, she was safe.

Skye sat.

The bread was being kept warm under a tea-cloth. Their glasses were filled with wine. The salad and potatoes were handy for self-serving. Luc came striding out with their steaks on a plate, placing it on the centre of the table with a flourish, inviting her to help herself.

He sat down, grinning from ear to ear. 'Isn't this nice?' he said.

It was...if the circumstances had been anywhere near normal. 'Yes. Thank you,' Skye replied, feeling swamped by the power of the man.

The dinner was irrelevant.

His eyes said he wanted to eat her up.

And in her heart of hearts, Skye knew she wanted to be eaten by Luc Peretti.

CHAPTER ELEVEN

SILENCE was the enemy. The romantic setting, Luc smiling at her, the sense of sharing an intimate dinner…silence seeded the longing to forget the lost years, forget what had parted them, slide back into that time of innocence when their joy in each other overwhelmed everything else, making the differences between them irrelevant.

Skye forced herself to plunge into conversation, instinctively targeting his family connection, needing to keep in the forefront of her mind why she couldn't allow herself to be tempted into setting it aside.

'What does your work entail these days, Luc?' she asked, forcing herself into normal action as well, piling some salad and a couple of potatoes onto her plate.

'Still designing buildings, though I'm now head of that department,' he answered easily, waiting for her to finish serving herself before doing the same.

'A fast rise,' she commented. He'd been a junior architect in the Peretti Corporation six years ago.

'I could say I had the talent and the brain for it,' he drawled with arrogant confidence.

'Not to mention being Maurizio Peretti's oldest son.'

The good humour instantly left his face, his expression hardening into cold pride, his dark eyes sharply challenging. 'You don't think I've earned my place?'

It pulled Skye back from the black judgement she had made. Because his family had not been fair to her, was no reason why she shouldn't be fair to Luc. 'I think you're capable of doing whatever you set out to do,' she said slowly. 'I just meant…well, you are tied to your father. Weren't both you and Roberto educated and groomed to fit into the places he planned for you to take?'

Architecture, engineering…perfect for a business centred on property development.

'I can't answer for Roberto who may well have pursued what pleased my father,' he said sardonically, 'but I was always interested in design, Skye, and chose my own career.'

Yes, he would, she realised, just as he had chosen to continue a relationship with her, despite his parents' disapproval. Only damning evidence of the worst infidelity she could have committed had stopped him. Luc was not his father's tool, yet being so strongly connected to the family business did leave him vulnerable to manipulation, and blood ties were not easily broken.

He felt he'd earned his place, was proud of filling it, probably with distinction—an important cog in the Peretti wheel. He wouldn't want to walk away from it. Skye suspected he'd fight to keep it, which could mean deadly conflict with his father who would definitely be opposed to the marriage Luc wanted. And she and Matt would be the meat in the sandwich.

Not a happy prospect.

'I report to my father at boardroom meetings but I

don't work under him,' Luc tossed at her to elucidate the situation. 'I have autonomy within my department.'

'Autonomy...' Skye seized on that word as though it was a lifeline out of the frightening problems that had been whirling through her brain.

It meant Luc was his own boss. He couldn't be manipulated where business judgements were concerned. And it was probably faulty reasoning to attach what had happened with the damning photographs to what might develop in his work situation. Emotional judgements were in a far more volatile territory.

'I'm sorry for implying...you could be pushed around,' she rushed out, suddenly feeling very much on the wrong foot. 'I guess your father is...something of a bogey-man to me.'

His face relaxed, his eyes softening to sympathetic understanding. 'I don't live in my father's pocket, Skye. He can't buy me away from you and Matt.'

Embarrassment—or was it something else? A deep treacherous pleasure?—sent a flood of heat to her cheeks. The commitment—conviction—in his voice, the possessive warmth in his eyes, the unswerving sense of purpose engulfing her... Skye teetered on the edge of giving him her trust, wanting him to take care of everything: her, Matt, the future...

She barely brought herself back from the brink, finding a brittle escape in focusing on the food on her plate, telling herself to keep talking.

Silence was the enemy.

Luc was filling it with temptations.

She was not even clear on why she had to fight them any more.

'What are you working on at the moment?' she asked, hoping his answer would be long and distracting.

He obligingly described his current project. The company had bought up old boatyards along the harbour shore at Balmain and Luc was designing a new apartment complex to be built on the site. She listened to the pleasure and satisfaction in his voice as he explained what he wanted constructed and how it would take advantage of the view, as well as catering for every modern aspect of living in the city.

Clearly he enjoyed his work and the opportunity to have such lavish projects to work on. He might not recognise how deeply he was tied to the Peretti Corporation since it had always been there for him to step into, but Skye did.

Big money at his fingertips.

Big money to invest how he saw fit.

Big money to spend how he pleased in his private life, as well.

As long as he stayed where he belonged.

Or was that being unfair, too? Luc had more than enough driving force to succeed in establishing himself anywhere, in any company, or on his own. Why couldn't she just accept that he didn't live in his father's pocket?

Because she couldn't make the fear go away.

It was too deeply rooted in past pain.

'Do you still live at Cronulla?' she asked, needing to know if he'd continued living with his family in the incredibly luxurious horseshoe compound facing the waterfront there.

He shook his head. 'Dad sold that place five years ago.'

The timing made Skye wonder if Maurizio Peretti had decided to shift his family right away from the neighbouring suburb of Caringbah where Luc's illegitimate child was possibly far too close for comfort.

Luc flashed her an ironic look. 'He upgraded to a heritage-listed mansion at Bellevue Hill.'

Mega-bucks, she thought, plus getting way out of the range of any accidental meeting with the unsuitable woman and her child.

'Big enough to house three generations of the family,' Luc went on, his voice carrying a sardonic edge.

Everything within Skye recoiled at the idea of living in the same house with his parents. It would be absolute madness to even consider marrying Luc if it meant co-habiting with his family. Regardless of how attractive he was to her, how good he was to Matt…

'It hasn't worked out that way,' he said, forestalling the tortured impulse to reject his proposal here and now.

'Oh?' It was more a choked gasp than a query. Skye was appalled at how wildly hope had galloped over despair.

'Roberto obligingly brought his bride home—' Luc's riveting dark eyes glittered derisively '—the bride my father had hand-picked for me, except I didn't oblige.'

'So Roberto married her instead?' She shook her head, shocked that such a switch would be made in so serious a life commitment.

Luc shrugged. 'He was happy to. And I'm sure Gaia found Roberto a more charming husband than I would have been. Besides which, it was a very advantageous marriage on both sides. Unfortunately, even the best-laid plans can go astray. Gaia was still childless when Roberto died, and has since returned to her own family.'

'You're not expected to...to console his widow?'

'I doubt my father would wish me to take a wife who might not be able to produce the grandchildren he wants,' he answered cynically. 'Gaia suffered two miscarriages in her short marriage to Roberto.'

It was revolting to Skye to think of any woman being regarded as a baby-making machine. On the other hand, Roberto's wife had probably been sadly disappointed herself not to have had a much-wanted child.

'I'm sure your father can find you another suitable wife for his dynastic ambitions,' she tossed at Luc, knowing she should never take on that role herself.

'I won't marry anyone but you, Skye.'

His eyes burned with unshakeable purpose, making her too agitated to even pretend to eat any more. She put down her knife and fork, willing herself to face him with her own determination. 'It won't work,' she stated bluntly.

He set down his cutlery and focused on her, the whole concentrated power of his energy coming at her full blast. 'I'll make it work.'

She leaned forward, fighting for her independence again. 'If you think, for one moment, I'd live under the same roof as...'

'I don't live there myself,' he added. 'I moved out when Roberto married. Bought my own apartment at Bondi Beach.'

Her mind whirled at this apparent disconnection to his family, though it quickly seized on the fact that the suburb of Bondi was right next to Bellevue Hill. 'Not far from them,' spilled from her mouth.

'Far enough to have separate lives,' he retorted.

Separate... Skye paused to catch her breath. Was she making bogey-men of everything, snatching at whatever fed her fear of the power his family had to hurt? Luc was proving at every point he was his own man. And he had been hurt, too, by the dreadful deception that had been played to make him turn his back on her.

'Why did you move out?' she asked, wondering if there had been some earlier rift between him and his family.

He shrugged. 'I didn't care to have the happiness of Roberto's marriage rubbed in my face every day.'

Her insecurities surged again. 'Regrets for rejecting it yourself, Luc?'

'None at all. I wished my brother well with it.'

'Then why did it upset you?'

'It didn't upset me. I knew my father would constantly use it as leverage to get me to fall into line with his plans, which would end up being unpleasant for everyone, so I removed myself from the situation.'

'While still maintaining your relationship with your family,' she said, pressing to ascertain just how important it was to him.

'I had the choice of coming and going as I pleased.'

'Did you ever miss a special family occasion?'

'I just did.'

Again she felt her defensive mat being swept out

from under her feet. 'What was it?' she asked, needing to know how much it meant.

His eyes glittered a joyless challenge. 'You remember the Easter Sunday luncheon you attended with me six years ago?'

The memory leapt vividly to mind—the huge luncheon party, and feeling like a fish out of water amongst all the Italian families, people engaging Luc in conversation and subtly ignoring her presence. Not obvious snubs, but definitely left out in the cold while warmth was overflowing everywhere else. It had been such a relief when Roberto had taken the time to charm her out of her sense of alienation.

Luc's brother...setting up the trap to get rid of her.

'You haven't told me how Roberto died.'

Luc frowned.

Realising she'd thrown him off-stride, Skye bitterly reminded him of the person who had betrayed them both. 'He was *nice* to me that Easter Sunday, making me feel welcome when no one else did.'

There was a flash of pain in his eyes. 'I'm sorry...sorry I subjected you to...' He shook his head. 'It won't happen again, Skye. I swear it. I won't take you anywhere near my family without an assurance that you will be welcomed.' He looked at her with searing intensity as he gave her his personal assurance. 'And I'd be watching. Watching every minute. If you're made to feel uncomfortable—'

'I would feel uncomfortable anyway, Luc,' she cut in bleakly.

He nodded, not pressing. 'You might find that Matt will break the ice,' he said hopefully.

She couldn't help thinking their only hope of having any happiness together was in living separate lives to his family. And was that really a possibility?

'Roberto died of extensive injuries from a car accident,' Luc said, grimacing as he softly added, 'He did regret what he'd done, Skye.'

'Not while he had his life to live,' she pointed out, her eyes sadly mocking Luc's view of the situation. 'I don't think your father is ever going to accept me.'

'I'd like to give him the time to take that option.'

'Time won't make any difference. I'm sure you challenged him over this Easter Sunday, asking if Matt and I would be welcome. He wouldn't come at it, would he?'

'I don't expect a quick turnaround. But the point was made, Skye.'

'And he made his. You're welcome. I'm not.'

Ruthless steel answered her. 'It will be his loss if he doesn't change his attitude.'

Your loss, too, Skye thought, and spelled out the most testing scenario of all. 'What if he threatens to cut you off?'

'So be it.'

Not the slightest dent in the steel. But Skye felt it was pride talking. In his heart of hearts, Luc didn't believe it would happen. To him, the family link was too strong. Blood would tell in the end. It was the argument he'd used to her for his parents' eventual acceptance of Matt as their grandchild. What he didn't take into consideration was how much *they* felt Matt's blood was tainted by hers.

A wave of sheer misery washed through her. Here she was sitting opposite a man she'd loved—a man she still couldn't help loving—the father of her child, wanting to marry her—and a decision about their future should be simple and straightforward, not hemmed around with the dark threat of endless pain.

'Skye...'

She had nothing left to say. The grief his family had already given her was swimming through her mind, carrying her towards rocks that would smash any happiness she might achieve with Luc. It startled her when his chair scraped back. Her heart leapt erratically as he rose to his feet, his eyes blazing with savage emotion.

'*You* come first with me!' he hurled at her, using his voice like a hammer, forcefully intent on breaking through anything that held him out of the centre of her existence.

The words rang in Skye's ears, drowning out the voices of doom that kept tugging her away from him...*first with me...first with me*. Not his son. Not his family. *She came first.*

In a few quick strides he was around the table, pulling her up from her chair, wrapping her in a fierce embrace, pouring out passionate pleas.

'Don't reject me, Skye...'

She didn't want to. Her whole body was flooding with the need to be held by him, loved by him, surrendering so utterly to his embrace, her head nestled onto his shoulder and her eyes closed to shut out the rest of the world.

'You know it's good between us. We connect on levels that no one else even touches.'

It felt good just feeling his chest rising and falling with each breath he took.

'I made myself forget that, told myself I'd only

imagined it to satisfy some need in me.' Harsh mockery in his voice, then powerful conviction. 'But I only had to meet you again to know we should never have been parted.'

Never echoed in Skye's mind, knocking out all the reasons why they should be parted.

'I've been like a hollow man all these years without you.'

The emptiness left after your heart has been torn out, she thought, and hers had only been punched back into chaotic life when Luc had re-appeared and the fear of being hurt like that again...and she might be...but right now, the need to have him was so paramount, it pushed the fear away to be dealt with some other time. Not now. The emptiness cried out to be filled, filled to overflowing.

'I want to make love to you, Skye.'

Yes...

Her whole body sighed in relief as the constraints she had willed on it were lifted.

Luc's imprisoning embrace eased a little, one arm still possessively pinning her to him while the other hand wove through the long fall of her hair, finding enough purchase to gently tug her head back, tilting it up to his.

'Look at me...'

She opened her eyes to see dark torment in his.

'It's not just sex, Skye. I can get that anywhere. You can, too. Don't belittle what we have together. I want you to remember how it was...how it can still be...'

He carried those last throbbing words to her mouth, making her feel them...how it still was...Luc kissing her, the wild surge of response shooting through her, wanting him so much, wanting all he'd ever given her before, everything so beautifully right between them.

They weren't forceful kisses, no taking in them at all, more a searching for the sense of mutual loving, the desire to establish it was so, overriding any urge to dominate. He was sexually aroused. She was, too. But it didn't matter, just a natural part of what was happening, the yearning of their bodies expressing the need for each other.

'Come to bed with me, Skye.'

It wasn't a command. Nor a plea. It was a softly murmured request for them to move to a private place where nothing else could intrude on the intimacy of being together.

'Yes,' she whispered, rebelling against the inhibitions that warned of consequences she would never be able to control.

The inhibitions sprang from Luc's world, but Luc was here with her, and if she truly came first with him, couldn't she let him come first with her?

He eased back and took her hand in his, leading her off the balcony, leading...not picking her up and carrying her off, letting her feet speak their consent to this move and they did, willingly walking through the apartment to his bedroom, though they faltered when she saw the bed, one high-risk consequence insisting on being acknowledged.

'I'm not protected, Luc.'

'I'll take care of it.'

The smooth reply was meant to soothe away the fear, but it was a sharp reminder that he hadn't cared last time, had actually hoped she'd fallen pregnant.

She turned to face him, her eyes searching for truth. 'Will you?' she asked, needing to know there was no manipulation of her vulnerability intended—no thought of future entrapment. The gift of love should be a free gift, if this was what it was.

He lifted a hand and gently stroked the anxiety from her facial muscles, his eyes promising safety with him as he answered, 'If we make another child, it will only be when we both want to. A planned baby, Skye, not conceived by accident nor a lack of fore-thought.'

'You came prepared for...for...'

'I hoped.'

'You aimed for it,' she wryly corrected him, run-ning her fingers down the bared strip of chest his un-buttoned shirt had left open for her touch—a temp-tation beyond bearing any longer.

'Why wouldn't I? You're the woman I want above all others.'

The man she wanted above all others.

He dropped his hand to her shoulder, fingertips drawing the strap of her sundress over to her arm. 'Do you want to stop me, Skye?'

'No.' She sucked in a deep breath, relaxing as it shuddered out again. 'No one can take this away.'

Maybe they could create a small world together—a place of survival for the love they could share, shel-tered from the storms that might rage around them, trying to break in and tear them apart.

She wanted it to be possible.

The magic of touching like this...making love...

Was it strong enough to hold against any destruc-tive intrusion?

Or was such a small world an impossible dream, bred from desires that craved satisfaction?

Skye didn't know.

Didn't want to think.

The need...simply to feel...made everything else fade away.

CHAPTER TWELVE

Luc found himself in two minds as he drove up to the Bellevue Hill mansion. It had been nine months since he had last set foot in it and he wasn't sure he wanted to make any rapprochement with his parents on a personal level. He might have a happier future with Skye if he kept them shut out of his private life.

Yet family was family.

Business forced him to deal with his father in boardroom meetings where all current property developments were reported on and future projects discussed. The subject of Skye was never mentioned between them. No doubt his father thought if he ignored the bone of contention long enough, it might go away, especially if the woman he regarded as unsuitable did not agree to marry his son. Or given enough time, Luc might have second thoughts about going through with his declared intention.

His mother had not made the effort to contact him—probably still wallowing in grief over Roberto. He had not been inclined to make the effort to visit her, either, remembering all too well her rigid disapproval of Skye—setting a foundation of rejection which Roberto had played on, creating a lethal structure of lies with supposedly just cause.

Luc could not bring himself to sympathise with his mother's grief when he was constantly conscious of the damage his brother had wrought, not to mention the years he'd missed of his own son's life. Besides which, her approval meant nothing to him any more.

He wondered if his mother knew about Matt or had his father *protected* her from any unsettling knowledge of an unwanted grandchild. If he had kept Matt's existence from her, the cat would certainly be out of the bag tonight!

He left his car parked near the front door which was promptly opened by the butler who informed him his parents were in the formal drawing room. Interesting, Luc thought grimly. Having called ahead, he was expected. No doubt his courtesy call had alerted his father to the possibility of serious news behind it so he was getting the grand treatment, designed to impress on him what he might be giving up in going against his parents' wishes.

Futile game-playing. He'd moved beyond any influence his father could bring to bear on him. Even professionally. He could walk away from the Peretti Corporation and start his own business, if necessary.

He didn't wait for the butler to usher him into the drawing room, moving ahead with quick purposeful strides, opening the door himself. His father was standing in front of the marble fireplace, the dominant figure amongst all his prized material possessions. His mother was sitting very upright in a nearby armchair. Still wearing black, he noted, but her regal demeanour telegraphed that her attention could be courted again.

She wore a full complement of jewellery and she'd obviously been to a beauty salon today, her thick wavy grey hair groomed to perfection, not a strand out of place, her fingernails buffed and polished. Her face was skilfully made up to presentation standard and Luc reflected on how imposing she could be when it suited her—totally intimidating to Skye.

'Mamma…more yourself again, I see,' he said dryly, walking forward to confront them more closely.

'No thanks to you, Luciano, since you haven't seen fit to come home for nine months,' his father remonstrated.

He shrugged. 'This isn't my home. You both know where I live…if I was needed,' he added in a pointed drawl.

'It's not a case of need,' came the brusque retort. 'Out of respect for your mother, you should have—'

'He is here now, Maurizio,' his mother broke in, giving Luc a gracious nod. 'Please sit down. It has been a long time.'

He propped himself on the well-cushioned armrest of a sofa, not about to let his father stand over him. 'I assume Dad told you what I've been doing. If you were interested in re-acquainting yourself with Skye Sumner and meeting our son, you could have called me, Mamma.'

Her lips compressed, whether in disapproval or frustration Luc wasn't sure, but clearly his words came as no shock to her. She knew all right. Her gaze turned straight to her husband in a sharp demand for him to deal with it.

Luc waited for his reply, wanting to be clued in on how they viewed the situation. His father wore his poker-face, not giving anything away. His reply was laced with careful diplomacy.

'We felt any *re-acquainting* was best left to you…to make a time…if it was what you wanted.'

So the policy had been to wait. No red carpet welcome was about to be rolled out. Not while ever there was an outside chance that Luc might come to his senses when there was no family support forthcoming, no turnaround to oblige his feelings. A complete stand-off.

Luc eyed his father with open scepticism. 'I did ask at Easter, Dad. You made it clear a meeting was not to your liking.'

'In front of all our friends?' he scoffed as though the idea was absurd.

'You could have put Skye and Matt at ease with you before your guests arrived.'

He waved an angry dismissal. 'The timing was wrong.'

'When will it be right?' Luc mocked. 'The truth is you had Skye unjustly trashed and can't bring yourself to offer her the apology she deserves, let alone acknowledge the beautiful person she is, and has always been.'

It earned a furiously resentful glare.

Luc shook his head and delivered the bottom line. 'If you're waiting for Skye to go away, you'll be waiting the rest of our lives.'

Thin-lipped silence.

His mother's hands fretted at each other as she waited for her husband's next move.

Luc didn't wait. He bluntly called the next move for him. 'You *took*, Dad. As far as I'm concerned, it's up to you—both of you—to come to reasonable terms with what I'm about to take back.'

His mother shifted uneasily, her face showing anxiety as she quickly asked, 'What does that mean?'

'It means that Skye and I are getting married.'

'No! This cannot be!' She rose in agitation, turning in protest to her husband. 'You said this would not happen, Maurizio. You said—'

He sliced a dismissive wave to silence the outpouring. 'It's not done yet, Flavia.' He turned a frown of intense disapproval to Luc. 'If you must marry this woman...'

'Her name is Skye. Skye Sumner,' Luc repeated, ramming her name down his father's throat.

'...a wedding must be planned...a proper church wedding...'

'More delaying tactics, Dad?'

'You are my son! Your marriage has to be celebrated in an appropriate manner.'

'Then you should have come to the party earlier. It's taken me all these months to win Skye's trust and I won't throw it away to accommodate a family who has made no gesture towards welcoming her into it. I've finally persuaded her to sign the necessary forms and we'll be getting married as soon as it's legally possible.'

'Which is when?' his father shot at him.

Luc gave a derisive laugh as he straightened up from the armrest. 'So you can use the time to stop it, Dad?' His eyes glittered out and out war. 'Take one step in that direction...'

'Enough!' his mother cried, swinging a fierce gaze from one to the other. 'Enough, Maurizio! I will not lose this son and I want my grandchild. If we have to accept this woman as Luciano's wife, we will.' She turned to Luc with an indomitable air. 'It *must* be a proper wedding with all the families invited. I will see to it myself.'

'Flavia...' Anger at her insubordination.

She rebelled against it, bristling with her own anger as she stated, 'I will not have Luciano shame us by marrying in a clandestine fashion. It is bad enough that his bride is not of the Italian community.'

'With a bastard child,' his father savagely reminded her.

'And whose fault is it that my son was born out of wedlock?' Luc sliced at him.

His father's chin jerked up in aggressive pride, ignoring the accusation to address his wife. 'It cannot be supported, Flavia. I will not support it.'

'You chose a wife for Roberto who could not carry a baby full-term,' she fired back at him. 'Where is our future, Maurizio?'

'In limbo until our son sees sense,' he said in disgust.

'Then in limbo it will stay,' Luc declared with steely resolve.

'Luciano...' his mother pleaded.

'No, Mamma, I will not change my mind. I am sorry to bring you shame by not having a traditional wedding, but you and Dad have chosen to keep Skye alienated, and as long as she remains *this woman* or *that woman* to you, I won't let you near her to plan a wedding or anything else.'

'She has to do it for you or you will be an outcast, Luciano,' came the fierce rejoinder. 'If she loves you...'

'Skye always loved me. And was put through hell for it. Because of any lack of caring from this family, she brought up our son alone. I need to prove my love for her, not the other way around, Mamma.'

'There *was* caring,' she argued. 'Your father set up a trust fund.'

'Which was not administered as it should have been.' He swung a hard gaze to his father. 'Right, Dad?'

'The intention was there,' he tersely countered.

'The intention to keep Skye and my son at a distance. Which you're still doing, regardless of how I feel about it.'

His father threw up his hands in exasperation. 'You were in shock at learning what was done for your own good. Making rash judgements. But to persist in this folly…to turn your back on your family…'

'A family that deceived me? Robbed me of five years of my son's life?'

'Stop!' his mother cried vehemently. 'You are like two bulls locking horns and I will not have it. There is the child to consider, Maurizio. He is our only grandchild.'

'There is Skye to consider, as well, Mamma. I will not let Matt near anyone who doesn't treat his mother with the respect she deserves. He's a happy little boy, very much due to his mother's caring, and I don't want any shadow put on his life. He knows nothing but love…'

'You think I won't love him?' his mother cried in obvious angst at the prospect of being kept from the only grandchild she had.

'I doubt that ignoring and disapproving of his mother will seem like love to Matt. He's a very bright, intelligent child.' Luc couldn't resist proudly adding, 'He could read books, even before he went to school.'

'You hear that, Maurizio? This child you thought would be no good? At five years of age he can read!'

'And he shot more goals at soccer this year than any other boy on his team,' Luc went on, deliberately rubbing in what his father was missing—the game of soccer being one of his passions, as it was with most Italians.

'It is as well you find some joy in the boy because you will find none in this marriage,' his father thundered, refusing to be moved from his stance.

'You're wrong, Dad,' Luc said quietly. 'I feel alive with Skye. She fills the emptiness I've known for far too long.'

'There will be an even greater emptiness when you find yourself ostracised from all the Italian families.'

It would happen, too. His father would make it happen. A line would be drawn, with no crossing over from either side. He remembered the conversation with Skye when she'd said they were prisoners of their backgrounds and he'd expressed a wish to be free of the oppressive constriction of his. She hadn't believed him—it wasn't how he was acting—and he realised now why she'd hung back from committing herself to marrying him.

Because he'd been still hanging on, working for the Peretti Corporation, maintaining at least that professional link, hoping for a change of attitude, a change of heart from his parents, wanting an acceptance of his reality, thinking he could force an acceptance—blindly tied to bonds that had to be broken, proving to Skye he was truly free of them.

An act of love for an act of faith.

He looked at his father who'd ruled so much of his

life, but would rule no more. 'My resignation will be on your desk Monday morning, Dad. Effective immediately.'

'You can't do that!' he blustered, clearly appalled by this decision and seizing on a cogent argument against it. 'You're under contract for the resort in Far North Queensland.'

'Then I'm giving notice that this will be the last contract I'll work on. As soon as it's done...'

'You'll give up everything for this woman?' he yelled, his face reddening with the intensity of his outrage.

Yes, he would.

He'd told Skye he would.

It was well past time he did it.

He shook his head over his father's total lack of understanding of what Skye gave him. There was no point in trying to explain what wouldn't be heard anyway. He simply said, 'I just won't be held by your expectations of me any longer. Your father emigrated to Australia on his own to build a new life for himself, Dad. I can make a new life elsewhere, too.'

'No! No! You must stop this!' his mother broke in again. 'You men and your headstrong pride! You are breaking my heart! Both of you!' She dropped back into her armchair, slumping over, her hands pressed to her chest.

'See what you've done? Upsetting your mother?' His father bellowed at him, striding over to the chair to put a comforting arm around her.

Emotional blackmail.

The weeping and wailing would start any second.

'I'm sorry, Mamma, but this situation was not of

my making,' Luc said, softening his tone while still holding to his own determination. 'We all have choices.' He cast one last look at his father to state unequivocally, 'I've made mine.'

Then he walked out.

Out of the drawing room.

Out of the multi-million dollar mansion.

Out of the lives of his parents.

He could start a new life elsewhere.

And he would.

His own family, making their own friends, completely free of the past.

CHAPTER THIRTEEN

IT WAS there again!

Skye's heart skipped a beat at the sight of the black limousine, parked directly across the street from her house, as it had been each afternoon for the past three days.

Her last client of the day noticed it, too—so totally out of place in this neighbourhood. As out of place as Luc's red Ferrari! 'Is there a wedding?' she asked, trying to find an explanation for its presence.

'I don't know,' Skye answered.

Her client shrugged, stepped off the front porch and headed towards the gate. The limousine had nothing to do with her. Skye couldn't feel quite so dismissive of it. The tinted windows made it impossible to see if anyone was seated inside the car, but she *felt* as though she was being watched.

She quickly shut the door, wishing her anxious tension could be blocked out as easily as the limousine which she found increasingly disturbing. Luc was away this week, having flown up to Cairns in far north Queensland for on-site meetings about a new project. His father would know that. Was someone from the Peretti family behind those tinted windows, looking for ammunition that could be used against her?

There was none.

But that didn't mean it couldn't be manufactured.

Or was she being hopelessly paranoid?

Skye tried to shake off her worry as she threw off her masseur clothes on which she'd spilled some oil, took a shower, then dressed in jeans and T-shirt to go and pick up Matt from school. Only three more weeks now and the school year would be over. Her life here at Brighton-Le-Sands would be over.

Luc wanted to get married before Christmas and once they were, she and Matt would move to his Bondi apartment where they'd live until this last contract with the Peretti Corporation was completed. Then they'd relocate, close to wherever Luc decided to set up business for himself.

It was all settled.

Except the black limousine made her feel unsettled.

Skye decided she would tell Luc about it tonight when he called, as he called every night to chat with her and Matt over the phone. He had informed his family about their forthcoming marriage. Predictably the news had not been met with joy. Luc had insisted it didn't matter. The future he wanted revolved around her and Matt.

Skye believed him. All this year he'd shown he was happy with them, persuading her that a marriage between them was workable, despite his family lurking in the background. His decision to resign from his position in his father's business empire was the ultimate proof of freedom from an influence she'd still feared. It gave her far more confidence in their future together.

But would his family leave them alone?

The limousine was still there when she left the house to walk to Matt's school. She could have driven the Alfa so as not to feel *exposed* to watching eyes, but it was a fine sunny afternoon and it wasn't her habit to drive when a walk would be pleasant. Besides, she had nothing to hide.

Matt was bubbling with news about the end of year school concert. They'd just had a rehearsal for it. His class was doing a selection of nursery rhymes in song and action and he was demonstrating how he twinkled like a star, singing away at the top of his voice as they turned into their street.

The limousine had not moved.

Matt broke off his song to comment, 'The big black car is there again, Mummy.'

'So it is,' she replied, trying to sound careless.

'Maybe a giant lives in it,' he speculated. 'His legs are too long to fit in an ordinary car.'

'You could be right,' Skye lightly agreed while her mind painted in a scary giant, like Maurizio Peretti whose great wealth gave him a very long reach.

'Look, Mummy! The door is opening!' Matt cried excitedly, delighted at the prospect of seeing the occupant.

The driver's door! So someone *was* inside behind the tinted windows! Skye felt herself tensing up but the chauffeur who emerged was not enough in himself to confirm her fears.

'It's just a man in a uniform,' Matt said in disappointment.

The man in the uniform rounded the bonnet of the limousine and opened the far side passenger door, perking up Matt's anticipation again.

'There must be someone else, too.'

Just keep walking, Skye told herself, determined not to be intimidated by the *someone else*.

'It's a lady,' came Matt's surprised commentary.

A lady, indeed, Skye thought bitterly, her spine instantly stiffening as she recognised Luc's mother. No doubt now that the limousine was associated with his family. The chauffeur escorted Flavia Peretti across the street and was dismissed by her when she was safely on the sidewalk, right next to the front gate where Luc had stood waiting, nine months ago.

'Is she coming to our place, Mummy?' Matt asked, curiosity enlivened by this strange visitor who was watching their approach.

'Maybe she wants to ask for directions, Matt,' Skye temporised, unsure what to expect from this meeting and unwilling to expose her son to a relationship that might prove harmful.

Flavia Peretti looked very imposing, elegantly dressed in black, her hair more grey than Skye remembered, though perfectly groomed as always. She had a strong-boned face and a very upright figure, tall enough to carry her weight well, very much an Italian Mamma, although the softness of her womanly curves belied the hardness of her judgemental character. She was staring at Matt, just as Luc had done—the son of her son, her only grandchild.

'Why is she looking at me?' Matt asked.

'Perhaps you remind her of someone,' Skye answered, worrying that an introduction was about to be forced.

And then what?

Her stomach was churning. Her mind was, too. Why had Flavia Peretti come now? What was the point of this visit? To try to stop her from marrying Luc? To get to her while her precious son was away, destroy her trust in their love?

All Skye's protective instincts told her to keep Matt out of any confrontation with Luc's mother. Needing to distract attention away from her son, as soon as they were close enough, she called out, 'Can I help you?'

Flavia Peretti lifted her gaze from Matt, looking at Skye with a determined directness that mocked any pretence of not knowing who she was. 'Miss Sumner...' she started, letting her own identification of Skye hang for a moment.

'Yes? Do you want to make an appointment?' Skye rushed out, hoping the evasive tactic might raise a decent sense of discretion. She put her hand pointedly on Matt's shoulder as they paused by the gate, waiting for an answer.

The intense dark eyes, so very like Luc's, flashed a rueful understanding. 'If I may come inside?' she replied with cool dignity, giving way to Skye's silent demand while exerting her own pressure for a private meeting.

'Of course,' Skye muttered, opening the gate and handing Matt the door-keys. 'Go ahead and change into play clothes while I see to business.'

Accustomed as he was to her dealing with clients, Matt didn't question the situation, and Skye breathed a sigh of relief when he obeyed without giving in to the temptation to question the lady about the extraordinary size of her car, either.

Skye watched him go inside before turning back to Luc's mother whose gaze was still trained on the opened front door which Matt had left ajar for them to follow. Inviting *the enemy* inside was certainly not to Skye's liking. She quickly asked, 'Why have you come here, Mrs Peretti?'

'I wanted to see my grandchild,' came the flat answer.

'You've seen him.'

'He's like Luciano.' The words were wistful, with an undercurrent of yearning.

'And me,' Skye stated fiercely, demanding her parenthood be recognised.

Luc's mother heaved a weary sigh as she returned her gaze to Skye. 'I knew nothing of how you and the child were dealt with until my husband informed me of it last Easter.'

'You didn't want me for Luc any more than your husband did,' Skye threw at her, certain it was true.

Flavia Peretti nodded. 'But Luciano will marry you nonetheless,' she said resignedly. 'He will not change his mind. For him it is a point of honour.'

'He loves me. And Matt,' Skye stated fiercely, resenting the implication that it was only honour driving Luc's desire to marry her. She did not believe it. Would not believe it.

'Do you love him?'

'Yes, I do. He's the only man I've ever loved. Ever will love. And I will not let you talk me out of marrying him, no matter what arguments you use, no matter what you might offer me, so your visit is a waste of your time and mine, Mrs Peretti.'

Skye's outburst seemed to make no impression on her. She bypassed it all, simply asking, 'When is the wedding date?'

'Soon.' Caution screamed not to name the day.

'Before Christmas?'

'It's none of your business, Mrs Peretti.'

'My son is getting married and it's none of my business?' It was a raw cry, scraped from a deep bank of emotion.

'You didn't care about what *he* wanted. You only care about what you want,' Skye retorted, fighting the possessiveness that had led to all her grief.

'I am Luciano's mother. As the mother of a son yourself...the only one I have left...'

Unbelievably, the haughty arrogance crumbled, tears welling into her eyes. And Skye couldn't help feeling sorry for her: this proud woman, weeping on a public street, this sad woman who had lost one son and was on the verge of losing the only one she had left. Regardless of the hurt she'd given in the past, she was Luc's mother, and Skye imagined her watching lovingly over Luc as a little boy, just as she did Matt.

It was impossible to leave her standing here like this. 'Come inside, Mrs Peretti,' Skye gently urged, taking her arm to steer her up the path and into the house.

Letting in the enemy.

Except it no longer felt like that.

Until she told Luc what had happened.

CHAPTER FOURTEEN

LUC'S call came through at seven o'clock that night, right on Matt's bedtime. Knowing this, he asked to speak to Matt first so he could say goodnight to him, and since Matt was jumping up and down in his eagerness to speak to his father, Skye passed the telephone receiver to him.

'Guess what, Daddy?' he cried excitedly. 'I met your Mummy today. She's my grandmother and she said to call her Nonna.'

He went on to describe the big black car this amazing new person in his life had come in, while Skye worried over how Luc was reacting to the news. She had strongly felt it would be wrong to gag Matt on the subject of his grandmother. It would have raised too many questions and none of the answers were appropriate for a little boy's understanding. Better to let him be happy about the relationship since there seemed to be a possibility that it could turn out good for him.

Matt prattled on, obviously prompted by questions Luc was putting to him about the meeting. His voice remained happy, signalling that Luc was carefully playing to their son's innocence. Skye hoped she had done the right thing with Flavia Peretti, but the difficult hump of past history was still playing on her mind. It was a relief when Matt finally said goodnight to his father and passed the receiver to her.

'Go on to bed now, Matt,' she instructed. 'You can read until I come in to say goodnight. Okay?'

'Okay, Mummy.' He shot her a proud grin. 'Nonna was surprised at how well I can read, wasn't she?'

Skye smiled back at him. 'Yes, she was. Off you go, Matt.'

She watched him skip out of the kitchen while she took a deep breath to ease her inner tension before speaking to Luc.

'Skye?' Urgency in his voice.

'Yes. I was just waiting for Matt to be out of earshot.'

'Tell me what happened.'

Skye recounted everything as best she could; the presence of the black limousine in their street for the past three afternoons, his mother's emergence from it today, the meeting on the sidewalk, her own stand about trying to keep the confrontation away from Matt, what was said and the reaction to it.

'My mother has a long habit of using tears to break down opposition and get her own way,' Luc commented tersely. 'She succeeded in getting you to let her meet Matt.'

Had it been deliberate manipulation? Skye hadn't thought so at the time. Surely it had been genuine distress. Besides, hadn't Luc himself said it would be her one and only grandchild who would bring his mother around?

'I thought you wanted her to, Luc.'

'Not like this, behind my back,' came the savage retort, making Skye cringe at having made a wrong judgement. Had she let in the enemy? Was this the thin edge of a wedge designed to drive her and Luc apart?

'I'm sorry. I…'

'No, I'm sorry,' he quickly cut in, tempering his tone. 'It's not your fault. I should have been expecting this, should have warned you.'

'Warned me of what?' Alarm tingled through every nerve in her body.

There was a long expulsion of breath at his end. 'Did my mother ask you to postpone our wedding?'

Giving his father time…to do what? How could anything be worse than what had been done to them six years ago? They were strong together now. Surely they could weather any attempt at interference.

'I didn't give her a date, Luc, but she did plead for us to wait until after Christmas. I said I'd have to discuss it with you.'

'Right! Why did she pinpoint Christmas?'

'She's offering Christmas Day as a day of reconciliation. For family mending.'

'Did you believe she meant it?'

Skye hesitated, but she had truly felt Flavia Peretti had spoken sincerely. 'Is there any reason why I shouldn't?' she asked warily. 'I thought you'd want this, Luc.'

'It depends on what it costs. What was her attitude towards you, Skye?'

'Stiff at first, but she wasn't…well, looking down her nose at me. It was more a kind of awkward acceptance. Her focus was more on Matt than on me, Luc. I think she truly wants Matt in her life and will do all she can to…to smooth things over.'

'There was nothing…offensive?'

'Not really. I don't expect a sudden flow of benevolence towards me from your mother. I never was what she wanted for you and I haven't miraculously changed into the perfect Italian bride. But I honestly felt she was making an effort today not to be disapproving of anything.'

'There's nothing to disapprove of,' he said fiercely, giving Skye the warm reassurance that he truly believed it and would fight to the death anyone who suggested otherwise.

It helped her relax, made her feel safe again. Luc was not being critical of her actions. He was being protective of her, angry that he had not been at her side to handle whatever was coming at her from his family.

'I don't like this…my mother visiting you behind my back,' he went on. 'Most probably behind my father's back, too. As if we haven't had enough deception messing us around!'

And they'd certainly both suffered from it. But giving suffering back did not right the wrong. Skye took a deep breath and tentatively suggested, 'She might have come as a go-between peace-maker.'

A harsh laugh. 'God knows! But I'll sure as hell find out before this goes any further. I've booked a four o'clock flight for tomorrow afternoon. Should be with you and Matt in time for dinner.'

'Do you want us to pick you up at the airport?'

'No. I'll catch a taxi, save the hassle. Don't worry about my mother's visit, Skye. I'll sort it out when I get home. Okay?'

She sighed, relieved to have this assurance, too.

'One thing,' he added in a determined tone. 'We

are not postponing our wedding for anything so don't even think about it. We love each other and we're going to get married on our agreed date.'

'That's good to hear,' she said, smiling over the fervour in his voice, though she was no longer sure it was a good idea to marry before Christmas. Flavia Peretti had raised issues that had made her feel very selfish about maintaining her small safe world with Luc.

'I'll let you go and tend to Matt now,' he said in a softer tone. 'Be with you soon.'

'Yes. 'Bye for now.'

'Love you.'

'Me, too.'

She did love him. But she was beginning to realise how much Luc's commitment to her was costing him and how blind she had been to that, only seeing that his family circle could hurt her. And Matt. It still could, but if she believed enough in Luc's love for her, wasn't there room for giving some kind of reconciliation a trial?

Watching his mother with Matt this afternoon…it had made her wish her own mother was still alive, taking pleasure in the grandchild she'd only known as a baby. Death was something no one could control—a final parting from which there was no turning back. Flavia Peretti had experienced that with Roberto. But the separation from Luc could be bridged if the prejudice against a non-Italian bride was set aside, and the pride of Luc and his father did not remain an ongoing battle-ground.

Big *ifs.*

And Skye knew she was right at the centre of them.

Moving from her own stance on Luc's family was absolutely essential if a truce was to be called. The big question was…and her heart quailed at facing it…how was she going to cope if she was continually made to feel not good enough for Luc? Good intentions could be very quickly undermined.

She had a bad night.

The next day wasn't much better, her tired mind still fretting over what should be done. At least every hour that dragged by was one hour less of being alone with her dilemma. It was a huge relief when Luc finally arrived home and wrapped her in his strong embrace, making her feel warm and secure in his love.

Matt, of course, was still full of his new Nonna over dinner, questioning Luc incessantly about his life as a child, learning that he'd had a younger brother and immediately deciding he'd like a brother, too. Which made Luc smile and cock a quizzical eyebrow at Skye.

'Maybe in another year or two, Matt,' she said, knowing Luc wanted at least one more child—one whose life he would be aware of right from the beginning, no missing out on anything. 'But your Daddy and I can't guarantee a brother. It might be a sister instead,' she cautioned.

'Oh!' He thought about it. 'That's all right, Mummy. I like girls, too.'

And no doubt they liked him, Skye thought. He *was* like Luc in lots of ways. Which made her feel all the more guilty about depriving Flavia Peretti of her grandchild, as well as her Luciano. She was glad when Matt's bedtime came and he was finally tucked in for the night, giving her and Luc the privacy needed to discuss the situation.

Luc wanted to sweep her off to bed but her need to talk first was paramount in Skye's mind, so she insisted they sit over coffee at the kitchen table. Which was not to his liking. His dark frown and suspicious eyes drove an instant flutter of apprehension through her heart.

'You're letting my mother's visit affect what we'd normally do,' he growled.

She looked at him in eloquent appeal. 'I can't discount it, Luc. Please?'

She made coffee and they sat, but the aggressive energy pouring from him made it difficult for Skye to know where to start. She felt Luc was going to pounce on anything she said and tear it apart. Did the harmony in their relationship depend on having no contact with his family? Or was this all her fault for making such a huge issue of it? It was impossible to forget the scars of the past, but weren't she and Luc strong enough together now to rise above them?

'My own mother is gone, Luc,' she began nervously. 'On my side there's no family, and no closely connected community forming an extension of family, either. There's only me and Matt.'

'And me,' Luc shot at her grimly.

'I'm not doubting that, Luc,' she hastily assured him.

'You're drawing lines, Skye.'

It forced her to choose her words more carefully. 'I just meant…you still have…other people who care about you.'

'Not so I've noticed,' he snapped, his face growing harder, his eyes angry.

'Because I haven't given you the chance to be with them,' she rushed out. 'I've been a coward, not facing up to your life, wanting to be safe in my own little world.'

'You have every right to want to feel safe,' he fiercely argued. 'As for chances, my father could have chosen any amount of chances to invite us into his home.'

Skye took a deep breath. 'Well, there might be a chance now.'

'According to my mother?' he flashed at her with deep scepticism. 'Along with her request to postpone our wedding? Can't you see she's dangling out an acceptance of you to stop what she and my father want to stop?'

'They can't stop us from getting married if we don't let them, Luc. I trust you on that. Can't you trust me?'

'It's taken me so long to convince you it's right for us…'

'And it is. I know it is. But I'm now feeling wrong about the way we're doing it.'

His jaw clenched. Skye sensed he was about to erupt from his chair, but the moment of shimmering violence passed. 'Why?' he bit out.

She shook her head over the realisation that her fears had driven Luc to an extreme stand, and he was not prepared to back down from it. He hadn't spelled out that in marrying her without his parents' blessing, he'd make himself an exile, but she had blindly accepted that sacrifice from him, accepted taking him away from others, too. She'd actually been intensely relieved that she didn't have to worry about *them* any more. Selfish relief.

'Your mother loves you, Luc,' she said quietly.

His head jerked aside as though he didn't want to be hit by that. He grimaced and turned his gaze back to her, eyes blazing with resolution. 'I won't have you hurt again, Skye. In all but law you're my wife now. My first allegiance is to you.'

She took another deep breath and said, 'Your parents didn't know how deeply you felt about me. They made a mistake.'

'That's putting it kindly,' he mocked, still not giving an inch.

'I'm not saying this to test you, Luc. I've thought about nothing else since your mother came.' She tried a smile to lighten the tension. 'As you just said, I'm your wife now in everything but the legality. Does it really matter if we postpone going to a registry office until after Christmas?'

His responding smile carried a load of irony. 'Did my mother promise you a big Italian wedding if we did?'

'No, she didn't.'

'Did she say if you loved me, you'd ensure that I come home for Christmas Day for the sake of family feeling?'

She sighed, regretting the huge barriers she had built. 'It wasn't like that, Luc. Your mother was very distressed at the rift that has developed. Can't you just accept that without colouring it as more deception?'

'And if it is deception?' he bored in.

'We'll know soon enough, won't we? Christmas is only five weeks away.'

'Don't count on my mother's peace-plan going through. I doubt my father knows about it. And I will not be going to Bellevue Hill again without his personal invitation.'

This was said with so much harsh pride, it made Skye wonder how much Luc himself had contributed to the rift. Her reaction to the deception with the photos and her acute awareness of being considered an undesirable in the Peretti family circle had certainly played its part. Given Luc's reaction to what she was saying now, perhaps he had drawn battle-lines with his father that couldn't be crossed by either side.

'He is your father, Luc,' she reminded him.

'No father has the right to do what he did.'

The vehemence in his voice left no room for argument. Besides which, what he said was true. His father had abrogated Luc's right to choose whether to know or deny his own child. It was a monstrous thing to do.

'What about your mother, then?' she asked. 'Must she pay for your father's decisions? She didn't know, Luc. She didn't know until Easter, when you didn't turn up for Easter Sunday.'

'But she doesn't turn up until now, trying to put off our wedding,' he pointed out, no softening at all in his expression.

It's gone too far, Skye thought, feeling totally miserable about it. 'I said she could come again, Luc,' she confessed on a heavy sigh. 'Matt was so excited about having a grandmother…'

'It's okay. Stop worrying about it, Skye.'

He was on his feet, coming around the table to her. She felt too drained to move, too torn by the conflicts that still raged around them to achieve any peace of mind. Luc stepped behind her chair and his hands slid over her shoulders and started a gentle massage.

'None of this is your fault,' he murmured, dropping a kiss on the top of her head, caring for her uppermost in his tone now. 'Try to relax, Skye. If my mother visits again…just let it be. Matt is her grandson. So long as the connection is good for him, no harm done.'

The tension in her shoulders eased under his expert manipulation. 'What about you, Luc? You're her son.'

'I'll welcome her if I'm with you and Matt. But don't be surprised if she never comes again. My father might forbid it. In which case…'

'Forbid?' She shook her head over the harsh concept.

'It's an old-fashioned Italian marriage,' Luc said wryly. 'Love, honour, obey…'

'Is that how you think, too? That you have the right to forbid me to do something you disapprove of?'

'No. I don't own you, Skye. I don't see marriage as a form of ownership. Nor do I see parenthood that way. There comes a time when you have to let a child choose his own path, even against what you think are his best interests.'

'What if your father honestly thought how he acted was in your best interests, Luc?'

'It doesn't excuse hurting you as he did.'

'He didn't know me.'

Caring too much about one person could make you

blind to others, Skye thought. And protecting the life you know can make you blind to others' lives, too. It was what she'd been doing.

Luc's thumbs pressed harder into her muscles as he said, 'He didn't *try* to know you.'

Anger again.

Anger built on her anger at what had been done to her. Perhaps anger at himself, as well, for believing what he should never have believed, knowing her as intimately as he had. But that was far in the past now, and Skye didn't want their future built on such a divisive foundation.

'What if he tries now, Luc?'

The movement of his hands halted. He dragged in a deep breath and exhaled it very slowly. 'Let's not talk about my father, Skye. It's you I need.'

The raw need in his voice compelled her to rise from her chair and give him whatever he wanted of her. He instantly caught her to him, one arm sweeping around her waist, one hand lifting to her face to stroke away any worry lines. His eyes searched hers with a searing intensity.

'I love you. Don't let anything come between us.'

The passionate plea carried the scars of their past experience, and Skye knew intuitively they'd been brought to throbbing life again by the intrusion of his family. She curled her arms around his neck and kissed him, not wanting him to feel any uncertainty about her love. That was strong and true, always had been, always would be.

They went to bed and made love long into the night.

Skye did not doubt Luc's commitment to her for a second.

But not even the secure comfort of being this close to him could banish the sense of wrongs which still had to be righted.

CHAPTER FIFTEEN

'PLEASE...sit with me.'

Flavia Peretti gestured to the two deck chairs on the small back verandah where Matt had led his Nonna to watch him kick the soccer ball around the backyard. Skye had hurried out to check there was no bird's mess on either of them before Luc's mother sat down. She had meant to leave her with her grandson, but it seemed too impolite to refuse such a direct request.

She sat, the old deck chair creaking as she did so, making her conscious of the huge difference between her living circumstances and that of the Peretti family. Everything about the cottage was old and shabby— she couldn't afford better—though she'd brightened it up with colour where she could. Here on the verandah, the petunias she'd potted were in full bloom, looking very pretty. A cheap little garden, Skye thought, but one that gave her pleasure.

Oddly enough, in her three visits to the cottage, Luc's mother had made no disdainful comment on Skye's relatively poor circumstances. Nor did she now.

'Matteo is a credit to you, Skye.'

Spoken with warm approval.

And actually using her first name.

Which made two firsts.

It was Flavia Peretti's third visit and she was finally

thawing from polite formality. Skye smiled. She didn't mind basking in her son's reflected glory. It was clearly difficult for Luc's mother to release the prejudice she had held against her son's non-Italian girlfriend and see the woman he loved.

'My husband...' Flavia gathered herself to look directly at Skye, a sad plea in her eloquent dark eyes. 'He says my invitation for Christmas Day is enough. If Luciano won't come, bringing you and our grandson, for my sake...' She gestured helplessly.

'I'm sorry, Mrs Peretti.'

'No...no...you have nothing to apologise for. It is we who must make up for what was done. But Maurizio...he has his pride. The father does not go to the son, you understand.'

'I can't say I do understand,' Skye said ruefully.

'You are not steeped in our traditions.' A deep sigh was heaved. 'Our marriage was an arranged one by our two families. That was how it was done. Maurizio came back to Italy for me and I came to Australia with him as his bride. He has been a good husband. And as a good father, he believed he was doing right by Luciano.'

Skye shook her head, seeing nothing right in what had been done to Luc and herself.

Flavia Peretti grimaced apologetically and rushed out an explanation. 'He did not understand the attachment to you. How could it be so when you were not one of us? To Maurizio it was a bad distraction from what should be Luciano's duty to the family. He asked Roberto to help and it was done. You were gone.'

'It was a terrible thing to do, Mrs Peretti,' Skye put in quietly.

'You were…a modern Australian girl. And—' she shrugged '—not a virgin.'

A heated protest sprang to Skye's lips. 'That doesn't make me a woman who jumps into any man's bed. I have only ever been with Luc.'

'Please…' Hands were raised in anguished appeal. 'I did not mean to insult you. I was trying to explain why it did not seem so terrible to Maurizio. When he learned of your pregnancy, he did make generous provision for the child so you would never be in need. In his mind, Luciano should understand all these things.'

The clash of cultures, Skye thought, wondering if there was any real chance of finding any meeting ground.

'A son should forgive his father a mistake which was made with his good at heart,' was the next pleading argument. 'Can you not speak to Luciano about this?'

'Why don't you speak to him yourself, Mrs Peretti?'

A weary roll of her eyes. 'He is a man. If anyone can get past his pride, it will be you, the woman he loves, the woman for whom he is turning his back on his family.'

This last statement hit Skye hard.

Luc would undoubtedly call it emotional blackmail, yet there was too much truth in it for her to dismiss it out of hand. In the end, family was family and the blood connection ran deep. It didn't go away, not even if one turned one's back on it. The memories were always there.

*   *   *

As Luc drove his Ferrari into Skye's street, a black limousine was turning the corner at the other end of the block.

His mother!

This was the third time she'd come without making any contact with him!

He put his foot on the accelerator in a burst of frustration, instinctively responding to the urge to chase her down and demand she stop bothering Skye. Only the sure knowledge that a confrontation between them would not achieve anything made him think better of going in pursuit. He slowed the car and pulled it in beside the kerb, thumping the driving wheel in anger as he switched off the engine.

The agreed wedding day was set for one week away. It was pointless to put it off until after Christmas. His father was never going to come around to accepting their marriage. He had made no attempt to arrange a private meeting with Luc at work. A reconciliation on Christmas day was definitely not on *his* drawing board.

And here was his mother meddling again!

Sure she probably wanted to see Matt—he was a wonderful grandchild for her—but it was Skye she was getting at, planting whatever seeds of dissension she could. Luc felt the difference each time she'd been; worries, tension, questions when there shouldn't be any questions.

Today had been Matt's last day at school for the year. As Luc alighted from his car, that time factor eased some of his own tension. There was no longer any need for Skye and Matt to stay at this house in

Brighton-Le-Sands. No excuse not to come and live with him at Bondi. Next year another school could be found for Matt, close to wherever they bought a suitable home—certainly a lot more suitable than this cheap little rental cottage where Skye had insisted on staying all year, clinging to her independence.

Which might well have given his mother hope that Skye wasn't completely committed to the marriage!

Luc strode across the street, setting his mind on a plan of action. He was not going to lose Skye now. No way. In fact, he'd help her start on packing her belongings tonight, sorting out what she wanted to keep and what could be given away to charity. Best to make the move to his apartment this weekend. That might stop his mother from sneaking visits behind his back.

He used the front door key Skye had given him and had no sooner stepped into the hallway than Matt came flying down it to meet him. 'Nonna was here again, Daddy. You've just missed her,' he cried, his happy face expecting Luc to feel both pleased and disappointed.

'Well, she should have timed her visit better,' he replied lightly, ruffling Matt's hair to project some fun into the moment. 'How was your last day at school?'

Skye was in the kitchen, cutting up vegetables for dinner. She smiled at him as he came in with Matt but there was a strained look in her lovely blue eyes and she didn't stop working to greet him beyond saying, 'Hi!' No hug. No kiss. A quick instruction to Matt. 'Let your father sit down and relax before you talk his head off.'

There was a tight restraint about her that knotted Luc's gut. He managed to drink the beer Matt brought him but it didn't relax him, and for once, his son's bright chatter did not give him joy. It took an act of will to respond to it. His gaze kept turning to Skye who just went ahead, preparing dinner, occasionally joining in the conversation, trying to act naturally as though nothing was wrong.

Luc wasn't fooled. However, it was impossible to say anything in front of Matt. Their son was a complete innocent in all of this, and should be kept so, unless circumstances forced knowledge on him that had to be dealt with. Luc had the feeling those circumstances were gathering around them very ominously at the moment.

He silently railed against his father's stubborn refusal to accept the woman he loved. Skye was everything he could possibly want in a wife. She had so many admirable attributes, far beyond her outer beauty. Was his mother seeing that now? Was she plotting to stop the marriage or was she beginning to recognise Skye's qualities?

Matt was still enthusiastic about his Nonna so there couldn't have been any unpleasantness between his new grandmother and his mother. Not in front of him. Yet something was seriously disturbing Skye. Luc could sense the anxiety behind her every look at him.

He forced restraint on himself all through dinner and the cleaning up afterwards. As soon as they'd bade Matt goodnight and switched the light off in his bedroom, Luc drew Skye straight into hers, closing the door behind them, wanting to close the door on anything that might separate them. He wrapped her in his arms, kissing her with all the deep passion she evoked in him, relief heightening his need for her as he felt her uninhibited response.

This, at least, was right.

It had always been right.

And she was as eager to strip off his clothes as he was to get rid of hers. He loved her. He took her to bed, determined on showing her how utterly and completely he did. She was so incredibly beautiful; the silky softness of her long glorious hair, the lush curves of her that were all woman, the smooth litheness of her legs, winding so possessively around him as he revelled in the sweet fire of her sexuality, knowing she was craving his.

He drove her through climax after climax, controlling his own excitement until it reached breaking point, bursting with the need to melt into her, be one with her, the ultimate sharing of themselves. Her sigh of fulfilment told him she was with him all the way and he kissed her to feel it even more intensely, to feel nothing could ever separate them. They belonged together, as deeply as any man and woman could.

The sense of blissful harmony carried over into their lying together afterwards, Skye's head resting contentedly over his heart as he leisurely caressed her back. 'I want to move you and Matt to my place this weekend,' he murmured. 'There's no reason for you to stay here any more, Skye, and I want you settled with me.'

'Yes,' she agreed, her warm breath fanning his skin, giving pleasure as her answer gave him pleasure.

Luc felt secure enough now to casually probe the concerns his mother's visit had raised. 'What's troubling you, Skye? Did my mother push again for us to postpone our marriage?'

She didn't lift her head. Her hand glided down to stroke the erotic area under his hipbone as she spoke. 'Those legal papers we signed...they're good for three months, Luc. We don't have to get married on the date we set.'

The delightful fuzz of sensual pleasure was instantly ripped from his mind. He grabbed her hand, squeezing it so hard she cried out his name in protest. But he was already rolling, slamming her hand into the pillow as her head came to rest on it, his heart pumping a much louder protest at what she was allowing to happen, what she was aiding and abetting.

'You asked me if I'd walk away from everything for you and Matt. I have,' he fiercely declared, seething over her inconstancy. 'Don't backtrack on me now, Skye. It's done. If you don't keep your word to me...'

'Luc, I will marry you. I will.' Alarm in her eyes. 'And I'll go with you wherever you choose to go. That's not in question.'

'Oh, yes it is.' Blood was pounding through his head with the urgent need to make her see what she was doing. 'You're actively betraying my love for you by listening to my mother, letting yourself be drawn into giving consideration to people who hurt you. Who will hurt you again. And do everything they can to take you from me.'

'They won't, Luc. I promise you. Nothing can tear me away from you now,' she said earnestly. 'But I shouldn't have asked you to give up everything, to sacrifice—'

'It's no sacrifice. It's freedom. Throwing off the shackles of an ownership I now refute in all its malevolent forms. I will not have it touch us.'

'Malevolent…' She repeated the word as though it tormented her. 'I made it so, Luc.'

'No.'

'What if it isn't?'

'My God!' he cried in exasperation. 'What more proof do you need? How can you forget what was done to us?'

'Your mother—'

'My mother has her own agenda. My father has not said one word to me about Christmas Day. Nothing is going to change in that court, believe me.'

'Please—' she sucked in a deep breath, her eyes searching his in frantic appeal '—will you just listen to me?'

He gritted his teeth, hating the fact there could be any issue about this.

'Please,' she begged.

He couldn't bear watching the damage already wrought by his mother's insidious visits. Yet to forbid Skye to give voice to it put him in the same frame his father occupied—the all too dominating male, leaning over her, leaning *on* her. He flung himself onto his back. Lying beside her was less threatening, giving her space to express what he didn't want to hear. His whole body was still keyed up to attack and forcing restraint was not easy.

'I'm listening,' he bit out.

She heaved a deep sigh. He could feel her distress

at his abrupt separation from her, but he couldn't bring himself to soothe it. Skye had to realise a wedge was being driven between them.

'Did you know your parents' marriage had been arranged by their families, Luc?'

His hands clenched at this harking back to a past which had nothing to do with them. 'What *they* accepted then—'

'Has a bearing on what was done to us, Luc,' she rushed out, rolling onto her side, propping herself up on one elbow, reaching out to lay her hand on his chest, softly stroking as though trying to soothe the savage beast in him.

He said nothing.

If she needed him to listen, he'd listen. And he did listen, trying to understand how she could forgive his father enough to even consider the prospect of a meeting with him, let alone tolerate it, especially when there was not one suggestion of an apology coming for what he'd done to her.

Her guilt over separating him from his family was absurd. She had done nothing to deserve their rejection. The fault lay entirely with his parents' prejudiced attitudes. *They* had to make the change.

This was Australia, not Italy, and they had made their lives here where the customs were different. If they couldn't face up to the difference—a difference Luc had grown up with, which was part and parcel of *his* thinking, then let them cling to their past and lose the future he and Skye could provide!

'I want you to go to your father, Luc.'

He closed his eyes. This was madness. For her to meet his father at all would be like walking into the lion's den, asking to be mauled. He couldn't let her do it. She had more than enough bad memories about his family. Adding freshly to them, connecting him to them...he didn't want to risk that.

'I've already been to him once,' he grated out.

'That was to tell him we were getting married.'

'And we are,' he stated determinedly.

She moved, lowering her body onto his, the softness of her breasts pressing into his chest, her arms burrowing under his neck, her warm breath tingling on his grimly tightened mouth. 'I love you,' she said with quiet fervour. 'And I'll marry you, no matter what.'

He opened his eyes. His hands slid over her back, up into her hair. An anguished wave of possessiveness swept through him. If they could just lose themselves in each other, make all these unnecessary issues go away...

'I'd just like to feel that everything's been done to...to mend fences, Luc.'

'They aren't our fences to mend, Skye,' he asserted, wanting her to turn aside from them, stay where she was safe. Where they were both safe.

'Does it matter if the move comes from you instead of your father?'

Yes, it mattered.

Her eyes probed his with a pleading intensity, wanting to find the giving that she was willing to give, yet everything in Luc resisted it. The giving should come from his father. Any softening from him would be interpreted as weakness, making them both vulnerable to attack.

'He hurt both of us very badly, Luc, but it was in not understanding the people we are,' she said softly.

'I'm his own son,' he bit out.

'And he thought you should be like him. You're not. Show him you're not by not being as rigid as he is.'

'He'll see it as crawling back to him, wanting what he can offer,' he argued in terse dismissal of the idea.

'*We* know it's not, Luc. It takes more strength to step over a battle-line and hold out a hand in peace than it does to keep fighting. If he doesn't meet you halfway, then I'll marry you whenever you want. But if he does...can we wait until after Christmas Day?'

He could see she wasn't going to let go of this idea. It would remain brooding in her mind if he refused to do what she asked, and perhaps he'd be the lesser man for it in her eyes.

He quelled the fierce rebellion in his heart. It went totally against his grain to go cap in hand for his father's blessing on a union which that same father had done his utmost to destroy. Even more critically, if a truce did eventuate, it gave his father the opportunity to undermine Skye's sense of security with him.

Nevertheless, if peace of mind on this issue was needed for them to achieve a happy future together, he had to take at least one step towards a reconciliation.

If his father turned away from it...no more!

He reached up to stroke the anxious line from between her brows. 'I'll speak to him about Christmas Day. Okay? If there's a positive response from him...'

She smiled. It was like sunlight bursting through clouds and his heart turned over. He didn't know how she could be so forgiving of the past. He knew only how much he loved her.

It was the last board meeting before Christmas. Luc watched his father work it with his usual commanding authority while treating his executives with the respect they deserved. As always it was an impressive performance, not missing a beat anywhere. If he was at all disturbed by personal family issues, it certainly didn't show.

Refreshments were wheeled in, along with bottles of champagne to toast another successful and highly profitable year for the Peretti Corporation. A festive mood took over, everyone happy to relax and socialise, the big boss playing the genial host to the hilt.

Luc wanted to walk out, turn his back on the whole scene. He'd done his job, given his end of year report, and he fiercely resented his father's bonhomie which telegraphed perfect peace of mind, while Skye fretted over an estrangement that *she* thought she'd caused. The irony was sickening.

Only his promise to her kept him there. He waited, circulating with every air of confidence himself, until most of the food had been eaten and the champagne bottles were empty. When he judged his father had done all the usual shoulder-clapping, he moved in with steely resolve.

'Could I have a private word with you, Dad?'

'Of course, Luciano,' he said genially, excusing himself from the group still gathered around him.

Luc followed him into the executive office adjoin-

ing the boardroom and closed the door, remaining beside it as his father moved around behind his desk,
apparently intending to sit down.

'This won't take long,' Luc warned, hating the
sense that he was in the position of a beggar.

His father paused beside his chair, seeming to
gather himself before meeting Luc's hard gaze. He
gestured open-handedly. 'I have as much time as you
want.'

On his terms, Luc thought, but he tempered his
tone to a less harsh note. 'You know Mamma has
been visiting Skye and Matt?'

'Yes, I know.'

No other comment. Not a hint of approval or disapproval. Just a flat stare at Luc, waiting for him to
make what he would of it.

'She extended an invitation for the three of us to
join you on Christmas Day,' he threw at his father.

'Your mother is free to invite anyone she wishes,'
came straight back at him.

Frustrated by the lack of any personal response,
Luc bluntly asked, 'Where do you stand, Dad?'

His chin lifted in aggressive pride. 'Beside your
mother. Where I have always stood.'

Again no personal comment on the invitation.

Luc studied his father's face, the whole indomitable
demeanour of the man, and knew this was as good as
he was going to get—a tacit acceptance, but no welcome mat rolled out and no apology for transgres-
sions, either. He realised that for his father, that would
be completely losing face, too humiliating. Yet there
was something in his eyes...an intensity of feeling
that was not pride.

Maybe it was a reaching out, or a wish to reach back to the time when his elder son had looked up to him. It struck a chord of sadness in Luc. He, too, wished for something different.

'We'll come,' he said. 'And I'll be standing beside Skye.'

It was both a challenge and a chance.

A great deal depended on how his father met it.

'I'll tell your mother,' he said, implicitly demanding trust.

Luc stared back at him, loath to give that trust without assurances. If Skye or Matt was abused in any way...

'Flavia is very taken with...our grandson,' his father stiffly added.

Our, not *her.*

A few more words were offered. 'I'm sure she will put some gifts for him under our Christmas tree.'

It was a start. The first concession. Luc didn't press for more. 'Christmas *is* for children,' he said, then nodded and left, telling himself at least Matt would be treated well. And Skye would risk it, since she was determined on trying to make peace with his family.

But be damned if he was going to stand by and see her hurt again!

CHAPTER SIXTEEN

CHRISTMAS Day...

Skye carefully attached the sapphire and diamond earrings to her lobes—Luc's Christmas gift to her. They matched the engagement ring he'd put on her finger when she'd finally agreed to marry him. There would have been a wedding ring already complementing it, but for the need she had to give Luc back his family.

She had no illusions about where she stood with his father and it was nerve-wracking having to face him today. But if Maurizio Peretti could tolerate her for the sake of having his son in the family fold again—and his grandson—she would somehow make herself tolerate him.

Besides, she knew Flavia Peretti would be working hard to smooth everything over. It was weird to think she and Luc's mother had become allies. Not friends. Friendship took a lot longer and might never eventuate. But it was good for Matt to have a grandmother who loved him.

Skye tucked the long fall of her hair behind her ear so at least one of the earrings showed, then stepped back to view her appearance in the mirror. She'd bought this dress especially for today, wanting to correct the impression she'd obviously given Luc's parents in the past when she'd worn more casual, form-fitting, *sexy* clothes—the in fashion—not realising she might be offending their sensibilities and possibly giving rise to the idea of her being a 'loose' woman.

The white linen shift was printed with turquoise and royal blue flowers with chartreuse leaves. The colour combination suited her very well, bringing out the blue in her eyes and contrasting nicely with the golden honey tan she had acquired since coming to live with Luc at Bondi Beach. The dress was sleeveless, befitting a hot summer day—which it was—the high scooped neckline was demure, and the simple style skimmed her figure rather than accentuating it.

Since rent for the Brighton-Le-Sands cottage no longer had to be paid and there was spare money to spend, she'd splashed out on turquoise sandals, as well, all in all making quite an elegant outfit, Skye thought. Her long blonde hair was smooth and shiny, her make-up minimal, and she couldn't see what else could have been done to make herself more presentable.

Luc's footsteps coming up the stairs of his two storey apartment alerted her to time going by, but a quick glance at her watch showed there was still a quarter of an hour before they had to leave for Bellevue Hill. Flavia Peretti had suggested a ten o'clock arrival, time for Matt to open gifts before morning tea.

Morning tea…

Nerves fluttered in Skye's stomach. Everything was bound to be terribly formal, not like the casual breakfast they'd had this morning with Matt too excited about his presents to sit at a table. They'd lounged around in Luc's lovely living room, eating raisin toast, sharing the fun of a beautiful Christmas morning together. Skye could only hope that what should be a joyful day remained so for Matt.

She turned around to face Luc as he entered their bedroom. 'Will I do?' she asked anxiously, thinking how perfect he looked in smartly tailored grey pants and a conservative white cotton shirt—acceptable anywhere and the light colours throwing up the striking attraction of his Italian heritage.

His dark eyes simmered with more than appreciation as they swept her from head to foot and back again. 'You look beautiful.'

'Luc, I was trying for respectable,' she appealed, feeling her skin flush under the heat of his appraisal and becoming unsure of her choice. Was it too colourful, too cheap-looking?

His expression instantly changed to thunderous. 'You don't have to prove anything to my parents, Skye. Absolutely nothing! If they don't...'

She moved quickly to place her hand over his lips, stopping the burst of angst. 'I want to look right for Christmas at their home, Luc. Just tell me if I do or don't.'

His breath hissed out from between clenched teeth. 'If it's making you feel like this, we shouldn't be doing it.'

She moved her hand to the tight muscles in his jaw, resting it there lovingly as she spoke a truth they had not discussed for a long time. 'When you saw the photographs of Roberto and the woman pretending to be me, you believed them, Luc. You believed what your father thought of me.'

'Skye...' It was a groan of pain, tortured regret in his eyes.

'Maybe part of it was my going to bed with you too easily, giving in to the desire we felt. And maybe part of it was the kind of clothes I wore, the wrong image for—' she grimaced at the term as she delivered it '—for a good girl.'

'Skye, I have wished a thousand times that I had believed you and not Roberto. I can't undo that…'

'It doesn't matter any more, Luc. It stopped mattering when you convinced me you really did love me this time around. And I'll never bring it up again.'

His arms swept around her, drawing her into a possessive embrace as his eyes begged her belief. 'You mean more to me than anything else.'

'I know. I know,' she repeated to assure him there were no doubts about his love in her mind. 'You walked away from your family, for my sake. I'll never forget you did that. But if I let this rift go on, you'll all be suffering a far greater loss than I did. A much longer loss. And that's not fair, Luc. Mistakes were made on both sides and I want to correct mine.'

He shook his head, still pained by her insecurities. 'You were just you, Skye.'

'I didn't know any better then.' She gave him an ironic smile, trying to lessen his concern for her. 'I'm older and wiser now and it doesn't hurt me to dress as appropriately as I can to please your parents on such an occasion as this. I'd like them to look at me and think…well, I won't completely shame them as their daughter-in-law.'

'They should be proud to own you as one of the family,' he asserted earnestly.

'I think that will take time. I'm not expecting much

today. You shouldn't, either. I think we should both
be very diplomatic.'

He grimaced, but the tense expression left his eyes,
giving way to a wry admiration. 'You are an incredibly giving woman, Skye Sumner. And you do...
beautifully. No one could possibly object to your appearance today. Not by any standard,' he fervently
assured her.

She took a deep breath to calm her nerves and
smiled her sunniest smile. 'Then I'm ready to go. Is
Matt okay?'

'Happily sorting out the edges and corners for the
Harry Potter jigsaw we're going to do together. I
guess we'd better go and collect him.'

Twenty minutes later, Luc turned the red Alfa
through a huge iron gateway and headed up a semi-
circular drive, past perfectly manicured lawns and
gardens to an incredibly large and imposing sandstone
mansion.

'It's as big as a castle, Daddy,' Matt remarked in
awe.

Was Maurizio Peretti going to be a gracious king,
or a giant ogre, Skye wondered, trying desperately not
to feel intimidated. Matt felt no fear at all. Once out
of the car, he bounded up the front steps, eager to
explore his Nonna's home, and when a formally
dressed butler opened the door, Matt looked him up
and down and promptly asked, 'Are you my grandfather?'

'No, Matt. This is Kirkwood, who's in charge of
the house,' Luc quickly introduced.

'It's a very big house, Kirkwood,' Matt said, showing his awe.

The butler unbent enough to smile. 'Indeed, it is, young sir.'

Skye instantly started worrying about Matt's clothes. She'd dressed *young sir* in dark blue shorts and a turquoise shirt printed with white sailing boats, navy sandals on his feet. He looked gorgeous—a perfect little boy outfit, she'd thought when she'd bought it for him—but perhaps she should have chosen something more formal, more in keeping with being the grandson of Maurizio Peretti.

They were ushered into a large drawing room furnished with elegant antiques and currently dominated by the most magnificent Christmas tree Skye had ever seen—a silvery-blue tree which matched the furnishings, well over two metres high, and covered with exquisite ornaments.

Maurizio Peretti was standing in front of a marble fireplace, imposingly attired in a dark grey suit, a red silk tie possibly adding a festive touch. Flavia Peretti rose from a nearby sofa, and amazingly she wasn't wearing black today. Her dark red dress made her look younger, as did the smile she bestowed on Matt as he rushed forward to greet her.

'Nonna! Your Christmas tree is beautiful!'

He put so much expression into *beautiful,* she actually laughed. 'I'm glad you like it, Matteo.'

'I brought this for you,' he proudly handed her his gift which Skye had wrapped up for him in gold paper and tied with red ribbon. 'Happy Christmas, Nonna! It's a picture I drew of the beach where Daddy lives.'

No holding back by Matt! He hadn't yet learnt how to contain himself.

'Thank you, Matteo. Now come and meet your

grandfather.' She took his hand to lead him over to her husband whose gaze had been exclusively trained on the little boy, not lifting to acknowledge Luc and Skye. 'You call him Nonno,' Flavia instructed.

Skye couldn't help tensing and Luc's hand squeezed hers so hard she knew if his father did not respond reasonably to their son, Christmas Day at Bellevue Hill would be over before it had barely begun.

Matt looked up at his formidable grandfather and without so much as a pause, brightly said, 'Hello, Nonno. I brought you a gift, too. Happy Christmas!'

He held out his offering and Maurizio Peretti's hand slowly reached out and took it. 'Thank you.' It was a gravelled rumble from his throat, which he then cleared. 'Is it another picture you drew?'

Matt nodded. 'It's me playing soccer.'

'Ah! Your father told me you'd kicked more goals than anyone else in your team.'

'Thirty-two,' Matt told him proudly. 'And I got a trophy for it, Nonno.'

'Well done!'—said with hearty approval. He opened the gift, unrolled the drawing and a smile gradually softened his hard face as Matt explained all the action in it to him. 'I shall have this framed and put on my desk at work, Matteo. Everyone who comes in will see what a clever grandson I have.'

Public acceptance!

Skye breathed a sigh of relief.

Luc's fingers relaxed.

His father gave them both a cursory glance as he tossed a greeting at them. 'Happy Christmas! Come and sit down.' He waved to a sofa, then fastened his attention on Matt again. 'Underneath that beautiful tree, you might find some gifts for you. Why don't you go and have a look?'

The next hour passed peaceably enough with all of them focusing more on Matt's pleasure in his Christmas booty than on each other. Morning tea was served by the butler. Pressed into eating something by Flavia, Skye managed to get through a small mince pie and a sliver of rich fruit cake.

She was very conscious of Luc watching his father like a hawk, ready to pounce on any discourtesy to herself, but Maurizio Peretti skirted carefully around her, not once addressing her directly by name. She wasn't exactly ignored but there was definitely some resistance to her presence, making her feel very much on edge.

What words were spoken between the men were few and far between, as well. As soon as the butler had cleared away the morning tea, Maurizio Peretti was on his feet, holding out his hand to Matt. 'Come and have a walk with me around the grounds. I'll show you the sailing boats in the harbour, and maybe we can find a good place for us to play cricket after lunch.'

A cricket set had been amongst the gifts and Matt was instantly up and grasping his grandfather's hand, eager to go along with his plan.

Luc rose to his feet, bristling with purpose. 'I'll come with you.'

'No, no…' His father waved him to sit down again. 'Let me get to know my grandson. Besides, your mother has plans she wants to put to you.'

Skye knew Luc wanted to challenge him over his

less than welcoming manner to her but she hoped his father might thaw more over lunch. 'Let them go, Luc,' she softly pleaded.

'Yes, we have much to talk about,' his mother leapt in anxiously.

Rather than raise an argument in front of Matt, he reluctantly conceded to the arrangement, resuming his seat beside Skye and seething with silent resentment as he watched his father take his son off for their walk. The moment the door was closed behind them he turned to his mother and flatly declared, 'I won't have Skye ignored, Mamma.'

'Your father is feeling awkward, Luciano,' she quickly excused. 'Give him time. It is not a feeling he is used to. Perhaps Matteo will ease him out of it.'

Luc shook his head in impatient frustration. 'Well, what is it you want to talk about, Mamma?'

Their wedding!

Flavia Peretti laid out a plan that had Skye's mind reeling at its grand scale. Firstly, she wanted Luc to bring Skye and Matt to the New Year's Day luncheon party which the Perettis held every year—a gathering of all their closest friends and associates. It could serve to introduce Skye as his fiancée and be turned into an engagement party, celebrating their forthcoming marriage.

Then the invitations to the wedding could be sent out—six weeks' notice was enough—and a suitable marquee could be hired and set up in the grounds to accommodate the hundreds of guests. She went on and on, covering every detail of a production designed to inform the whole Italian community that

Luc's bride was to be acknowledged as a welcome addition to the Peretti family.

'Has Dad approved of this plan?' Luc tersely asked.

'You know it must be so, Luciano,' his mother pleaded rather than replied.

'You've discussed it with him?' Luc bored in, refusing to take anything for granted.

'Yes, of course.'

'Mamma, he stole Skye from me once. If this putting her on public display is meant to make her feel less than she is…if its purpose is to alienate her from me…'

'I swear it is not, Luciano,' his mother cried in alarm.

Luc beetled a frown at her. 'I see no sign of Dad treating Skye with respect.'

'He will. He *will*,' came the insistent reply.

'This plan may be his way of making amends, Luc,' Skye murmured, though she quailed at the thought of being put under such a spotlight in front of people whom she didn't know, people who didn't know her, people who were bound to look askance at the woman who'd borne a child out of wedlock and was probably forcing this unsuitable marriage because of it.

'Then why isn't he offering it himself?' Luc queried, his eyes searching hers for the truth of how she felt. 'You can't want to do this, Skye.'

'If it means a happier outcome all around…' She looked to his mother for guidance, believing that Flavia understood the complexities of the situation far better than she did. 'Is it necessary, Mrs Peretti?'

'No, it's not,' Luc cut in vehemently. 'We can get

married as planned. Privately. No more postpone-
ments.'

'Luciano, please…' his mother begged. 'I will help
Skye all I can. Do everything. She need only be here
for you.'

'Don't put this on me!' he fiercely retorted. 'I'm
not asking it of Skye. And you have asked too much
of her already, Mamma.' He rose to his feet, too
pumped up with aggressive energy to remain seated.
His hands flew into furious gesticulation as he fired
more shots at his mother. 'All these months ignoring
her…and now you expect her to perform for you. It's
too much. We get married how we want to get married.'

Flavia Peretti turned imploring eyes to Skye.
'Please…it is a matter of family honour.'

'And where was honour when Matt was born?' Luc
hurled at her. '*My* son!'

'Luc!' Skye's sharp cry switched his attention back
to her but his eyes were still blazing with turbulent
emotion. She shook her head at him and dredged up
the courage to do what had to be done. 'No more. It
has to stop now. Matt loves having his Nonna. He's
taken to your father, too. Let it be, Luc. I'll do it—'
her smile was meant to appeal to his strong, protective
instincts '—if you'll hold my hand.'

A few fast strides and he was back on the sofa with
her, holding both her hands. 'You don't have to do
this.'

'It doesn't matter. We're getting married, aren't
we?'

'Yes, but…'

'Your mother said she'd help me.'

'As I would a daughter,' Flavia Peretti swiftly promised.

'You see? It will be all right.'

The storm passed, though it left an unease which both women worked at glossing over; Luc's mother asking for Skye's input on everything to do with the wedding, Skye saying she was happy to go along with whatever Flavia advised. At the end of the day, she and Luc would be married, and if what she agreed to won his parents' blessing, that was what she had set out to achieve for him.

'Skye will choose her own wedding dress,' Luc insisted at one point, glowering at both of them.

His mother instantly agreed. 'Of course, she must. She is the bride.'

The bride...

It was weird to be called that. Skye didn't feel like a bride. Being a mother to Matt, living with Luc, having suffered through all they had to be together...a wedding like this felt very unreal to her. She had no guests to invite, no father to give her away. To her this whole plan was simply a process to ensure Luc would not lose anything by marrying her. But... maybe she would feel like a bride on her wedding day.

Matt came racing in ahead of his grandfather, full of exciting news. 'Mummy, you should see. There's a swimming pool and a tennis court and lots of flowers you'd like. Not just in pots.'

Maurizio Peretti strolled into the drawing room and Skye smiled at him, hoping he would share her pleasure in his grandson's happy list of wonderful things. His gaze skated right past her to his wife who nodded, apparently in answer to some silent question. His mouth twitched into a grim little smile and the mocking look he turned to Skye—his first direct look at her—made her own smile falter and die.

'I take it you're happy with the wedding arrangements.'

'Yes,' she agreed, though his attitude was swiftly giving her second thoughts.

'I had no doubt you would be,' he said with arrogant cynicism. 'Having no family yourself, and seeing all we can offer here...'

The implication was so gross, Skye completely lost sight of the purpose that had brought her to this monstrous castle of money—blood money that had got rid of her and paid for Matt's exclusion from their lives.

All the most negative emotions she'd ever had about the Perettis churned through her, driving her to her feet, Matt's hand firmly grasped in hers. She heard her voice shaking with a fierce primitive passion that literally burst from her.

'I do have family, Mr Peretti. I have my son. And believe me, I'm perfectly happy to take him away from everything you have here. I only came for Luc. Because I love him. I love him...'

Luc was suddenly beside her, his arm around her shoulders, hugging her tight, and to her intense mortification, a gush of tears welled into her eyes.

'Maurizio, you have this wrong!' his wife wailed, rushing forward to grab his arm to press her own belief, shaking it in her angst. 'The cottage she lived in...she would not even take from Luciano!'

'Mamma, you waste your breath.' Luc growled. 'I'm taking Skye home.'

'No…no…' In panicking protest, his mother whirled past her husband to block their way, flapping her hands in distress. 'I don't want you to go. Maurizio, this is not right. You must see it is not.'

It was a horribly painful situation.

Skye could feel Luc's father glaring at her, hating the dissension she had brought to his household. Luc was holding her protectively. She was hanging on to Matt's hand, savagely possessive of him in her own distress. Flavia Peretti made it impossible for Luc to manoeuvre all three of them past her.

The wretched impasse pulsed with enormous stress. Into the dreadfully fraught silence came Matt's little boy voice, quavering with incomprehension and fright at what was going on around him, yet incredibly homing in on the heart of the problem.

'Nonno…why don't you love my Mummy?'

A hysterical bubble of laughter almost broke over the terrible lump in Skye's throat. *Love* her? Luc's father had hated her all along! It didn't matter what she did, however many concessions she made…

'Matt, we're just going to take your mother home,' Luc said firmly.

'But, Daddy…'

'I'll explain later, Matt. We must leave now. Mamma, if you'll just step aside…'

'No!' The emphatic command from Maurizio Peretti was followed up by his moving to stand by his wife, ensuring their departure was blocked. 'The boy has a right to ask,' he declared, challenging Luc before turning his gaze down to their son.

'Dad…' Luc threatening.

'Matteo…the reason why I do not love your mother

is because I do not know her. I have not taken the time to know her. And for that—' he lifted his gaze directly to Skye '—I apologise.'

Silence.

The apology might have been wrung from him but it was hanging out there to be accepted, completely confusing Skye. Was it sincere or...or what? He had certainly spoken the truth. He did not know her.

'You could get to know my Mummy now, Nonno,' Matt reasoned in his innocence. 'Daddy knows her real good and he loves her.'

'Yes, he does,' Maurizio Peretti conceded to Matt, then looked directly at Luc before adding. 'I know he does.'

Skye had no idea what passed between the two men. Her vision was hopelessly blurred, but she could feel the tension of absolute war slightly easing.

'Mummy likes flowers,' Matt informed helpfully. 'You could take her for a walk, Nonno, and show her your garden.'

'That sounds like a very good idea, Matteo. Perhaps after lunch, your mother would agree to accompany me. And I can apologise more fully for not knowing her.'

Matt tugged on her dress. 'Please don't cry, Mummy. Nonno didn't mean to upset you. He just didn't know.'

Skye brushed the wetness from her cheeks with the back of her hand, still too choked up to speak.

Maurizio Peretti cleared his throat. 'Skye...if I may call you that...'

'It's her name,' Luc fiercely muttered.

'Will you offer me…an olive branch…for the sake of those we love?'

It was why she had come.

Maybe the sentiment was genuine, maybe it wasn't. She still had to try.

In her hands was the power to build a family or destroy one.

She swallowed hard, sucked in a deep breath, lifted her head to hold it high, and said, 'Yes, I will, Mr Peretti.'

'Bravo!' he murmured, and for the very first time, she saw a glint of admiration in Maurizio Peretti's eyes.

For her.

'What's an olive branch, Daddy?' Matt asked.

'It's the gift of love, Matt. Your mother is telling your grandfather how much she loves both of us. And I hope he understands it.'

'Do you, Nonno?'

'Yes, I do, Matteo.'

'Mummy could love you, too.'

'That, my dear child, would be a miracle, but since it's Christmas Day, miracles can happen.'

'Indeed, they can,' Flavia breathed in relief. Then quite briskly, 'Come, Matteo, we'll go and wash your hands before lunch. Maurizio, you'd best check the wine with Kirkwood.'

Which neatly left Luc and Skye alone to have some private time together. He turned her to face him, gently tilting her chin up to look into her eyes. 'Are you really okay with this, Skye?'

'No. Not yet. But I'll get there,' she answered shakily.

'You're determined on it?'

'So long as you hold my hand.'

'All my life,' he promised.

And she knew he would keep that promise, regardless of whatever happened today, tomorrow, next week, next month, next year, all their future together.

CHAPTER SEVENTEEN

THE wedding day…

Skye sat quietly in the white limousine as it was driven to the city centre. Opposite her sat Karin Holmes, the wedding planner Flavia had hired to ensure everything was done to perfection—a very pleasant woman who took all the angst out of getting things right. Skye was intensely grateful to her for all her instructions and advice.

Luc's mother sat beside Karin, facing Matt who was delighted to be riding in this very long car, chattering away to Nonna without the slightest sign of being nervous about this highly momentous occasion. His Nonna was clearly enjoying the conversation she was having with her grandson.

Skye reflected on how amazingly well Matt connected with both his grandparents. She had no worries about leaving him with them while she and Luc were away on their honeymoon, no worries about accepting Flavia's offer to collect Matt after school and mind him on the days she'd be at university this year, finishing her physiotherapy degree.

Luc had withdrawn his resignation and was staying on as head of his department in the Peretti Corporation. Where he truly belonged, Skye thought. And they'd purchased a house at Rose Bay, with a backyard for Matt to play in and a boathouse for the sailing yacht Luc wanted to buy. Living in his parents' mansion, as Roberto had with his wife, was not an option to be considered as far as Luc was concerned, much to Skye's relief.

It was only two months since Christmas and she was still getting used to the turnaround from Luc's father. She found Maurizio Peretti perhaps too much like Luc in some ways. Once he set his mind on a course, there were no holds barred. As Luc's fiancée, she was treated like an honoured princess in public, possibly an exercise in saving face. In private, he was still getting to know her. Cautiously. Occasionally testingly.

It had been the right decision to take the chance, Skye thought with satisfaction. So much had changed for the better. Luc was more relaxed now. She was more relaxed. They were even going off on a honeymoon together. To Italy. The romantic island of Capri.

And today she truly did feel like a bride. She loved her dress—a stunning beaded gown in blush silk and ivory French lace. With it, she'd bought a matching beaded lace skullcap to sit over her forehead and frame her face. Her hair was pulled back and woven into elegant loops at the back, under which her veil was cleverly attached to the cap—a wonderful long veil that extended into a lace-edged train. Even her shoes were special, high-heeled pearl sandals, glittering with the same beads used on the dress.

Flavia had taken her to her hair stylist, hired a beautician to do her make-up, and a manicurist to buff and varnish her nails with a dusky pink polish. 'A perfect bride!' her future mother-in-law had happily declared, looking Skye over before they'd stepped into the limousine. Which was now pulling up outside St Mary's Cathedral.

No ordinary church for a Peretti marriage. No ordinary celebrant to conduct the ceremony, either. The Archbishop of Sydney was officiating, and inside were four hundred guests, many of whom were very prominent people far beyond the close Italian community that mainly formed the Peretti social circle. Skye had been amazed at some of the names on the wedding list.

It had struck her forcibly that this was what she was marrying into. This was Luc's heritage, what he would have given up for her—a nobody on any social scale. It also gave her more understanding of why his parents had been against the relationship, and how far they'd had to bend to accept that she was the woman Luc had chosen as his wife.

Background was important.

But love was more important.

Love was what held it all together, despite the differences.

Skye was very conscious of this as Karin Holmes helped her out of the car. Now that they were here, Luc's mother was to go ahead into the cathedral first, taking Matt with her. Skye gave her bouquet to Karin to hold and took Flavia's hands in hers, leaning forward to kiss her on the cheek.

'Thank you for all you have done for me. My own mother could not have done more,' she murmured gratefully.

'My dear…you do Luciano proud. You go to him now with my blessing. And his father's.'

*   *   *

Flavia Peretti left Skye to the wedding planner's competent handling, took her grandson's hand and entered the cathedral. Heads turned to watch the two of them walk down the aisle. She heard the whispers, knew tongues were wagging about Luciano's illegitimate child, but she refused to care what anyone thought.

Matteo was a wonderful little boy. She adored him. And she now had him firmly in her life. Perhaps more grandchildren, as well, further down the track—babies whose births could be celebrated with Luciano and Skye properly married. The empty future would be filled as she needed it to be filled.

She had no quarrel with Skye any more. Flavia was sure she would be a good daughter-in-law. Her giving nature made everything much easier than she had anticipated, thank God! And Maurizio…finally understanding what a husband should understand for his wife. It was all very well, being a big businessman and accumulating a great deal of wealth, living in a fine house, but without family…yes, he finally understood.

Maurizio Peretti smiled at the child who had walked into his life and grabbed his heart. Flavia seated them both beside him in the front pew, their grandson between them.

'Mummy looks beautiful, Nonno,' Matteo whispered.

'I think your Daddy looks fine, too,' he answered, nodding to where his son stood, waiting for his bride—the only bride he would accept.

A fine woman, too, Maurizio thought, intensely relieved that he had been wrong about Skye Sumner.

She would make a true life partner for Luciano, caring about his needs, just as Luciano cared about hers. It was also very generous of her to let the past go, not that Maurizio had meant to give her so much suffering. If her stepfather had been a decent man...though he himself had been wrong, very wrong in misjudging his own son's feelings, as well as Skye's.

Perhaps, he should acknowledge these things in his speech at the wedding reception. Nothing embarrassing, but a few words that expressed the real truth—a love that had already spanned many years, proving it was deep and steadfast, the best basis for a long, lasting and happy marriage. Although he and Flavia had done very well with hardly knowing each other before they were married. On the other hand, there had certainly been a spark between them—difficult to wait until their wedding night.

Luciano and Skye had not waited.

Yet how could he regret their having Matteo?

A fine grandson.

It was right to celebrate this marriage.

He would say so.

Luc was conscious of a sea of faces in front of him, hundreds of guests seated in the pews, waiting for the arrival of his bride. Undoubtedly it was an interesting occasion to them—Maurizio Peretti's eldest son marrying a woman who'd already borne his child. It was not interesting to him. It was vital. And every second of waiting was hell.

The last time he had been in this cathedral was for Roberto's funeral. Was his brother resting in peace now? Skye had been found. The child he hadn't known about was now a proudly acknowledged grandson. And he himself felt brilliantly alive again with Skye back in his world.

Smile, brother, he thought on a wave of love for the Roberto who had cared so much for him at the end. *The wrong has been righted.*

The boys' choir finished singing. The pipe organ started playing the first chords of Mendelssohn's Wedding March. At last, he thought, every nerve in his body electrified by the intense energy pouring from his need for Skye to be his wife.

His heart thundered in his chest as she began the walk down the aisle towards him—a vision of such loveliness his breath was caught in his throat. This is the woman I love, he told himself, not a dream. And she smiled her love at him, making the moment wonderfully real—Skye coming to him, his bride.

He no longer saw anyone else. He didn't even hear the music. His hand reached out for her and she took it—took his hand in marriage, for better and for worse, from this day forth. Luc didn't need to say the vows, didn't need to hear Skye say them. The big production his parents had wanted to make of this wedding meant nothing to him. Every bit of meaning in this ceremony was encased in the hand holding his.

A simple bonding...yet it meant they were one with each other.

It meant he and Skye owned a future together—a future no one could steal from them.

They were one.

THE MARCHESE'S
LOVE-CHILD

by

Sara Craven

Sara Craven was born in South Devon and grew up surrounded by books in a house by the sea. After leaving grammar school she worked as a local journalist, covering everything from flower shows to murders. She started writing for Mills & Boon in 1975. Apart from writing, her passions include films, music, cooking and eating in good restaurants. She now lives in Somerset.

Sara Craven has appeared as a contestant on the Channel Four game show *Fifteen to One* and is also the winner of the 1997 *Mastermind of Great Britain* championship.

Don't miss Sara Craven's exciting new novel, *Ruthless Awakening*, available in June 2009 from Mills & Boon® Modern™.

CHAPTER ONE

'YOU'RE going back to Italy?' There was outrage in Lily Fairfax's voice as she turned on her daughter. Anger too. 'Oh, I don't believe it. You can't—you mustn't.'

Polly Fairfax sighed soundlessly. 'Mother, I'm escorting an elderly lady to Naples, where she'll be met by her family, upon which—I catch the next flight home. I'll be gone for a few hours at most. Hardly *Mission Impossible*.'

'You said you'd never return there,' her mother said. 'You swore it.'

'Yes, I know,' Polly acknowledged wearily. 'But that was three years ago. And circumstances change. This is a work assignment, and there's no one else to do it. Since Safe Hands was featured on that holiday programme, we've been snowed under with requests.' She adopted a persuasive tone. 'And you enjoyed seeing me on television—you know you did.' She added a smile. 'So you can't complain if I'm in demand as a consequence.'

Mrs Fairfax wasn't pacified. 'Is this why this woman—this Contessa Whatsit wants you? Because you've been on television?'

Polly laughed. 'I shouldn't think so for a moment. She's far too grand to bother with anything so vulgar. And her name's the Contessa Barsoli.'

Her mother dismissed that impatiently. 'I didn't think you liked her very much.'

Polly shrugged. 'I don't particularly. She's been a total pain the whole week I've been with her. And I'm damned sure she doesn't care for me either,' she added musingly. 'She always looks at me as if I'm a slug in her salad. Believe me, I shan't be tempted to linger.'

'Then why did she choose you?'

'The devil she knows, perhaps.' Polly shrugged again. 'As opposed to some stranger. Anyway, she needs someone to see to her luggage, and make sure she's got all her documentation. Which is where Safe Hands comes in, of course.'

She leaned forward. 'To be honest, Mum, I don't know how much longer I can go on turning down jobs in Italy, just because of something that happened three years ago. I like my job, and I want to hang on to it. But Mrs Terence is running a business here, not an agency for people who've been crossed in love.'

'It was,' her mother reminded her tightly, 'rather more than that.'

'Whatever.' Polly bit her lip. 'But I can't pick and choose my clients, and I think Mrs T has made all the allowances over Italy that she's going to. So I have to treat it as just another destination from now on.'

'And what about Charlie?' Mrs Fairfax demanded fiercely. 'What's going to happen to him while you're gadding off?'

It hardly seemed to Polly that enduring another twenty-four hours in the company of a disdainful Italian autocrat counted as 'gadding'.

And her mother had never objected to her role as child-minder before, even when Polly was absent on other, much longer trips. In fact she'd declared that Charlie's presence had given her a new lease of life.

She looked out of the window to where her cheerful two-year-old was trotting about after his grandfather, picking up hedge clippings.

She said slowly, 'I thought he would stay with you, as usual.'

There were bright spots of colour in her mother's face. 'But it's not usual—is it? You're deliberately defying my wishes—yet again. I was totally against your taking that job in Sorrento three years ago, and how right I was. You came slinking home pregnant by some local Casanova, who didn't want to know about you any more. Can you deny it?'

'To be fair, Sandro had no more idea that I was expecting a baby than I did myself,' Polly said levelly. 'Although I agree it would have made no difference if he had known. But that's all in the past. I've—rebuilt my life, and he'll have moved on too.' She paused. 'All the same, I promise not to go within ten miles of Sorrento, if that will make you feel better.'

'I'd feel better if you didn't go at all,' her mother returned sharply. 'But if it really is just a day trip, I suppose I can't stop you.'

'You'll hardly know I've gone,' Polly assured her. 'Thanks, Mum.' She gave her a swift hug. 'You're a star.'

'I'm an idiot,' Lily Fairfax retorted, but she sounded slightly mollified. 'Are you going to stay for supper? I've made one of my steak pies.'

'It's good of you, darling,' said Polly, mentally bracing herself for another battle. 'But we must get back. I have this trip to prepare for.'

Mrs Fairfax gave her a tragic look. 'But I've got Charlie's favourite ice-cream for dessert. He'll be so disappointed.'

Only because you've already told him, Polly thought without pleasure.

Aloud, she said, 'You really mustn't spoil him like that.'

Her mother pouted. 'It's a sad thing if I can't give my only grandchild the occasional treat.' She paused. 'Why not leave him here—if you're going to be busy this evening?' she coaxed. 'It'll save you time in the morning if you have a plane to catch.'

'It's a kind thought.' Polly tried to sound positive. 'But I really look forward to my evenings with Charlie, Mum. I—I see so little of him.'

'Well, that's something your father and I wanted to discuss with you,' her mother said with sudden briskness. 'There's a lot of unused space in this house, and if we were to extend over the garage, it would make a really nice flat for you both. And it would mean so much less disruption for Charlie.'

She emptied the carrots she'd been scraping into a pan. 'We've had some preliminary plans drawn up, and, if you stayed, we could look at them over supper perhaps.'

Polly supposed, heart sinking, that she should have seen it coming—but she hadn't. Oh, God, she thought, is this the day from hell, or what?

She said quietly, 'Mum, I do have a flat already.'

'An attic,' her mother dismissed with a sniff, 'with a room hardly bigger than a cupboard for Charlie. Here, he'd have room to run about, plus a routine he's accustomed to. And we're in the catchment area for a good primary school, when the time comes,' she added. 'I think it's the perfect solution to all sorts of problems.'

My main problem, Polly thought wearily, is prising Charlie out of this house at the end of the working day. Of staking a claim in my own child. She'd seen trouble looming when her own former bedroom was extensively redecorated and refitted for Charlie, despite her protest that he wouldn't use it sufficiently to justify the expense.

Her mother must have had this in mind from the first.

She rallied herself, trying to speak reasonably. 'But I need my independence. I'm used to it.'

'Is that what you call the way you live? You're a single mother, my girl. A statistic. And this glamorous job of yours is little better than slavery—running around all over the place at the beck and call of people with more money than sense. And where did it lead? To you making a fool of yourself with some foreigner, and ruining your life.' She snorted. 'Well, don't come to me for help if you mess up your life a second time.'

Polly's head went back in shock. She said unsteadily, 'That is *so* unfair. I made a mistake, and I've paid for it. But I still intend to live my life on my own terms, and I hope you can accept that.'

Mrs Fairfax's face was flushed. 'I can certainly see you're determined to have your own way, regardless of Charlie's well-being.' She sent her daughter a fulminating glance. 'And now I suppose you'll take him with you, just to make your point.'

'No,' Polly said reluctantly. 'I won't do that—this time. But I think you have to accept that I do have a point.'

'Perhaps you'd send Charlie indoors as you leave.' Her mother opened a carton of new potatoes and began to wash them. 'He's getting absolutely filthy out there, and I'd like him to calm down before he eats.'

'Fine.' Polly allowed herself a small, taut smile. 'I'll pass the message on.'

As she went into the garden, Charlie headed for her gleefully, strewing twigs and leaves behind him. Polly bent to enfold him, the breath catching in her throat as she inhaled his unique baby scent. Thinking again, with a pang, how beautiful he was. And how painfully, searingly like his father...

Her mother had never wanted to know any details about his paternity, referring to Sandro solely as 'that foreigner'. The fact that Charlie, with his curly black hair, olive skin and long-lashed eyes the colour of deep topaz, was also clearly a Mediterranean to his fingertips seemed to have eluded her notice.

But it was the details that only Polly could recognise that brought her heart into her mouth, like the first time her son had looked at her with that wrenchingly familiar slow, slanting smile. His baby features were starting to change too, and she could see that he was going to have Sandro's high-bridged nose one day, and the same straight brows.

It would be like living with a mirror image before too long, Polly told herself, thinking forlornly that nature played cruel tricks at times. Why couldn't Charlie have inherited her own pale blonde hair and green eyes?

She smoothed the hair back from his damp forehead. 'Gran wants you to go inside, darling,' she whispered. 'You're sleeping here tonight. Won't that be fun?'

Her father came to join them, his brows lifting at her words. 'Will it, my love?' His voice was neutral, but the glance he sent her was searching.

'Yes.' Polly cleared her throat, watching Charlie scamper towards the house. 'It—it seems a shame to uproot him, when I have to start work early tomorrow.'

'Yes.' He paused. 'She means it all for the best, you know, Poll,' he told her quietly.

'He's my child, Dad.' Polly shook her head. 'I have to have an opinion on what's best for him, too. And that doesn't include moving back here.'

'I know that,' her father said gently. 'But I'm also aware how hard it must be raising a child without any kind of support from his father—and I'm not simply talking about the economics of it.'

He sighed. 'You were so precious to me, I can't imagine a man not wanting to involve himself with his own flesh and blood.'

Polly's lips moved in a wintry little smile. 'He didn't want to know, Dad—about either of us. It was best to leave it that way.'

'Yes, love,' he said. 'So you told me. But that hasn't stopped me from worrying—or your mother either.' He gave her a swift hug. 'Take care.'

Polly's thoughts were troubled as she rode home on the bus alone. Her mother's attempts to totally monopolise her grandson was becoming a seriously tricky situation, and she wasn't sure she had sufficient wisdom to resolve it.

The last thing she wanted was for Charlie to become a battleground, but even a mild suggestion that she should enrol him at a local nursery for a few hours a week so that he could mix with other children had provoked such an injured reception from Mrs Fairfax that she hadn't dared raise the subject again.

Her mother's hostile attitude to her work was a different thing.

Safe Hands had proved the job of her dreams, and she knew, without conceit, that she was good at it.

The people who made use of the company were mainly female and usually elderly, people who needed someone young, relatively strong and capable to deal with their luggage, guide them through airports and escort them safely round unfamiliar foreign cities.

Polly was the youngest of Mrs Terence's employees, but she had a gift for languages, and her brief career as a holiday rep had taught her patience and tolerance to add to her natural sense of humour—qualities she soon found she needed in abundance.

She knew how to diffuse potentially explosive situations with overseas Customs, find restaurants that were sympathetic to delicate digestions, hotels in peaceful locations that were also picturesque, and shops prepared to deliver purchases to hotels, or post them on to addresses abroad. She could also discover which art galleries and museums were prepared to arrange quiet private tours for small groups.

And she never showed even a trace of irritation with even the most high-handed behaviour from her charges.

After all, she was being paid for acceding to their whims and fancies, and part of her skill was in making them forget that was how she earned her living, and persuading them that she was there for the sheer pleasure of their company.

But with the Contessa Barsoli, it had been a struggle from day one.

Polly had long accepted that not all her clients would like her, but she did need them to trust her, and, from the start, her senses had detected an inflexible wariness, bordering on hostility at times, in the *contessa*'s attitude which she was at a loss to account for.

Whatever the reason, there had never been any real warmth between them, so Polly had been genuinely astonished to hear that the *contessa* had specifically requested her services again for the homeward leg of her journey to southern Italy, and was prepared to pay her a generous cash bonus too.

Surprised—but also alarmed enough to ask herself if the money was really worth the damage to her nervous system.

Her previous visit—the first and last—had left her scarred—and scared. And there was no way she'd have dared risk a return, if there'd been the slightest chance she might encounter Sandro again. But the odds against such a meeting must run into millions to one. But irrational as it might seem, even the remotest possibility still had the power to make her tremble.

They said time was a great healer, but the wound Sandro had dealt her was still agonisingly raw.

She'd tried so hard to block out the memories of that summer in Sorrento three years ago. The summer she thought she'd fallen in love, and believed she was loved in return. But the images she'd hoped were safely locked away forever had broken free, and were running wild in her brain again.

Her room, she thought, wincing, during the hours of siesta, the shutters closed against the beat of the sun, and only the languid whirr of the ceiling fan and their own ragged breathing to break the silence.

And Sandro's voice murmuring soft, husky words of passion, his hands and mouth exploring her naked body with sensuous delight. The heated surge of his body into hers at the moment of possession.

She had lived for those shadowed, rapturous afternoons, and warm, moonlit nights, which made the pain of his ultimate betrayal even more intense.

What a gullible little fool I was, Polly thought with self-derision. And I can't say I wasn't warned. The other reps said that he was just looking for some easy summer sex, and cautioned me to be careful, but I wouldn't listen because I knew better.

I knew that he loved me, and that when the summer was over we were going to be married. I was convinced of it—because he'd said so.

I thought it was that innocent—that simple. I should have realised that he wasn't what he seemed. He told me he worked at one of the big hotels, but he always had too much money to be just a waiter or a barman. And these jobs were usually taken by younger men, anyway, while Sandro was thirty at least.

I knew from the first that there were depths to him that belied the seaside Romeo tag—and that the latent power I always sensed in him was part of his attraction for me.

But I liked the fact that he was something of an enigma. That there were questions about him still to be answered. I thought I would have the rest of my life to find out the truth.

Yes, I was a fool, but it never once occurred to me that I could be in any real danger. That there was another darker side to his life, far away from the sunlight and whispered promises.

Not until he got bored with me. Not until his friend arrived—the man in the designer suit with the smile that never reached his eyes. The man who came to tell me that it was all over, and to suggest, smiling suavely and icily, that it would be better for my health to get out of Sorrento, and away from Italy altogether.

The man who told me that I'd become an inconvenience, and that it would be much safer for me to quit my job and go back to England.

And that I should never try to contact Sandro, or come back to Italy again—ever.

In return for which I was to receive the equivalent of fifty thousand pounds.

Polly shuddered. Even now the memory made her shake inside. But what had crucified her then, and still hurt today, was that Sandro hadn't had the guts to come to her himself—to tell her in person that it was finished between them. And why...

She'd rejected his money with anger and contempt, unable to believe that he could insult her like that. Ordered his confederate out of her room.

But, all the same, she'd obeyed and left, because she was too heartbroken—and also too frightened to stay. She didn't know what Sandro could be involved with to afford a bribe of that size—and she didn't want to know. But something had reached out from the shadows around him, which had touched her life, and destroyed her hope of happiness.

She had been at home for several weeks before it dawned on her that she was pregnant—a knowledge born slowly from grief, bewilderment and unbelievable loneliness. At first she'd told herself that it could not be true—that they'd always been so careful—except for one night when their frantic, heated need for each other had outweighed caution.

And that, she had realised, stunned, must have been when it happened. Another blow to deepen the agony of pain and betrayal. Yet, although the prospect of single-motherhood had filled her with dread, she'd never once considered the obvious alternative and sought an abortion.

Her mother had thought of it, of course. Had urged her to do it, too, cajoling one minute, threatening the next. Railing at Polly for her stupidity, and for bringing shame on the family. Swearing that she would have nothing further to do with her daughter or the baby if the pregnancy went ahead. A resolution that had lasted no longer than an indrawn breath from the moment she had seen her newborn grandson.

Charlie had instantly taken the place of the son she'd always longed for. And there'd never been any question about who was going to look after him when Polly recovered and went back to work.

But, as Polly ruefully acknowledged, the arrangement had become a two-edged sword. Over the months, she seemed to have been sidelined into playing an elder sister's role to Charlie. Any slight wail, bump or graze brought her mother running, leaving Polly to watch helplessly while Mrs Fairfax hugged and comforted him. And that was not good.

She had to admit that her mother had not been too wide of the mark when she'd described Polly's flat as an attic. It had a reasonable-sized main room, a basic bathroom and a minuscule kitchen opening out of it, plus Charlie's cubby-hole. Polly herself slept on the sofa bed in the living room.

But she couldn't deny it was a weary climb up steep and badly lit stairs to reach her front door, especially when she was encumbered with Charlie, his bag of necessities and his buggy, which she didn't dare leave in the entrance hall in case it was stolen.

Once inside, she kept her home space clean and uncluttered, the walls painted in cool aqua. Most of the furniture had been acquired at auction sales, including the sofa bed, for which she'd bought a new cover in an Aztec print of deep blue, crimson and gold.

It wasn't flash, but the rent was reasonable, and she always felt the place offered comfort and a welcome as she went in.

And tonight she was in sore need of both.

It was a warm evening, so she unlocked the living-room window and pushed up the lower sash, sinking down onto the wooden seat beneath. There was some cold chicken and salad in the fridge, and it would be a moment's work to put a potato to bake in her second-hand microwave.

But she was in no hurry to complete her supper preparations. She felt tired and anxious—and more than a little disheartened. It seemed strange not to hear the clatter of Charlie's feet on the stripped boards as he trotted about, or his incessant and often unintelligible chatter.

She missed, too, his sudden, unsteady gallop to her arms. That most of all, she thought, her throat tightening.

I should have brought him home, she told herself restlessly, and not let myself be out-manoeuvred like that.

She felt, she realised, totally unsettled, for all kinds of reasons, so maybe this would be a good time to review her life, and see if she needed to make some changes.

And, first and foremost, she needed to be able to spend more time with Charlie.

When she began working again, after he was born, Safe Hands had seemed ideal, more of a career choice than an ordinary job. Having her cake, and eating it—or so she'd thought then.

She had been able to go on with the travelling she loved, and, as well as her salary, the majority of the clients paid her a cash bonus as well. Even at London prices, she could afford to live, and provide Charlie with what he needed, although there was never much left over for extras.

But his needs were changing, and so, she realised, were hers.

For one thing, it wasn't essential to work, or even live, in London. In fact, it would be sheer relief to be able to say goodbye to those stifling journeys on the underground and buses.

She could move to a totally different area altogether, away from the south-east of England. Deliberately select a place where it would be cheaper to live, and find a job in local tourism. Something strictly nine-to-five, with no time away from home, so that she could spend her leisure hours with her son.

During the day she'd need a minder for him, of course. There was no way out of that. But she'd look for someone young and lively, caring for other children too, so that Charlie would have playmates. Maybe, in time, she could even get a foot on the housing ladder—find somewhere small and manageable, hopefully with a garden. Something she would never be able to afford in London.

She would miss this flat, she thought, sighing, and it would be a wrench leaving Safe Hands but reason was telling her it would be for the best.

I have, she thought, to make a life for us both. For Charlie and myself. I need to build a proper relationship with him. And I can't do that if we stay here. Because I won't be allowed to.

But she wasn't delusional enough to think she could strike out on her own without a struggle, she told herself, wrinkling her nose. Her mother would fight her every step of the way, coming up with every possible reason why she should not do this thing—and a few impossible ones, too.

And when she saw Polly could not be moved, she would be very bitter. There might even be an open breach between them.

But that won't last forever, she thought. Whatever Mum thinks of me, she'll still want to maintain contact with Charlie.

She got to her feet. She would eat now, and when supper was over she'd use her laptop to go internet-exploring, looking at house prices in different parts of the country. Now that she'd made up her mind, there was no time to be lost.

Strange, she thought, how I can suddenly be so sure of that.

Yet the pressure on her to accept the Italian assignment must have contributed to her decision. It had left her feeling uneasy— and awoken too many bad memories.

A clean break with the past was what she needed. New job— new home—new friends.

She would never be able to forget, of course, that Sandro was Charlie's father. But in time, it might begin to hurt less. And she might even be able to stop being afraid. One day.

'See Naples and die, eh?' The man in the adjoining seat emphasised the originality of his remark with a slight dig in Polly's ribs, as their plane descended towards Capodichino Airport. 'That's what they say, isn't it?'

Polly gritted her teeth as she gave a wintry smile in acknowledgement.

But I don't care what 'they' say, she told herself fiercely. Naples is going to be my jumping-off point for a whole new life. And I plan to live every moment of it.

She couldn't say she'd enjoyed the flight. The *contessa* might need her physical assistance, but she certainly hadn't wanted her company. Which was why she was seated in first class, while Polly herself was in economy, with a neighbour who considered her presence his personal bonus.

Never mind, she thought. In a few moments I'll never have to see him again, or the *contessa* either.

She'd sipped mineral water throughout the flight, in spite of her fellow traveller's unceasing efforts to buy her what he called a proper drink. And the irony was that she'd have welcomed some alcohol, to dispel the shaky chill which had settled in the pit of her stomach. The closer they had got to their destination, their progress cheerfully marked by the captain, the more nervous she'd become.

I shan't relax until I'm safely back in Britain, she thought.

On the surface, she was calmness itself. She was wearing the company uniform of a slim-fitting, button-through dress in navy linen, with the distinctive silver brooch showing a pair of clasped hands pinned to her left shoulder. Her pale hair was in a loose knot on top of her head, and she wore her usual dusting of powder, and soft pink lipstick.

As they touched down, and the plane began to taxi to its stand, Polly reached under the seat, and extracted the navy leather satchel which held the travel documents and a few basic necessities in case of delay. Her client, she was sure, would have an eagle eye for the slightest lapse in efficiency.

Her companion nudged her again. 'Dangerous city, they say,' he whispered. 'If you're on your own tonight, I'd be happy to show you around.'

'Tonight,' she told him, 'I intend to be back in London.' And left him gaping.

Contessa Barsoli was a tall woman, rake-thin, with immaculately coiffed white hair and still handsome in a chilly way. A member of the cabin staff was permitted to help her descend the aircraft steps while Polly followed, instinctively lifting her face to the brilliant warmth of the southern sun.

Once inside the terminal, she found her charge a chair, retrieved her luggage and guided her through the formalities.

'There has been a small change of plan,' the older woman informed her abruptly. 'I am too tired to undertake a long car journey down to the Campania, so my cousin has arranged a suite for me at the Grand Hotel Neapolitana. You will accompany me there.'

Polly knew resignedly that she shouldn't be surprised. Most of the arrangements she'd made for the *contessa* during her stay in Britain had been subject to alteration, usually at the last moment. Why should this time be any different?

But this wasn't just irritating, she reminded herself, schooling her expression. It was seriously inconvenient. She had a return flight to catch, and the *contessa* knew it.

'Do you wish me to get us a taxi?' she asked quietly. If she could find a driver who knew a few short cuts through Naples' crowded streets, she might still be in with a chance.

'A taxi?' The *contessa* made it sound like a tumbrel. 'My cousin has sent a car and chauffeur for us. Oblige me by finding him.'

That was easily achieved. Transferring the *contessa* and her luggage to the roomy depths of the limousine was a completely different matter. The lady liked to take her time, oblivious to Polly's simmering frustration as the minutes ticked past.

The traffic was a nightmare, and when they did reach the hotel at last, Polly accepted that she probably wouldn't make it back to the airport in time for her flight.

I haven't a prayer, she told herself resignedly. It'll take me half an hour to get her to the lift.

But to her astonishment, the *contessa* suddenly became quite sprightly. She conducted her own registration at the desk, waving Polly regally away, and made no fuss about the prompt unloading of her luggage.

An under-manager escorted her, bowing, to the lift, where Polly caught up with her.

She said awkwardly, 'I need to say goodbye now, *contessa*, if I'm to get my flight.'

She got a severe look. 'But I wish you to accompany me to the suite, *signorina*. I have ordered coffee and *biscotti* to be served there. Besides,' she added, seeing that Polly was on the verge of protest, 'there is still the question of the money I offered you. I do not conduct such transactions in the foyers of hotels. If you want to be paid, you will come with me now.'

Groaning silently, Polly stood beside her as the lift made its way upward. They emerged onto a crimson-carpeted corridor, opposite a heavily carved door.

The under-manager produced a key with a flourish, and unlocked the door, and, still bowing, showed them ceremoniously into the suite.

Polly found herself in a large drawing room, shaded by the shutters which had been drawn over the long windows to combat the force of the mid-June sunlight. She had a confused impression of brocaded sofas and fresh flowers in elaborate arrangements, their scent hanging languidly in the air.

And realised suddenly that the room wasn't empty as she'd first thought. Because someone was there—someone standing by the windows, his figure silhouetted against the slatted light. Someone tall, lean and unforgettably—terrifyingly—familiar.

Even before he spoke, Polly knew who he was. Then his voice, low-pitched and faintly husky, reached her, and there was no longer room for any doubt. Or any hope, either.

He said, 'Paola *mia*. So, you have come to me at last.'

He moved—came away from the window, and walked towards her with that long, lithe stride she would have known anywhere, his shadow falling across the floor as he approached.

She tried to speak—to say his name, but her trembling mouth could not obey her and shape the word.

Because this could not be happening. Sandro could not be here, in this room, waiting for her.

As he reached her, she cried out and flung up her bare and unavailing hands in a desperate effort to keep him at bay. Only to find the shadows crowding round her, welcoming her, as she slid helplessly downwards into the dark whirl of oblivion.

CHAPTER TWO

AWARENESS returned slowly, accompanied by an acrid smell that filled her nose and mouth with its bitterness, making her cough and mutter a feeble protest.

She lay very still, fighting against a feeling of nausea, hardly daring to open her eyes. Her senses told her that she was cushioned on satiny softness, and that she was not alone. That in the real world behind her closed eyelids, there was movement—people talking. And the heavy noise of traffic.

She propped herself dizzily on one elbow, and looked around her. She was lying in the middle of a vast bed, covered in deep gold embroidered silk. She was shoeless, she realised, and the top buttons of her dress had been unfastened.

The first person she saw was the *contessa*, as she stepped back, replacing the stopper in a small bottle. Smelling salts, Polly thought, dazedly. The older woman always insisted on having some handy in case travel motion upset her.

And, standing in silence a few yards away, was Sandro, head bent, his face in profile.

Not a figment of her imagination, as she'd hoped, but a nightmare that lived and breathed, and would not go away.

And not the laughing, dishevelled lover, wearing frayed shorts and an old T-shirt, and badly in need of a haircut, that she'd once known and desired so passionately, but that other, hidden man whose identity she'd never even suspected as she lay in his arms.

This other Sandro wore a dark suit that had clearly emanated from a great Italian fashion house. The dark curling hair had been tamed, to some extent at least, and there wasn't a trace of stubble, designer or otherwise, on what she could see of the hard, tanned face, only a faint breath of some expensive cologne hanging in the air.

His immaculate white shirt set off a sombre silk tie, and a thin platinum watch encircled his wrist.

Whatever path he'd chosen to follow, it had clearly brought him

21

serious money, Polly thought, anger and pain tightening her throat.
And she didn't want to contemplate how it might have been ob-
tained. Who said crime didn't pay?

Nor was he staying silent out of weakness, or any sense of guilt.
Instinct told her that. He was simply exercising restraint. Under
the stillness, Polly could sense his power—and the furious burn
of his anger, rigorously reined in. Could feel the violence of his
emotions in the pulse of her blood and deep within her bones, just
as she'd once known the naked imprint of his skin on hers, and
the intimate heat of his possession.

As if, she thought with a sudden sick helplessness, she lived
within his flesh. Part of him. As she had once been.

Now that the impossible had happened, and she was face to
face with him again, she was shocked by the intensity of her physical reaction to him. Ashamed too.

She had to make herself remember the cruel brutality of his
rejection. The cynical attempt to buy her off, and the explicit threat
that had accompanied it.

She needed to remind herself of the abyss of pain and loneliness
that had consumed her after she'd fled from Italy. And, most important of all, she had to get out of here, and fast.

She sat upright, lifting a hand to her head as the room swayed
about her.

The movement riveted everyone's attention, and Sandro took a
hasty step forward, pausing when Polly flinched away from him
involuntarily, his mouth hardening in an icy sneer.

'No,' he said. 'It is not pretty. You should have been prepared
in advance, perhaps. Warned what to expect.'

As he came closer, Polly saw his face clearly for the first time.
Saw the jagged scar that had torn its way from the corner of his
eye, across the high cheekbone and halfway to his jaw.

For a brief moment she was stunned, as shocked as if she had
seen some great work of art deliberately defaced.

He looked older too, and there was a weariness in the topaz
eyes that had once glowed into hers.

Oh, God, she thought, swallowing. He thinks that I find him
repulsive, and that's why I turned away just now.

A pang of something like anguish twisted inside her, then she
took a deep breath, hardening herself against a compassion he did
not need or deserve.

Let him think what he wanted, she thought. He'd chosen his life, and however rich and powerful he'd become he'd clearly paid violently for his wealth. And she'd been fortunate to escape when she did, and keep her own wounds hidden. That was all there was to be said.

She looked away from him. 'I don't understand.' Her voice was small and strained. 'What am I doing here? What—happened?'

'You fainted, *signorina*.' It was the *contessa* who answered her. 'At my cousin's feet.'

'Your cousin?' Polly repeated the words dazedly, her mind wincing away from the image the older woman's words conjured up of herself, unconscious, helpless. She shook her head, immediately wishing that she hadn't. 'Is that supposed to be some kind of joke?'

The *contessa* drew herself up, her brows lifting in hauteur. 'I do not understand you, *signorina*. There is no joke, I assure you. Alessandro is the son of my husband's late cousin. Indeed, his only child.'

'No,' Polly whispered. 'He can't be. It's not possible.'

'I am not accustomed to having my word doubted, Signorina Fairfax.' The *contessa*'s tone was frigid. She paused. 'But you are not yourself, so allowances must be made.' She handed Polly a glass of water. 'Drink this, if you please. And I will ask for some food to be brought. You will feel better when you have eaten something.'

'Thank you, but no.' Polly put down the empty glass and moved to the edge of the bed, putting her feet to the floor. She was still feeling shaky, but self-preservation was more important than any temporary weakness.

She'd fainted—something she'd never done in her life before, and a betraying sign of vulnerability that she could ill afford.

She spoke more strongly, lifting her chin. 'I would much prefer to leave. Right now. I have a flight to catch.'

'You are not very gracious, Paola *mia*.' Sandro's voice was soft, but there was a note in it that made her quiver. 'Especially when I have had you brought all the way from England just to see you again.'

Had you brought... The words echoed in her head, menacing her.

'Then you've wasted your time, *signore*.' Was that how you

addressed the supposed cousin of an Italian countess? Polly had no idea, and didn't much care. 'Because I have no wish to see you.'

There was a bitter irony in this, she thought. This was supposed to be the first day of her new life, and instead she seemed to have walked into a trap.

Ironic, inexplicable—and dangerous too, she realised, a shiver chilling her spine.

The *contessa* had deliberately set her up, it seemed. So she must be in Sandro's power in some way. But however scaring that was, it couldn't be allowed to matter, Polly reminded herself swiftly. She didn't know what was going on here, nor did she want to know. The most important thing, now, was to distance herself, and quickly.

'"*Signore*"?' Sandro questioned, his mouth twisting. 'Isn't that a little formal—for us, *bella mia*?'

Her pulses quickened at the endearment, putting her instantly on the defensive.

'To me this is a formal occasion,' she said tautly. 'I'm working—escorting the *contessa*. And there is no "us",' she added. 'There never was.'

'You don't think so?' The topaz eyes were watchful. 'Then I shall have to jog your memory, *cara*.'

'I can remember everything I need to, thanks.' Polly spoke fiercely. 'And it doesn't change a thing. You and I have nothing to say to each other. Not now. Not ever again.' She took a deep breath. 'And now I wish to leave.'

Sandro shook his head slowly. 'You are mistaken, *carissima*.' His voice was soft. 'There is a great deal to be said. Or else I would not be here. But perhaps it would be better if we spoke alone.'

He turned to the *contessa*. 'Would you excuse us, Zia Antonia?' His tone was coolly courteous. 'I think Signorina Fairfax and I should continue our conversation in private.'

'No.' Polly flung the word at him, aware that her voice was shaking. That her body was trembling too. 'I won't stay here—and you can't make me.'

He looked at her, his mouth relaxing into a faint smile. 'You don't think so, Paola *mia*? But you're so wrong.'

'*Contessa!*' Polly appealed as the older woman moved towards the door. 'You had no right to do this. Don't leave me alone—please.'

The *contessa* gave her a thin smile. 'You require a chaperone?' she queried. 'But surely it is a little late for that?' She paused, allowing her words to sting, then turned to Sandro. 'However, Alessandro, Signorina Fairfax might feel more at ease if you conducted this interview in the *salotto*. A suggestion, merely.'

'I bow to your superior wisdom.' Sandro spoke briskly.

Before Polly could register what he intended, and take evasive action, he had stepped forward, scooping her up into his arms as if she were a child. She tried to hit him, but he controlled her flailing hands, tucking her arms against her body with insulting ease.

'Be still,' he told her. 'Unless, of course, you would prefer to remain here.' He glanced significantly back at the bed.

'No, I would not.' She glared up into the dark, ruined face. 'But I can walk.'

'When you are shaking like a leaf? I think not.'

In spite of her continuing struggles, Sandro carried her back into the now deserted drawing room. The *contessa* had disappeared, Polly realised with a stab of panic, and, although neither of them were her company of choice, it meant that she and Sandro were now alone. Which was far worse...

'This was easier when you were unconscious,' he commented as he walked across the room with her. 'Although I think you have lost a little weight since our last meeting, Paola *mia*.'

'Put me down.' Polly was almost choking with rage, mingled with the shock of finding herself in such intimately close proximity to him. 'Put me down, damn you.'

'As you wish.' He lifted a shoulder nonchalantly, and dropped her onto one of the sofas flanking the fireplace. She lay, winded and gasping, staring up at him.

'You bastard,' she said unevenly, and he clicked his tongue in reproach as he seated himself on the sofa opposite.

'What a name to call the man you are going to marry.'

'Marry?' The word strangled in her throat. Polly struggled to sit up, pulling down the navy dress which had ridden up round her thighs. 'You must be insane.'

He shrugged. 'I once asked you to be my wife. You agreed.' He watched as she fumbled to re-fasten the buttons he'd undone, his lips slanting into faint amusement. Looking so like Charlie that she almost cried out. 'That makes us *fidanzato*. Or am I wrong?'

'You're wrong,' she bit back at him, infuriated at her own awkwardness, and at the pain he still had the power to cause her. 'Totally and completely mistaken. And you know it, as well as I do, so let's stop playing games.'

'Is that what we're doing?' Sandro shrugged again. 'I had not realised. Perhaps you would explain the rules to me.'

'Not rules,' she said. 'But laws. Laws that exist to deal with someone like you.'

'*Dio*,' he said. 'So you think our government interests itself in a man's reunion with his woman? How enlightened of them.'

'Enlightened enough to lock you up for harassment,' Polly said angrily. 'And I am not your woman.'

He grinned at her, making her realise that the scar had done little to diminish the powerful sexual charisma he'd always been able to exert, which was as basic a part of him as the breath he drew. He was lounging on the sofa opposite, jacket discarded and tie loosened, his long legs thrust out in front of him, totally at his ease. Enjoying, she thought bitterly, his control of the situation. While she remained shaken and on edge, unable to comprehend what was happening. Or why. Especially why...

'No? Perhaps we should have stayed in the bedroom after all, *cara mia*, and continued the argument there.' The topaz eyes held a familiar glint.

'You dare to lay a hand on me again,' Polly said, through gritted teeth, 'and I'll go straight to the police—have you charged.'

'With what offence? The attempted seduction of my future bride?' He shook his head regretfully. 'A girl who once spent a summer as my lover. I don't think they would take you seriously, *carissima*.'

'No,' she said. 'I expect they have to do what you want—like the *contessa*. And where is she, by the way?'

'On her way back to Comadora, where she lives.'

'But she was supposed to be staying here.'

He shook his head. 'No, Paola *mia*. I reserved the suite for myself.' He smiled at her. 'And for you to share with me.'

'If this is a joke,' Polly said, recovering herself from a stunned silence, 'I don't find it remotely funny.'

'And nor do I,' Sandro said with sudden curtness. 'This is no

CHAPTER ONE

'REMEMBER Skye... Skye Sumner...'

It was a shock to hear the name, falling from his brother's lips in a laboured whisper. Luciano Peretti frowned at the dark anguish in Roberto's eyes. Why speak of *her* now? Why waste any time at all on *her* when time was so precious?

In a few minutes Roberto would be wheeled out of this intensive care cubicle for the surgery that might or might not save his life. A fifty-fifty chance, the doctors had told the family. Their parents were out in the waiting room with the priest and Roberto's wife because of his brother's request to speak to him alone, and it seemed crazy to bring up Skye Sumner—an old wound between them that Luc had long since set aside for the sake of family harmony.

'Water under the bridge,' he muttered, wanting to dismiss whatever lingering guilt Roberto felt over the betrayal involved. 'Forgiven and forgotten,' he added for extra assurance.

'No, Luc.' It obviously pained him to speak but the determination to get out what he wanted to say demanded respect for the effort. 'I lied. It wasn't Skye...in the photos. She was never with me...like that. I set it up...to get her out of your life.'

Not Skye?

Luc's whole body clenched in denial. It couldn't be true. It was too...monstrous! Yet why would

5

game, believe me. I am entirely serious.' He paused. 'Do you wish to test my determination?'

He hadn't moved, but suddenly Polly found herself remembering the strength of the arms that had held her. Recognised the implacable will that challenged her from his gaze and the sudden hardening of the mobile, sensuous mouth which had once stopped her heart with its caresses.

She bit her lip, painfully. 'No.'

'You begin to show sense at last,' he approved softly.

'Not,' she said, 'when I agreed to come to Italy today. That was really stupid of me.'

'You must not blame Zia Antonia,' he said. 'She shares your disapproval of my methods.' He shrugged. 'But if you and I had not met again tonight, then it would have been at some other time, in some other place. Or did you think I would simply allow you to vanish?'

She said coldly, 'Yes, of course. In fact, I counted on it.'

His head came up sharply, and she saw the sudden tensing of his lean body. 'You were so glad to be rid of me?'

You dare to say that—to me? After what you did?

The words trembled on the tip of her tongue, but she fought them back. He must never know how she'd felt in those dazed, agonised weeks following his rejection. How she'd ached for him, drowning in bewilderment and pain. Pride had to keep her silent now. Except in defiance.

She shrugged in her turn. 'Do you doubt it?' she retorted. 'After all, when it's over, it's over,' she added with deliberate *sang-froid*.

'You may think that, *mia cara*.' His voice slowed to a drawl. 'I do not have to agree.'

She looked down at her hands, clamped together in her lap. 'Tell me something,' she said in a low voice. 'How did you find me?'

'I was at a conference on tourism. A video was shown of a British company which looks after single travellers. You were its star, *cara mia*. I was—most impressed.'

Polly groaned inwardly. Her one and only television appearance, she thought, that her mother had been so proud of. It had never occurred to her that it might be shown outside the UK.

She said coldly, 'And you were suddenly overwhelmed by nostalgia, I suppose.'

'If so,' Sandro said with equal chill, 'I would have sighed sentimentally and got on with my life. But it reminded me that there are issues still unresolved between us.' He paused. 'As you must know, also.'

She moistened her dry lips with the tip of her tongue. 'I need to say something. To tell you that—I've never talked about you. Never discussed anything that happened between us. And I wouldn't—I give you my word...'

He stared at her, frowning. 'You wished to wipe me from your memory? Pretend I had never existed? But why?'

She swallowed, her throat tightening. *Because it hurt too much to remember,* she thought.

'Once I discovered your—your background,' she said, 'I realised it was—necessary. The only way...'

His gaze became incredulous. 'It disturbed you to find that I was rich. You'd have preferred me to be a waiter, existing on tips?' He gave a short laugh. *'Dio mio.'*

Polly sat up very straight. She said coldly, 'It was the way you'd acquired your money that I found—unacceptable. And your—connections,' she added bravely, controlling a shiver as she remembered the man who had confronted her. The scorn and menace he'd exuded.

'Unbelievable,' he said slowly. 'But if you expect me to apologise for my family, Paola, you will wait a long time.' The look he sent her was hard—unrelenting. 'I am what I am, and nothing can change that. Nor would I wish it to.'

He was silent for a moment. *'Certamente,* I hoped—at one time—that you would find it possible to live in my world. Understand how it works, and accept its limitations.'

But you soon changed your mind about that, Polly thought painfully. In fact, once you realised that I'd never be suitable, you were willing to pay a small fortune to get me out of your life altogether—and I should be grateful for that. Relieved that you sent me away, and saved me from an impossible moral dilemma. Prevented me from making a choice I might have hated myself for later, when I was sane again...

And knowing that has to be my salvation now. Has to...

She said stiltedly, 'That could—never have happened. It was better—safer for us to part.'

'You think so?' He drew a harsh breath. 'Then how is it I have been unable to forget you, Paola *mia*, no matter how hard I have tried? Or how many other women there have been in my life since you?'

She lifted her chin, resisting the sudden anguish that stabbed her. 'Am I supposed to feel flattered?'

'You ask me about your emotions?' Sandro asked derisively. 'What did I ever know about your thoughts—your feelings? I saw what I wished to see—believed what I needed to believe.'

He shook his head. '*Madonna,* how many times in these long months I have wished I could simply—dismiss you from my mind.' He paused. 'Forget you as easily as you have rejected the memory of me.'

Oh, God, Polly thought numbly, how little you know...

She tried to speak evenly. 'Life doesn't remain static. It moves on—and we have to go with it.'

'Do you go alone?' Sandro enquired, almost negligently studying his fingernails. 'Or do you have company on your journey?'

Polly tensed. 'That,' she said, 'is no concern of yours.'

'Then let us make it my concern,' he said softly. 'Because I wish to know the truth. Do you live alone?'

The question seemed to hang in the air between them while her mind ran in frantic circles, looking for a way out.

Useless to go on telling him it was none of his business. That would not deter him. On the other hand, it would be a humiliation to admit that since him, there had been no one in her life. That she existed in self-imposed celibacy.

She could invent a lover, but she'd always been a terrible liar, and the risk of him seeing through her story was too great.

And then, as if a light had dawned, she realised there was no need for invention after all.

Polly lifted her chin, and faced him. 'No,' she said, very clearly. 'I don't live alone.'

It was no more than the truth, she thought. And it might just set her free...

Sandro was very still suddenly, little golden fires leaping in his eyes as his gaze met hers. He said, 'And, naturally, your companion is male?' He watched her swift, jerky nod.

There was another silence, then he said harshly, 'Do you love him?'

Unbidden, an image of Charlie's small sleeping face invaded

her mind, and her mouth curved involuntarily, instinctively into tenderness.

'Yes,' she said. 'And I always will.'

As soon as she spoke the words, she knew they were a mistake. That she'd snatched at a means of escape from him, without fully considering the consequences. And that she could have gone too far.

'You dare to tell me that?' His voice crackled with suppressed anger.

Her heart jolted nervously, but she knew that she had to finish what she'd started. That she had no other choice.

She tilted her chin defiantly. 'What did you expect? That I'd stay single in memory of you? Like you remained celibate for me?' she added scornfully. 'Dream on—please.'

Sandro's eyes were fixed on her, a slow flame burning in their depths. 'And how long has he been part of your life? The truth.'

She touched the tip of her tongue to her dry lips. 'Two years—or so.'

'So,' he said slowly. 'You went from my arms to his.' His gaze went over her, measuring and contemptuous. 'I see you wear no ring.'

She swallowed. 'That's my own choice.'

'And have you whispered the same promises to him that you once made to me?' His voice was quiet. Compelling.

She hesitated, choosing her words with care. 'He knows that I'll—always be there for him.'

'How touching,' Sandro said softly. 'Yet you left him to come to Italy.' His sudden smile was cool. Dangerous. 'And to me.'

'I believed I was working for the *contessa*,' Polly returned fiercely, trying to conceal the fact that she was shaking inside, nearing the edge of panic. 'I had no idea that she could be a relation of yours—or that you were even in the region. If I'd known, I wouldn't be here.'

She flung back her head. 'So, how did you persuade her to do your dirty work? Bribery—or blackmail?'

His mouth thinned. 'You are not amusing, *carissima*. Be very careful.'

'Why?' she challenged recklessly. 'I already know the lengths you're prepared to go to—when there's something you want.'

Or when you've stopped wanting...

You sent me away, she thought. *So why are you here now, tormenting me like this—reviving all these unwanted memories?*

Her throat ached suddenly at the thought of them. But that was a weakness she couldn't afford, because the room seemed to be shrinking, the walls closing in, diminishing the space between them. A space she needed to maintain at all costs.

'I wonder if that's true.' Sandro's voice was quiet—reflective. 'Perhaps you don't know me as well as you think.'

'Well,' she said, 'that hardly matters any more.' She paused. 'And I don't think there's much point in continuing this discussion either.'

His smile twisted. 'Then we agree on something at last.'

'So, if you can tell me where to find my shoes and jacket, I'll go.'

'Back to him? Your *innamorato*?'

'Back to my life,' Polly said, lifting her chin. 'In which you have no part, *signore*.'

'I can hardly argue with that,' Sandro shrugged. 'You will find your belongings in the bedroom, Paola *mia*.'

He did not, she noticed, offer to fetch them for her, as the Sandro she'd once known would have done.

Don't fool yourself, she thought as she trod, barefoot, into the bedroom and paused, looking around her. As he said—you never really knew him at all.

Her jacket and bag were on a small sofa by the window, her shoes arranged neatly beneath it. As she reached them she was aware of a sound behind her, and turned.

Sandro had followed her, she realised, her heart missing a beat. She hadn't been aware of his approach, because he too had discarded his shoes. But the noise she'd heard was the sound of the door closing behind him, shutting them in together.

And now he was leaning back against its panels, watching her with hooded eyes, his expression cool and purposeful as, with one hand, he began to unfasten the buttons on his shirt.

Polly felt the breath catch in her throat. With a supreme effort, she controlled her voice, keeping it steady. 'Another game, *signore*?'

'No game at all, *signorina*.' Cynically, he echoed her formality. 'As I am sure you know perfectly well.'

She had picked up her bag, and was holding it so tightly that the strap cut into her fingers. 'I—I don't know what you're talking about.'

Sandro tutted. 'Now you're being dishonest, *bella mia*, but I expected that.' He allowed his discarded shirt to drop to the floor, and began to walk towards her.

She swallowed. 'I think you must be going crazy.'

'Possibly,' he said with sudden harshness. 'And I want to be sane again.' He halted, the topaz eyes blazing at her. 'You are under my skin, Paola. In my blood, like a fever that refuses to be healed. And that is no longer acceptable to me. So, I plan to cure myself of you once and for all—and in the only possible way.'

'No.' She stared back at him, her appalled heart thudding frantically. 'No, Sandro. You can't do this. I—I won't let you.'

'You really believe you have a choice?' He gave a short laugh. 'I know better.'

She backed away until her retreat was cut off by the wall behind her. Until he reached her.

'Please, Sandro,' she whispered. 'Please let me go.'

He laughed again, touching a finger to her trembling lips, before outlining the curve of her jaw, and stroking down the delicate line of her throat to the neckline of her dress.

'Once I have finished with you, *carissima*,' he drawled insolently, 'you are free to go anywhere you wish.'

'Do you want me to hate you?' Her voice pleaded with him.

'I thought you already did.' Almost casually, he detached her bag from her grasp and tossed it to one side, his brows snapping together as he saw the marks on her skin.

He lifted both her hands to his lips, letting them move caressingly on the redness the leather strap had left.

'I had almost forgotten how easily you bruise.' His voice was low and husky. 'I shall have to be careful.'

Her whole body shivered at the touch of his mouth on her flesh, the aching, delirious memories it evoked. And the promise of further, dangerous delights in his whispered words.

A promise she could not allow him to keep.

She snatched her hands from his grip, and pushed violently at the bare, tanned wall of his chest, catching him off balance. As Sandro was forced into a step backwards, she dodged past, running for the door.

With no shoes and no money, she was going nowhere, but if

she could just get out of this bedroom it might be possible to reason with him—deflect him from his apparent purpose.

She flung herself at the door handle, twisted it one way, then the other, trying to drag the door open, but it wouldn't budge an inch, and she realised with horror that he must have locked it too—and taken the key.

'Trying to escape again.' His voice was sardonic, his hands hard on her shoulders as he swung her relentlessly to face him. 'Not this time, *bella mia*.' His smile mocked her. 'Not, at least, until you have said a proper goodbye to me.'

'Sandro.' Her voice cracked. 'You can't do this. You must let me go...'

'Back to your lover? Surely he can spare me a little of your time and attention first. After all, he has reaped the benefit of our previous association, wouldn't you say?' He paused. 'And, naturally, I am intrigued to know if your repertoire has increased since then.'

Her face was white, her eyes like emerald hollows, as she stared up at him, her skin seared by his words.

She said chokingly, 'You bastard.'

'If you insist on calling me bad names,' Sandro said softly, 'I have no option but to stop you speaking at all.' And his mouth came down hard on hers.

She tried to struggle—to pull away from him, so that she could talk to him—appeal, even on the edge, to his better nature. Tell him that his actions were an outrage—a crime. But what did that matter to someone who lived his life outside the law anyway? her reeling mind demanded.

Her efforts were in vain. The arm that held her had muscles of steel. At the same time, his free hand was loosening the dishevelled knot of her hair, his fingers twisting in its silky strands to hold her still for the ravishment of his kiss.

Her breasts were crushed against his naked chest. She could feel the warmth of his skin penetrating her thin dress. Felt the heat surge in her own body to meet it.

She heard herself moan faintly in anguished protest—pleading that this man, to whom she'd once given her innocence, would not now take her by force.

But Sandro used the slight parting of her lips for his own advantage, deepening the intimacy of his kiss with sensual intensity as his tongue invaded the moist sweetness of her mouth.

No sign now of the tenderness with which he'd caressed her fingers only moments ago. Just the urgency of a need too powerful to be denied any longer.

A fever in the blood, he'd called it, she thought in a kind of despair, her starved body craving him in turn. And how was it possible that she could feel like this? That she could want him so desperately in return?

When at last he raised his head, the scar on his face was livid against the fierce burn of colour along his taut cheekbones.

He said, 'Take off your dress,' his voice hoarse, shaken. And when he saw her hesitate, 'Or do you wish me to tear it off you?'

'No.' She sounded small and breathless. 'I—I'll do it.' She turned away from him, as her shaking fingers fought with the buttons. When half of them were loose, she pushed the navy linen from her shoulders, freeing her arms from the sleeves as she did so, and letting the dress fall to the floor.

She faced him slowly, her arms crossed defensively across her body, trying to conceal the scraps of white broderie anglaise that were now her only covering.

'But how delicious,' he said, softly. 'Bought for your lover?'

Polly shook her hair back from her face. 'I dress to please myself.'

'Ah,' he said. 'And now you will undress to please me. *Per favore*,' he added silkily.

She could hear nothing but the wild drumming of her own pulses, and the tear of her ragged breathing. See nothing but the heated flare of hunger in his eyes. A hunger without gentleness, demanding to be appeased.

And his hands reaching for her—like some ruthless hawk about to seize his prey.

Not like this, she thought in anguish. Oh, dear God, not like this. Not to lie naked in his arms and be taken—enjoyed for one night alone. To be used, however skilfully, just so that he could get her out of his system, only to find herself discarded all over again when his need for her was finally assuaged. And to be forced to go through all that suffering a second time—unappeased.

It was unthinkable—unbearable.

Her voice shook. 'Sandro—please—don't hurt me...'

She paused, knowing she was on the edge of complete self-betrayal here. Realising too that she must not let him see that he still had the power to inflict more misery on her.

The sudden silence was total. He was completely still, apart from a muscle which moved swiftly, convulsively in his throat.

When at last he spoke, his voice was hoarse. '*Dio mio*, you think that I'm going to rape you? That I might be capable of such a thing?' He shook his head. 'How could you believe that? It is an insult to everything we have ever been to each other.'

He lifted his hand, and touched the scar. 'This has only altered my face, Paola. It has not turned me into a monster.'

'I—I didn't mean...' Polly began, then bit her lip. This was a misunderstanding that she could not put right—not without the kind of explanation she was desperate to avoid, she told herself wretchedly.

'*Basta,*' Sandro said sharply. 'Enough.' He bent and retrieved his shirt from the floor, dragging it on with swift, jerky movements.

'Now dress yourself and go,' he instructed icily. 'And be quick. Otherwise I might lose all self-respect, and justify your low opinion of me. Punish you in the way you deserve,' he added grimly.

He went to the door, unlocked it, then turned.

'Remember this, *mia bella*.' His voice grated across her taut nerve-endings, just as his contemptuous gaze flayed her skin. 'Even if I had taken you there on the floor like the *sciattona* you are, it would still not have been rape.' He smiled at her with insolent certainty. 'You know it as well as I do, so do not fool yourself.

'Now, get out of my sight,' he added curtly, and left, slamming the door behind him.

CHAPTER THREE

SHE had missed her plane, but eventually managed to catch the last flight of the evening, thanks to a no-show.

Her escape from the hotel had been easier than she could have hoped. She had dressed quickly, her shaking hands fumbling so badly with the buttons on her dress that she had to begin again.

Then she'd wasted precious moments listening tautly at the door for some sound from the room beyond. Dreading that Sandro might be waiting there for her, still angry and possibly vengeful.

But when she had finally risked taking a look, the room was completely deserted, and she left on the run. The hotel commissionaire had summoned a cab for her, allotting her dishevelled state a discreetly impassive glance.

She had prowled around the airport, her eyes everywhere. Terrified that he might change his mind, and come to find her. To prevent her from leaving. Even when she presented her boarding card, she was half expecting his hand to reach over her shoulder and take it from her.

When the plane finally took off, she was almost sick with relief. She ordered a double brandy from the stewardess, and fell asleep before she'd drunk half of it.

She took a cab from the airport to her flat, unlocking the door and falling inside in the same movement. There was a strange empty chill about the place that she had never experienced before, that seemed to match the cold hollow inside her.

A voice in her head whispered, 'You're safe—you're safe...' But somehow she couldn't believe it. She even found herself picking her way in the darkness to her living-room window, and drawing the curtains before she switched on the lights.

Then she sank down on the sofa, and tried to stop trembling.

I didn't suspect a thing, she thought. To me, the *contessa* was simply another very demanding client, nothing more—but it was all a trick.

She had to be deeply in Sandro's power to agree to something

36

like that, Polly told herself, and shivered as she remembered how nearly she'd surrendered to that power herself.

Oh, God, she thought. He only had to touch me...

But it had always been like that. From the first time his hand had taken hers as they walked together, her body had responded with wild yearning to his touch. She had hungered and thirsted for his mouth on hers—for the brush of his fingers over her ardent flesh. For the ultimate mystery of his body joined to hers.

Sandro had enraptured her every sense, and she had mistaken that for love. And he had cynically allowed that—had said the words she wanted to hear—whispered the promises that would keep her enthralled until he chose to leave her.

She'd been just one more girl in his bed, easily discarded, instantly replaced. Except that he'd caught a fleeting glimpse of her on television and discovered, for some inexplicable reason, that he still wanted her.

Sandro Domenico, she thought painfully. A man rich enough to pay for his whims, and powerful enough to pull the strings that would satisfy them.

And yet he'd let her go, outraged at the idea that he could rape her physically, but too arrogant to realise he'd already done far worse damage to her emotionally.

Still, it was over now, and she had nothing more to fear. She'd insulted his sense of honour, such as it was, and he would never come near her again.

In fact, she'd got off comparatively lightly, she told herself. Yes, she was bruised by his anger and disgust, but she'd recover from that—given time. And her future held plenty of that.

In some ways, it all seemed like a bad dream—some torment dredged up from the depths of her unconscious. But the faint lingering tenderness of her lips forced her to face reality.

Wincing, she touched her mouth with her fingertips, telling herself that it could all have been so much worse. That at this moment, she might have been in his bed, and in his arms, with a whole new cycle of heartbreak and regret to endure.

For all she knew he could be married to someone 'suitable'. A dynastic union from the criminal network he belonged to, she thought with a pang.

But she—she was all right, she rallied herself. She'd had a narrow escape, that was all.

Just the same, her vague plans for a change of location had become a firm resolve as a result of the past twenty-four hours.

She and Charlie would move, somewhere anonymous and preferably far away. And, to ensure she could never be so easily traced again, she'd find out the legal implications of changing her name.

Drastic measures, she thought, but, in view of her recent scare, perfectly justified.

She stripped in her tiny bathroom, putting her clothing in the laundry basket, then took a shower, scrubbing herself from top to toe, and even shampooing her hair to make sure she erased every trace of him.

She only wished she could wash away the memories of the heated pressure of his mouth, and the familiar, arousing scent of his skin just as easily.

Dear God, she thought, towelling her hair with more than necessary vigour, that is—frighteningly pathetic.

She put on her cotton housecoat, belting it securely round her slim waist, and trailed into the kitchen.

She needed a hot drink, but not with the additional stimulus of caffeine. She'd have enough trouble sleeping as it was through what little was left of the night.

No, she'd have a herbal tea instead, she decided. A *tisana* at bedtime was a habit she'd acquired in Italy. One of the good ones, she amended wryly.

While the kettle was boiling, she wandered back into the living room, and, for reasons she couldn't properly explain, crossed to the window, and pulled back the edge of the curtain slightly.

The road below seemed empty, or was there an added density among the shadows opposite, in a gateway just out of the range of the street light?

No, she thought, hurriedly letting the curtain fall back into place. It was simply her imagination. Sandro had traced her through her work, simply and easily, so there was no need for him to compile a complete dossier on her.

Because if he'd done so, he'd have realised at once that her 'live-in lover' was pure invention, and told her so. And he'd have known, too, about Charlie...

She turned her head, staring at the chest of drawers, and the framed photograph that occupied pride of place. Charlie, on his second birthday. His father's image smiling at her.

Sandro's out of your life, she told herself feverishly. He's gone.

Nevertheless, on the way back to the kitchen, Polly found herself taking Charlie's portrait off the chest, and stowing it in the top drawer instead.

Better, she thought, safe than sorry, and shivered again.

Polly slept badly, in spite of her *tisana*. When morning came, she telephoned Safe Hands, said quite truthfully that she felt like death, then crawled back into bed and slept until lunchtime.

She woke with a start, thinking of Charlie. Why was she wasting time, when she could have the bonus of a whole afternoon in his company without the distractions of shopping and housework?

She rang her mother's house but there was no reply, so she left a message on the answering machine to say she would be over to collect him in an hour.

She took a quick shower, then dressed in a casual blue denim skirt, topping it with a crisp white cotton shirt, and sliding her feet into flat brown leather sandals. She brushed her hair back from her face and secured it at the nape of her neck with a silver barette, and hung small blue enamel cornflowers on delicate silver chains from her earlobes.

She had some work to do with the blusher and concealer she kept for emergencies, or her mother would guess something was wrong. And Polly had enough bad news to give her without mentioning Sandro's shock reappearance in her life.

But that was all over, so there was no need to cause her further distress, she told herself firmly, applying her lipstick and attempting an experimental smile which, somehow, turned into a wry grimace.

Positive thinking, she adjured herself, and, grabbing her bag, she left.

The house seemed unusually quiet when she let herself in, and Polly paused, frowning a little. Surely her mother hadn't taken Charlie out somewhere, she thought, groaning inwardly. Was this the latest move in the battle of wits between them? She hoped not.

She kept her voice deliberately cheerful. 'Mum—Dad—are you there?'

'We're in the living room.' It was her mother's voice, high-pitched and strained.

Her frown deepening, Polly pushed open the door and walked in.

It wasn't a particularly large room, and her instant impression was that it had shrunk still further in some strange way.

The first person she saw was her mother, sitting in the chair beside the empty fireplace, her face a mask of tension, and Charlie clasped tightly on her lap.

The second was a complete stranger, stockily built with black hair and olive skin, who rose politely from the sofa at her entrance.

And the third, unbelievably, was Sandro, standing silently in the window alcove, as if he had been carved out of granite.

For a moment the room seemed to reel around her, then she steadied herself, her hands clenching into fists, her nails scoring her palms. She was *not*, under any circumstances, going to faint again.

She said hoarsely, 'What the *hell* are you doing here?'

'Is it not obvious?' The topaz eyes were as fierce as a leopard's, and as dangerous. His voice was ice. 'I have come for my son. And please do not try to deny his parentage,' he added bitingly. 'Because no court in the world would believe you. He is my image.' He paused. 'But I warn you that I am prepared to undergo DNA testing to prove paternity, if it becomes necessary.'

Polly stared at him, her stomach churning, her heart pounding against her ribs. 'You must be mad.'

'I was.' His smile was grim. 'Before I discovered quite what a treacherous little bitch you are, Paola *mia*. But now I am sane again, and I want my child.'

Her low voice shook. 'Over my dead body.'

He said softly, 'The way I feel at this moment, that could easily be arranged. Do not provoke me any further.'

'He's going to take him away from us,' her mother wailed suddenly. 'Take him to Italy. I'll never see him again.'

Horror caught Polly by the throat. She turned on Sandro. 'You can't do that.'

'And what is there to stop me?' His glance challenged her.

'It—it's kidnapping,' Polly flung at him. She took a breath. 'Although I suppose that's an everyday occurrence in your world.'

And it was more common than she wanted to admit in her own,

she thought numbly. There'd been numerous headlines in the papers over the past few years where children had been snatched and taken abroad by a parent. They called them 'tug of love' babies...

She looked with scorn at the other man, who had got quietly to his feet. 'And what are you—another of his tame thugs?'

His brows rose. 'My name is Alberto Molena, *signorina*, and I am a lawyer. I act for the *marchese* in this matter.'

Polly gave him a scornful glance. 'Don't you mean you're his *consigliere*?' she queried with distaste.

He paused, sending Sandro a surprised look. 'May I suggest that you sit down, Signorina Fairfax, and remain calm? It would be better too if the little boy was taken to another room. I think he's becoming frightened.'

'I have a better suggestion,' Polly flared. 'Why don't you and your dubious client get out of here, and leave us alone?'

His tone was still quiet, still courteous. 'I'm afraid that isn't possible. You must understand that your child is the first-born son, and thus the heir of the Marchese Valessi, and that he intends to apply through the courts for sole custody of the boy. Although you will be permitted proper access, naturally.'

He looked at Charlie, who was round-eyed, his knuckles pushed into his mouth. 'But, believe me, it would be better if the little boy was spared any more upset from this discussion. We have a trained nanny waiting to look after him.'

He walked to the door and called. A pleasant-faced girl in a smart maroon uniform came in and removed Charlie gently but firmly from his grandmother's almost frenzied grasp, talking to him softly as she carried him out of the room.

'Where's she taking him?' Polly demanded shakily.

'Into the garden,' the lawyer told her, adding less reassuringly, 'For the time being.'

She swallowed convulsively, turning to the silent man by the window. 'Sandro.' Her voice was pleading, all pride forgotten. 'Please don't do this. Don't try to take him away from me.'

'I have already been deprived of the first two years of his life,' he returned implacably. 'There will be no more separation.' His lip curled. 'How remiss of you, *cara mia*, not to inform me of his existence. Even last night, when we talked so intimately about your living arrangements, you said nothing—gave no hint that you had borne me a child. Did you really think you could keep him hidden forever?'

She moistened her dry lips. 'How—how did you find out?'

He shrugged. 'I employed an agency to trace you. They suggested broadening the scope of their enquiries.' His voice was expressionless. 'I received their full report last night after you left. It made fascinating reading.'

She stared down at the carpet. 'So there was someone watching me when I got back,' she said almost inaudibly.

'Can you wonder?' Sandro returned contemptuously. 'I have a beautiful son, Paola, and you deliberately barred me from his life. You preferred to struggle alone than ask me for help—or give me the joy of knowing I was a father.' His gaze was cold, level. 'How can such a thing be forgiven?'

'It was over between us.' Polly lifted her chin. 'What did you expect me to do—beg?'

'I think,' he said softly, 'that is something you may have to learn for the future.'

There was a silence. Polly could hear her mother weeping softly.

'No court in the world,' she said huskily, 'would take a baby away from his mother.'

'Yet it is his grandmother who has the care of him each day.' His tone was harsh. 'I was watching when you came into the room, and he did not try to go to you. Is he even aware that you are his mother?'

Polly gasped, and her head went back as if he had slapped her.

She said unsteadily, 'I go out to work to support us both. As the *contessa* has probably told you, the hours can be long and difficult. But I needed the money, so I had no choice.'

'Yes,' he said, his voice quiet and cold. 'You did. You could have chosen me. All that was needed was one word—one sign.'

There was an odd intensity in his voice, which startled and bewildered her. And also rekindled her anger.

He talks, she thought, as if I deserted him.

A sudden noise from her mother—something between a sigh and a groan—distracted her, and she went over and sat on the arm of her chair, putting an arm round her shoulders.

Oh, God, she thought. To think I was going to tell her that I was taking Charlie away. But how could I have guessed this was going to happen?

'It's going to be all right, Mum,' she said softly. 'I promise.'

'How can it be?' Mrs Fairfax demanded, almost hysterically. 'He's going to take my little treasure to Italy, and I can't bear it.' She reared up from Polly's sheltering arm, glaring venomously at Sandro, who was regarding her with narrowed eyes, his mouth hard and set. 'How dare you come here, ruining our lives like this?' she stormed. 'Get out of my house. And never come back.'

'You are not the only one to suffer, *signora*.' His tone was almost dismissive. He looked at Polly. 'But it would be better for my son to be looked after by someone else until the custody hearing. The nanny I have engaged will move in with you.'

'She can't,' Polly told him curtly. 'My flat is far too small for that.'

He shrugged. 'Then you will be found somewhere else to live.'

'I don't want that,' she said raggedly. 'I don't want anything from you. I just need you to go, and leave us in peace.'

'The *marchese* is being generous, Signorina Fairfax,' Alberto Molena intervened unexpectedly. 'He could ask for the child to be transferred to the care of a temporary guardian while the custody issue is decided.'

'And, of course, he's so sure he'll get custody.' Polly got to her feet, her eyes blazing. 'So bloody arrogant and all-conquering. But what court's going to hand over a baby to someone with his criminal connections? And I'll make sure they know all about his underworld background,' she added defiantly. 'Whatever the cost.'

There was a stunned silence. Then Sandro muttered, *'Dio mio,'* and turned sharply, walking back to the window, his fists clenched at his sides.

Signor Molena's voice was hushed. 'I think you're making a grave mistake, *signorina*. Since the death of his father, the *marchese* has become head of an old and much respected family in southern Italy, and chairman of a business empire with strong interests in the tourist industry among other things.'

He spread his hands almost helplessly. 'You must surely have heard of the Comadora chain of hotels? They are internationally famous.'

'Yes.' Polly had to force suddenly numbed lips to form the words. Her shocked gaze went from his embarrassed face to Sandro's rigid back. 'Yes, I know about them.'

Signor Molena paused, awkwardly. 'And *marchese* means

''marquis'' in your language. It is an aristocratic title, not what you seem to think.' He shook his head. 'To suggest that any member of the Valessi family has ever been linked with criminal elements would be a serious slander if it were not so laughable.'

Polly had never felt less like laughing in her entire life. If she'd been cold before, she was now consumed in an agony of burning humiliation, blushing from her feet to the top of her head.

She wrapped her arms defensively round her body. 'I—I'm sorry,' she mumbled.

Behind her, her mother moaned faintly, and sank back in her chair.

Sandro turned slowly and studied them both reflectively. When he spoke his voice was calm but there was no sign of softening in his attitude.

'That is what you thought?' he asked. 'What you really believed, in spite of everything? It almost defies belief. Almost,' he added quietly, 'but not quite. And it explains a great deal.'

He paused. 'I understand from the *signora*, your mother, that your father is at his office. Perhaps he could be fetched. I do not think that she should be alone.'

Polly shook herself into action. 'Yes—yes, I'll telephone him. And her doctor...' She went out into the hall, standing helplessly for a moment as she tried to remember the number. Realising her mind was a blank.

Sandro followed, closing the door of the living room behind him.

She didn't look at him, doggedly turning the leaves of the directory. 'What—what will happen now?'

'The legal process will begin. But for tonight you may take Carlino to sleep at your *appartamento*.'

'Thank you,' she said with irony.

'The *bambinaia*, whose name is Julie Cole, will accompany you to put him to bed,' he went on, as if she hadn't spoken. 'Then she will return in the morning at seven o'clock to take care of him.'

He spoke as if he was conducting a board meeting, Polly thought incredulously, rather than trying to destroy her life.

She said, 'We could all stay here, perhaps. There's—plenty of room.'

'No,' he said. 'This is not an environment I want for my son.'

Why? she wanted to cry. Because it's an ordinary suburban

house rather than a *palazzo*? Just as I was an ordinary girl, and therefore not deemed as a suitable candidate to become your *marchesa*?

She could see now why it had been so important to pay her off, in order to get rid of her. There was too much at stake dynastically to allow a mistake like herself to enter the equation.

The old pain was back like a knife twisting inside her. A pain that her pride forbade her to let him see. So she would never ask the question 'Why did you leave me?' because she now knew the answer to that, beyond all doubt.

Besides, it would expose the fact that she cared, and that he still had the power to hurt her. And she needed that to remain her secret, and her solitary torment.

Besides, at the moment she was faced with all the suffering she could handle.

Unless she could divert him from his purpose somehow, she thought. Unless...

She picked up the phone irresolutely, then put it down again. She said quickly, before her courage ran out, 'Sandro, it doesn't have to be like this. Surely we could work something out. Share custody in some way.'

His mouth thinned. 'I am expected to trust you? When you have deliberately kept our child from me and even claimed to have a lover to sustain the deception? How much do you think your word is worth?'

Polly swallowed. 'I don't blame you for being angry.'

'*Mille grazie.*' His tone was sardonic.

'And maybe doing my best to be Charlie's mother hasn't been good enough,' she went on, bravely. 'But he doesn't know you at all, and if he was just whisked off to another country among strangers, however well-meaning, he'd be disorientated—scared. He—he's shy with people at first.'

'A trait he shares with you, *mia bella,* if memory serves,' Sandro drawled with cool mockery.

She remembered too. Recalled how gentle and considerate he had been that first time in bed together. How he'd coaxed her out of her clothes and her initial inhibitions.

She flushed hotly and angrily. 'May we cut out the personal reminiscences?' she requested curtly.

He shrugged. 'It is difficult to see how. Making a child together is an intensely personal matter.' He paused. 'And by the time I take Carlino to Italy, we will be well acquainted with each other. I guarantee that. And my own old nurse, Dorotea, will be waiting to look after him. The transition will not be too hard.'

But it will be agony for me, she thought, her throat tightening convulsively. First I lost you, and now you're trying to take Charlie away. And already I feel as if I'm dying inside.

She said tonelessly, 'I'd better make those calls.'

He inclined his head courteously, and went past her, and out into the garden.

Presently, distant but gleeful, Charlie's laughter came to her on the light summer wind, and she stood, staring in front of her unseeingly, her teeth sunk so deeply into her lower lip that she could taste blood.

She wanted to hate Julie Cole, but it was impossible. She was too kind, too tactful, and she thought that Charlie was heaven on legs.

And if she knew that her job was more for security than enjoyment, she kept that to herself.

The creamy scrambled eggs she made for supper were good too, and Charlie loved the triangles of buttered toast that went with them, although Polly could barely force her portion past the sick, scared lump in her throat.

She had wanted to wait at the house to talk to her father, or perhaps just put her head down on his shoulder and cry out her fear, but suddenly there was a car and driver at the gate, and Sandro was insisting quietly but implacably that she should take Charlie home.

She'd begun a protest, but Sandro had simply looked at her, his brows lifted haughtily, questioningly, and the words seemed to stutter and die on her lips.

'You begin to learn,' he had approved coldly.

She had been shaken to find him carrying Charlie down to the car in his arms, and found herself hoping that the little boy would have one of his infrequent tantrums, kicking, screaming and reaching for her as proof that no one else would do.

He didn't; nor did he burst into tears when Sandro had gently but firmly removed his thumb from his mouth.

She had said defensively, 'He doesn't really do that any more. Only when he's tired—or frightened.'

'All the more reason, then, to take him home,' Sandro had retorted unarguably.

She could only imagine the kind of scene that would erupt once her father returned, and her mother had some solid support.

'I'll make your father sell the house,' she'd hissed at Polly as she was leaving. 'Marquis or not, I'm going to fight this man through every court in the land.'

Polly sighed silently. She really doesn't know what she's up against, she thought unhappily. And I'm only just beginning to find out, too.

Only twenty-four hours ago or less, she'd been planning for her life to change, but not to this extreme, catastrophic extent. She'd seen a period of struggle ahead, but never the bleak desert of loneliness that now threatened her.

'He may not win,' she thought. And only realised she'd spoken aloud when Julie said, 'Are you all right, Miss Fairfax?'

Polly jumped, then mustered an attempt at a smile. 'Yes, fine,' she lied.

Julie studied her dubiously. 'I saw some white wine in the fridge while I was getting the eggs. Why don't you sit down and put your feet up, while I do the dishes, and then I'll bring you a glass?'

I don't want a glass, thought Polly. I want a bottle, a cellar, a whole vineyard. I want the edges of my pain blurred, and to be able to stop thinking.

She cleared her throat. 'I know Sandro—the *marchese*—instructed you to put Charlie to bed, but I'd really like to do it myself, if you wouldn't mind.'

'Sure, Miss Fairfax.' Was that compassion in the other girl's voice? 'Anything you say.'

Charlie was tired, and more than a little grumpy, especially when he realised his usual playtime in the bath was going to be curtailed. By the time she'd wrestled him into his pyjamas, Polly felt limp, and close to tears.

'Let me take him.' Julie spoke gently behind her. 'You look all in.'

Polly submitted, standing in his doorway, while her grizzling son was tucked in deftly and firmly.

He'll never settle, she told herself with a kind of sour triumph, only to be confounded when he was fast asleep within five minutes.

She stood at the side of the cot, watching the fan of dark lashes on his cheek, and the small mouth pursed in slumber. She ached to snatch him up and hold him. To run with him into the night to a place where they would never be found.

But she was crying for the moon, and she knew it. Even if there was such a place, she hadn't enough money to go on the run, or enough skill to outwit Sandro for long. And she couldn't afford to provoke his wrath again. She needed to reason with him—to persuade—even to plead, if she had to. Besides, on a purely practical level, instinct warned her that if she attempted to leave, whoever waited in the shadows opposite would step out and prevent her from going.

She sank down onto the floor, and leaned her head against the bars of the cot, listening to Charlie's soft, even breathing. And thinking of all the nights of silence that could be waiting for her.

When she finally returned to the other room, she discovered gratefully that the sofa bed had been opened and made up for the night, and the glass of wine was waiting with a note that said, 'See you in the morning. J.'

She took a first sip, then carried the wine into the bathroom, and began to half fill the tub with warm water, softened by a handful of foaming bath oil. No shower tonight, she told herself. She wanted to relax completely.

She took off her clothes and slid with a sigh into the scented water, reaching for her wineglass.

It would help her sleep, she thought. And tomorrow, when she was more rested, things might seem better. After all, she knew now the worst that could happen to her, and there must be a way of dealing with it that would not leave her utterly bereft.

She leaned back, resting her head on the rim of the bath, and closing her eyes.

Yes, tomorrow she would make plans. Find out if she qualified for legal aid, and get herself a lawyer of her own. Someone who would negotiate with Sandro on her behalf, and allow her to maintain some kind of distance from him.

I really need to do that, she thought. To stay calm—and aloof. I can fight him better that way.

And at that moment, as if he were some demon she'd conjured

up from her own private hell, she heard his voice, low, mocking and far too close at hand.

'Falling asleep in the bath, *mia bella*? That will never do. Surely you don't wish Carlino to become motherless so soon?'

CHAPTER FOUR

POLLY started violently, giving a strangled cry of alarm as the glass jerked and the wine spilled everywhere.

She looked round and saw Sandro leaning in the doorway, watching her with cool amusement.

She tried to sit up, remembered just in time that there weren't enough bubbles to cover her, slipped on the oily surface, and was nearly submerged. She grabbed the rim of the bath, gasping in rage, and saw Sandro walking towards her.

'Keep away from me.' Her voice rose in panic.

'I am coming to rescue your glass, nothing more,' he countered silkily. 'If it breaks, you could hurt yourself badly.' He took it from her hand. 'Besides, how shameful if I had to tell people that the mother of my child drowned while drunk,' he added, his mouth slanting into a grin.

'Just keep me out of your conversations,' Polly said hotly, aware she was blushing under his unashamed scrutiny. 'How the hell did you get in here?'

'I told Julie not to lock the door when she left.'

'You did what?' Polly almost wailed. 'Oh, God, how could you? You realise what she'll think?'

He shrugged. 'I am not particularly concerned.' He gave her a dry look. 'Anyway, I imagine one look at Carlino told her all that she needs to know. We cannot hide that we once had a relationship.'

'Yes,' she said. 'With the emphasis on the "once". But not now, and not ever again, so will you please get out of here? Before I call the police,' she added for good measure.

Sandro shook his head reprovingly. 'Your skills as a hostess seem sadly lacking, *cara mia*. Perhaps you feel at a disadvantage for some reason?'

'Or maybe I prefer company I actually invited here,' Polly threw back at him. 'And you'll never be on any guest-list of mine.'

'You entertain much, do you—in this box? I'm sure you find

the sofa that turns into a bed a convenience—for visitors who linger.'

'This is my home,' she said. 'And I assure you it caters for all my needs.' She paused. 'Now I'd like you to go.'

Quite apart from anything else, it was uncomfortable and undignified crouching below the rim of the bath like this. And the water was getting colder by the minute, she thought angrily.

His brows lifted. 'Without knowing why I am here? Aren't you a little curious, Paola *mia*?'

'I can't think of one good reason for you to inflict yourself on me again,' she told him raggedly. 'Can't you understand you're the last person I want to see?' She sent him a hostile glance. 'Unless you've come to tell me that you've had a change of heart, and you've decided not to proceed with the custody application.'

'No,' Sandro said gently. 'I have not. I simply felt that we should talk together in private. Maybe even in peace. Who knows?'

'I know.' Her voice was stormy. 'And we have nothing to discuss. You want to rob me of my son? I'm going to fight you every step of the way. And my parents will be behind me.'

'No.' Sandro inclined his head almost regretfully. 'They will not.' He raised the glass he was still holding. 'Now, I am going to pour you some more wine. I think you are going to need it.'

He allowed her to absorb that, then continued. 'So, I suggest you stop trying to hide in that inadequate bath, and join me in the other room.' He took a towel from the rail and tossed it to her, then walked out, closing the door behind him.

Polly scrambled to her feet, holding the towel defensively against her as she stepped out gingerly onto the mat. She began to dry herself with hasty, clumsy hands, keeping an apprehensive eye on the door in case Sandro chose to return.

Not that she could do much about it even if he did, she thought, grimacing. And it was ridiculous, anyway, behaving like some Victorian virgin in front of a man who'd seen her naked so many times before. Someone who'd kissed and caressed every inch of the bare skin she was now so anxious to conceal.

Instead of this burning self-consciousness, she should have pretended it didn't matter. Demonstrated her complete and utter indifference to his presence whether she was dressed or undressed.

Fine in theory, she thought. But much trickier in practice.

Especially if Sandro had interpreted her apparent sang-froid as provocation...

Her mouth felt suddenly dry, forcing her to abandon that train of thought for one just as disturbing. What was that comment about her parents meant to imply? What had been said in her absence—and, dear God, what pressure had been brought to bear?

She needed to find out, and quickly.

She looked down at the small pile of clothing she'd discarded earlier. Common sense suggested she should put it back on. Use it as part of the armour her instinct assured her that she was going to need.

But in the end, she opted for the elderly cotton robe hanging on the back of the door. It was plain and prim, without an ounce of seduction in its unrevealing lines, she thought, fastening the sash in a tight double bow. Her equivalent of a security blanket, perhaps.

Then, drawing a deep breath, she squared her shoulders and marched defiantly into the living room, only to halt, disconcerted, when she found it deserted.

The door to Charlie's room was ajar, however, and she ran, stumbling slightly on the skirts of her robe, and pushed it open.

Sandro's back was to the door, but he was bending over Charlie's cot, his hands reaching down, and she felt her heart miss a beat. Was he planning to snatch her baby while he thought she was safely in the bathroom?

'What are you doing in here?' she hissed. 'Don't touch him. Don't dare.'

Sandro straightened, and turned. 'I saw this on the floor.' He held up a small brown teddy bear. 'I was replacing it.' He paused. 'And I came in simply to watch my son sleep. A pleasure that has been denied me for the past two years,' he added coldly.

'And which you want to deny me permanently,' Polly flung at him, tight-lipped.

His smile was wintry. 'Just as you would have done to me, *mia cara*, if fate had not intervened,' he returned unanswerably.

He held the door, allowing her to precede him back into the living room.

He looked round him, his expression disparaging. 'And this is where you have allowed him to spend the beginning of his life? In this *conigliera*?'

'And what precisely does that mean?'

'A hutch,' he said. 'For rabbits.'

She bit her lip. The room did seem to have shrunk suddenly, or was it just the effect of Sandro's presence? And the bed being open and made up didn't help either. In fact it was a serious embarrassment.

'It was all I could afford at the time,' she said. 'And it works,' she added defiantly, thinking of the hours she'd spent painting the walls, and stripping and stencilling the small chest of drawers which held Charlie's things, and which just fitted into his room. He gave no credit, either, she thought bitterly, for the way she kept the place neat and spotless.

'One word from you,' he said harshly, 'one hint that you were *incinta*, and it would all have changed. My son would have come into the world at Comadora, in the bed where I was born, and my father and grandfather before me.' He took her by the shoulder, whirling her to face him. His voice was passionate. '*Dio*, Paola, why did you not tell me? How could you let me exist without knowing?'

'Because we were no longer together.' She freed herself from his grasp. 'I made a decision that my baby was going to be part of my life only, and that I wanted nothing from you.' She paused. 'Didn't I make that clear enough at the time?'

'More than clear.' His mouth twisted. 'What I could not understand was—why.' He frowned. 'You could not have truly believed I was Mafioso. That is impossible—*assurdo*.'

'Why not? It was evident there were things you hadn't told me,' Polly countered. 'Things you didn't want me to know.' She shrugged. 'What was I supposed to think?'

'Not, perhaps, to give me the benefit of the doubt?'

'No,' she said. 'Any more than you decided to tell me the truth. And I expect we both had our reasons.'

'*Sì*,' Sandro said quietly. 'But I also have regrets, which you do not seem to share.'

'You're wrong.' She looked down at the floor. 'I wish very much that I had never met you.'

'Unfortunately for us both, the situation cannot be changed.' His voice was a drawl. He picked up her refilled glass from the chest of drawers and handed it to her. 'Shall we drink to our mistakes?'

Polly realised she was holding the glass as if it might explode. 'This isn't a social occasion,' she reminded him tautly. 'You said you came here to talk.'

'And I would do so,' he said, 'if I thought you were in any mood to listen.' He paused. 'I had better fortune with your parents.'

Polly stiffened. 'What have you been saying to them? If you've threatened them...'

He gave her a weary look. 'With what? A cattle prod, perhaps?' His mouth curled. 'Once again, you are allowing your imagination to run away with you, *mia cara*.'

She flushed. 'You're trying to tell me they gave up without a fight. I don't believe it.'

'Your mother, I think, would have gone to any lengths to thwart me,' he said. 'Your father, however, was more reasonable.'

'He thinks I should simply hand Charlie over to you?' Her voice broke on a little sob. 'Oh, how could he?'

'No, he knows that even if he made the kind of sacrifices your mother was demanding, he would still not have the financial resources for a lengthy court battle.' His smile was brief and hard. 'Especially if it took place in Italy,' he added softly.

The colour deepened in her face. 'You'll go to any lengths—pull any dirty trick to win, won't you?' she accused in a stifled voice.

Sandro shrugged. 'I see little point in losing, *bella mia*,' he returned. 'But I am prepared to offer a draw—a negotiated settlement.'

She stared at him. 'Would it mean that Charlie stayed with me?'

'That would depend on you,' he said. 'Carlino is coming to Italy with me. As my son, he needs to learn about his heritage. I am merely inviting you to accompany him.'

'As what? Some kind of glorified nanny?' she demanded. She shook her head. 'I think I'd rather have my day in court.'

'He already has a nanny,' Sandro told her evenly. 'And another waiting in Italy to love him. But what he really needs is the stability of both parents in his life. So, Paola *mia*, I am asking you once again, as I did three years ago, to be my wife.'

For a long, dazed moment Polly was too shaken to speak.

At last, she said huskily, 'Is this some grotesque joke?'

'No,' he said. 'We are, if you remember, already engaged to each other,' he added cynically.

Her breathing quickened. 'Was I really supposed to believe that—that nonsense? I—I don't think so. And whatever happened between us, it was all over a long time ago, and you know it. You can't simply revive it—on a whim.'

'Very well, then,' Sandro returned equably. 'Let us forget it ever took place. Pretend that, for the first time, I am making you an offer of marriage, Paola *mia*.'

She shook her head. 'But you don't—you can't want to marry me.'

'I have no particular desire to be married at all,' he retorted. 'But there are good reasons why I should sacrifice my freedom.'

'Your freedom?' Polly almost choked. 'What about mine?'

He looked around him. 'You call this liberty? Working long hours. Living in little more than one room? I don't think so.'

'I could always sue you for child support.' She drew a breath. 'That would improve my circumstances by a hundred per cent.'

'But I am already offering to support our child—as the Marchese Valessi,' he said silkily. 'Besides, our marriage would remove any possible objections to Carlino's right to inherit when the time comes, and it would mean that his well-being and nurture becomes the concern of us both from day to day.' He paused. 'I suggest it as a practical alternative to a custody battle.'

'Which I might win,' she said swiftly.

'You might, but could you fight the appeal which would follow?' Sandro countered. 'Or the appeal against the appeal?' His smile was chilly. 'The case might last for years.'

'Or until I run out of money, of course,' she said bitterly. 'You don't need a cattle prod, *signore*.'

His brows lifted. 'You regard marriage to me as some kind of torture, *signorina*?' he asked softly. 'Then perhaps I should make something clear to you at once. What I am offering is only a matter of form. A way of legalising the situation between us. But it would not be a love match. Too much has taken place for that. We would share nothing more than a roof, if that is what concerns you.'

He gave her a level look. 'I accept now that any feelings we had for each other belong in the past. That we are different people, and we have both moved on.'

'You say that now.' Her voice was husky. 'Yet only last night you told me I was still in your blood.'

'But a lot has happened since then,' Sandro said harshly. 'And my feelings towards you have naturally changed as a result.' He paused. 'Now our child remains the only issue between us, and his ultimate welfare should be our sole consideration. You agree with that, I hope?'

Polly nodded numbly.

'*Bene,*' he said briskly. 'In return, I promise that your life as the Marchesa Valessi will be as easy as I can make it. You will be made a suitable allowance, and asked occasionally to act as my hostess.' His smile was hard. 'But you may spend your nights alone.'

She swallowed. 'And—you?'

'I hardly think that concerns you,' he said coldly. 'However, I will ensure that any liaisons I have are conducted discreetly.'

She bit her lip. 'As ours was?'

'*Davvero,*' he nodded. 'Precisely.'

She said with difficulty, 'And what about me—if I met someone?'

His brows lifted. 'I should require you to behave with equal discretion. I would tolerate no open scandal in my family.'

He paused. 'So what is your answer, Paola? Will you be my wife?'

'I don't know what to say.' Concealed by the skirts of her robe, her hands were clenched painfully into fists. 'I mean—you might want more children at some point.'

'I have a son to safeguard the inheritance. That was always my priority in such matters. As to the rest...' He shrugged again. 'I have cousins, both married with *bambini*. At times my house seems full of children. Although that, of course, will be good for Carlino,' he added thoughtfully. 'He does not talk as well as he should, and he hardly knows how to kick a ball. That must change.'

Polly's lips parted in sheer outrage. 'How—dare you? Last week you didn't even know you were a father. Now you're a bloody expert on child-rearing.'

'I made no such claim,' Sandro returned mildly. 'But Julie had concerns which she mentioned to me.'

'Then she had no right,' Polly flared. 'Charlie's absolutely beautiful, and he can do all kinds of things,' she added hotly, burying the memory of various clashes she'd had with her mother on that very subject.

'And could do far more, I suspect.' Sandro's smile was cold, 'if he was allowed to—and once keeping his clothes clean from every speck of dust is no longer a major priority.' He allowed her to absorb that, then went on, 'Can he swim?'

She reddened, still stung by his last comment, but honestly unable to refute it. He hadn't missed much during his first encounter with her mother, she thought ruefully.

'No, not yet,' she said in a subdued voice. 'I meant to take him to the local baths, but weekends are always so busy.'

'It's not a problem,' he said. He smiled at her for the first time that night without edge, the sudden unforced charm making the breath catch in her throat. 'I shall enjoy teaching him myself in our own pool.'

She caught her lower lip in her teeth, struggling to regain her equilibrium. Trying to disregard the image his words had presented. 'Yes—I suppose...'

'So,' he said, after a pause, 'shall we settle this thing now? Will you marry me, and come to Italy with our son?'

'I don't seem to have much of a choice,' she said in a low voice.

Something unreadable came and went in his face. 'And if you could choose? What then?'

'I would wish to be as far from you,' she said passionately, 'as it's possible to get.'

His head went back, and his eyes narrowed. 'Well, do not despair, *bella mia*,' he drawled scornfully. 'My home at Comadora is large, a *palazzo*, with thick walls, and many rooms. You should be able to avoid me easily.'

'Thank you,' she said huskily.

'Tonight, however, you will not be so fortunate,' he added.

She stiffened. 'What are you talking about?'

'I intend to spend the night here.'

She gasped. 'But—but you can't...' She tried not to look at the all too obtrusive sofa bed. 'There's no room.'

'It will be cramped,' he agreed. He took off his jacket, and began to loosen his tie. 'But it is only for one night.'

She said in a choked voice, 'You promised me—you swore this wouldn't happen. Oh, why did I think I could trust you?'

'The boot is on the other foot, *cara mia*.' He began unhurriedly to unfasten his shirt. 'I do not trust *you*. Who knows what you might be tempted to do, if you were left alone?

'But I have no intention of breaking my word,' he added. 'This armchair looks comfortable enough, so I shall use that.' His smile grazed her skin. 'And you can have that *congegno* quite undisturbed. I hope you sleep well.'

He draped his shirt over the back of the chair, sat down and removed his shoes and socks, while Polly watched in growing alarm. But when he stood up, his hands going to the waistband of his trousers, she intervened.

'Kindly stop right there,' she said grittily.

'You have some problem?'

'Yes.' Her green eyes were stormy. 'Of course I do.'

'Then deal with it.' He unzipped his trousers, stepped out of them, then placed them, folded, with the rest of his clothes. He was wearing brief silk shorts, and the rest of him was smooth tanned skin. For one burning moment of self-betrayal she found herself remembering the taste of him, and felt her body clench in uncontrollable excitement.

'Why, Paola, you are blushing,' he jeered softly. 'But not even to spare you will I sleep in my clothes. And you were not always such a prude,' he added drily. He indicated his shorts derisively. 'These, as you know, are a concession. But if the sight of me is still too much, you could always close your eyes.' He paused. 'Have you a towel I can use?'

Dry-mouthed, she muttered acquiescence, and went to the chest of drawers. As she reached for a towel, she uncovered Charlie's photograph.

'What is that?' Sandro came to her side, and took it from the drawer. He studied it for a moment, brows lifted, then turned to her. 'Is this where you usually keep it?'

'No,' she admitted reluctantly.

'You hid it,' he asked, incredulously. 'In case I came here?'

'Think whatever you wish,' she flung at him. 'I don't give a damn.'

He set the photograph carefully on top of the chest of drawers. 'And you wonder why I do not trust you,' he said silkily. He rescued the towel from her nerveless hand and went into the bath-room, closing the door behind him.

For a moment she stood irresolutely, trying to decide what to do. She could hardly go to bed in her robe, without exciting the kind of comment from him she most wished to avoid. And what nightgowns she possessed were far too thin and revealing.

However...

Polly knelt, opening the bottom drawer of the chest, searching with feverish fingers. There were some oddments of winter cloth-ing here, she knew. Among them...

She drew out the pyjamas with a sigh of relief. They were worn out, washed out, and she'd never liked them, but they were good old-fashioned winceyette, and they covered her from her throat down to her feet.

She was just fastening the last button on the mandarin-style jacket when Sandro returned, and stopped dead at the sight of her.

'*Santa Madonna,*' he breathed, with a kind of fascinated horror. 'No wonder you sleep alone. I think I shall have to choose your trousseau myself, particularly the *biancheria intima.*'

'Thank you,' Polly returned icily. 'But I prefer to pick my own lingerie. And if you don't like the way I look, you can close your eyes too,' she added triumphantly.

'That is one solution,' he admitted musingly. 'But I can think of others that I would enjoy more.' He saw her blench, and grinned. 'Calm down, *cara mia.* I intend to keep my word. But sometimes to cover too much can be a mistake, because it excites the imagination.' He paused. 'I suppose a spare blanket is too much to hope for.'

She wanted to scream at him that she hoped he caught galloping pneumonia and died alone in a ditch. Instead she heard herself say unwillingly, 'Yes, there is one.'

She fetched it from the corner cupboard, pale blue and still in its wrappings. 'I bought it for Charlie,' she told him, gruffly. 'For when he moves into a bed instead of his cot.'

There was a silence. 'Then I am doubly grateful,' he said quite gently. 'Because this is a sacrifice for you. And I will make sure it goes with us to his new home.'

For a moment, there was a note in his voice that made her want to cry. She turned away hurriedly, and got into bed, pulling the covers over her, the metal base creaking its usual protest as she settled herself.

'*Dio,*' Sandro muttered. 'And that—atrocity will remain here.'

Well, she wasn't going to argue about that, Polly thought wearily. Aloud, she said, past the constriction in her throat, 'Will you turn the light off, please? When you're ready.'

'I am ready now.'

She lay, eyes tight shut, as he went past her, and the room was plunged into darkness. Waited for him to return to the chair.

Instead, she was aware of him standing beside her. He said quietly, 'Paola, do you ever wish you could turn back the clock? Wipe out what has been?'

'No,' she said. 'Because I know it's impossible, and I prefer to deal with reality.'

He sighed. 'Then could we not declare a truce for this one night? Be together for old times' sake?'

She wanted so badly to yield. To reach up and draw him down to her. She was starving for him, her body quivering with need, aching for him. Reminding her that she'd never shared a room with him before without eventually falling asleep in his arms in the drugged sweetness of sensual exhaustion.

But if she surrendered, she would be lost forever. And if she resisted, as she knew she must, at least she would retain what remained of her pride. Which might be all she had left to sustain her in the weeks, months, even years ahead.

'Even if I was in the mood for casual sex,' she said stonily, 'you gave me your word.' And paused. 'Besides, you flatter yourself, *signore*,' she added, coolly and distinctly. 'The old times weren't that special.'

She heard his swift intake of breath, and flinched, knowing she had gone too far. Waiting for a retribution which seemed inevitable.

But there was nothing.

She felt rather than heard the moment he moved away. Listened, all her senses tingling, as he wrapped himself in the blanket. Then, in the heavy silence which followed, she turned her face into the single pillow, and lay like a dead thing.

It had never occurred to her that she would sleep. She was too aware of his even breathing only a few feet away, demonstrating quite clearly, she realised, that her rejection couldn't have weighed too heavily with him after all.

She sighed silently, searching for a cool place on the pillow. She needed to look calm and rested in the morning, not wan and heavy-eyed.

Because Sandro must not be allowed to think that he still mattered to her.

That was what she needed to remember above all. Anything else would be a disaster, because, as those few moments in the darkness had proved all over again, it was going to be difficult to remain immune to the devastating allure of his sexuality.

But that, she thought, had always been her downfall from their first meeting. She had been too much in love, too blinded by the passion and glamour of him to ask the right questions and demand answers that made sense.

Her first major surprise had been his brilliant command of English, but when she'd asked him about it he'd simply said he'd had good teachers.

Polly had wondered, with a pang, whether he meant other women, and decided not to probe any further. Now she suspected that he'd gone to school in England, and probably university too, either here or in America.

He'd told her too that he worked at the Grand Hotel Comadora, but she'd never gone there to see him because its sheer expensive exclusivity discouraged casual visitors. The entrances were controlled by security guards, and the staff were subject to strict rules, so she'd stayed away. Otherwise she'd have soon found out that he wasn't simply an employee, but the owner. And that had been the last thing he wanted her to know.

Her own *naïveté* made her cringe now. The way she'd trusted him with all her small, loving dreams of their future.

'I'd like a tiny house,' she told him once. 'In one of the villages high above the sea, with a terraced garden, and its own lemon tree.'

'Mm.' He'd stroked her hair back from her love-flushed face with gentle fingers. 'And will you make me *limoncello* from our tree?'

He was talking about the lethally potent liqueur that was brewed locally, and she'd laughed.

'Well, I could try.'

God, what a fool she'd been, and how he must have been secretly amused at her, knowing full well that he was going to dump her once their warm, rapturous summer together was over.

He'd found himself an inexperienced virgin, and cynically turned her into an instrument for his pleasure.

I bet he couldn't believe his own luck. I must have been the perfect mistress, she thought, wincing. Easily duped, and ecstatically wanton. He didn't even have to kiss me. The sound of his voice—the warmth of his skin as he stood next to me were enough.

And, as she'd discovered tonight, they still were.

So how was she going to deal with the bleak sterility of the future that awaited her in Italy? A wife who was not a wife, she thought, living in a house that would never be her home. Her only link with Sandro, the child he had made in her body. A child, at the same time, who had driven them further apart than any years or miles could have done.

Sandro blamed her for keeping her pregnancy from him, but what else could she have done when she'd been dismissed so summarily from his life? And the accompanying threat might have been veiled, but it was real enough to have kept her from Italy ever since. Or until yesterday, at least.

And that had been all his own doing.

And now amazingly she was going to return to the Campania at his side. Somehow, she was going to have to learn to be his *marchesa*. To sit at his table, wearing the clothes and probably the jewellery he provided. To be pleasant to his family, and welcoming to his guests. And never by word, look or gesture let anyone suspect that she was bleeding slowly to death.

She supposed there would be compensations. She knew there would be heartbreak. And she was scared.

Scared of the inevitable isolation that awaited her—the power he still exerted over her trembling senses—and the ever-present danger of self-betrayal.

She needed to work on her anger—her bitterness at his desertion. They would protect her. Build a barrier that not all his sensual expertise could breach. That was the way she must go.

All the same, she found her mind drifting wistfully back to the tiny dream house and its lemon tree, and she saw herself walking beneath it with Sandro, her hand in his, as the sun glinted through the leaves.

And though her mouth smiled, there were tears on her face as she finally fell asleep.

CHAPTER FIVE

SHE was weighed down, sinking into the depths of a dark and bottomless sea, unable to move or save herself.

Polly opened her eyes, gasping, to the familiar surroundings of the flat, bathed in early-morning light through the thin curtains, but the sensation of being pinned down persisted. Even increased.

Slowly, and with foreboding, she turned her head, and saw that Sandro was lying next to her, on top of the covers. The blue blanket was thrown lightly over him, and, she realised incredulously, Charlie's small pyjamaed form was also present, sprawled across his father's bare chest, his dark head tucked into the curve of his shoulder. Both of them were fast asleep.

For a moment Polly was transfixed by this unexpected tableau. And deep within her, she felt such a stir of tenderness that she almost cried out.

She swallowed deeply, reclaiming her self-control. Reminding herself that she would have to get accustomed to seeing them together, although not in such intimate circumstances. And, at the same time, knowing a pang of jealousy that Charlie, usually awkward with strangers, should have capitulated so readily. She overcame an impulse to snatch him back.

Slowly and stealthily, she began to ease her way towards the edge of the bed. It was still early, but her need for coffee was evenly matched with her desire to extract herself from a difficult situation.

Besides, she wanted both Charlie and herself to be ready by the time Julie arrived.

Julie, she thought, her mouth tightening, who was going to get a piece of her mind. And yet was that really fair to the girl, who'd only been doing the job she was hired for?

Yes, she had concerns, but so had Polly. She'd been worried about her mother's apparent resolve to keep Charlie a baby for as long as possible, and therefore more dependent than he should be at his age. Mrs Fairfax had lavished presents on 'my little prince' and 'Gran's sweet little man', most of them in the form of expensive clothing which she fussed to keep pristine. Even helping his grandfather to gather up hedge clippings seemed to be on the forbidden list, Polly recalled wryly. Hardly any wonder that Charlie didn't shine at outdoor activities.

And he was lazy about feeding himself, and doing simple tasks that Polly set him, probably because he was used to having everything done for him at other times.

I knew there were problems, she admitted as she slid with infinite care from under the covers, but at the same time I wanted to avoid another confrontation with my mother. So I have only myself to blame.

She stood up, then paused, suddenly aware of movement behind her. Stiffening as Sandro's voice said a husky, '*Buongiorno*'.

'Good morning.' She didn't look at him. 'I was going to make coffee—if you'd like some. I—I don't have espresso,' she added stiltedly.

'Coffee would be good,' he said. 'If I can free myself sufficiently to drink it.' She could hear the smile in his voice, and bit her lip.

'Shall I put him back in his cot?' she asked.

'Why disturb him for no cause?'

'Perhaps I should ask you the same thing.' Polly stared down at the floor. 'What is he doing here?'

'He was crying,' Sandro said shortly. 'He wanted a drink, which I gave him. Should I have left him thirsty?'

'He'd have needed changing too.' God, she thought, she sounded so carping—like a miserable shrew.

'I even managed that,' he returned. 'After a struggle. Although I do not guarantee my handiwork,' he added drily.

'You did that?' Polly turned then, staring down at him.

'But of course. He was uncomfortable.'

'Well—thank you for that,' Polly said reluctantly. She shook her head. 'I can't understand why I didn't hear him myself. I always do...'

'You were dead to the world.' His voice gentled a little. 'You did not even scream "rape" when I joined you on the bed. Perhaps you sensed Carlino was there to act as chaperone.'

'Maybe so,' she agreed stiffly.

'A friend warned me that when you have a child, the concept

of ''three in a bed'' takes on a new meaning,' he went on. 'I now know what he means.'

Polly looked away, her mouth tightening, and he sighed. 'That was a joke.'

'An inappropriate one,' she said, hating the primness in her voice. 'I'll get the coffee now. And—thanks again for helping with Charlie.'

'It was my pleasure,' he said, his voice faintly weary.

By the time she returned, Charlie had woken and was in a grizzly mood.

'You are sour in the mornings, *figlio mio*,' Sandro told him. He slanted a faint grin at Polly. 'Like your *mammina*.'

She sipped the strong, scalding brew she'd made. 'I'm sorry.' Her voice was defensive. 'But this isn't easy for me.'

'Or for me, *cara mia*,' he said. 'Or for me.'

He swallowed his own coffee with the complete disregard for its temperature that she remembered so well, then rose, swinging Charlie up into his arms. 'Come, my little grumbler. Come and take a bath with Papa and see if it improves your temper.' He glanced at Polly. 'You have no objections, I hope.'

'No,' she said. 'None.'

She occupied herself with stripping the bed and turning it back into a sofa, while attempting to ignore the noise of splashing and Charlie's gleeful squeals coming from the bathroom. Trying hard, too, not to feel envious and even slightly dejected, because that would get her nowhere.

Her path might have been chosen for her, but she had to follow it, whatever the cost.

What would happen next? she wondered. She supposed she would have to see Mrs Terence and tell her that Safe Hands would be losing her earlier than planned.

And she would have to visit her parents and break the news to them too—a situation which had all the makings of a Class A nightmare.

And if Sandro was serious about moving her into a larger flat, and so far he seemed to have meant everything he said, then she would have to pack.

She wandered into the tiny kitchen and poured herself some orange juice. She felt as if she needed all the vitamins she could get.

It was as if her life had been invaded by a sudden whirlwind, all her plans and certainties swept away.

And at some point she would have to stand beside Sandro in a church or registry office, and listen to him making promises he had no intention of keeping as he put his ring on her finger.

Three years ago, all my dreams were of marrying him, she thought unhappily. And now it's happening at last, but not in a way I could ever have hoped. Because I'm being offered the façade of a marriage, without its fulfillment. And, for Charlie's sake, I have to find some way—to endure.

She rinsed out her glass and put it on the draining board.

What was the old saying? she wondered drearily. Be careful what you wish for, in case your wish comes true?

Well, she had wished so hard to be Sandro's wife—once.

She gave a small wretched sigh, then went into Charlie's room to choose his clothes for the day, and that was where Sandro found her a few minutes later. He was fully dressed, while Charlie, capering beside him, was in a towel draped like a Roman toga.

'Do you have a mop, or a cloth, perhaps? I need to dry the bathroom floor.' Sandro's tone was faintly rueful.

'It doesn't matter,' Polly said too brightly. 'I'll clear up when I have my own bath.' She paused. 'You seemed to be having fun together,' she went on with an effort. 'Somehow—he's not shy with you.'

'Why should he be?' Sandro lifted a hand and touched his scarred cheek. 'Did you think, perhaps, that this would terrify him—make him run away from me screaming, and force me to think again?' he added sardonically.

'No—oh, no,' Polly stammered. 'But he can be tricky with people he's only just met. But not you.'

Sandro shrugged. 'Blood calling to blood, perhaps.'

'Yes,' she said. 'That must be it.'

He was watching her. He said quietly, 'Paola, I am not trying to take your place. You will always be his mother. But he needs us both.'

Her throat closed. She nodded, unable to speak, her hands restlessly folding and unfolding a little T-shirt.

His hand closed on her shoulder. His touch was gentle, but she felt its resonance through her blood and bone.

'Go and dress yourself,' he directed quietly. 'I will see to our son.'

She didn't want his kindness, his consideration, Polly thought wildly as she fled. She needed antagonism to feed her anger—her determination to stay aloof from him at all costs. To blank out forever the memories of those days and nights when her universe had narrowed to one room, and the bed where she lay in his arms.

She needed to hate him.

The state of the bathroom was a spur to that, of course. It looked as if it had been hit by a tidal wave, and it took ten minutes' hard graft with a mop and bucket, and a roll of paper towels, to render it usable again.

But even then the recollection of Charlie's crows of delight diffused her resentment.

And it occurred to her, too, that next time Sandro chose to play submarines or whatever with his son it would be someone else's task to do the clearing up after them.

It was clear that her life was going to change at all levels, not just the strictly personal. And would she be able to cope?

Although she would not be Sandro's wife in the accepted sense, she would have some practical role to play in his life, and maybe she should ask to have it defined.

She sighed. So many things she needed to know—not least how he'd acquired the scar on his face. Her own assumptions had been totally and embarrassingly wrong, of course, but she'd been offered no other explanation for an injury that must have gone dangerously deep.

She could only suppose that Sandro found the circumstances surrounding it too difficult and painful to discuss. So what could possibly have happened, and could she ever persuade him to talk about it?

Then there was his family. It seemed that he had other cousins apart from the *contessa*. How much did they know about her existence? she wondered. And what would they feel about her arrival—an interloper with a child?

Polly sighed again. She was just beginning to realise there were problems she hadn't even imagined awaiting her in Campania.

When she emerged from the bathroom, freshly attired in jeans and a pale blue shirt, she found Sandro standing by the window with

Charlie in his arms, apparently having a murmured conversation about the traffic in the street below.

'Have you pointed out the security men watching the flat?' Polly asked caustically.

'I sent them away last night,' Sandro told her, unfazed. 'From now on, *cara*, I shall be watching you myself.' He paused, watching the swift rush of colour to her face. 'So, what are your plans for the day?'

'Principally, giving up my job, and trying to calm my mother.' Polly thrust her hands into the pockets of her jeans in an effort at nonchalance. 'She's probably looking for a hit man right now to take you out of the equation.'

'What a pity I am not Mafioso as you thought,' he murmured. 'I could perhaps have suggested someone.'

Polly's mouth tightened. 'I suppose I should also start packing—if you really intend to move us out of here. Or was that simply a threat?'

'I do intend it,' he said. 'And as quickly as possible. But do not bring too much, *cara*. I plan to provide you and Carlino with everything you need, including new wardrobes.'

She lifted her chin. 'And I prefer to choose my own things.'

He looked her up and down, brows raised. 'Of which those are a sample?'

'There was a time,' Polly said, 'when you would have found these clothes perfectly acceptable.'

'But then we are neither of us the same people,' he said, gently. 'Are we, Paola?'

'No,' she said. 'We're not. And, as a matter of interest, who was the Sandro Domenico you once claimed to be?'

'You are interested?' His brows lifted mockingly. 'A step forward, perhaps. Domenico was the name of my late father, and was given to me as a second name at my christening. I used it when I did not wish to reveal my true identity.'

'Of course,' she said. 'Why didn't I guess?'

'So, will you allow me to make reparation for that, and accept that I wish to show my gratitude to you for agreeing to marry me, and how better than with a *corredo di sposa*?'

'I don't want your gratitude,' she said stonily. 'Or a trousseau of designer dresses. Just the space you promised me.'

'Does that exclude you from having lunch with me at my hotel—the Grand Capital? There are things we need to discuss.'

Polly bit her lip. 'If I must.'

Sandro shrugged. 'You overwhelm me,' he told her drily. 'Shall we say one o'clock in the bar?'

'Lunch in a restaurant?' Polly gave her angelically smiling son a dubious glance. 'I'm not sure Charlie could manage that.'

'He does not have to,' Sandro said briskly. 'I have arranged for him to spend some time with friends of mine, Teresa and Ernesto Bacchi, so we can talk without distraction.'

Polly drew a swift breath. 'That's very arbitrary,' she said mutinously. 'I might not like these friends of yours.'

'Well, you will meet them later today, so you can judge for yourself,' he said, shrugging.

'And it might upset Charlie, too.'

'I doubt that,' he said. 'They have twins his age. And he is more adaptable than you think.' Sandro smoothed the little boy's hair back from his forehead. 'Tell Mammina,' he whispered. He pointed to himself. 'Who am I?'

'Papa,' Charlie said promptly, and hid his face on his father's shoulder.

Polly made herself laugh and applaud. How easily Sandro had won him over, she thought. But why should she wonder at that?

Before he'd even spoken to her that first day in Sorrento, she'd been aware of the intensity of his gaze, her own mouth curving shyly—involuntarily—in response to his smile. Her heart had thudded in anticipation of the moment when he would come to her side.

Dear God, she thought wearily. She'd been seduced with just a look. A number-one, first-class pushover.

She turned away blindly, murmuring about finding her bag, and then the door buzzer sounded to announce Julie's arrival.

She'd decided it would be hypocritical to have a battle with the nanny over concerns that she actually shared, so she greeted her with a polite word, and smile instead.

She took herself into the kitchen to make more coffee while Julie received her instructions for the day.

At the moment Sandro ruled, and there was nothing she could do about it, she thought, leaning against the cramped work surface while she waited for the kettle to boil.

She was still inwardly reeling from the shock of his return, and its traumatic aftermath, but her confusion wouldn't last forever. Soon, she would be back in control of herself, and she'd make damned sure that more of a partnership was established over Charlie's parenting than existed at the moment.

Something that might be easier once she was officially Sandro's wife—and one of the few advantages of the forthcoming marriage, she thought painfully.

When she returned to the living room, Sandro came over to her, having relinquished Charlie to his nanny.

'I must go,' he said. He took out his wallet, and extracted what seemed to be an obscene amount of money, which he placed next to Charlie's photograph on the chest of drawers. 'For taxis,' he said. 'Tomorrow there will be a car and driver for your use.'

'Public transport has always been perfectly adequate,' Polly informed him loftily, conveniently forgetting how often she had cursed its delays and overcrowding.

Sandro shrugged. 'Then spend it as you wish,' he said. 'In this, at least, the choice is yours.'

Ignoring her mutinous glance, he took her hand and bowed over it.

'I will not kiss you, *bella mia*,' he said softly. He lifted her imprisoned fingers, drawing them lightly over his unshaven chin, the topaz eyes meeting hers in open challenge. 'I would not wish to mark your exquisite skin.'

Polly mumbled something incoherent, and withdrew her hand from his with more haste than courtesy, aware that Julie, in spite of her training, was watching open-mouthed.

And probably thinking every inch of me is grazed to the bone, she thought, cringing inwardly.

If you only knew, she told the other girl silently. If you only—truly—knew...

And found herself sighing under her breath.

She handed in her notice at Safe Hands, aware that she was causing a slight shock wave, but unable to explain or defend her decision. Far too tricky, she thought.

And then, of course, she had her parents to face.

She'd expected her mother to be instantly on the attack when she arrived at the family home, but Mrs Fairfax was upstairs, lying on her bed with the curtains drawn. The look she gave Polly was subdued, almost listless.

'So, he's persuaded you,' she said heavily. 'I supposed he would. A man like that. I—we didn't realise what we were taking on.'

Polly took her mother's cold hand in hers. 'It won't be so bad,' she said, wondering which of them she was trying to convince. 'And Italy's such a beautiful country. You'll be able to come and visit as often as you like. I'm sure Sandro will want that,' she added, mentally crossing her fingers.

'Crumbs from the rich man's table,' her mother said with a harsh laugh. 'How could I ever have imagined it would end like this—that he'd come to find you?'

'She'll be all right,' her father told Polly comfortingly as they went downstairs. 'I'm going to take her down to Cornwall for a few days. She loves it there, but we haven't been able to go recently.'

'No.' Polly bit her lip. 'Because you've been too busy looking after Charlie. Maybe the break will do her good—stop her brooding.' She hesitated. 'Dad—about the wedding—when it happens...'

'You want us to stay away?'

She shook her head vehemently. 'I'm counting on you to give me away, but how is Mum going to feel about it?'

'Let's cross that bridge when we come to it,' he said gently. He gave her a searching look. 'Sweetheart—tell me something.'

'If I can.'

'Charlie's father,' he said. 'Was it just a temporary fling, or did you really care about him?'

She looked away. 'I—cared,' she said in a low voice. 'But I discovered that—he didn't.'

'Well, at least he's trying to put things right now, no matter what your mother says.' He gave an awkward chuckle. 'Even asked my permission, which threw me.' He put his hand on her shoulder. 'It won't be easy, I know, but maybe you could try meeting him halfway?'

But he would have to want that too, she thought. *And he doesn't. Besides, how can I meet him anywhere when I don't even know who he is? And never did...*

She suppressed a sigh, and her little smile was wintry. 'Perhaps that's a bridge I have to cross.' She kissed his cheek. 'Good luck with Cornwall. I'll be in touch.'

She didn't want to be late for lunch, so she reluctantly spent some of Sandro's money on a taxi after all.

She hadn't changed into anything more formal for their meeting, just added her favourite pair of earrings—the tiny enamelled cornflowers on delicate silver chains. But she began to wish she had dressed more smartly as she walked across the Grand Capital's marble foyer, skirting the fountain and the groups of elegant women who'd gathered there to chat before lunch.

Sandro was already sitting at the bar when Polly entered. He was laughing at something the barman had said, and she hesitated, almost stunned, as the full force of his attraction hit her once more like a punch in the throat.

Nor was she the only one, she realised, recovering her breath. Women were sending him predatory looks from all over the room. No change there, then, she thought drily, remembering the same reaction every time she'd walked down a street with him in Sorrento.

And the scar on his cheek had not detracted from his appeal in any way. On the contrary, thought Polly, he looked like some Renaissance swordsman injured in a duel.

At that moment, he looked round and saw her. He slid off the stool, coming across to her, his mouth curling in faint cynicism as he registered her instant tension.

'*Cara,*' he said softly, and took her hand. 'So you have decided to join me. I could not be sure. But I am delighted.' He leaned towards her, his gaze travelling to her mouth, and Polly flinched, freeing her fingers from his grasp.

'Still no kiss?' His tone was mocking. 'Even though I have learned my lesson from this morning, and shaved more closely in anticipation?'

'I don't consider that any particular inducement,' Polly responded stonily. 'I've agreed to marry you, and I see no need for any—embellishments.'

'Now, there we disagree. I see I shall have to teach you the difference between public and private behaviour, my reluctant bride.' He smiled as he spoke, and only Polly was aware of the ice in his voice. 'But we will discuss that later.'

He took her to a corner table, and signalled to a hovering waiter. 'What would you like to drink. Is it still Campari and soda?'

More unwanted memories, she thought, biting her lip. She said coolly, 'Just a mineral water, please.'

'Last night you drank white wine.'

'Today I need to keep a clear head.'

He gave her a thoughtful look, then turned to the waiter. 'Mineral water, *per favore*,' he directed. 'For both of us.'

The waiter departed, leaving a silence behind him that Sandro was the first to break.

'Have you had a productive morning?' he asked.

'I suppose so.' Polly gave a slight shrug. 'I resigned from my job, and visited my parents, who are planning a holiday in Cornwall.'

'I have not been idle either,' he said. 'The legal requirements for our marriage are being fast-tracked, so I have decided it would be best if you moved here to my suite until the wedding.'

'I—move in with you?' she repeated blankly. 'What are you talking about?'

'Finding a flat to rent for such a short time could be a problem,' he explained. His mouth curled slightly. 'But do not be too disturbed, *cara*. The suite has two large bedrooms.'

She said in a hollow voice, 'There are three of us. Four with Julie.'

'The *bambinaia* will work only in the daytime. At night, we will care for Carlino ourselves. You have been doing that since he was born,' he added. 'So it is scarcely a hardship. He can decide whose room he shares each evening.' He gave her a cool smile. 'An excellent arrangement, don't you think?'

Her voice shook. 'You don't want to know what I think.'

'Probably not,' he agreed drily. 'But you will not be forced to endure my company for too long. We shall leave for Italy and Comadora immediately after our wedding, and, once there, I will do my best to keep out of your way. In view of my work commitments, it should not be too difficult.'

Polly gave him a pleading look. 'Can't we do a deal over this? As it's only for a short time, couldn't Charlie and I stay at the flat?'

'Unfortunately that is impossible.' His hand closed over hers, his thumb stroking her soft palm, sending tiny tremors through her senses which she was unable to ignore or control. 'You see, *carissima*, I need you near to me,' he whispered huskily. 'Especially at night. Just in case you decided to try and escape me after all.'

At that moment, the waiter arrived back with their drinks, and a colleague came hurrying with menus and a wine list.

Polly withdrew her hand from his clasp, not trusting herself to speak, longing for a sliver of ice long and sharp enough to pierce her tormentor to the heart.

She took refuge behind her menu while she regained her equilibrium.

Last night had been bad enough, she thought broodingly. She'd never envisaged having to move in with him, but she realised now that she'd been naïve. There were probably plenty of other options, but his will was paramount, and he was letting her know it.

Yet he'd been so different once; gentle, humorous, patient—and adoring, or so she'd believed.

Now, she thought, wretchedness gnawing at her, it seemed that treacherous, deceitful and arrogant were more accurate descriptions.

He'd simply played the part of the sincere lover, as a ploy to keep her in his bed, trusting and eager, all summer long.

Yet, while she knew this, how was it possible that his lightest touch still had the power to stir her to the depths of her being, reigniting needs and longing that should be dead?

It was madness, and she needed to become sane again, or her existence, even on the outskirts of his life, would become intolerable.

She'd never felt less hungry in her life, but she knew she should eat something, so decided on consommé and chicken in wine sauce to follow. Fuel, she thought, for the next battle.

'So,' Sandro said when they were alone again, 'you will stay here with me, and no more arguments?'

She nodded abruptly, and he smiled at her. 'I am charmed by your obedience,' he told her, and raised his glass. 'Shall we drink to marital harmony?'

'No,' Polly said grittily, 'thank you. Not even in water.'

'Che peccato,' he said lightly. 'What a shame. Then, instead, let us drink to your earrings.' He put a hand out as if to touch one of the little cornflowers, and Polly shrank back.

He stared at her, his brows snapping together. When he spoke, his voice crackled with anger. 'Tell me, Paola, do you intend to cringe each time I come near you?'

'Isn't that the whole point?' she demanded huskily. 'I don't want you near me. You've promised to keep your distance, but can I believe you?'

'And how can I make you see that some contact between us is inevitable, and that you must accept it?' he asked coldly. 'I am letting it be known among my family and friends that we are reunited lovers.'

She said thickly, 'You can't expect me to go along with that. Not after everything that's happened...'

'I do expect it,' he said harshly. 'In fact, I insist on it. There is bound to be talk—even scandal—when our marriage, and our child, become public knowledge. I wish to minimise that for Carlino's sake. Make people believe that we were victims of fate who have been given a second chance together.'

She gave him a scornful look. 'That is such hypocrisy.'

'You would prefer to have the whole truth broadcast?' His voice bit. 'I can tell you my cousin Emilio would be delighted. He publishes a whole range of cheap gossip magazines, exposing secrets that the rich and famous would prefer to remain hidden.

'Until yesterday, he considered himself my heir, and will not be pleased to find himself demoted,' he added cuttingly. 'If he finds out that ours is simply a marriage of convenience, then our sleeping arrangements will be headline news in every trashy publication he puts on the streets. Is that what you want?'

'Oh, God.' Polly put down her glass. 'He couldn't, surely.'

'Think again,' he said. 'We have never liked each other, so he would do it and revel in it. So I prefer to safeguard my pride and my privacy, *cara mia*. And you would be well advised to co-operate too, unless you wish to feature as a discarded mistress—and the unwanted wife that Alessandro Valessi threw out of his bed. Is that what you choose?'

'No,' she said, staring down at the table. 'I—I don't want that.'

'Then play your part, and stop behaving as if I were a leper,' he told her. 'Because it bores me.' He paused. 'It also makes me wonder,' he added softly, 'what you would do if, some night, I—tested your resolve. *Capisce?*'

'Yes.' Her voice was a thread.

'*Bene.*' He gave her a swift, hard smile. 'Now let us go, happily united, into lunch.'

CHAPTER SIX

SHE walked into the restaurant beside him, moving like an automaton. His hand was under her arm as if she was in custody, as they followed the head waiter to yet another corner table.

'They have a new chef here,' Sandro told her as he took his place beside her. His sleeve, she realised, was only a few inches from her bare arm. Altogether too close for comfort. 'And the food is said to be very good,' he added.

'You seem to know a lot about it,' she said. 'Is this hotel part of the Comadora chain, by any chance?'

'We acquired it six months ago.'

'I see.' She played nervously with the cutlery. 'Will—will you tell me something?'

His gaze sharpened. 'If I can,' he said, after a pause.

'When we first met—why didn't you tell me who you really were? Why did you let me think you were simply a minor hotel employee?'

'Because that is exactly what I was,' he said. 'I had been travelling round all the hotels in the group to learn the trade, working in every department, so I could see what shape they were in.

'Traditionally my family has always been involved in agriculture and banking. The hotels were acquired in the nineteenth century by one of my ancestors who is said to have won them in a poker game.

'When my father inherited them, he wanted to get rid of them. He had no interest in tourism. But I felt differently. I thought managing the chain—updating and improving it—would be more interesting than citrus fruit and olive oil, or sitting in some air-conditioned office in Rome.

'So I was working incognito, and compiling a report that I hoped would convince my father to keep the hotels and invest in them.'

'But I wasn't involved with any hotels,' Polly protested. 'I worked for an independent tour company. You could have told me the truth.'

He said quietly, 'Paola, as the Valessi heir, I brought a lot of baggage with me. We are a wealthy family, and there had been women in my life whose sole priority was my money. I had become—wary.'

He spread his hands. 'You had no idea who I was, and yet you wanted me—for myself. For Sandro Domenico. I found that— irresistible. Can you understand that?'

'I understand.' There was a constriction in her throat. 'But your money must have been useful when you needed to be rid of— someone.'

His mouth hardened. 'Yes,' he said. 'In the end, it usually came down to—money.' He paused. 'Is that all you want to ask?'

'No.' She shook her head. 'I have a hundred questions. But I'm not sure you'd be prepared to answer them all.'

'No?' He sent her a meditative look. 'Try me.'

She took a deep breath. 'Well—the scar on your cheek. I was wondering how that happened.'

'I was in an accident,' he said expressionlessly. 'In the hills above Comadora. My car left the road on a bend and plunged into a ravine. I was thrown clear, but badly injured. My life was saved by a local man who found me, and administered some rough first aid before the ambulance got to me.'

It was a bald recital of the facts—something he'd clearly done many times before. He spoke as if it no longer had the power to affect him, but Polly could sense the tension in him.

She stared down at the immaculate white tablecloth. She said quietly, 'You were—lucky.'

You could have died, she thought, the breath catching in her throat. You could have been killed so easily. And I—I might never have known just how much I had to mourn.

'Yes,' he agreed. 'Fortunate, indeed.' His eyes were hooded as he looked at her. 'Do you require further details?'

Oh, God, Polly thought. I know what I have to ask—but I don't want to hear the answer.

She took a deep breath. She said, 'When did it happen? Was anyone else involved—in the crash?'

'Three years ago. I had a passenger,' he said levelly. 'A girl called Bianca DiMario. She—did not get clear.'

Polly stared at him, aware of the sudden chill spreading through her veins. She said hoarsely, 'That's—terrible.'

She wanted to stop there—to ask nothing more. But that was impossible, of course.

I have to go on, she thought, steeling herself. I—I have to know.

'You—you were close? You knew her well?' *She was a casual acquaintance? You were just giving her a lift? Please say that's all it was—please...*

'I had known her for most of my life,' he said quietly. 'She came to live at the *palazzo* with her aunt, the *contessa*, at my father's invitation. Bianca's parents were both dead, and the *contessa* was a widow who had been left with little money.

'My father had a strong sense of family, and he considered it a duty and an honour to care for them both.' He paused. 'Bianca was also intended to be the next Marchesa Valessi,' he added, evenly. 'The announcement of our engagement had been planned for the week after the accident.'

Polly was reduced to stricken silence as the pain returned, twisting inside her. She could see so clearly now why he'd had to get rid of her with such indecent haste—and offered such a high price to achieve that.

She'd become an embarrassment, she thought. Their affair an insult to his future wife.

She bent her head. 'I—I'm sorry,' she said huskily. 'It must have been utterly ghastly—to lose the girl you were going to marry in such a way.'

'Yes,' he said. 'It was the worst time of my life. Something I cannot let myself forget.' His faint smile was grim. 'So I keep the scar to remind me how I was robbed forever of my chance of happiness.'

How can I listen to this? she asked herself imploringly. How can I let him hurt me all over again? She wanted to throw herself at him, hitting him with her fists, and screaming that she mattered too.

She wanted to weep until she had no tears left.

With a supreme effort, she mastered herself.

'The accident,' she said. 'Does anyone know what caused it?' How could she speak normally—discuss this terrible thing when she was falling apart inside? When she had to face all over again that everything he'd ever said to her—promised her—had been a lie?

Sandro shrugged. 'The inquiry found a burst tyre on my car, so I was—exonerated. But I still have to live with the memory.'

And I, Polly thought, shall have to live with your betrayal of me—and I don't know if I can do that. I think you may be asking the impossible.

She met his gaze. 'Bigamy,' she said clearly. 'Is that another Valessi family tradition? Because you seem to have been engaged to two women at one time.'

He sighed harshly. 'I should never have let things go so far, and I know it.' His mouth twisted. 'Believe me, I have been well punished for my silence.'

'Bianca.' She forced herself to say the name. 'Did she—know about me?'

A muscle moved beside his mouth. 'Yes.' One small, uncompromising word.

'I see,' she said. She was silent for a moment. 'So—I was the only fool.'

'No,' he said. 'I meant to tell you everything. To explain, and ask you to forgive me. But then the crash came, and after that— everything changed.' His smile was icy. 'As you know.'

'Yes,' Polly said almost inaudibly. She paused. 'It must have been awful for the *contessa* too—to lose her niece.' She forced a smile. 'No wonder she doesn't like me.'

He sighed again. 'Paola *mia*, Bianca has been dead for three years. Zia Antonia has to accept that.'

'And she still lives at the *palazzo*—in spite of it all?'

'Of course,' he said. 'I could hardly ask her to leave. Besides, I am often away, and she currently manages the house and estate for me.'

'So she's bound to have constant reminders of Bianca.' Polly hesitated. 'And three years isn't all that long—when you care deeply for someone.' She took a breath. 'After all, you must think about her too.'

She saw his face harden, his hand lift as if to touch his scarred cheek, then fall again.

'*Sì,*' he said harshly. 'I think about her. And three years can seem an eternity.'

I asked for that, Polly thought wretchedly. A self-inflicted wound.

She said in a low voice, 'I'm sorry. I shouldn't have pried.'

'You had to know,' he said. 'And I wished to explain. But up to now, you have shown no curiosity about the past.' His mouth twisted. 'Who knows? I might have spent all these years in the Regina Coeli prison for robbery with violence.' He put his hand briefly over hers. 'So, is there nothing else you wish to ask me?'

For a moment, she thought she detected a note of pleading in his voice. But that was ridiculous. Sandro had never pleaded in his life.

And there were questions teeming in her brain, falling over themselves to escape. But she knew she could not bear to hear the answers. The news about Bianca had been as much as she could take today.

She shook her head. 'There's nothing I need to know. After all, it's not as if ours will be a real marriage. It's just an arrangement, for Charlie's sake. So, it's better if we can keep our lives separate—and private.'

He was silent for a moment, then he inclined his head almost wryly. 'As you wish.'

The food when it came was delicious, but Polly might as well have been chewing sawdust. She had to force every mouthful past the tightness in her throat, helped down by the Orvieto Classico he'd chosen. Because she couldn't allow Sandro to glimpse her inner agony.

He broke my heart once, she thought. I can't allow him to do that again. Especially when I know that he could—all too easily. And she sighed quietly.

When the largely silent meal was finally over, Polly found her next ordeal was accompanying Sandro up to the penthouse to inspect her temporary home.

She'd hoped she would find some insoluble problem with the accommodation, but the bright, airy rooms with their masses of fresh flowers seemed just about perfect.

To her unspoken relief, the bedrooms were well apart, facing each other from opposite sides of the large and luxurious drawing room. And each had its own bathroom, so she could hardly complain about a lack of privacy.

'Will you be comfortable here?' he asked, watching her prowl around. 'I hope it has everything you want.'

'Everything,' she said. 'Except the freedom to make decisions, and live my own life.'

'A trifle, surely.' Sandro's tone was solemn, but his eyes were glinting in sudden amusement. 'When the cage you occupy is so beautifully gilded. Also unlocked.' He produced a key from his pocket. 'For your bedroom door,' he said. 'In case I walk in my sleep.'

Her heart missed a beat, but she spoke lightly. 'You'd soon wake up when Charlie started yelling.' She glanced at her watch. 'When are we picking him up from your friends? Time's moving on, and I still have to go back to the flat and pack our things.'

'I have arranged for two of the girls from Administration here to do that for you,' Sandro said calmly, meeting her fulminating gaze head-on. 'I told them to bring the minimum. I will have the remainder suitably disposed of.'

'My God,' she said furiously. 'You take a lot upon yourself. Is this part of your campaign to force me to buy new clothes?'

He smiled at her. 'No, I am relying on Teresa to do that,' he said. 'She cannot wait to take you shopping.'

'I can buy my own damned things,' Polly threw at him. 'And I don't need a minder.'

'I hope she will be much more than that,' he told her with a trace of chill. 'Her husband is one of my greatest friends, and I was best man at their wedding. They have been—good to me in return.'

He paused. 'You are going to a new life, Paola, with its own demands. As my wife, you will be expected to patronise Italian designers. How many do you know? What formal clothes will you need? How many dinner dresses—how many ballgowns?

'This is a world Teresa knows, and you can trust her advice.' He paused. 'She can also help you in another way. Before she married Ernesto, she worked as a linguist. So you may practice speaking Italian to her. Start to regain your former fluency.'

Her face warmed suddenly as she recalled precisely how that proficiency had been acquired during those long, hot afternoons a lifetime ago. The things he had whispered to her as she lay in his arms—and taught her to say to him in return.

She was suddenly aware that he was watching her, observing

the play of embarrassed colour on her skin, before he added softly and cynically, 'But with a rather different vocabulary, *carissima.*'

She said with deliberate coldness, 'Do you have any other orders for me?'

He was unfazed. 'If I think of any, I will let you know.'

'How nice it must be,' she said, 'to always get your own way. Think about it.' She ticked off on her fingers. 'You need an heir—you have one ready-made. You require somewhere convenient to keep us—and you own a hotel with a vacant suite. You don't wish to be married—and you find a wife who doesn't want to be anywhere near you either. You're ahead on all points.'

'Am I, *bella mia*?' His tone was cordial. 'How interesting that you should think so. But perhaps you should refrain from mentioning my good fortune to Teresa and Ernesto. They might not agree with you.'

He paused. 'One more thing before we go to meet them.' He reached into the inside pocket of his jacket and extracted a small velvet box.

As he opened it, Polly drew an unsteady breath at the coruscating fire from the enormous diamond it contained.

'Give me you hand.' It was a command, not a request, but she still hesitated.

'Surely—this isn't necessary...'

'On the contrary, it is essential,' Sandro contradicted her. 'So—*per favore...*'

Mutely, reluctantly, she allowed him to slide the ring onto her finger. A moment, she thought in anguish, that she'd imagined so many times during the summer of their love. But not like this. Never like this.

Her voice shook slightly. 'It's—beautiful.'

At the same time its dazzling brilliance seemed almost alien on her workaday hand, she thought, making her feel like some latter-day Cinderella.

But Sandro was no Prince Charming, she reminded herself soberly. And his diamond was altogether too magnificent a symbol of the cold, sterile bargain they had made with each other.

As if Sandro had read her thoughts, he said quietly, 'You will soon accustom yourself to wearing it.'

She bent her head. 'Along with everything else, it seems.'

'There will be compensations,' he told her. 'Tomorrow I shall open a bank account for you.'

She shook her head almost violently. 'I don't want that.'

'*Dio mio.*' His voice was weary. 'Paola, do you have to fight me each step of the way? Do you wish our child to be brought up in a battlefield?'

She looked away. 'No, of course not.'

'Then please try and accept the arrangements that must be made.'

'I can—try,' she said unsteadily. 'But it's not easy when your whole world has suddenly been—turned upside down.'

'You think you are alone in that?' There was a note of harsh derision in his voice. 'I too am obliged to make—adjustments.'

'But you don't have to.' She faced him with new determination, hands clenched at her sides. 'I—I understand that you need to see Charlie, to spend time with him, and I swear I'll co-operate in any way over this. But why tie yourself to an unwanted marriage when you could meet someone to love—someone who knows how to be a *marchesa*?' She paused. 'Someone the *contessa* might even approve of.'

'You think that is an essential quality in my bride?' His mouth twisted.

'I think that, otherwise, there'll be problems,' Polly said flatly. 'You must see that. After all, she runs your home—and she'll see me as an interloper. A poor substitute for the girl she loved.'

'Then she too will have to adjust.' His voice hardened. 'Believe this, Paola. My son will grow up in my home with the knowledge that his mother is my wife. Nothing else will do—either for him, or for the world at large.'

He walked to the door, and held it open. 'Now begin to play your part. My friends expect to meet a girl happily reunited with her lover—so pretend,' he added flatly. '*Avanti.*'

The serial killer was on the move, and the heroine was alone in her apartment, with a thunderstorm growling overhead. Any minute now she was going to run herself a bath or take a shower, Polly thought wearily, because that was what always happened.

I need, she thought, blanking out the television screen with one terse click of the remote control, to be distracted, not irritated.

She also wanted to relax—but her inner tensions were not so easily dispelled.

Besides, she could do without artificial horrors. Her mind was full enough already of disturbing sounds and images—bleached rock in the blazing sun, the squeal of tyres, the screech of brakes and wrenched metal. A girl screaming in fright, and then an even more terrifying silence, with Sandro lying unconscious and bleeding under a pitiless sky.

Perhaps this was why she was still up and restless, when common sense suggested she should be in bed, with Charlie fast asleep in his cot near by. She'd wondered if he would react badly to his new surroundings, but he'd settled with little more than a token protest.

Perhaps I should be more like him, Polly thought with a grimace. Learn to deal with six impossible things before breakfast.

However, liking Teresa and Ernesto had not proved impossible at all. She was tall, and slim as a wand, with long dark hair and laughing eyes. And although she was the epitome of chic, that did not stop her indulging in a rough-and-tumble on the floor with Charlie and the twins.

Ernesto was quieter, with a plain, kind face, observing his wife and children with doting fondness through his silver-rimmed glasses.

In other circumstances, Polly would have loved to have them as friends. As it was, she felt a total fraud. And sitting next to Sandro on one of the deeply cushioned sofas in their drawing room, with his arm draped casually round her shoulders, had proved unnervingly difficult.

Blissfully married herself, Teresa, left alone with Polly, had made it clear that she thought Sandro was glamorous and sexy beyond belief, in spite of his scarred face, and that she was assisting at the romance of the century.

And even if I told her that marrying Sandro was simply a rubber stamp on a legal arrangement I want no part of, Polly thought sadly, she wouldn't believe me.

'Ah, but shopping will be such fun, *cara*,' Teresa had told her buoyantly. 'Particularly as Alessandro has put no limit on our spending,' she added with glee.

And although she must have been brimming with curiosity

about Sandro and Polly's former relationship, she nobly refrained from asking questions that her guest might find difficult to answer.

There had been only one awkward moment, when Teresa had been admiring Polly's engagement ring. 'A diamond?' she exclaimed. 'But I thought...' She encountered a swift glance from Ernesto, and hastily went on, 'I thought, as your bride has green eyes, you would have chosen an emerald for her. Or do you believe they are unlucky? Some people do, I think. And a diamond is forever, no?'

Sandro had smiled lazily. 'Forever,' he agreed.

But Polly found herself wondering what Teresa had meant to say.

'So, was that such a hardship?' he'd asked as their chauffeur-driven car took them back to the hotel, with Charlie bouncing between them.

'No,' she admitted. 'They were lovely. I hate making fools of them like this.'

He gave her a dry look. 'Do not underestimate Teresa, *cara*. She is a shrewd lady.'

Is she? Polly thought. Yet she clearly thinks Sandro and I will be having an intimate dinner for two in our suite, followed by a rapturous night in each other's arms. How wrong can anyone be?

'Then I'll take care to be extra-careful,' she said. She paused. 'Why did she query my engagement ring being a diamond?'

'You noticed,' Sandro gave a shrug. 'She would expect you to wear the Valessi ruby, which is traditionally passed to each bride.'

'But not to me.'

'No,' he said, his mouth hardening. 'It was found in the wreckage of the car. My father had it buried with Bianca.'

'I see.' She swallowed. 'Well, that's—understandable.' She paused, desperate for a change of subject. 'I—I wonder if the box containing my life has been delivered yet?'

He looked at her thoughtfully. 'That has made you angry,' he said. 'Which was not my intention. I thought I had simply relieved you of a tedious job.'

'It would have been,' she admitted. She forced a smile. 'I'm just accustomed to my independence.'

'Then it may please you to know that you will not be burdened with my presence at dinner tonight,' he told her drily. 'I am going out. Would you prefer to dine in the suite, or go down to the restaurant?'

'I'll stay in the suite. It will be better for Charlie.'

'As you wish. I will arrange for Room Service to bring you a menu.'

Polly wondered where he was planning to spend the evening, but knew she could never ask. Because she did not have the right. This was the life she had agreed to for Charlie's sake. A life of silences. No questions asked, or information volunteered. A life where to be blind and deaf might be a positive advantage.

'I shall come to say goodnight to Carlino before I leave,' he added. 'If you permit, of course.'

'I can hardly prevent you.'

'You have a key to your room,' he reminded her. 'There could be a locked door between us.'

Yes, Polly had thought, her mouth drying. But would that really keep you out, if you wanted to come in?

Remembering that now, she got up with a shiver, and, walking over to the long glass doors which opened on to the balcony, she pushed them open and stepped out into the sultry night, tightening the sash on the towelling robe as she did so.

Her elderly, much-loved cotton dressing gown had not survived the Great Pack, so she'd had to use the one hanging on the bathroom door in its plastic cover. She missed her old robe badly. She'd had it for years—even taken it to Italy with her, when she worked for the travel company, and now it was gone. Like a symbol of her old life, she thought sadly.

But at least they'd brought Charlie's blue blanket—and the brown teddy bear, both of them now adorning his cot. She would have to find something else to comfort herself with.

How peaceful everything looked in the moonlight, she thought, leaning on the stone balustrade. How normal. And how deceptive appearances could be.

She would not be welcome at Comadora, and she knew it. The *contessa* would be bound to resent her savagely, but at least she knew she had not imagined the older woman's hostility to her.

It was probable that Bianca had confided her hurt over Sandro's affair to her aunt. And now the *contessa* had to watch the hated mistress elevated to wife.

I'd hate me too, she thought soberly. But it's still going to be a problem.

She turned restlessly to go back inside, and cannoned into Sandro, who had come, silent and completely unsuspected, to stand behind her.

She recoiled with a little cry, and immediately his hands gripped her arms to steady her.

'Forgive me,' he said quietly. 'I did not mean to startle you.'

She freed herself, her heart thudding. 'I—I didn't expect to see you.'

His brows lifted. 'You thought I would celebrate our *fidanzamento* by staying out all night,' he asked ironically.

Polly lifted her chin. 'Even if you did,' she said, 'it would be no concern of mine. Do whatever you want.'

'You are giving me permission to stray, *cara mia*?' Sandro drawled. 'How enlightened of you, but totally unnecessary. Because I shall, indeed, do as I please.' He paused. 'I thought you would be in bed.'

'I'm just going,' she said hastily.

She wanted to escape. With his arrival, the night was suddenly too warm and the balcony too enclosed as if the balustrade and surrounding walls had shrunk inwards.

And Sandro was too close to her, almost but not quite touching. She felt a bead of sweat trickle between her breasts, and dug her nails into the palms of her hands.

'Then before you do, perhaps you will allow me to steal another look at my son.'

'Of course,' Polly said, edging past him into the living room. 'And he's my son too,' she added over her shoulder.

'I have not forgotten,' he said. 'What were you doing out there, Paola? Gazing at the moon?'

'Just—thinking.' She paused, looking down at the floor. 'Will—will the *contessa* be returning for the wedding?'

'No,' he said. 'She will remain at the *palazzo* to make sure everything is ready for our arrival.'

'And afterwards?'

He paused. 'She will stay, at least until you are ready to take over the running of the household.'

'Or even longer?' She still did not look at him.

'Perhaps.' He sighed. 'Paola, my father promised her a home.

Out of respect for his memory, I cannot honourably deprive her of it, unless she wishes to go, no matter what has happened.' He paused. 'I hope you can accept that.'

'It seems I shall have to.' *And more easily than she will ever accept me...*

She turned and walked into her dimly lit bedroom. Sandro followed, and stood by the cot, an expression of such tenderness on his face that her heart turned over.

She thought, Once he looked at me like that, and winced at the wave of desolation that swept over her. Ridiculous reaction, she told herself fiercely. Unforgivable, too.

She went back to the door and waited, her arms hugged defensively round her body.

Sandro looked at her meditatively on his way past to the living room.

'Yes?' She felt suddenly nervous, and her voice was more challenging than she intended. 'You have something to say?'

'Our son,' he said quietly. 'How curious to think we should have made a child between us, when, now, you cannot even bear to stand next to me.' His voice changed suddenly—became low, almost urgent. 'How can this have happened, Paola *mia*? Why are you so scared to be alone with me? So frightened that I may touch you?'

'I'm not scared,' Polly began, but he cut across her.

'Do not lie to me.' There was a hard intensity in his tone. 'You were a virgin when you came to me, yet, even then, you never held back. From that first moment, you were so warm—so willing in my arms that I thought my heart would burst with the joy of you.'

Oh, God, she thought wildly. *Oh, dear God...*

She could feel the slow burn of heat rising within her at his words, at the mcmories they engendered, and had to fight to keep her voice deliberately cool and clear.

'But that,' she said, 'was when I was in love with you. It—makes—quite a difference.'

Her words seemed to drop like stones into the sudden well of silence between them. The air seemed full of a terrible stillness that reached out into a bleak eternity.

Polly felt her body quiver with tension. She had provided the lightning flash, and now she was waiting for the anger of the storm to break.

But when he spoke, his voice was calm. 'Of course,' he said. 'You are right. It—changes everything. I am obliged to you for the reminder. *Grazie* and goodnight.'

She was aware of him moving, turning away. Then, a moment later, she heard his own door open and close, and knew she was alone. And safe again.

Her held breath escaped her on a long, trembling sigh.

She'd had a lucky escape and she knew it. Now all she had to deal with was the deep ache of traitorous longing that throbbed inside her.

But she could cope, she told herself, shivering. She had things to do. Clothes to buy. Italian lessons to learn. Long days with Charlie to enjoy for the first time since he was a baby.

So much to keep her busy and banish all those long-forbidden thoughts, and desires. And, for her own sake, she should make a start at once. Telephone Teresa in the morning. Make a list of all the books she'd not had time to read. She could even have parcels of them, she thought, sent to her in Italy. She might even book for a theatre matinée, now that she had a nanny. Go to the cinema. Something. Anything.

While, at the same time, she underwent the painful process of turning herself into some stranger—the Marchesa Valessi. The wife that no one wanted—least of all Sandro himself.

CHAPTER SEVEN

'So,' TERESA said, 'in two days you will be married. It is exciting, no?'

'Wonderful,' Polly agreed in a hollow voice.

She didn't feel like a bride, she thought, staring at herself in the mirror, although the hugely expensive cream linen dress which Teresa had persuaded her to buy, and which would take her on to the airport and her new life after the ceremony, was beautifully cut and clung to her slenderness as if it adored her, managing to be stunning and practical at the same time. While her high-heeled strappy shoes were to die for.

It wasn't just the usual trappings of tulle and chiffon that were missing, she thought. It was radiance she lacked.

And at any moment, Teresa would be ordering her to relax, because otherwise the tension in her body would spoil the perfect line of her dress. But the other girl would never understand in a million years that this was not merely bridal nerves, but sheer, blind panic.

Since their confrontation on her first night in the hotel Sandro had taken her at her word and left her strictly to her own devices, except when they were with Teresa and Ernesto, when he continued to play the part of the charming, attentive bridegroom.

On the other occasions when they encountered each other, he was polite but aloof. But these were rare. Except for the sacrosanct hours he devoted to Charlie, he spent very little time at the hotel.

Well, she could not fault him for obeying her wishes, she thought. But she alone knew that she was lonely, and that her sense of isolation would only increase once she reached Comadora.

'Now take the dress off and hang it away,' Teresa cautioned. 'Sandro must not see you in it before the wedding.' She paused. 'Is all well with you, Paola? You are quiet today.'

Polly stepped out of the dress, and slipped it onto a padded hanger. 'Well, for one thing, there's Julie.'

'Oh?' Teresa's eyes twinkled. 'Has she fallen in love with Alessandro?'

'No, of course not,' Polly said. 'At least, I don't think so.'

Teresa giggled. 'They all do. I had a nanny from Australia when the twins were born, and each time Alessandro came into the house she would go pink—like a carnation—and refuse to speak for hours.'

Polly's brows lifted. 'And how did he react?'

'*Ahime,* he did not even notice.' Teresa shrugged. 'It is endearing how little vanity he has in such matters.'

'Well, his arrogance in other ways more than compensates for that,' Polly said crisply, zipping herself into a pretty blue shift dress.

'You would not think so if you had known his father, the Marchese Domenico,' said Teresa. 'Now, there was a supreme autocrat. And of course that old witch he brought to the house after his wife died encouraged him to think he could do no wrong. She and Bianca, her secret weapon.'

Polly put her wedding dress away in the wardrobe. She said, 'What was she like—Bianca? Was she beautiful?'

'An angel.' Teresa waved a languid hand. 'A dove. Submissive and so sweet. I longed to bite her and see if there was honey in her veins instead of blood. And taught by nuns,' she added darkly. 'She wore her purity like a sword—every inch of her being saved for the marriage bed.'

She sighed. 'No wonder Alessandro looked for amusement elsewhere.' She stopped dead, clapping a hand over her mouth, looking at Polly in round-eyed horror. '*Dio,* Paola. My mouth will be my death. Forgive me—please.'

Polly sat down at her dressing table, and ran a comb through her hair. She said quietly, 'There's nothing to forgive. I'm really under no illusion about Sandro—or myself.'

'*Cara,*' Teresa shot off the bed where she'd been sprawling, and came to kneel beside Polly. 'Listen to me. Ernesto—myself—every friend Sandro has—we are so happy that you are together. And that you have given him a son that he adores. Let the past rest. It does not matter.'

'Bianca died,' Polly said. 'That makes it matter.'

'You think he wished to marry her?' Teresa demanded. 'No, and no. It was the *contessa,* who saw to it that Bianca had the old *marchese* twisted round her little finger. With Sandro, he was always harsh, but Bianca was his sweetheart, his darling child. And Bianca wanted Alessandro.'

'Yet you say they weren't lovers.'

Teresa gave her a worldly look. 'But whose choice was that? Ernesto, who has known Alessandro since they were children, told me that she used to watch him constantly—try always to be near him. He said—forgive me, this is not nice, and Ernesto is never unkind—that she was like a bitch on heat.' She shrugged. 'And for her, he was unattainable.'

'Then why did he agree to marry her?'

'His parents' marriage had been an arranged one,' Teresa said. 'It was made clear to him what was expected of him in turn. And perhaps he felt it was a way to please his father at last. He was only twelve when his mother died, and after that his relationship with the *marchese* became even more troubled. And Sandro was wild when he was younger,' she added candidly.

She gave Polly a serious look. 'But you can understand, *cara*, why his relationship with Carlino is so important to him. Why he wishes to make his own son feel loved and secure.'

'Yes,' Polly said quietly. 'I can—see that.'

Teresa got to her feet, brushing the creases from her skirt. 'But you were telling me of Julie. There is some problem?'

'She's having some time off this afternoon to go for a job interview.' Polly sighed. 'Apparently, she's only on a temporary contract with us, which lasts until we get to Italy and then Sandro's staff take over, and she flies back. I—I'm going to miss her badly, and so will Charlie. And she's someone I can talk to in my own language.'

'Then ask him if you may keep her on.' Teresa shrugged. 'It is quite simple.' She gave Polly a wicked grin. 'I am sure that you can persuade him, *cara*. Do as I do. Wait until you are in bed, and you have made him very happy. He will give you anything. And the rest of the servants will be pacified when they have your other *bambini* to care for.'

Polly's blush deepened painfully, but she made herself speak lightly. 'That's the kind of cunning plan I like.'

The way things were between them, he was more likely to fire Julie instantly, she thought ruefully when Teresa had gone. But she could always ask, although it wouldn't be in the way the other girl had suggested.

Not that she had the opportunity for the rest of the day. In the afternoon, she went to visit her parents in a last-ditch effort to get them to come to the wedding.

But Mrs Fairfax, still in her dressing gown and looking pale and wan, was adamant, insisting she wasn't well enough to go, and needed her husband with her in case of emergency.

And she alarmed Charlie by hugging him too tightly, and weeping.

Polly got back to the hotel feeling as if she'd been run down by a train, her only comfort her father's quiet, 'She'll come round, sweetheart. She just needs time.'

Sandro was out, and, although she planned to tackle him about Julie on his return, he was still missing by the time she eventually admitted defeat and went to bed.

He was spending the eve of his wedding with Teresa and Ernesto, who were going to act as their witnesses, so she would just have to catch him first thing in the morning before he left, she told herself.

Charlie had already been collected by Julie, and taken down to the dining room for breakfast, when she woke, so she had the bathroom to herself.

She bathed and put on one of her new dresses—primrose silk with a scooped neck, and slightly flared skirt. Nailing her colours to the mast, she thought with faint defiance as she crossed the drawing room to his door.

'*Avanti.*' The response to her knock was cool and casual, and Polly, drawing a deep breath, opened the door and went in.

The curtains were drawn back, filling the room with sunlight, and Sandro was in bed, lying back against the piled-up pillows, reading a newspaper and drinking coffee from the breakfast trolley beside him. His skin looked like mahogany against the pristine dazzle of the white bed linen.

He glanced up, his brows snapping together as he saw her.

'*Buongiorno,*' he murmured after a pause. 'You will forgive me if I do not get up,' he added, indicating the sheet draped over his hips which was quite clearly his only covering. 'Would you like coffee?'

'No, thank you.' Polly shifted uneasily from one foot to the other, praying she would not blush, and wondering if it was possible to look at someone without actually seeing them. And certainly without staring. And particularly without feeling that treacherous excitement slowly uncurling inside her. 'I've had breakfast.'

'How virtuous of you, *cara*,' he drawled. 'They bring an extra cup each morning, presumably because they hope I will eventually get lucky. I think I shall have to tell them to stop.' He refilled his own cup. 'So—to what do I owe this extraordinary pleasure?'

Polly gritted her teeth. 'I—I've come to ask you a favour.'

His brows rose. 'You fascinate me, *bella mia*. Especially when you choose my bedroom to make your request.'

'Well, don't read anything into that,' Polly said shortly. 'It's just that I seem to see so little of you these days.'

Sandro moved, stretching slowly and indolently, letting the concealing sheet slip a little. 'You are seeing enough of me this morning, *carissima*,' he drawled. 'Or do you want more?'

She glared at him. 'No.'

'You disappoint me,' he murmured. 'But if it is not my body, I presume it is money. How much do you want?'

'Money?' Polly repeated in bewilderment. 'Of course it isn't. I haven't spent half the allowance you made me.'

'I would not grudge more.' Folding his arms behind his head, Sandro studied her through half-closed eyes, frankly absorbing the cling of the silk to her body, a faint smile curving his mouth. 'You seem to be spending it wisely.'

She flushed under his scrutiny. 'Thank you—I think.'

'*Prego.*' He continued to watch her. 'I hope you do not wish me to persuade your mother to attend the wedding. I should hate to disappoint you.'

She bit her lip. 'No. I've accepted that it's a lost cause. Besides, she wouldn't listen to you. You—you seem to make her nervous.'

'*Mi dispiace,*' he returned without any real sign of regret. 'I seem to have the same effect on you, *cara mia*. So—what is it?'

She swallowed. 'I'd like Julie to stay in Italy with us, and go on looking after Charlie—please.'

Sandro moved slightly, adjusting the sheet to a more respectable level. He sent her a meditative look.

He said, 'Paola, I have a houseful of staff who are dancing for joy at the prospect of looking after the future *marchese*. He will not lack for attention, I promise you.'

'No,' she said. 'But he's used to Julie, and he likes her. Anyway, the others will speak Italian to him, and he might feel lost at first.' She hesitated. 'And I like Julie too, and I can talk to her in English. In spite of Teresa's coaching, I'm going to feel pretty isolated.'

'*Davvero?*' His tone was sardonic. 'You do not feel that you could talk to me, perhaps?'

That was what Teresa had said, she thought, biting her lip again. She looked at the floor. 'That isn't very likely,' she said constrictedly. 'After all, we're not marrying for any kind of companionship, but for Charlie's sake.'

'Does one rule out the other?' He was frowning slightly.

'I think it has to,' Polly countered, with a touch of desperation. 'And after all, you—you won't always be there,' she added, feeling dejectedly that she was losing the argument. 'You have your work—your own life to lead.'

'No,' he said, quietly. 'That is true.' He shrugged a naked shoulder. '*Va bene.* If that is what you want, I agree.'

'Oh.' Polly found herself blinking. 'Well—thank you.'

'Is that all? I am disappointed.' The topaz eyes glinted at her. 'I was hoping for a more—tangible expression of gratitude.'

Polly stiffened. 'I don't think I understand.'

'And I think you do.' He smiled at her, and held out a hand in invitation. 'Is one kiss too much to ask?'

She wanted to tell him to go to hell, but there was too much riding on this transaction.

She said coldly, 'You're not as generous as I thought.'

'And nor are you, *carissima*,' he said gently. 'Which is why I have so far asked for so little. Besides, you will have to kiss me tomorrow at the wedding. It is tradition.' His smile widened. 'And you certainly need the practice.'

There was a taut silence, then Polly trod awkwardly to the side of the bed. Ignoring his proffered hand, she bent to brush his cheek with swift, unyielding lips.

But before she could straighten, Sandro had grasped her wrists in an unbreakable hold, and she was being drawn inexorably downwards, losing her balance in the process. She found she was being turned skilfully, so that she was lying across his body, the outrage in her eyes meeting the mockery in his. Mockery mingled with something altogether more disturbing. Something that, in spite of herself, every pulse in her body leapt to meet.

He said softly, 'But I will not settle for as little as that, Paola *mia*.'

And her instinctive cry of protest was stifled by the warmth of his mouth on hers.

He kissed her deeply and thoroughly, holding her imprisoned in one arm, while his other hand twined in her hair to hold her still, defeating any attempt she might make to struggle. Forcing her to endure the sensuous and unashamedly possessive invasion of his tongue, as his mouth moved on hers in sheer and unashamed enticement.

Robbing her, she realised numbly, of any real desire to fight him. Awakening very different memories—and longings.

The heat of the sun pouring through the window—the unforgettable scent of his naked skin—the pressure of his lithe, muscular body against hers sent the last three years rolling back, and they were lovers again, their bodies aching and melting to be joined together in the ultimate intimacy, yet deliberately holding back to prolong the sweetness of the final moments.

He had always wooed her with kisses, she remembered dazedly, arousing her with a patient, passionate tenderness that splintered her control, and sent her reason spinning, so that she clung to him mutely imploring his possession.

Why else had she been unable to see that bringing her to eager, quivering acquiescence was the work of a practised seducer?

Yet even now, it seemed, she was unable to resist him, or the sensual magic of his lips.

When he lifted his head she was breathless, her heart thudding unevenly against her ribcage—which he must have known, because his hand had moved and was gently cupping her breast, his thumb stroking her hardening nipple to a rapturous peak through the silk of her dress.

He looked down at her, his eyes glittering and intent, asking a question which she was too scared and confused to answer. She only knew that if he kissed her again, she would be lost. And as he bent to her once more, a soft moan, half-fear, half-yearning, parted her lips.

And then, swiftly and shockingly, it was over, as the telephone beside the bed suddenly rang, its stridency shattering the heated intensity within the room like a fist through a pane of glass.

Sandro swore softly and fluently, but his hold on her relaxed, and she forced herself out of his embrace and off the bed, and ran to the door.

She flew across the intervening space, snatching at the door handle to her own bedroom, but as she did so it opened anyway, and she half fell into the room beyond.

As she struggled to recover her balance, there was a cry of 'Mammina' and Charlie, looking angelic, came scampering towards her from the bathroom, with Julie close behind.

'He had a little accident with his cereal this morning,' she told Polly, trying to look severe. 'I've just had to change his top and trousers. You wouldn't believe how far he can spread one small bowl.'

As Polly bent to him, fighting for calm, the door opposite was flung wide, and Sandro came striding towards them, his face like thunder, tying the belt of a robe he'd clearly thrown on as an afterthought.

Polly scooped Charlie up in her arms, and turned to face him defensively.

He halted, staring at her, his ominous frown deepening. He said in Italian, 'We need to talk, you and I. Now.'

'There's nothing to talk about,' Polly said, nervously aware that Julie had vanished with discreet haste back into the bathroom. She reverted to her own language. 'I should have known I couldn't trust you.'

His mouth twisted contemptuously. 'No,' he said. 'I think, my beautiful hypocrite, that you realised you could not trust yourself. It is that simple. So why, for once in your life, can't you be honest?'

He took a step towards her, and she recoiled, still clutching Charlie, who was beginning to wriggle. She said hoarsely, 'Don't touch me. Don't dare to come near me. You—you promised to leave me alone.'

'That will be my pleasure,' Sandro hit back. 'Now, be silent. You are frightening our son.' Charlie was squirming round, his lip trembling, holding out his arms to his father, and Sandro took him from her, soothing the little boy quietly.

He said, 'He will spend the day with me. I will telephone to say when he may be collected.' He carried him back to his own room, where he turned and looked back at Polly, his eyes icy with warning.

He said too softly, 'And, as long as you live, *signorina*, never— never again use our child as a barrier between us.'

The door closed behind them both, leaving Polly shaking and alone in the middle of the room.

'Are you all right, Miss Fairfax?' Julie was regarding her anxiously from the doorway.

Polly mustered her reserves. 'Yes,' she lied. 'Fine. A—a misunderstanding, that's all.'

'I thought at first that the *marchese* had come to give you the good news,' Julie said. 'He spoke to me as I was going off duty yesterday evening, and suggested that I should go to Italy as well, to help Charlie to settle in. Isn't that great? I was going to tell you myself, first thing, only his lordship there did his trick with the cereal.'

Polly's hands slowly curled into fists. He knew, she thought, fury uncurling inside her. He knew exactly what I was going to ask, and used it against me. A ploy to get me into bed with him. And—dear God—I was almost fool enough to fall for it. To give in.

'Miss Fairfax?' Julie was looking puzzled. 'I thought you'd be pleased.'

'Yes,' Polly said, summoning a hurried smile. 'I'm delighted. That's—absolutely wonderful. Just what we both wanted.'

She paused. 'And Charlie's spending the day with his father, so you have some free time to go and pack for the Campania. Mind you take a couple of bikinis too,' she added over-brightly. 'Apparently the *palazzo* has a pool.'

Julie's face lit up. 'Well—if you don't mind...'

When the other girl had gone, Polly walked over to one of the sofas and sat for a long time, with her face buried in her hands.

She was angry, but her anger was mixed with guilt too. It was wrong of her to use Charlie like that, but the truth was she hadn't dared allow Sandro to touch her again. Or come within a yard of her, for that matter.

As it was, she felt sick with shame at how easily he'd drawn a response from her. And how her unfulfilled body now felt torn apart by frustration. Like the first time he had made love to her, she thought wretchedly, when she'd been wild for him, his caresses exciting her to the point of desperation. When, at last, he'd entered her, her body had been molten with need, and there'd been no pain.

Just a rapturous sense of total completion, she thought wretchedly. And what she'd believed was utter love.

I know better now, she told herself, her mind raw. I know he was just using me for sex—nothing more, but that's something I'll learn to live with.

But I can't let it happen ever again—and I won't.

She hadn't taken his money, she thought harshly. Nor would she accept the false coin of his lovemaking, no matter what the cost to her as a woman. And no matter how she might ache for him, as she did now.

The next day, she married Sandro in a ceremony so brief she could hardly believe it was legal. As they were pronounced man and wife, and he turned to her, she closed her eyes, bracing herself for the promised kiss, only to feel his lips brush her cheek swiftly and coldly.

As she stepped back she glimpsed Teresa and Ernesto exchanging astonished glances, and moved to them to be hugged with real warmth. Teresa drew her to one side. 'A little gift, *cara*,' she whispered, handing her a flat parcel, wrapped in silver tissue with violet ribbons. 'Do not open it now. Wait until tonight.'

Polly forced a smile of thanks, and put the package in the soft leather shoulder bag which served as her hand luggage.

There were no problems on the flight itself. Polly had never travelled first class before, and sitting in comfort, being served champagne, at least gave a veneer of celebration to the day's proceedings.

Charlie chatted in wonder about 'big planes', gave an imitation of a jumbo jet taking off, then fell asleep, but he awoke grouchily when they reached Naples, and the subsequent journey soon disintegrated into nightmare.

Polly discovered, dismayed, that her son did not enjoy travelling by car, even an air-conditioned limousine, and that he was constantly and miserably sick throughout the trip.

Every few miles they were forced to stop, so that Charlie could be cleaned up and comforted, and eventually Julie, who'd borne the brunt of the little boy's misery, was sent to sit in the passenger seat beside the chauffeur, and Sandro took her place, cradling Charlie on his lap and talking to him gently.

'Why not give him back to me?' Polly suggested, aware that her linen dress was already ruined. 'I'm worried that he'll spoil your beautiful suit,' she added awkwardly.

He gave her a look of faint impatience. '*Che importa?*' he demanded, and Polly subsided, biting her lip and turning to look out of the window.

Up till now, she'd been totally unaware of the scenery she was passing through, all her attention given to Charlie's woes. But now she had a breathing space to take in the reality of her surroundings. The road they were travelling had been carved out of the rock-face which towered above them. On the other side was the eternal blue of the Mediterranean, serene today, reflecting the cloudless sky. And straight ahead, nestling in the curve of the bay, a cluster of terracotta roofs round a boat-studded marina.

Beyond it, a rocky promontory jutted into the sea, dominated by a large rectangular building with faded pink walls, made even more imposing by the tower at each of its corners.

She did not need Sandro's quiet 'Comadora at last' to recognise that this place, more a fortress than a palace, was to be her home, and Charlie's inheritance.

She said, 'It—it looks a little daunting.'

'That would have been the intention, when it was built,' he agreed drily. 'This coast was often attacked by pirates.'

'Yes,' she said, her tone subdued. 'That was part of the local history I had to learn when I was here—before.' She hesitated. 'I suppose I must learn not to mention that.'

'*Perche?*' His brows lifted. 'Why should you think so?'

She said stiffly, 'I didn't think you'd want your family to know that your wife used to be a travel rep.'

'Why, Paola,' he said softly, 'what a snob you are.'

Polly bit her lip. 'How did you explain why I was back in your life? It might be better if I knew.'

He shrugged. 'After the crash, I suffered memory problems for a while, something they all know. Once I recovered fully, you had disappeared, and it took time for me to find you.' He looked at her over Charlie's sleeping head, his smile mocking. 'And now we are together again—united in bliss forever.'

Polly drew a breath. 'Your restored memory seems to have been pretty selective.'

'You have a better version?'

'No,' she admitted unwillingly. 'But no one's ever going to believe that we're—blissfully happy.'

'Then pretend, *cara mia.*' There was a sudden hard note in his voice. 'Pretend like you did three summers ago, when you let me believe you found pleasure in bed with me.'

'Sandro—please...' She felt her face warm, and turned away hurriedly, her body clenching in swift, intimate yearning.

That jibe of hers, uttered purely in self-defence that first night at the flat, seemed to have hit a nerve, she thought unhappily. But it didn't mean anything. After all, no man liked to have his expertise as a lover challenged.

'Do I embarrass you?' he asked coldly. 'My regrets.'

There was a silence, then he said, 'Will you tell me something, Paola? When you went back to England, did you already know that you were carrying my child?'

'No,' she said. 'No, I didn't.'

'Ah,' Sandro said quietly.

The car turned in between tall wrought-iron gates, and negotiated the long winding drive which ended in a paved courtyard before the main entrance to the *palazzo.*

It was bright with flowers in long stone troughs, and in the middle was a fountain sending a slender, glittering spire of water into the air.

Thank God, Polly thought as the car drew up. Peace at last. She stretched, moving her aching shoulders, longing for a bath and a change of clothing, hopefully with a cold drink included somewhere too.

The car bringing their luggage would have arrived ages ago, she thought.

It seemed that if she was going to be unhappy, at least it would be in comfort. But for now, that thought brought no solace at all.

The massive arched double doors opened, and a man, short and balding, dressed in an immaculate grey linen jacket came hurrying across the courtyard to meet them, looking anxious.

He looks like the bearer of bad news, thought Polly. Perhaps there's been another accident and our luggage is all at the bottom of the Mediterranean.

Clearly Sandro was concerned, because he deposited Charlie on her lap and got out.

The little man, hands waving, launched himself into some kind of diatribe, and Polly watched Sandro's expression change from disbelief to a kind of cold fury, and he turned away, lifting clenched fists towards the sky.

When he came back to the car, he was stony-faced as he opened Polly's door.

'The *contessa*,' he said, 'has decided to surprise us with a welcome party, and has filled the *palazzo* with members of my family, including my cousin Emilio,' he added with a snap. 'Tonight, Teodoro tells me, there will be a formal dinner, followed by a reception for some of the local people.'

'Oh, God, no.' Polly looked down in horror at her stained and rumpled dress. 'I can't meet people like this. Is there no other entrance we could use?'

'There are many,' he said. 'But the Marchesa Valessi does not sneak into her house through a back door. Give me Carlino, and we will face them all together.'

Stomach churning, she obeyed, pulling her dress straight and pushing shaking fingers through her dishevelled hair.

Then Sandro's hand closed round hers, firmly and inflexibly, and she began to walk beside him towards the doorway of the *palazzo*. As they reached it, she lifted her chin and straightened her shoulders, and was aware of his swift approving glance.

She was fleetingly aware of a hall hung with tapestries, and a wide stone staircase leading up to a gallery. A clamour of voices abruptly stilled.

People watching her, eyes filled with avid curiosity or open disapproval, a few smiling. And, for a moment, she almost froze.

Then Charlie lifted his head from his father's shoulder, and looked at all the strange faces around him. In a second his expression had changed from bewilderment to alarm, and he uttered a loud howl of distress, and began to sob.

Polly felt the atmosphere in the great hall change instantly. Censure was replaced by sympathy, and the marked silence that had greeted them changed to murmurs of, 'Poor little one, he is tired,' and, 'He is a true Valessi, that one.'

The crowd parted, and a small, plump woman, her hair heavily streaked with grey, came bustling through. Arms outstretched, voice lovingly scolding, she took Charlie from his father's arms and, beckoning imperiously to the wilting Julie to follow, disappeared just as rapidly, the sobbing Charlie held securely against the high bib of her starched apron.

'That was Dorotea,' Sandro said quietly, his taut mouth relaxing into a faint smile. 'Don't worry, Paola, she has a magic touch. Carlino will be bathed, changed, fed and in a good mood before he knows what is happening. And Julie also,' he added drily.

Lucky them, Polly thought, and groaned inwardly as the crowd parted again for the *contessa*.

'*Caro* Alessandro.' She embraced him formally. 'Welcome home. As you see, your family could not wait to meet your beautiful wife.'

'I am overwhelmed,' Sandro said politely. 'But I wish you had allowed Teodoro to give me advance warning of your plans.'

She gave a tinkling laugh. 'But then there would have been no surprise.'

'No,' he said. 'That is precisely what I mean.'

He looked about him. 'I am delighted to welcome you all,' he began. 'But as you can see we have had a bad journey with a sick child, and my wife is exhausted. She will meet you all when she has rested.' He turned to Polly. 'Go with Zia Antonia, *carissima*, and I will join you presently.'

Polly was aware of an absurd impulse to cling to his hand. 'Don't leave me with her,' she wanted to say. Instead she forced a smile and nodded, and followed the *contessa*'s upright figure towards the stairs.

From the gallery, they seemed to traverse a maze of passages until they arrived at last at another pair of double doors, elaborately carved.

The *contessa* flung them open and motioned Polly to precede her. 'This is where you are to sleep,' she said.

Polly paused, drawing a deep breath. She had never imagined occupying such a room, she thought dazedly. It was vast and very old, its ceiling beamed, and the walls decorated with exquisite frescos.

It was dominated by one enormous canopied bed, with crimson

brocade curtains and a magnificent bedspread in the same colour, quilted in gold thread, but little other furniture.

'That door is to the bathroom.' The *contessa* pointed a manicured hand. 'I think you will find all you need.' And the sooner the better, her tone of voice seemed to indicate. 'The other leads to the dressing room, where your clothes have been unpacked for you.' She paused. 'Would you like some tea to be brought to you?'

'That would be kind.' Polly hesitated. 'If it's not too much trouble—as you have all these other guests, I mean.'

'How can it be a difficulty?' The thin lips wore a vinegary smile. 'After all, *cara* Paola, you are the mistress of the house now, and your wish is our command.' She indicated a thick golden rope. 'Pull the bell, if you wish for the services of a maid to help you dress. Or perhaps your husband will prefer to assist you himself—as this is your *luna di miele*.'

'I can manage,' Polly said quietly, conscious of the faint sneer in the older woman's voice, and the swift pang of alarm that her words engendered. 'But I would like to make sure my son is all right, and I don't know where the nursery is.'

'I will instruct Dorotea to take you to him later.' She looked Polly up and down with faint disdain. 'Now, I recommend that you do as Alessandro suggests, and take some rest. After all, this will be your wedding night, officially at least,' she added, with another silvery laugh, and left the room, closing the door behind her.

Left to herself, Polly walked over to the long windows and opened the shutters. She knelt on the embrasure, lifting her face to the heavy golden warmth of the late afternoon.

If the *contessa* had deliberately plotted to present her at her worst, she could not have done a better job, she thought bitterly. But there was no way the older woman could have known how badly Charlie would react to the long journey from the airport.

I wish I could stay here, she thought, because I think I've already got '*null points*' from the jury downstairs.

Instead, she had to put on one of the evening dresses Teresa had made her buy, and play her unwanted role as *marchesa* with whatever style and grace she could summon. And undo, if possible, that first unfortunate impression.

And talking of Teresa... Polly fetched her shoulder bag, and retrieved the parcel it contained. As she undid the ribbons, the tissue parted to reveal a cascade of the finest black lace.

Polly's eyes widened as she examined it. It was a nightgown, she realised, low-necked, split to the thigh on one side, and almost transparent. Provocation at its most exquisite. An expensive, daring tease.

Any girl who wore it would feel irresistibly sexy. And any man who saw it couldn't fail to be aroused.

It seemed clear that Teresa had sensed the tensions in her relationship with Sandro, and decided the honeymoon could need a kick-start.

As Sandro said, you're shrewd, Polly addressed her friend silently, bundling the delicate fabric back into its wrappings, and wondering where she could hide it. But this time you've misread the situation badly.

She left the package on the bed for the time being, and went to investigate the bathroom. The room itself probably dated from the Renaissance, she thought, but the plumbing was strictly twenty-first century, and luxurious in the extreme.

The walls were tiled in shades of blue, interspersed with mother-of-pearl, which gave the impression that the room was under shimmering water.

There was a deep sunken bath, and a capacious shower cubicle in the shape of a hexagon, with a pretty gilded roof.

Thankfully Polly slipped out of her clothes, and stepped behind its glass panels. There was a corner shelf holding toiletries, and she chose some scented foam, lathering her body sensuously. The jet was powerful, but reviving, and she twisted and turned under it, feeling some of the tensions of the day seeping away.

She dried herself slowly, her body refreshed and glowing, then took another bath sheet from the pile and wound it round herself, sarong-style, securing it just above her breasts.

If only her tea was waiting, she thought, opening the bathroom door, then, however briefly, life might be perfect.

She walked into the bedroom, and stopped dead, lips parted in shock, and her heart beating an alarmed tattoo.

Because Sandro was there, stretched out across the bed, his coat and tie discarded, and his shirt unbuttoned to the waist.

'Ciao, bella,' he said softly, his eyes lingering on her bare shoulders in undisguised appreciation. 'You look wonderful, and smell delicious,' he went on. 'And now there is this.' He held up the black nightgown with a soft whistle. 'Perhaps marriage may have its compensations after all.'

And as she watched, transfixed, he lifted himself lithely off the bed, and began to walk towards her, the black lace draped over his arm.

CHAPTER EIGHT

POLLY took a step backwards. She said hoarsely, 'What are you doing here?'

'I want to take a shower,' he said. 'I decided you would probably not wish me to join you, so—I waited.'

She took a breath. 'How—considerate.' Her voice stung. 'Perhaps you'd be even kinder and go to your own room, and use your own shower. I'd like my privacy.'

'So would I, *cara*, but we are both to be disappointed. Thanks to Zia Antonia, all the rooms in the *palazzo* are occupied by other people and will remain so for tomorrow—the day after—who knows?' He paused. 'Also you are under a misapprehension. This is my room—and my shower.'

He paused to allow her to digest that, his mouth twisting in sardonic amusement at her shocked expression.

'The accommodation intended for you is currently taken by my aunt Vittoria, a pious widow with a hearing problem,' he went on. 'She does not like to share either. Also, she snores, which, as you know, I do not.'

He smiled at her. 'But she is certainly leaving tomorrow, so you will only have one night to endure in my company,' he added lightly.

She stared at him, her hands nervously adjusting the towel. 'You really imagine I'm actually going to sleep here—with you?' Her voice rose stormily. 'You must be mad. I can't—I *won't*...'

'You will certainly spend the night with me,' he interrupted, a harsh note in his voice. 'I cannot predict whether or not you will sleep. That is not my concern.'

'Then what does concern you?' She glared at him. 'Certainly not keeping your word.'

He flung exasperated hands at the ceiling. '*Dio*—you think I planned this? That I have deliberately filled my house with a pack of gossiping relatives, including my cousin Emilio, may he rot in hell,' he added with real bite, 'just so that I can trick you into bed with me?'

He gave her a scornful look. 'You overestimate your charms, *bella mia*. You will stay here tonight, without fuss or further argument, for the sake of appearances, because it is our wedding night, and because we have no choice in the matter.

'But let me attempt to allay your obvious fears,' he went on cuttingly. Clasping her wrist, he strode back to the bed, with Polly stumbling after him, tripping on the edge of her towel. He dragged back the satin coverlet, dislodging the huge lace-trimmed pillows to reveal a substantial bolster. 'That,' he said, pointing contemptuously, 'placed down the middle of the bed, should deter my frenzy of desire for you. I hope you are reassured.'

He paused. 'May I remind you, Paola, you agreed to co-operate in presenting our marriage as a conventional one.'

'Yes.' Polly bit her lip. 'But—I didn't realise then what could be involved.'

His smile was thin. 'Well, do not worry too much, *carissima*. There are enough willing women in the world. I see no need to force someone so clearly reluctant.'

He held up the nightgown. 'Although your prudishness hardly matches your choice of nightwear. Why buy a garment so seductive, if you do not wish to be seduced?'

'I didn't buy it,' Polly said stonily. 'It was a present from Teresa.'

'Indeed,' he murmured. 'I never guessed she was such a romantic. Or such an optimist,' he added, his mouth curving in genuine amusement.

'Don't tear it,' he told her mockingly, as Polly made an unavailing attempt to snatch it from him. 'That is a privilege I might prefer to reserve for myself.'

She glared at him. 'Not in this lifetime,' she said defiantly.

'And certainly not unless I wish to do so,' he reminded her softly. 'However, for now, I shall have to console myself with imagining how it might look if you wore it, *bella mia*.' He gave it a last, meditative glance. 'Like a shadow falling across moonlight,' he said quietly, and tossed it to her. 'I must write to Teresa and thank her,' he added with a swift grin, as he straightened the bedclothes.

'And I,' she said coldly, 'shall not.' She swallowed. 'I would like to get dressed now, please.'

His brows lifted, as he scanned the slipping towel. 'You want assistance?'

'No.' She managed just in time to avoid stamping her bare foot on the tiled floor. 'Just some privacy.' She shook her head. 'Oh, can't you see how impossible this all is?'

'I can only see that I shall have to stop teasing you, *cara mia*,' he said with unexpected gentleness. 'Get dressed if you wish, but there is no need for you to face the inquisition downstairs, unless you want to do so. And it is a long time until dinner, when you will be expected to make an appearance, so why not rest quietly here until then? I promise you will not be disturbed,' he added levelly. 'By anyone.'

As she hesitated there was a knock on the door, and a small, round-faced girl came in carrying a tray with Polly's tea. She stopped, her mouth forming into an embarrassed 'o'.

'*Mi scusi, excellenza,*' she stammered. 'I thought the *marchesa* was alone.'

Sandro smiled at her. 'Come here and meet your new mistress, Rafaella.' He turned to Polly. 'I have arranged for this child to become your personal maid, *cara mia*. She is the granddaughter of an old friend, so be kind to her.'

Polly, about to flatly deny any need of a personal maid, saw the girl's eager face, and subsided.

'Once you have had your tea,' Sandro went on, 'I hope she can persuade you to sleep for a while, even if I cannot,' he added wryly. 'And I shall ask her to return at eight to help you to dress for dinner.'

Polly nodded resginedly. 'Thank you. Darling,' she added as an afterthought, and saw his lips twitch before he turned away, heading for the bathroom.

Rafaella set the tray down on one of the old ornamental tables that flanked the bed, then flew to the dressing room, returning with a dark blue satin robe, which Polly awkwardly exchanged for the towel.

'*Parli inglese?*' she asked as the girl folded back the coverlet to the foot of the bed, and plumped up the pillows.

Her face lit up. '*Sì, vossignoria.* I worked for an English family, *au pair*, for two years. I learn much.'

'Yet you came back to work at the *palazzo*?'

Rafaella nodded vigorously. 'It is an honour for me, and for my grandfather, who asked for this post for me, when his *signoria* wished to reward him.'

'Reward him?' Polly queried.

'It was my grandfather who found the *marchese* when his car crashed into the ravine,' Rafaella explained. 'He saw it happen, and ran to help. At first he thought his *signoria* was dead, because he did not move, and there was so much blood, but then he could feel his pulse and knew that he lived, so my grandfather went to the car to rescue the lady.' She shrugged. 'But it was too late.'

Polly winced. 'It must have been a horrible experience for him.'

'*Sì, vossignoria*. He spoke about it to the inquiry, and also to his *signoria* when he was in hospital, but never since. There is too much pain in such memories.'

She bent to retrieve the discarded bath sheet, then straightened, beaming. 'So it is good that the *marchese* is now happy again.'

'Yes.' Polly realised with acute embarrassment that the girl was holding up the black lace nightgown, which must have been entangled in the folds of the towel. 'I—I suppose so.'

She tried to concentrate on her tea, and ignore Rafaella's stifled giggle as she carried the nightdress off to the dressing room.

No doubt the rumour mill at the *palazzo* would soon be in full swing, she thought, swallowing. But at least it would support the idea that this was a real marriage, which would please Sandro.

She put down her cup and turned on her side, shutting her eyes determinedly, and, presently, she heard Rafaella's quiet departure.

It would be good to relax, she thought, burrowing her cheek into the lavender-scented pillow. To recover from the stress and strain of the past days and weeks, and re-focus on this extraordinary new life, to which, for good or ill, she now belonged.

Thanks to the *contessa*, it was proving a more difficult start than she'd anticipated, she told herself, sighing.

For one thing, and in spite of the closed bathroom door, she could clearly hear the sound of the shower, reviving all kinds of past associations, and she pressed her hands over her ears, in an attempt to shut them out.

She didn't want to remember those other times when Sandro had been showering, and she'd joined him, their bodies slippery under the torrent of water, her mouth fierce on his skin, his arms strong as he lifted her against him, filling her with the renewed urgency of his desire.

But the memories were too strong, too potent to be dismissed, and for a moment, as her body melted in recollection, she was pierced once more with the temptation to abandon all pride and go to him.

But it would pass, she thought. It had to. Because she would not be drawn again into the web of sensuality where she'd been trapped before. It was just a moment of weakness because she was tired—so very tired...

And gradually, the distant rush of water became a lullaby that, against all odds, soothed her to sleep.

She had never really dressed for dinner before, Polly thought as she sat in front of the mirror, watching Rafaella apply the finishing touches to her hair. The other girl had drawn the shining strands into a loose knot on top of Polly's head, softening the look with a few loose tendrils that were allowed to curl against her face, and the nape of her neck.

Her dress was a sleek column of black silk, long-sleeved, with a neckline that discreetly revealed the first swell of her breasts, and gave her skin the sheen of a pearl.

She'd kept her make-up deliberately muted, faintly emphasising the green of her eyes, and curving her mouth with a soft rose lustre.

Whatever her inward inadequacies, this time she would at least look the part of the Marchesa Valessi, she thought.

She had hoped that Sandro would be beside her again, to guide her through her second entrance, but Rafaella had told her that he had changed for dinner and rejoined his guests while she still slept.

So, she'd have to brave them all alone.

Sighing under her breath, she rose. 'Rafaella, I'd like to say goodnight to my son before dinner. Can you take me to the nursery, *per favore*?'

'*Sì, vossignoria.* Of course.'

'And that "*vossignoria*" is a terrible mouthful,' Polly went on. 'Maybe we could change it. What did you call your last boss?'

Rafaella looked a little startled. '*Signora*, sometimes, but usually *madame*.'

Polly smiled at her. 'Then that will be fine with me, too.'

'But I was instructed, *vossignoria*, by the *contessa*.'

'And now you're getting further instructions from me,' Polly advised her crisply. 'From now on it's *madame*, and that's final.'

'As you say, *madame*.' Rafaella's agreement was subdued.

Polly was expecting another maze of passages, but the nursery turned out to be only round a corner, and up a flight of stairs.

It wouldn't have been far for Dorotea to come, she thought as she opened the door and walked in.

She found herself in a spacious room lined with cupboards. There was a table in the middle, and a young girl was tidying up, placing toys in a large wicker basket.

Her jaw dropped as Polly entered in a rustle of silk, and she hurried over to a half-open door on the other side of the room, and said something in a low voice. A moment later, Dorotea joined them. She inclined her head stiffly to Polly, then turned to Rafaella and launched herself into a flood of half-whispered Italian, complete with gestures.

Rafaella looked at Polly with an awkward shrug. 'She regrets, *madame*, but your son is asleep. She was not expecting a visit from you. She understood that your duties to your guests came first.'

'Nothing comes before my little boy,' Polly said quietly. 'And I thought it was arranged that she would come and fetch me once he was settled. I have been waiting.'

She paused. 'Clearly, there has been some misunderstanding tonight, but explain to her, please, that we will speak in the morning about Carlino's future routine. And now I would like to kiss my son goodnight.'

Dorotea listened to Rafaella's translation, but it brought no lightening of her expression. And she stood unwillingly aside to give Polly access to the night nursery.

A nightlight in a holder shaped like a shell was burning near his cot, and Charlie was lying on his back, his arms flung wide, his breathing soft and regular.

Polly stood looking down at him, then bent and brushed a strand of hair back from his face with gentle fingers. At the same time she became aware that Dorotea, who'd been watching from the doorway, arms folded across her bosom, was bobbing a kind of curtsy and muttering a deferential *'Excellenza'* as she backed out of the room. And she realised that Sandro had come to join her.

She had never seen him in dinner jacket and black tie before, and the breath caught in her throat, because this new formality conferred its own kind of magnificence. It also set him at a distance, which was all to the good, she told herself.

She summoned a smile. '*Buonasera.* I came to say goodnight. Maybe even goodbye, just in case they tear me to pieces downstairs.'

'They will not do that. They are all eager to meet you.'

She looked back at the cot. 'How—how beautiful,' she said, softly. 'Don't you think so?'

'*Sì,*' he agreed quietly. 'Beautiful indeed.' And she realised that he was looking at her, and turned away as she felt her body quiver in instinctive response, walking past him into the now-deserted day nursery.

He followed. 'But I did not come simply to see Carlino,' he went on. 'I have something for you, *cara mia.*' His hands touched her shoulders, halting her, and Polly felt the slide of something metallic against her throat, and glanced down.

The necklace was nearly an inch wide, a flat, delicate network of gold, studded with the blue-white fire of diamonds. She touched it with a wondering hand. 'Sandro—it's lovely. But there's no need for this.'

'I am permitted to give you a wedding present,' he told her drily.

'I—suppose.' She shook her head. 'But I feel dreadful because I have nothing for you.'

'You don't think so?'

He turned her slowly to face him, then bent towards her, and she felt his lips rest softly, briefly on her forehead. She had not expected that, and his intense gentleness made her tremble.

'My beloved girl,' he whispered. 'You are here with me at last.'

The sudden flash of light from the doorway was a harsh, unbearable intrusion. Stunned and dazzled, Polly pulled free, looking round wildly. 'What was that?'

'My cousin Emilio,' Sandro said with a shrug. 'Armed with a camera, and searching for some moment of intimacy between us to thrill his readers.'

She stared at him. 'You *knew* he was there?'

'I was aware he had followed me upstairs,' he said. 'And guessed his motive. I think we provided what he wanted,' he added, casually. 'And you did well, Paola *mia*. You almost convinced me.'

Hurt slashed at her like a razor. Just for a moment, she'd believed him—believed the tenderness of his kiss.

She said colourlessly, 'I'm starting to learn—at last.'

She paused, taking a steadying breath. 'And while I'm on a roll, why don't you take me downstairs and present me to your family? Because I'm ready.'

'And no more only children,' Zia Vittoria boomed authoritatively. 'In Alessandro's case, it was understandable. His mother was a delicate creature, and no one expected too much, but you seem to be a healthy young woman, and Alessandro's first born is a fine child, in spite of his irregular birth. I commend you,' she added graciously.

Polly, seated at her side, with her smile nailed on, murmured something grateful, and wondered what the penalty might be for strangling a deaf Italian dowager. She was aware of sympathetic smiles around the room, and a swift glance, brimming with unholy mirth, from Sandro.

I should have known it was going too well, she thought grimly.

Dinner in the tapestry-hung banqueting hall had been a splendid occasion. She had sat opposite her husband at the end of a long candlelit table shining with exquisite silver and crystal, and been formally welcomed to the family by Sandro's ancient great-uncle Filippo. Her health had been drunk with every course served, and her neighbours had vied with each other to talk to her, delighted when she'd attempted to reply in Italian. Only the *contessa* had stayed aloof from the talk and laughter round the table, sitting like a marble statue, her mouth set in a thin, unamused smile.

At the reception which followed, Polly had been presented to various local dignitaries, and invited to serve on several charity committees. Sandro, standing at her side, his arm lightly encircling her waist, explained with great charm that, with a young child, his wife's time was limited, but she would consider all proposals in due course.

After which the visitors left expressing their good wishes for the happiness of the *marchese* and his bride, and Polly had felt able to relax a little. Until, that was, she'd found herself summoned by Zia Vittoria, and subjected to an inquisition on her background, upbringing and education in a voice that was probably audible in the marina, even before she tackled Polly's suitability to add to the Valessi dynasty.

When the good lady was finally distracted by the offer of more champagne, Polly seized the opportunity to escape. It was a warm night, and the long windows of the *salotto* had been opened. Polly slipped through the filmy drapes, and out onto the terrace, drawing a shaky breath of relief when she found herself alone.

The air was still, and the sky heavy with stars, just as she remembered. Even before she met Sandro, she had always loved the Italian nights, so relaxed and sensuous.

Polly moved to the edge of the terrace, and leaned on the stone balustrade, inhaling the faint scents that rose from the unseen garden below. Tomorrow, she would explore the *palazzo*'s grounds with Charlie—find the swimming pool perhaps. Take hold of this new life with both hands, and make it work somehow.

As she stared into the darkness, she suddenly became aware of another scent, more pungent and less romantic than the hidden flowers. The smell of a cigar.

She turned abruptly, and saw a man standing a few yards away from her. He was of medium height, and verging towards the plump. Handsome, too, apart from the small, petulant mouth beneath his thin black moustache. And well-pleased with himself, instinct told her.

She met his bold, appraising stare, her chin lifted haughtily.

'Forgive this intrusion, *marchesa*.' His English was good, if heavily accented. 'But I could not wait any longer to meet my cousin's bride. My name is Emilio Corzi.'

'I think we've encountered each other already, *signore*.' Polly paused. 'Earlier this evening—in my son's nursery.'

He laughed, unabashed. 'I hope I did not offend, but the moment was irresistible, if surprising. Not unlike yourself, *vossignoria*,' he added softly. 'I have been watching you with interest, and you have much more charm and style than I was led to believe.'

'Really?' Polly raised her eyebrows. 'I don't need to ask who was doing the leading.'

'You are right, of course.' Emilio Corzi sighed. 'Poor Antonia Barsoli. She has never recovered from the death of that unfortunate girl, Bianca. It must be hard for her to see someone set in her place, especially when Alessandro swore after the accident that he would never marry.' He paused. 'Although she has less reason to be bitter than I have.'

'Ah.' Polly gave him a level look. 'You mean the loss of your inheritance.'

He sighed elaborately. 'It is unfortunately true. His late father had two brothers and a sister, my mother, who produced ten children between them, all girls except for myself, and I was the youngest of three. Alessandro, of course, was an only child, and I dare say too much was expected of him, at too early an age.'

Polly knew she should walk away, but against her better instincts, she lingered.

'Why do you say that?'

'Relations between him and his father were always strained.' Emilio drew reflectively on his cigar. 'And became worse once his mother was no longer there to act as mediator. As you know, she died when he was twelve.' He looked at her, brows raised. 'Or did you know?'

'Of course.' Polly lifted her chin.

'I could not be certain,' he said. 'There are so many areas of his life about which he is silent. Although I am sure he has his reasons.'

'Probably because he doesn't want the details splashed all over your magazines,' Polly suggested shortly.

'But he wrongs me, my dear cousin.' Emilio's tone was plaintive. 'I have not made capital out of his forbidden affair with you—or his secret love-child. I am treating it as a romantic story with a happy ending. My family loyalty is real.' He paused. 'I have not even expressed my doubts in public over the mystery of Bianca DiMario's death. Or not yet anyway.'

'Mystery?' Polly repeated. 'What are you talking about? It was a tragic accident.'

'That was the decision of the inquiry, certainly. But I am fascinated by the reticence of the only witness who was called— Giacomo Raboni.' He smiled at her. 'But after all, his family have served the Valessi faithfully for generations. Who knows what someone less partisan might have said?'

Polly stiffened. 'That is—a disgusting implication. There was a burst tyre on the car. These things happen.'

'But the inquiry was held so quickly,' Emilio countered. 'While Alessandro was still seriously ill in hospital, and unable to give evidence. But perhaps they thought he never would,' he added swiftly. 'It was still possible that he would end his days in a wheel-chair, and that there might be permanent brain damage.'

He shrugged. 'But in the end he suffered only some temporary amnesia, and he made a full recovery—to everyone's enormous relief,' he added piously.

'Yes,' Polly said stonily. 'I bet you were thrilled to bits.' She was leaning back against the balustrade, shaking like a leaf, her stomach churning, as she thought of Sandro trapped, perhaps, in a helpless body. Unable even to understand, maybe, that he had fathered a child, let alone hold him or love him.

'But even when he was well again, he was never questioned about that afternoon in the mountains,' Emilio said softly. 'The advantage, I suppose, of being the son of a rich and influential man. And there was much sympathy, too, for my uncle Domenico, who had lost a young girl he cherished as a daughter. So, many questions were left unanswered.'

'Such as?' she demanded curtly.

'What did Giacomo Raboni know, but not speak about? I know he was well rewarded at the time by my uncle. And now, I find, his granddaughter has been given a position of prestige as your personal maid.'

She said hoarsely, 'But gratitude is quite natural. Sandro told me that Giacomo had saved his life. That's quite a service.'

He shrugged. 'I think his silence has been a greater one. And they say too that generosity is often prompted by a guilty con-science.' He lowered his voice conspiratorially. 'Have you ever wondered whether the scar on your husband's cheek might be the mark of Cain?'

'I think you've said enough.' Her tone was ice. 'You're supposed to be Sandro's guest. It would be better if you left.'

He tutted reproachfully. 'You are harsh, my dear Paola. And your loyalty to Alessandro is misplaced, believe me. I am simply trying to be your friend, and one day you may need me.'

'I can't imagine that,' she returned curtly.

'But then did you foresee finding yourself Marchesa Valessi, with Alessandro's diamonds on your hand and circling your throat? I note he has not given you the jewels that have been in the Valessi family for centuries, but these trinkets are valuable enough.'

'Thank you,' Polly said grittily. 'I'll tell him you approve.'

'Oh, no,' he said. 'I do not think you will discuss our conversation with him at all.' He paused. 'So, what will you do when the little Carlo becomes his legal heir, and Alessandro tires of playing husband, and wants you out of his life a second time?'

Shock was like bile in her throat. 'What the hell do you mean?'

He sighed. 'I hoped you would be honest at least. Your days and nights with my cousin are numbered, and you know it. He has never wished to be married. Not to the unfortunate Bianca. Not to you. No one woman will ever fill his need for variety.' His lip curled. 'Do you wish to know the name of his mistress in Rome?'

'That,' she said huskily, 'is it. Go, please. Just pack and—get out.'

There was sudden venom in his voice. 'Did you make him sign a pre-nuptial agreement, or will he make you settle for the same paltry sum as last time's parting price before he sends you home? If so, you may be glad to turn to me. I would pay you well for a personal view of your association with him.'

'You,' Polly said, steadying her voice, 'are completely vile.'

'And he, Paola *cara*, is totally ruthless, as you must know, else why are you here?' He made her a little bow. 'I will leave you to your solitary contemplation. We shall meet again—once you have learned sense.'

He turned and walked along the terrace, disappearing from view into the darkness.

Polly found she was gasping for breath. She stood, a hand pressed to her throat as she fought for self-control.

She could not stay out here on the terrace forever. Soon, now, she would have to go back inside, and she needed at least the appearance of serenity to fool the sharp eyes that would be watching her.

All the vicious things Emilio had said to her were tumbling around in her head. She might tell herself they were ludicrous, vindictive lies of a disappointed man, but in some ways they seemed like the confirmation of all her worst nightmares.

What had really happened the day Sandro's car went into the ravine? Rafaella had told her that her grandfather refused to speak about it. What had he seen—or heard—that prompted him to silence?

Somehow or other, she thought, I'm going to have to ask him—and make him tell me the truth. Because I need to know.

As for Emilio's comments about her marriage... A little shiver ran through her. He was probably right about that. After all, it was only a means to an end, as Sandro had made clear. And once he had Charlie established as his heir, why would he bother to keep her around? Especially when he had other interests?

Do you wish to know the name of his mistress in Rome?

The words ate at her like some corrosive acid.

The fact that there was another woman in his life had not stopped him trying to seduce her back into his bed, she thought, hurt and anger warring inside her. 'A fever in the blood' he'd once called it. And once the fever had been quenched, what then? Had he expected her to be so much in thrall to him that she was compliantly prepared to share him with his Roman beauty?

She bit her lip so hard that she tasted blood. I can't think about that, she told herself desperately. I dare not go there...

But there was another problem, too, that she had to confront. Was it just Emilio or did other members of the family know that he'd tried to pay her off three years before? If so, that was the ultimate humiliation, and she wanted to run somewhere and hide, away from the smiles and sneers that would accompany such knowledge.

But most of all, she wanted to hide from Sandro. And instead she was obliged to go upstairs, and get into one side of the extravagantly wide bed she had to share with him tonight. And be expected to sleep.

Oh, God, she thought, her fists clenching convulsively. It's all such a charade. Such total hypocrisy.

And if I had any guts, I'd get Charlie, and make a run for it back to England, and see how Sandro deals with a scandal like that.

But, realistically, how far would she get? She was here in this—fortress in a foreign country, where he had power, and she had none. Even the money in the bank account he'd opened for her had been transferred to Italy.

She was helpless—and she was suddenly afraid too.

'So, here you are.' Sandro was walking across the terrace towards her. 'What are you doing out here alone?'

She swallowed slowly and deeply, aware of the frantic thud of her heart at the sight of him.

'I needed some fresh air.' She forced herself to sound light and cool. 'Pretending to be pleasant is hard work, and every actress needs an interval.'

'Is it really so hard to meet such goodwill halfway?' he asked unsmilingly.

'I think it exists for Charlie, not myself,' she returned curtly. 'I'm your wife by accident not design, and they must know that.'

He said drily, 'In the eyes of most of my family, you are not yet my wife at all. I am being given embarrassingly broad hints that I should take you upstairs without further delay and rectify the matter.'

'Oh, God.' Polly pressed her hands to her burning cheeks.

'I am truly sorry, *cara mia*.' His voice was suddenly gentle. 'I never meant you to be subjected to this. We had better face them.'

'Very well.' Ignoring his outstretched hand, she walked stiffly beside him towards the open windows of the *salotto*.

'I can give you ten minutes' privacy,' he added quietly. 'But no longer, or Zia Vittoria will be demanding to know why I am not with you, doing my duty by the next generation.'

Her throat muscles felt paralysed, but she managed a husky, 'Thank you.'

In spite of her tacit resistance, Sandro slid an arm round her waist, holding her against his side, as they went into the brightness of the room and paused to meet the laughter and faint cheers that awaited them.

Then she felt his lips touch her hot cheek, as he whispered, 'Go now, *bella mia*.'

The door seemed a million miles away, especially when she had to reach it through a sea of broad grins and openly voiced encouragement. She was aware that people were swarming after her into the hall, watching her walk up the stairs.

She glanced back once, and saw Sandro standing a little apart from them all. He was unsmiling, his eyes bleak, as he looked at her, raising the glass he was holding in a cynical toast. Then he drained the contents in one jerky movement, and went back into the *salotto*.

Leaving Polly to go on, feeling more alone than she had ever done in her life before.

CHAPTER NINE

THE bedroom was empty, but it was prepared and waiting for her. And, she thought, her senses tautening, for him.

Lamps on tall wrought-iron stands were burning on either side of the bed. The coverlet had been removed and the white lace-edged sheets turned down and scattered with crimson rose petals.

And, she supposed, inevitably, the black lace nightdress was draped across the bed in readiness too.

Well, that she could deal with, she thought, folding it with quick, feverish hands into a tiny parcel of fabric. She went into the dressing room, and stowed it away in her wardrobe in the pocket of a linen jacket against the moment when she could dispose of it for good and all. Otherwise it was going to haunt her.

She also needed an alternative to wear, she thought, rummaging through the exquisitely arranged contents of her lingerie drawer. She decided on a plain ivory satin nightgown, cut on the bias, its neckline square across her breasts, and supported by shoestring straps.

Discreet enough to be an evening dress, she thought as she slipped it over her head after showering briefly in the bathroom. Especially with the diamonds still glittering round her neck. Where they would have to remain, as the clasp resisted all her efforts to unfasten it.

Sighing, Polly shook her hair loose, ran a swift brush through it, and went back into the bedroom.

She was aware the minutes had been ticking past, but she'd still hoped she might be granted a little more leeway than Sandro had suggested. Prayed that it might be possible to be in bed, pretending to be asleep before he came to join her.

But her hopes were dashed, because Sandro was there already, dinner jacket removed and black tie loosened, walking towards the bed. He turned, surveying her without expression as she hesitated in the doorway.

He said, 'Do you not think you are a little overdressed, *bella mia*?'

Her heart skipped. 'What are you talking about?'

His mouth twisted. 'I was referring to the diamonds, naturally.'

She lifted her chin. 'I couldn't unfasten them—and Rafaella wasn't here.'

'She would not risk her life by intruding.' He beckoned. 'Come to me.'

She went slowly towards him, waiting, head bent, while he dealt with the clasp, his touch brisk and impersonal.

'Take it.' He dropped the necklace into her hand.

She said, 'But shouldn't you have it?'

'It was a gift, Paola,' he said shortly. 'Not a loan.'

'I meant—wouldn't it be better in a safe...somewhere?'

'There is a place in the dressing room for your jewellery. Rafaella will show you in the morning.' Sandro turned back to the bed, and began brushing away the rose petals. One of them drifted to Polly's feet, and she bent and retrieved it, stroking the velvety surface with her fingertips.

She said, 'Someone has taken a lot of trouble. Perhaps you were right about the goodwill.'

'The wedding night of a *marchese* and his bride is always a great occasion.' Sandro dragged out the bolster from under the pillows, and arranged it down the centre of the bed. 'How fortunate they will never know the truth,' he added sardonically.

'There,' he said, when he had finished. 'Will that make you feel safe?'

'Yes,' Polly said stiltedly. 'Yes—thank you.'

He walked away towards the dressing room, and Polly switched off her lamp and got hastily into bed. She slid her necklace under the pillow, then lay down, her back turned rigidly towards the bolster. The scent of the roses still lingered beguilingly, and she buried her face in the pillow, breathing in the perfume, and relishing the coolness of the linen against the warmth of her skin.

When at last she heard Sandro returning, she burrowed further down under the sheet, closing her eyes so tightly that coloured lights danced behind her lids.

She sensed that the other lamp had been extinguished, then heard the rustle of silk as he discarded his robe, and the faint dip of the bed as he took his place on the far side of the bolster.

There was a silence, then he said, 'Paola, you are permitted to stop acting when we are alone together. And I know you are not asleep.'

She turned reluctantly, and looked at him over her shoulder. In the shadows of the room, she could see the outline of him, leaning on the bolster, watching her, but she was unable to read the expression on his face.

She kept her voice cool. 'But I'd like to be. This has been one hell of a day.'

'Crowned, I imagine, by your meeting with my cousin Emilio,' he drawled. 'Where did you encounter him?'

Polly, unprepared for the question, hunched a shoulder. 'He happened to be on the terrace while I was there,' she said evasively.

'Emilio does not "happen" to be anywhere, *cara*,' he said drily. 'His locations are always intentional.' He paused. 'Did you share a pleasant conversation?'

'No,' she said. 'Not particularly. I hope he isn't a frequent visitor.'

'I believe he comes mainly to see Zia Antonia,' he said. 'Usually when I am not here. As he is leaving early in the morning, he has asked me to pass on a message to you.'

Polly shifted uncomfortably. 'Oh?'

'He sends you his homage,' Sandro went on silkily. 'And hopes that tonight will provide you with wonderful memories for the rest of your life.'

She punched the pillow with unnecessary vigour, and lay down again. 'Well, neither of us are likely to forget it,' she said shortly.

'That is true,' he said. 'But I am surprised to find you on a level of such intimacy with Emilio.'

'I'm not,' she returned heatedly. 'He's a loathsome little worm, and I'm amazed that someone hasn't dealt with him by now.'

'They have tried,' Sandro said drily. 'He has been pushed off a balcony in Lucca, and thrown into the Grand Canal in Venice. And he was nearly the victim of a drive-by shooting in Rome, but it seems that was a case of mistaken identity.'

Polly was surprised into a giggle. 'What a shame.'

'As you say,' he agreed solemnly. 'But, in a way, he can be pitied. For years he has been waiting confidently for me to break my neck on the polo field, be caught in an avalanche or drown while sailing. The car crash must have made him feel that his dream could come true at last.

'Yet here I am with a wife and a son, and his hopes of the Valessi inheritance are finally dashed.'

She put up a hand to her pillow, hugging it closer. Her voice was faintly muffled. 'Is that why you were so determined to take Charlie? To put Emilio out of the running?'

'It played its part. But I wanted him for his own sake, too.' His voice sharpened. 'Paola, you cannot doubt that, surely.'

'No,' she said. 'I—know you did.'

It was almost her only certainty, she thought. Emilio's vile insinuations were still turning like a weary treadmill in her brain, reminding her yet again just how tenuous her position was. And how easily she might lose everything in the world that mattered to her.

And in spite of the warmth of the night, she gave the slightest shiver.

He noticed instantly. 'Are you cold? Do you wish for a blanket?'

'It's not that.' She sat up, making a little helpless gesture. 'I—I just don't know what I'm doing here—why I let myself do this. I don't understand what's happening.'

He was silent for a moment, then he said wearily, a trace of something like bitterness in his voice, 'Currently, you and I, *cara mia*, are about to spend a very long and tedious night together. When it is over, we will see what tomorrow brings, and hope that it is better. Now, sleep.'

He turned away, and lay down with his back to her, and, after a pause, she did the same.

Time passed, and became an hour—then another. Polly found herself lying on the furthermost edge of the bed, listening to Sandro's quiet, regular breathing, scared to move or even sigh in case she disturbed him.

She felt physically and emotionally exhausted, but her brain would not let her rest. She was plagued by images that hurt and bewildered her, images of fear and isolation, but she found them impossible to dismiss, however much she wanted to let go, and allow herself to drift away into sleep.

At one point, she seemed to be standing at one end of a long tree-lined avenue, watching Sandro, who was ahead of her, walk-

ing away with long, rapid strides. And she knew with total frightened certainty that if she allowed him to reach the end of the
avenue, that he would be gone forever. She tried to call out, to
summon him back, but her voice emerged as a cracked whisper.

Yet somehow he seemed to hear, because he stopped and looked
back, and she began to run to him, stumbling a little, her legs like
leaden weights.

She said his name again, and ran into his arms, and they closed
round her, so warm and so safe that the icy chill deep inside her
began to dissolve away as he held her.

And she thought, This is a dream. I'm dreaming... And knew
that she did not want to wake, and face reality again.

When she eventually opened her eyes the following day, that same
feeling of security still lingered, and she felt relaxed and strangely
at peace.

The first thing she saw was that the bolster was back in its
normal place, and that the bed beside her was empty. She was
completely alone, too, with only the whirr of the ceiling fan to
disturb the hush of the room. Sandro had gone.

Well, she thought, I should be grateful for that.

She sat up, pushing her hair back from her face. It was very
hot, she realised, and the shutters at the windows were closed to
exclude the molten gold of the sun. At some moment in the night,
she'd kicked away the covering sheet, but her satin nightdress was
clinging damply to her body.

She glanced at her watch, and gasped. No wonder the temperature was soaring—the morning was nearly over. She felt as if
she'd slept for a hundred years, and that, if she left this room, she
would find the passages choked with cobwebs.

And, as if on cue, there was a knock on the door and Rafaella
came in carrying a tray.

'*Buongiorno*, madam.' Her smile was wide and cheerful.

Polly spread her hands helplessly. 'It's almost afternoon!' she
exclaimed. 'Why did no one wake me?'

'The *marchese* said that you needed to sleep, and should not be
disturbed,' Rafaella returned demurely, her eyes straying to the
tray she had just placed on the bed.

Polly followed her gaze, and saw that in addition to the orange juice, the fresh rolls, the dish of honey, the bowl of grapes and the silver coffee pot, there was a red rose lying across the snowy tray cloth, and a folded note beside it.

Swallowing, she reached for it. It said simply, *'Grazie, mi amore,'* and was signed with his name.

Polly realised she was blushing to the roots of her hair, and hurriedly crushed the paper in her hand. Everyone in the *palazzo*, she thought, would know about his message by now, and the remembered passion implied in its words.

It was simply another brick in the wall of pretence around their marriage, and she knew it, but that didn't make it any easier to take.

She had also seen the faintly puzzled glance that the girl had sent the ivory nightgown.

Maybe I should have left the black one shredded on the floor, she thought ruefully. Silenced any lingering doubts that way.

She cleared her throat. 'Where—where is the *marchese*?'

'He has been bidding goodbye to his guests, madam. Now he has gone down to the port with his son and the *bambinaia*.' She beamed. 'The little Carlo wished for ice-cream, I think.'

'His father has a short memory,' Polly commented crisply. 'Charlie, ice-cream and a car ride could be a lethal combination.'

'Ah, no, *signora*. The *marchese* was also ill on journeys when he was a *bambino*, and Dorotea has her own special remedy,' Rafaella reassured her cheerfully. 'Shall I pour *signora*'s coffee?'

Dorotea? Polly thought, as she sipped the strong brew. Then where was Julie?

'The *maggiordomo*, Teodoro, sends his respects to *vossignoria*,' Rafaella reported when she returned from running Polly's bath. 'The *marchese* has instructed him to show you the *palazzo*, and he awaits your convenience.'

'Oh,' Polly said, slowly. 'Well, please thank him for me. It will be my pleasure.' She paused, spreading a roll with honey. 'I was also thinking, Rafaella, that I would really like to meet your grandfather.' She made her tone casual. 'Thank him for all he did for the *marchese*. Could you arrange that for me?'

'It would be his honour, *signora*,' Rafaella's dark eyes shone. 'But at the moment he is away, visiting my sister in Salerno, who is expecting her first child. When he returns, perhaps?'

'That would be fine,' Polly agreed. 'I'll hold you to it.'

An hour later, bathed and dressed in a knee-length white skirt and a sleeveless navy top, she made her way to the nursery, hoping that Charlie might be back. Instead, she found Julie sitting alone at the big table, listlessly leafing through the pages of a magazine.

'Oh.' Polly checked at the sight of her. 'So you didn't go to the port.'

Julie sighed. 'Dorotea may not speak much English, but she made it plain I wasn't wanted,' she said wryly. 'Instead, I've been cleaning out these already spotless cupboards.'

Polly frowned. 'Doesn't she realise you're here to be with Charlie?'

'That's the problem. Apparently there's only one way to look after his excellency's son, and it's not the way I do it. And the Contessa Barsoli was here earlier, asking when I planned to go home.' She looked squarely at Polly. 'I think my coming here was a big mistake.'

Polly forced a smile. 'I'm hardly the flavour of the month with them either. I was only just allowed to say goodnight to him yesterday,' she added candidly, then paused. 'But please hang in there, Julie. I'm sure things can only get better.' And mentally crossed her fingers.

Teodoro was waiting in the hall for her, still looking anxious, but his face cleared a little when Polly spoke to him in his own language. Overall, she thought afterwards, the tour of the *palazzo* went well, although there were too many rooms, too many glorious works of art on the walls, too many priceless tapestries, statues and ceramics on display to be assimilated all at once. And most of the furniture in everyday use would have graced any museum. Becoming familiar with it all would be a life's work. And her days here were limited.

If she had a criticism, she thought, it would be that it all seemed incredibly formal and curiously lifeless. Everything appeared to have its own place, which it had occupied for centuries.

The exception was Sandro's study, and the small office which adjoined it, staffed by a severe woman with glasses called Signora Corboni. This was where the work was done, Polly surmised, surveying the computers and fax machine, and metal filing cabinets, but even here the past intruded in the shape of a massive antique desk.

And she had never seen so many fireplaces. Every room seemed to have one, and the largest often had two. But there was no central heating, so logs would be burned to dispel the chill and damp of an Italian winter.

There was only one door locked against her. The room, Teodoro told her with faint embarrassment, occupied by the *contessa*. And Polly smiled and shrugged to indicate that there was no problem— that the *contessa* was an elderly woman entitled to her privacy.

Teodoro had clearly been keeping the best until last, flinging the final door open with a flourish. 'And this, *vossignoria*, this is all for you.'

It was far from the largest room she'd been shown, yet her flat in England would probably have fitted into it quite comfortably. And comfort was the theme, with a carpeted floor, two deeply cushioned sofas covered in a blue and cream floral design flanking the stone hearth, and matching curtains hanging at the large window.

'Oh.' Polly knelt on the window seat, looking down over a sloping riot of dark green trees and shrubs to the azure sea beyond. 'Oh, how lovely.'

Teodoro beamed in satisfaction, and began to point out the other amenities, which included a television set, a state-of-the-art music centre with a rack of CDs, and a tall case stocked with the latest English fiction and non-fiction titles.

There were no old masters on the walls, but some delightful water-colours. There were roses filling the air with scent on a side-table, and the ornaments, although undoubtedly valuable, had clearly been selected for their charm.

'This was the favoured room of the *marchese*'s late mother, may God grant her peace,' Teodoro said, crossing himself devoutly. 'Messere Alessandro ordered it to be specially prepared for you. He wished you to have somewhere quiet and private for yourself alone, to sit and read, perhaps, or play music.'

And be out of his way? Polly wondered wryly. But, whatever Sandro's motives, she couldn't deny her pleasure in the room, or fail to appreciate the thought that had gone into it.

She said quietly, 'That's—very kind of him.'

He nodded, pleased. He indicated the telephone standing on a small, elegant writing desk. 'If you wish to make a call, our switchboard will connect you. And if there is anything else *vossignoria* requires, be gracious enough to pull the bell by the fireplace.'

After that there were more practical matters to be dealt with. There were food stores and the wine cellars to be inspected, plus the laundry and the bakery to be visited.

The *palazzo* was a little world of its own, she thought, and pretty much self-sufficient, probably dating from the days when it was regularly besieged by its enemies.

Not a lot of change there, she thought ironically as she refused lunch, but gratefully accepted Teodoro's offer of iced lemonade served on the terrace.

She had just seated herself in a cushioned chair under the shade of a sun umbrella when Sandro appeared, walking up the steps from the garden.

He was wearing shorts, and an unbuttoned cotton shirt, his feet thrust into canvas shoes, and was carrying an excited Charlie on his shoulders.

'*Ciao.*' His greeting was casual, but the look he sent her was curiously watchful. 'Did you sleep well?'

She forced a smile. 'Better than I could have hoped. And you?'

He said laconically, 'I survived.' And lowered Charlie down to the flags.

The little boy came rushing to Polly. 'Mammina, I went in a boat, with *big* sails.' Waving arms indicated a vast expanse of canvas. 'And a man give me a fish all of my own. Doro says I can eat it for supper.'

Polly sent Sandro a surprised look. 'What's this?'

'I took him to meet an old friend of mine, called Alfredo.' Sandro poured himself some lemonade. 'When I was a young boy, I used to escape whenever I could down to the port, and Fredo would take me fishing with him. A pleasure I would like Carlino to share.'

'But he can't swim,' Polly protested. 'Supposing the boat had capsized?'

Sandro shrugged, his face hardening. 'Supposing we had all been abducted by aliens?' he countered impatiently. 'And I intend to give him his first swimming lesson later today, after siesta.' He paused. 'Perhaps you would like to come and make sure his life is not endangered again.'

She said stiffly, 'I suppose you think I'm making a fuss about nothing.'

'Yes,' he said, 'if you think I would allow harm to come to one hair on his head.'

Biting her lip, she turned back to Charlie and gave him a big hug. 'So, tell me about your fish, darling. What colour is it?'

He gave it frowning thought, then, 'Fish-coloured,' he decided.

Sandro's lips twitched. '*Avanti,*' he said. 'Let us go and find Doro, *figlio mio*. It is time you had a rest.'

'Let me take him,' Polly said quickly. 'To Julie.'

'But I am already going upstairs,' he said. 'So there is no need for you to do so. Unless, of course, you wish to share the siesta with me,' he added with touch of mockery.

'Thank you,' Polly acknowledged, stonily. 'But no.'

His mouth twisted. 'You seemed to find it enjoyable once.'

'Perhaps,' she said. 'But I really don't need to be constantly reminded of my mistakes—especially those in the distant past.'

'Last night is not so distant, *cara*,' he said softly. 'And you slept happily in my arms for most of it.'

Polly put her glass down very carefully. 'What are you talking about?'

'Think about it,' he advised, then swung Charlie onto his hip and went indoors, leaving her staring after him, alarm clenching like a fist inside her.

He was teasing her, Polly told herself, pacing backwards and forwards across her living room. For reasons of his own, he enjoyed needling her—seeing how far he could push her before the explosion came. That was all it was. She was sure of it.

And yet—and yet...

She couldn't forget that curious feeling of well-being that had surrounded her when she'd awoken that morning. How rested she'd felt. How completely relaxed.

And remembered, too, those times when they were lovers that he'd joined her in bed when she was already asleep, and she'd woken to find herself wrapped in his arms, her head tucked into the curve of his shoulder, and her lips against his skin. And, smiling, had slept again.

There was a strange familiarity about it all.

Oh, no, she groaned silently. Please—no...

And, all too soon now, she had to face him again, she thought glumly. She couldn't hide away anywhere, so the only thing she could do was bluff it out. Pretend that nothing had happened, which might even be true, and never refer to it again.

She was halfway to the door, when it opened abruptly and the *contessa* came in.

So much for privacy, Polly thought wryly.

She said, politely, '*Buongiorno, contessa*. Is there something I can do?'

The older woman stared around her for a long moment, then turned back to Polly, smiling stiffly. 'On the contrary, dear Paola. I came to make sure that you had everything you wanted—in your new domain.'

She gave the room another sharp, appraising look. 'I confess I have not visited it since Alessandro gave orders for its total renovation. I—I find it painful to see the changes, indeed I can barely recognise it, but I know I must not be a foolish old woman.'

Polly said quietly, 'I don't think anyone would ever see you in that light, *contessa*.' She paused. 'Were you very close to Sandro's mother? I didn't know.'

'Close to Maddalena?' the older woman queried sharply. 'I knew her, of course, but we were never on intimate terms. No, I was speaking of my cherished Bianca, who was also given this room by Alessandro's father as her personal retreat. She loved it here.' She sighed deeply. 'Now every trace of her has gone, even the portrait of her that my cousin Domenico had painted.' She paused, and a note of steel entered her voice. 'I am astonished that your husband should have so little regard for his father's wishes.'

'I'm sorry you feel like that,' Polly said, caught at a loss. 'Maybe you should take up the matter with Sandro himself.'

'My poor Bianca.' The *contessa* swept on regardless. 'How much she loved him—and what she endured for his sake. And how soon she is forgotten.' And she sighed again.

'I'm sure that's not true,' Polly told her quietly. 'I know he has the greatest respect for her memory, *contessa*.'

'Dear child, you are kind to say so. But the evidence makes that so hard to believe. She was such an innocent, and her only sin was to love Alessandro too much. And because of that—she died.'

She shook her head with the appearance of someone labouring under more sorrow than anger.

'He drove too fast—always. And that terrible day, he was in a temper—a wicked, dangerous rage. He had quarrelled with his father, so Bianca followed him, like the angel she was—insisted on going in the car with him to reason with him. To persuade him to return and make peace with his father.'

Her voice broke a little. 'Only for her, there was no return. He was too angry—too reckless to judge the bend correctly, and the car went into the ravine.

'He was never made to answer for what he had done, of course. His own injuries saved him from possible charges.

'But it is guilt he feels, my dear Paola—not respect—and that is why he has had every remnant of my poor Bianca's presence removed—even her portrait.'

She paused, looking keenly at Polly, who was standing with her arms wrapped round her body in an instinctive gesture of defence. 'I am sorry if I grieve you, but it is as well you should know the truth.'

Polly said quietly, 'I am sure my husband blames himself just as much as you could wish, *contessa*.'

The older woman's tone was almost purring. 'But call me Zia Antonia, I beg you. We cannot be strangers. Your position in this house is hardly an enviable one,' she added. 'Alessandro is so— unpredictable, and I fear you may find yourself much neglected. I hope that when problems arise, you will know you can always turn to me.'

'Thank you,' Polly said. 'I—I'm very grateful.' *Or am I?* she asked herself silently as she watched the *contessa* walk to the door, bestow another thin, honeyed smile and leave. *It's like feeling obligated to a cobra that's already bitten you once.*

But the *contessa*'s words had left her shaking inside. She was clearly implying that Sandro was guilty of manslaughter at the very least.

This, coupled with Emilio's comments about a possible cover-up at the official inquiry, painted a frightening picture, and one Polly did not even want to contemplate.

If he had been recklessly speeding and made a fatal error of judgement which caused the accident, then surely he had been well-punished for it. *The mark of Cain,* she thought, and shuddered.

But, at the same time, the power of the Valessi family was being highlighted for her in an awesome way, she realised unhappily.

Money was waved, and things happened. A girl who could prove a nuisance was dismissed back to her own country. An eyewitness to a car crash was persuaded to doctor his account of the tragedy to protect the heir to a dynasty. An expensive court action was threatened, and that same heir acquired a wife and child.

He would have hated the scandal of a court appearance, she thought. If I'd listened to my mother and stood up to him, maybe he'd have backed off. And I would not be here now, torn apart by doubts. Tormented equally by my fears and longings.

She looked down at the glow of the diamond on her hand. A symbol of a fever in the blood? she wondered. Or a cold flame that would consume her utterly, reducing her to ashes? As it might have destroyed Bianca three years earlier, she thought, and shivered.

And once she had gone, would she be so easily forgotten too?

There was a tap on the door, and Teodoro appeared.

'Please excuse me.' He inclined his head respectfully. 'But the *marchese* is asking for you to join him at the swimming pool. I should be happy to show you the way, *marchesa*, if you will accompany me.'

'Yes,' she said, and took a deep breath. 'Yes, of course.'

She got slowly to her feet, pushing her hair back with a mechanical gesture. Life went on, and whatever her mental turmoil, it seemed she was required to join Sandro, and needed to obey the summons. Accept the situation that had been forced upon her, she thought, and all its implications.

Because, after all, what other choice did she have?

And, straightening her shoulders, she reluctantly allowed Teodoro to escort her from the room, and out into the sunlight.

CHAPTER TEN

THE pool was an oval turquoise set in creamy marble, created, Polly guessed, out of a former sunken garden and reached by a series of shallow steps, which wound their way downwards through banks of flowering shrubs. And where Teodoro left her to make the rest of her way alone.

As she descended, she saw that the pool was surrounded by a broad sun-terrace with cushioned loungers and parasols, and, at the far end, there was a flamboyant piece of statuary, depicting some sea god surrounded by leaping dolphins.

And with equal flamboyance, a large inflatable duck with a coy smile and long eyelashes was bobbing quietly at the pool's shallow end.

Sandro was stretched out under one of the umbrellas, reading. He was wearing a pair of brief black trunks, which set off his lithe, bronzed body in a way that made her heart skip a momentary beat. His only other covering was the pair of designer sunglasses which he removed at her approach.

'*Ciao.*' He surveyed her with a faint frown. 'Are you all right?'

'Never better,' Polly lied too brightly. She looked around her. 'What—what a wonderful spot this is. And so peaceful.'

'I think the peace will be broken when Dorotea arrives with Carlino,' he said drily.

'Dorotea?' Polly asked, her own brows creasing, seating herself on an adjoining lounger. 'Why not Julie?'

He shrugged. 'Perhaps she is still learning her way about—or tired from the events of yesterday.'

'Yes,' she said. 'Perhaps.' She hesitated. 'I should apologise for my failure to join you this morning, and say goodbye to your guests. I hope no one was offended.'

'I explained you needed your rest,' he said. 'They understood completely.'

Faint colour invaded her face. 'Oh, I expect you made sure of that.'

136

'It was hardly a lie,' he said. 'You did not sleep well, because you were clearly troubled by bad dreams. Otherwise, why would you have spoken my name and reached for me, as you did?'

Her flush deepened. She said coldly, 'I wasn't aware of it, believe me. And I've had nightmares before,' she added.

'Not,' he said softly, 'when you have been in bed with me, *carissima.*'

She bit her lip. 'Perhaps not. But there was no need for any—intervention on your part.'

'Well,' he said lightly, picking up his book again, 'it will not occur again. From tonight, you will sleep alone, *bella mia.* I have given the necessary orders.'

'Thank you,' she said. 'My own bedroom as well as a personal living room. What luxury.' She paused. 'But can I ask not to be allocated another shrine to Bianca?'

His gaze sharpened. 'What are you talking about?'

'Your cousin Antonia visited me earlier. She was upset about the changes you'd made to your mother's room—especially the removal of Bianca's portrait.'

'I will tell Teodoro to rescue it from storage,' he said. 'And hang it in her own suite, if it means so much to her. But she already maintains a shrine to Bianca,' he added coldly. 'It is on the mountain road at the place where the car went over. There is a photograph, with a candle burning in front of it, and fresh flowers which she places there regularly. I am sure she would show it to you, if you asked.'

She said, 'I'll bear it in mind.' She paused. 'Not that it matters, but don't your servants find it a little strange that we're having separate rooms?'

'They are not paid to question my decisions,' he drawled. 'And they will not find it so extraordinary. My parents and grandparents had the same arrangements, and probably every generation of my family before that.

'And you are also under a misapprehension,' he added. 'You will not be moving. You will continue to sleep in the master bedroom, which is quite free of any connection with Bianca.' His tone was expressionless. 'As far as I know, she never entered it.'

She said uncertainly, 'But surely that's your room, and you should keep it.' She tried to smile. 'After all, you're very much the master here.'

'I can sleep anywhere,' he said. 'And besides, I shall be away from the *palazzo* a great deal.'

'You will?' She looked at him uncertainly.

'*Naturalamente*. My work involves a great deal of travelling, and this trip has been planned for a long time.' He slanted a look at her. 'If circumstances were different, I would take you with me, *cara*. But I cannot guarantee there will always be convenient bolsters in our accommodation.'

'Not that they seem to make much difference to you,' she flashed.

He hunched an indifferent shoulder. 'I held you, Paola, while you slept, and because you seemed to need comfort. If you wish me to apologise for that,' he added deliberately, 'you will wait forever.'

He looked her over. 'You are not dressed for swimming. You do not intend to join your son in the pool for the first time?'

She bit her lip. 'I didn't bring any swimwear with me. I—I suppose Teresa thought there was no need...that I would buy something when I got here.'

'It's not a problem.' He pointed to the pair of changing cabins that stood on the opposite side of the pool. 'You will find a selection there. I hope there will be something to your taste.'

'Or yours anyway,' she returned coolly.

He picked up his book. 'Then keep your clothes on,' he said with cool indifference, 'if you do not want to swim. And also if you do not care about the disappointment to Carlino,' he added silkily, offering the killer blow.

Oh, but she did want to swim. The sun seemed to be pouring its full intensity into this secluded marble bowl, and she could feel the sweat trickling down her body. The thought of cool water against her skin was irresistible.

She said, 'I care very much, and you know it. I—I'll go and change.'

Feeling self-conscious, she crossed to the women's cabin, but a swift glance backwards revealed that Sandro was absorbed in his book again.

The swimwear was displayed in a cupboard, a whole row of bikinis on padded hangers. There was one in black, and the rest were in a range of clear, pretty colours. To her surprise, all of them were in her size, and, even more astonishing, none of them were nearly as revealing as they might have been.

The violet bikini she eventually picked had sleek, simple lines, with cups that lifted and enhanced her breasts without undue exposure, and briefs that discreetly skimmed her hip bones. She slipped on the gauzy jacket that matched it, and slid her feet into white canvas mules before venturing outside again.

Sandro watched her walk towards him, his face enigmatic. 'I am glad at least one met with your approval,' he commented.

'They were all—lovely.' She hesitated. 'And not what I'd expected you to choose for your ladies.'

Sandro sighed, and put down his book. 'I chose them for you, Paola, this morning at the marina. You, and no one else,' he told her with a touch of harshness. 'This is my home, and I have never invited my "ladies", as you call them, here for poolside orgies, whatever you may believe.

'Finally, you are my wife,' he added cuttingly. 'And, in theory, I am permitted to see you in private in any state of undress I wish. In public, however, I prefer a certain decorum. Do I make myself clear?'

She bent her head. 'Perfectly. It's all down to appearances again.'

His smile was cynical. 'Of course, *cara mia*. Because appearances are all we have. So accustom yourself, as I am doing.'

He paused. 'And now try to smile, because here comes our son.'

Against all the odds, thought Polly as she pulled herself out of the water and reached for a towel, the session in the pool had turned out to be one of the happiest times she could remember in her life.

To her surprise, Charlie, his armbands securely in place, had taken to the water as if he belonged in it, and his wide-eyed enjoyment of this new environment had prompted a more relaxed response from herself as well. They played with a ball in the shallow end, and after some rowdy splashing games Polly steered her son carefully round the pool on the back of the duck, as he squealed with delight. Afterwards, she watched and encouraged as Charlie, under Sandro's patient guidance, managed his first uncertain swimming strokes.

It was, however, apparent that Sandro was strictly avoiding any but the most fleeting physical contact with herself, which created a few moments of awkwardness.

The only other drawback was the presence of Dorotea, who sat with her knitting at the poolside, uttering faint cries of alarm at intervals, in the apparent belief that Charlie was about to be allowed to drown by his negligent and uncaring parents.

If she really found it all so nerve-racking, why on earth hadn't she let Julie, who had swimming and life-saving qualifications, bring him down to the pool instead? Polly wondered with faint irritation.

As it was, Dorotea could not wait to get her charge out of the water and towelled down, as she clucked over him.

My mother all over again, Polly thought wryly. And something I shall have to watch.

Charlie was furious to discover that the inflatable duck would not be permitted to accompany him back to the *palazzo* or sleep with him that night, and threatened a tantrum. But Sandro diverted this by reminding the little boy that he was to have his special fish for supper, and that the duck might steal it from him. Besides, he added, improvising rapidly, the duck would also miss his pool, and keep them all awake during the night with his homesick quacking.

Polly, vigorously rubbing her dripping hair, watched Charlie depart, his hand in Dorotea's.

She glanced across at Sandro, who was also drying himself. She said on impulse, 'He's going to miss you terribly while you're away.'

'This time it is unavoidable, but it will not be for long,' Sandro said. 'And next time he will not miss me at all, because I shall take him with me.'

Polly folded the towel she'd been using with immense care.

She said, 'I'm sorry. What are you saying? Because I don't think I quite understand.'

'It is perfectly simple, *cara*,' he drawled. 'My next trip is a much shorter one, and I intend Carlino to accompany me.'

Polly looked at him, stupefied. 'But he's only a baby,' she whispered.

'He will not be asked to make any boardroom decisions.' Sandro tossed his towel aside and sat down on the lounger, raking back the tousled dark hair.

'It's still ludicrous,' she protested. 'You—you can't take him away.'

He smiled faintly. 'And who is going to stop me? You, *bella mia*?' He shook his head. 'I don't think so.'

She took a deep breath. 'Why are you doing this?'

'Because I love his company,' he said. 'And I wish to strengthen the bond between us, now that it has been established.'

'But I've never been without him for more than a night,' Polly said desperately.

'Then you are fortunate,' he said with sudden harshness. 'I have already missed too much of his life, and I do not mean him to grow up a stranger to me, as I was to my own father for so long.'

She went over and knelt beside him, her hands gripping his arms. 'Sandro.' Her tone was pleading. 'Don't do this to me, please. Or to him. He's too young.'

His face expressionless, he freed himself gently but inexorably from her clasp.

'My mind is made up,' he said. 'He would be travelling with me tomorrow, but my arrangements are already made.'

'Including a trip to Rome, no doubt.' The words were out before she could stop them.

His brows lifted. 'Rome, yes,' he said, with faint mockery. 'That is unmissable, of course. Afterwards—Milan, Florence, Turin and Venice. The next time will involve a simpler route.'

She stayed on her knees, looking up at him. She said huskily, 'Let me go with you.'

For a long moment he was silent, then very slowly and with infinite care his finger traced the curve of her breast above the cling of the soaked bikini cup, then slid under the strap, pulling it down without haste from her shoulder.

He said quietly, the topaz eyes intent and watchful, 'But when do you offer your company, *carissima*? In a few weeks with Carlino? Or tomorrow—alone—with me? On a honeymoon?'

The vivid sunlight seemed to enclose them both in a golden breathless cloud, where she could hear nothing but the trembling hurry of her own heart. Feel nothing but the burn of his touch on her cool, damp skin. See in his eyes the urgency of another, deeper question that she dared not answer.

She longed to tell him 'Yes', she realised dazedly, and with shame.

Because she knew that tiny tendrils of sensation were uncurling at his touch, arousing potent memories of her nakedness explored and exquisitely enjoyed. Igniting the urgent need to yield herself once more to the pleasure of his hands and mouth. To lose herself, trembling, in the totality of his powerful masculinity. A woman reunited with the only man she had ever known. Ever wanted.

Her nipples ached to be free of their flimsy covering and offered to the balm of his tongue.

She wanted to give up the struggle, and surrender. To forget the unhappiness of the past, and abandon the remnants of her pride to the passionate delight of the moment.

Instead she snatched, drowning, at the last vestige of sanity and self-respect she possessed. Because a moment in time was all he might have to give her. And she could not bear to be taken and then discarded once again on a whim.

Especially when he had just made it more than clear that it was only their child he wanted and valued.

He said softly, 'Paola, I need you to answer me.'

'I'm sure you know already,' she said. 'It has to be—Charlie, and always will be.'

Hand miraculously steady, she hitched her bikini strap back into place, and got to her feet.

'After all, a business trip is scarcely a honeymoon, *excellenza*,' she went on with forced lightness. 'And, as you say, your arrangements for tomorrow are already made—including some I am sure you would not wish to alter. And for which I would be—surplus to requirements.'

Tell me it's not true, her heart cried out to him silently. Say that you want me, and only me. That you love me. Beg me—just once—please—please...

But: 'How understanding you are, *cara*,' he drawled. 'The perfect wife for a man who does not wish to be married.'

'I wish,' she said, 'that I could pay you the same compliment. Say that you're the ideal husband for a reluctant wife.' She paused. 'And now perhaps you will excuse me?'

She turned away, walking to the changing pavilion, but before she had gone three yards Sandro was beside her, swinging her round to face him.

'Tell me one thing.' His voice was soft and savage. 'Who will you reach for in the nights ahead, when the bad dreams come?'

She tore herself free. 'No one,' she answered hoarsely. 'A lesson I should have learned three years ago, because all my bad dreams are about you, *signore*.' She paused. 'Now let me go.'

His mouth curled. 'With pleasure, my sweet wife. Enjoy your freedom, because it is all you will have from me.'

He went back to his lounger, and lay there face downwards, and motionless, pillowing his head on his folded arms.

Suddenly, getting back to the *palazzo* seemed a safer option than retrieving her clothes, and Polly found herself going up the stone steps two at a time, as a voice in her head whispered breathlessly, It's over—finished—done with.

And wishing with all her heart that she could feel relief, instead of the desolation that stalked her like a shadow through the late-afternoon sun.

The *palazzo* without its master was a different proposition altogether, and Polly became aware of that within forty-eight hours of Sandro's departure.

Following the afternoon at the pool, he had not joined her for dinner, informing her through a bewildered Teodoro that he had an engagement in town. And the next morning he was gone almost before the sun was up, so there was no opportunity to say goodbye.

Polly gathered from Rafaella that a courteous reluctance to disturb her through his early departure had been used to explain his move to another bedroom. She also realised, almost at once, that the excuse had fooled nobody, and that being regarded as the *marchese*'s unwanted bride was not an enviable situation to be in.

How else to explain the none-too-subtle shift in attitude by the rest of the household almost as soon as Sandro had gone? The thinly veiled hostility she'd encountered in the nursery seemed to have spread through the *palazzo* like a miasma.

The food she was served was often cold, her attempts to speak Italian were ignored, her bell left unanswered, and once, in a mirror, she'd caught a glimpse of one of the maids making the sign to ward off the evil eye behind her back.

It was no comfort to realise that Julie was faring even worse. She saw hardly anything of Charlie, being designated instead to hand-wash and iron all his clothes, and even his bedding, in between scouring the nursery itself.

And when Polly told Dorotea firmly that this had to stop, and Charlie's things must be sent to the laundry, so that Julie could bring the little boy down to the pool each afternoon, she was met with shrugs and looks of incomprehension.

And each time Polly herself entered the nursery, she could feel the resentment in the air.

Even Rafaella seemed oddly subdued, and it was hard to get a smile out of her.

Perhaps she resents working for someone who's a *marchesa* only in name, and a second-class citizen in reality, Polly thought wryly.

But it wasn't just the attitude of the staff that she found difficult to take. It was missing Sandro.

She thought of him all the time, found herself listening for his step, and the sound of his voice. She had no idea when he was to return, and there was no one she could ask.

Least of all himself, she acknowledged, even though he telephoned the *palazzo* each day to speak to Charlie. On the occasions when he asked to speak to her too, their exchanges were cool and stilted.

Strangers, she thought achingly. With nothing to say to each other.

But even living a separate existence under his roof was preferable to his continuing absence, she thought. And her imagination worked overtime in picturing where he was, and what he might be doing. And with whom...

The nights were the worst. In spite of the summer heat, the vast bed she occupied seemed as wide and chilly as a winter ocean, and sleep was a deep pit of loneliness which swallowed her up, then released her, restless and unrefreshed when morning came. And often, when she woke, her face was wet with tears.

She wished with all her heart that she'd been the one to move out. Everything that belonged to him had been scrupulously removed, but it had made little difference. His presence still seemed to linger, invisible but potent.

He had been gone nearly a fortnight when Polly received a pleasant surprise—a flying visit from Teresa, Ernesto and the twins, who had come to visit his parents in Naples.

They were clearly stunned to discover Sandro's absence, but quickly concealed their shock under a flood of chatter and laughter.

Polly knew that Teresa would have picked up immediately on her wan face and shadowed eyes, but that good manners would keep her from asking awkward questions.

But when Ernesto was down at the pool with the children, and Polly was alone with Teresa in her living room, she did confide in the other girl about her staff problems, and saw her frown.

'Your Italian is good,' she said. 'And will become better with practice. So, there should be no misunderstandings—especially with Dorotea. She has worked at the *palazzo* longer than anyone, and is devoted to the Valessi family. You are the mother of Alessandro's heir, so she should be your greatest supporter.' She patted Polly's hand. 'I will go and ask for some coffee and almond cakes to be brought, and see what I can find out.'

When she returned, her face was solemn. 'They believe they are going to lose their jobs,' she said. 'That you intend to replace them all with your own servants from England, and that Julie is only the first of many.'

'But that's complete nonsense.' Polly stared at her, aghast. 'I haven't got any servants in England, for heaven's sake. And Julie's here on a strictly temporary basis. In fact, I'm surprised she hasn't walked out already.'

She shook her head. 'And even if I wanted to make changes—which I don't—Sandro would never allow it. Surely they know that?'

Teresa shrugged. 'They know only that he is a man with a new bride,' she commented drily. 'And that you have powers of persuasion with him that they lack.'

She hesitated. 'Dorotea has been the most deeply hurt. She believes you think her too elderly to have charge of Carlino, and too old-fashioned in her ways, and that is why she will be the first to be replaced.'

'No wonder it's like walking into a brick wall whenever I go near the nursery,' Polly said bitterly. 'Oh, God, how can this have happened?'

Teresa chose her words carefully. 'It is clear to me, Paola, that these rumours have been started by someone with authority, whose word they feel they can trust. I think you have an enemy, *cara*,' she added gently.

Polly had been staring at the floor, but now her head came up sharply. 'Don't tell me,' she said with sudden grimness. 'The *contessa*.'

'It seems so. She has offered to be their champion, and fight their cause with you. No doubt she is already telling them that you are intransigent, and will make no concessions.

'You need to do something, Paola, before they walk out,' she added candidly, 'and Alessandro returns to find his house deserted.'

'Perhaps I'm the one who should leave,' Polly said in a low, unhappy voice. 'I'm clearly out of my depth here. I thought they just despised me because I didn't know how to be a *marchesa*.'

'But you have one great advantage over any lies that Antonia Barsoli tells,' Teresa said quietly. 'You are Alessandro's chosen wife, and they love him.' She smiled encouragingly at Polly. 'Make it clear their jobs are not threatened, and fill that big nursery with more babies for Dorotea to cherish, and they will love you too.'

Easier said than done, Polly thought, forcing a smile of agreement. On both counts.

She was smiling again when she waved them off a few hours later, but she felt bleak as she went slowly back indoors. For a while, she'd been let off the hook, and allowed to put her troubles aside to enjoy their company.

Now her temporary reprieve was over, and her problems were crowding round again. But at least she now knew what she was up against, she thought. And Teresa's advice had been practical as well as bracing, so she had a plan of action too.

It had done her so much good to have them here, and she'd extracted a serious promise from them to come for a proper visit later in the summer. If, of course, she was still here, she amended with a pang.

However, just for a few hours, she hadn't felt quite so isolated, and she missed them all badly now that they'd gone back to Naples.

Nor was she the only one.

Charlie, Julie reported ruefully, had screamed blue murder when he realised the twins were leaving, and had subsequently cried himself to sleep.

'He really needs other children to play with on a regular basis,' she added, with a swift sideways glance at Polly, who flushed, guessing that the other girl was thinking in terms of brothers and sisters for him.

Clearly, because she was part of the opposition, any gossip about the separate rooms had passed her by completely.

Perhaps, as time went on, she would establish some kind of social life, Polly thought, trying to be hopeful, and meet other young mothers whose children could provide Charlie with companionship.

Meanwhile, she would simply have to go on enduring all these none-too-subtle hints, she told herself and sighed.

The next morning dawned overcast and heavy, with even a hint of thunder in the air.

Good day for starting a different kind of storm, perhaps, Polly thought as she drank the tea that Rafaella had brought to her bedroom.

As the girl emerged from the dressing room with the pale blue linen trousers and matching jersey top that she'd been asked to fetch, Polly gave her a quick smile.

'Has your grandfather come back yet from Salerno?' she asked. 'Because I'd still like to talk to him.'

'I have not forgotten, *madame*.' There was a faintly evasive note in Rafaella's voice. 'I will ask again.' She paused. 'Shall I run your bath now?'

'Yes—please.'

Polly took another reflective sip of tea. It sounded as if Giacomo had already been approached and returned a negative response, she thought, troubled. Which seemed to suggest that he might well have something to hide over Sandro's accident.

For good or ill, I need to know, she told herself.

In the mail that was brought to her living room later that morning was a postcard from Cornwall. 'Just like old times,' ran the message. 'Keep well. Be happy.' The handwriting was her father's, but her mother had signed it too, she noticed thankfully.

She took out the notes that she'd made the previous day with Teresa's help, and read them through several times, committing them to memory, before she put them in the empty grate and set fire to them.

Then she rang for Teodoro. 'Will you tell all the staff that I wish to see them in the *salotto* at three o'clock?' she instructed quietly. 'And I mean everyone.'

'Even Dorotea? The little Carlino is upset because he cannot swim today, and she plans to take him out in the car this afternoon.'

'Certainly Dorotea,' Polly said crisply. 'Julie can look after my son.'

'*Sì, Vossignoria.*' He hesitated, studying her with worried eyes. 'Is there some problem?'

She smiled at him. 'Nothing that can't be fixed, I hope. Three p.m., then.'

Teodoro had done his work well, because the *salotto* seemed full of people when Polly entered.

She had decided not to change into more formal clothes, because that might look as if she was trying too hard. Instead, she had simply combed her hair and applied some colour to her lips.

She stood in front of them all, her back to the open door, and spoke slowly using the Italian phrases that Teresa had written down for her. 'I have called you here today to clear up a serious misunderstanding. Some of you may have heard a rumour that I plan to take your jobs from you, and have you dismissed from the *palazzo*. I wish to set your minds at rest, and assure you that there is no truth in this story, and I cannot understand where it has come from, or why it has been spread in this malicious way.'

She heard faint gasps from her audience, but went quietly on. 'I am sorry that none of you felt able to come to me and ask if it was true, but we are to a large extent still strangers to each other. I intend to change that, and take on much of the everyday management of the household myself.'

More gasps, and louder.

'One thing I must make clear at once,' she continued, raising her voice a little above the whispering that had also broken out. 'In the last few weeks, the life of my little boy has changed completely. He has a new environment to learn, and a new language, too.'

She paused. 'Julie, who came with us from England, is not simply a *bambinaia*, but a friend who is helping him come to terms with all these puzzling changes. But it was always the plan of the *marchese* that Dorotea, who cherished him in childhood, should ultimately take full charge of his son in turn. And this is my wish, also.'

She looked directly at Dorotea, who was staring back, her mouth working, and her hands twisting in her white apron.

'My husband, the *marchese*, has a demanding career,' Polly continued. 'And I wish him to have a peaceful and well-run home to return to. I hope we can work together to achieve this, but anyone who cannot accept my regime is, of course, free to leave.'

She smiled around her, keeping it positive. Letting them see she expected their co-operation. 'Although, naturally, I hope you will all stay. And that you will bring any future difficulties straight to me. Because I am the mistress of the house.'

But it appeared she had lost them, because nearly all eyes were looking past her to the door behind.

And then she heard Sandro's voice, cool and slightly mocking. '*Bravo, marchesa.* I am impressed.'

She swung round, her heart thumping, and saw him, leaning against the massive doorframe, watching her steadily with a smile that did not reach his eyes.

CHAPTER ELEVEN

THE almost agonised leap of her heart at the sight of him stilled and died. She checked the impulsive step towards him she'd been about to take, waiting rigidly instead for him to come to her side.

As he did, his cool gaze sweeping the room, his hand lightly clasping her shoulder. 'So,' he said, 'I suggest that anyone wishing to remain in our employ gets back to work—*subito*.'

Polly had never seen a room empty so quickly or silently.

'Teodoro,' Sandro added as the majordomo approached, 'be good enough to bring us coffee—in the *marchesa*'s own living room, I think, if you permit, *cara mia*?'

As if she had any real choice in the matter, thought Polly, finding herself led gently but firmly by the hand to the room in question.

Sandro waved Polly to one of the sofas, and seated himself opposite, long legs stretched out in front of him as he loosened his tie. He looked tired, she thought, and he needed a shave.

She looked down at her clasped hands. 'I wasn't expecting to see you.'

'I did not anticipate returning so soon.'

She cleared her throat. 'Did—did you have a successful trip?'

'So far,' he said. 'Unfortunately, it was curtailed before I reached Rome.'

'Oh.' She felt a stab of fierce pleasure. 'Why was that?'

'Because last night I received a telephone call from Teresa and Ernesto telling me that you had problems here, and might need me.'

She looked at him, stunned. So, they knew where to find you, she thought, biting her lip. And I didn't.

'Therefore, I came to you at once,' he went on. 'Only to find you coping admirably alone.'

She said, 'It's kind of them to be so concerned, but they've already been of great help. They—they shouldn't have dragged

150

you into this. Interrupted your trip.' She shrugged. 'Really, it was all pretty trivial. A storm in a teacup.'

His mouth twisted. 'If it is like the storm outside, Paola *mia*,' he said as a sudden flash of lightning illuminated the room, followed almost at once by a reverberating clap of thunder, 'then it may get worse before it is better.'

He paused. 'So, has your rallying call halted the revolution, *cara*?' he asked softly. 'Or are there still matters to be dealt with?'

She met his gaze with as much composure as she could muster. 'I think it's—settled.'

'Ah,' he said. 'Then Zia Antonia is at this moment packing her bags.'

She swallowed. 'No, of course not. I—I couldn't do that.'

'But you are the mistress here,' he said. 'I heard you say so.'

'Yes.' Her hands tightened on each other almost painfully. 'But perhaps I was presuming too much.'

'Or not enough,' he returned drily. 'While I have been away, I have had time to think, and I realise that the situation here cannot be allowed to continue.'

Before she could even ask what he meant, the door was flung open and the *contessa* came in, all smiles.

'*Caro* Alessandro.' He rose at her entrance, and she reached up to embrace him. 'But what a wonderful surprise for us all. I should have been here to greet you, but I was resting in my room. This weather—so dreadful. I shall be fortunate to avoid a migraine.'

She turned to Polly, a reproving note in her voice. 'But, my dear child, you have ordered no refreshment for your husband on his return. A little remiss of you, if you will forgive me for saying so.'

'I am sure she will do so,' Sandro said quietly. 'And coffee is being brought, so do not concern yourself.'

The *contessa*'s tone became steel covered by honey. 'But I must express my anxieties, my dearest cousin. Your household is in my charge after all, and yet my maid had to inform me of your arrival.' She tutted smilingly. 'She also informs me that our dear Paola summoned all the staff to a meeting a little while ago, to harangue them on the subject of loyalty. If she had issues to raise on that or any other matter, then surely she should have come to me first.'

The smile she bestowed on Polly was pure acid. 'One must make allowances for your inexperience, dear girl. You are not accustomed to dealing with servants, of course. But, in future, there is certainly no need to indulge in such...ludicrous histrionics—or to send for your husband, while he is away on important business, and involve him in a purely domestic matter.'

'I hope Alessandro is not too angry with you,' she added on a teasing note that set Polly's teeth on edge.

'I am not angry at all,' Sandro corrected her courteously. 'And nor did Paola send for me. I had other reasons for my return.' He moved across to Polly and put his arm round her, drawing her close to his side.

'I felt, you understand, that I had left my bride alone for too long, and could not bear to spend another night away from her. A very different domestic matter,' he said softly.

Polly looked down at the floor, aware that every drop of blood in her veins had moved to her face and was tingling there.

The *contessa*'s little laugh was husk-dry. 'Why, Alessandro, how marriage has tamed you,' she said. 'You have become quite a romantic, *caro mio*.' She paused theatrically. '*Dio mio*. Tell me that I have not intruded on a private moment.'

Sandro smiled back at her. 'Not,' he said softly, 'while the key for that door remains unaccountably missing. Perhaps you would have the goodness to search for it again.'

Just open, Polly told the floor silently. Just open and swallow me—please.

'In fact,' Sandro went on remorselessly, 'you may bring my wife all the keys. She can hardly embark upon her new duties without them.'

The delicate blusher that the *contessa* wore was suddenly like a stain on her white face. Her drawn breath was a hiss.

'You intend *her* to manage the *palazzo*. A girl from nowhere, without family or position? A girl for whom you sacrificed my Bianca, and broke your father's heart? And whose only accomplishment has been to bear your bastard?'

Her strident laugh broke in the middle. 'Are you insane? You see for yourself that she cannot handle your servants. And who will ever accept her?'

'I have,' Sandro said with deadly quietness. 'Nothing else is necessary.' He paused. 'Ever since Paola came here you have attempted to undermine her, but each time she has proved to be more than your equal. Today was one such moment. Nor will I allow her to endure your insults any longer.'

He looked at the older woman, his mouth hard and set. 'My father offered you a home, and I acceded to his wishes and permitted you to remain, setting convenience against my better judgement. But my tolerance is now exhausted.'

'No,' she said hoarsely. 'No, Alessandro. You cannot do this.'

He went on as if she had not spoken. 'Out of respect for my father, I shall provide you with a house. I shall also consult with my lawyer on a suitable supplement to your income. But you must and will leave Comadora.'

'But I helped you find her.' Her fingers were twisting together like claws. 'I searched for this—*sciattona* in England because you still wanted her.'

'No, *contessa*,' Sandro said softly, 'you discovered somehow that I wished to find her, and told Emilio. What did you do, I wonder? Listen at a door? Read my correspondence?' He shook his head. 'It would not be the first time.

'And Emilio sent you to England on his own behalf, hoping to buy lurid details of my affair with Paola, and discredit me at last.' He shrugged. 'But, unluckily for both of you, I guessed what you were doing, and found her first. So you had to pretend you had been working for me all the time.'

His mouth twisted. 'How galling that must have been. How much had Emilio offered for your services?'

Her thin body was as taut as a wire. 'I would have done it for nothing,' she spat back. 'How could I have known you would forget everything that was due to your name, and marry your discarded whore?'

There was a terrible silence. Polly turned away, feeling sick, her hands pressed to her burning face. Sandro walked to the fireplace and reached for the bell rope, but as he did so there was a knock on the door, and Teodoro came in with the tray of coffee.

He checked instinctively, his glance darting from one to another, but Sandro beckoned him forward. 'Please escort the *contessa* to her room,' he said. 'She is unwell. Call her doctor, and tell her maid to stay with her.'

Teodoro set the tray on a side-table, and offered the *contessa* a deferential arm which she ignored, walking slowly and stiffly to the door. Where she turned.

'You will be sorry for this.' Her tone sounded almost conversational. 'In the past I have argued against Emilio's wish to have the inquiry into Bianca's death reopened. But no longer. This time, *marchese*, you will appear and answer for what you did. And your loyal accomplice, Giacomo Raboni, will be made to tell all he knows—in public. Emilio will see to that.'

Another lightning flash lit up the room. In its momentary glare, Sandro's face looked carved from granite, the scar livid against his cheek.

He said, 'If he hopes to buy Giacomo, he is wasting his time.'

The *contessa* shrugged. 'Everyone has their price, my dear cousin,' she said softly. She sent Polly a malevolent glance. 'Including, if you remember, the little gold-digger you call your wife. Where will she be, I wonder, when you come out of jail?'

Teodoro, his face rigid with shock, seemed to grow another six inches in height. He took the *contessa*'s arm without gentleness and hustled her from the room.

The thunder roared again, and rain began to fall, huge, heavy drops beating a tattoo on the terrace, and hurling themselves in gusts against the window.

Polly sank down on one of the sofas, because her legs would no longer support her. Resting her elbows on her knees, she buried her face in her hands and waited for the shaking to stop.

Eventually she became aware that Sandro had come to sit beside her, and she raised her head and looked at him.

She said in a small, quiet voice, 'That was so—terrible.'

'I am sorry, Paola.' He spoke gently. 'You should not have had to endure that. I did not realise she was so near the edge.' His hand covered hers and she realised he was trembling a little too.

She said on a rush, 'I—I should go up to the nursery. Charlie may be frightened of the storm.'

'In a moment,' he said. 'But stay with me now. We need to talk.'

'Yes.' She ran the tip of her tongue round her dry mouth. 'I—I suppose we must.' She paused. 'I always knew the *contessa* didn't like me,' she said slowly. 'But—it was more than that. It was hatred. Not just for me—but also for you.'

His mouth tightened. 'Until now, I only saw the bitterness, and thought I understood. When she came here twenty years ago, I think she believed that my father would eventually offer her marriage. Only he had no such intention. His relationship with my mother had brought happiness to neither, and, after her death, he was content with an occasional discreet liaison.

'When Antonia saw she had nothing to hope for from him, she diverted all that fierce energy into preparing Bianca as a bride for me. Perhaps she felt her own thwarted dreams would be fulfilled by the next generation. But it was not the usual matchmaking that older women sometimes indulge in. Even as young as I was, and as careless, I sensed there was something wrong. Something obsessive—and dark. Just as I felt...' He paused. 'Well, that is not important. Let me say that I began to spend as little time as possible at Comadora.'

'But why did your father go along with her scheme if he saw how you felt?'

Sandro hesitated. 'He saw marriage as a business arrangement, not a matter of emotion,' he told her slowly. 'Also I believe he felt guilty, so his encouragement was a form of recompense to Antonia for having disappointed her so deeply himself.'

Polly thought of the portrait of the late *marchese* which hung at the top of the stairs, remembering the harsh lines of the dark face beneath the grizzled hair, the thin mouth and piercing eyes that she felt followed her as she passed. Not a man, she thought, who looked as if he ever suffered from remorse, and she repressed a shiver.

'When the accident happened to Bianca, the *contessa* must have felt as if she'd died herself,' she said quietly. 'Perhaps we shouldn't blame her too harshly. Especially...' She stopped hurriedly, aware that she'd been about to say *when there are so many questions over what really happened.*

'Especially?' Sandro had noticed her hesitation.

She said, 'Especially when you have lost someone that you love so much.' She remembered the weeks after her return to England. The greyness of her life as one bleak day followed another. The nights she'd spent in bitter weeping, her eyes and throat raw with grief and bewilderment. Her stunned sense of isolation, caught as she was between her mother's anger and her father's disappointment.

'She'll feel as if she's in an abyss,' she went on, half to herself. 'With no way out, and no one to turn to. Facing an eternity of emptiness.'

Her own turning point had come when she'd felt the first faint flutter of her baby moving inside her, she realised. And from somewhere she'd found the strength to reclaim her life and sanity.

If there hadn't been Charlie, she thought, I could have ended up like the *contessa*, corroded with anger and bitterness.

He said with faint grimness, 'Almost you persuade me, *cara*, but not quite. She cannot remain here.'

'But you can't make her go,' Polly said passionately. 'Can't you see she means what she says? She and Emilio will rake up everything that happened three years ago and use it against you. You know that they will.'

He was very still suddenly. And when he moved, it was to release her hand.

He said quietly, almost conversationally, 'You speak, *cara*, as if I had something to fear. Is that what you think?'

'How do I know what to think?' The loss of the gentle clasp of his fingers round hers made her feel suddenly bereft. 'All I hear is that the inquiry wasn't told everything. That Rafaella's grandfather, who found you, is sworn to secrecy. My God, you've just admitted as much.' She swallowed. 'So I have to believe you have something to hide—and that the *contessa* and your vile cousin will move heaven and earth to uncover it. And once these things start, who knows where they can lead?'

'Clearly you imagine they could lead to prison,' Sandro drawled. 'Unless I decide instead to submit to blackmail. Neither option has much appeal, *bella mia*. And I would not be much of a man if I were to choose either of them without a fight.

'But then you do not have a very high opinion of me, anyway,' he added with a shrug. 'Is that why you have been trying to persuade Giacomo to meet you through Rafaella? And why you have had no success?

'Unfortunately for you, whenever an attempt is made to contact him, he immediately informs my lawyers, and they tell me. And that, my loving wife, is one of the other reasons I decided to make an early return, to suggest that you waste no more time on these fruitless enquiries.

'But then, what does it really matter?' He got to his feet, stretching lithely. 'Except that I am once again the villain,' he added mockingly. 'But that is something I shall have to live with.'

He paused. 'And now I am going to shower and change,' he

went on. 'Under the circumstances, I shall dine in the town tonight. I would not wish to spoil your appetite by forcing you to eat with a murderer.'

'I never said that,' Polly protested. 'I never would.'

His smile was grim. 'But I swear it must have crossed your mind, *mi adorata*. And the knowledge of that might turn my stomach too.'

As he strode to the door, she said huskily, 'Sandro—please. I just need to know the truth.'

'Truth,' he echoed contemptuously. 'It is just a word, Paola, like so many others. Like love, for example, and loyalty. Like honour and faith. Just words to be used and forgotten, as we will eventually forget today ever existed.' He inclined his head curtly, and was gone.

Polly sat staring at the closed door. She knew she should go after him, pour out all her doubts and fears—all her confused emotions. Make him listen. Make him, somehow, understand.

He had clearly expected her to trust him without question, but how was that possible when she was still dealing with the nightmare of the past, and his betrayal?

We both loved him, she thought wretchedly. Both Bianca, and myself. And he wanted neither of us. The only difference is that I survived, and she didn't. The margin is that small.

And I still love him, no matter what he does, or what he is. And I know now that beyond logic, beyond reason, I always shall, because I can't help myself. He's part of me—my flesh, my blood, the pulse of my heart. Because, in spite of everything, I only feel safe with his arms around me.

And, like the *contessa*, that's a tragedy I have somehow to endure.

She gave a long, shaking sigh. The abyss was back, it seemed, and deeper than ever. And with as little hope for escape.

After a while she got up wearily, and went to the table where the forgotten coffee waited. It was still hot, and it provided her momentarily with the jolt she needed.

She and Sandro might be a million miles apart, but upstairs was a child who might need her.

When she reached the nursery she paused, taking a deep breath before she went in. If she walked into the usual wall of resentment, she wasn't sure she could bear it.

Dorotea was there, seated in one of the big rocking chairs that flanked the hearth, knitting busily, while opposite her sat Julie with Charlie on her lap, fast asleep.

The older woman looked up at Polly hovering in the doorway, and her plump face creased into an equally hesitant smile.

She got to her feet, indicating respectfully that Polly should take her seat, then signalled to Julie to transfer the little boy to his mother's arms.

This safely achieved, Dorotea stood for a moment, and patted Polly awkwardly on the shoulder as Charlie murmured drowsily and pushed his small round head against the familiar curve of her breast. '*Bene,*' she said. 'Is good now, *vossignoria, sì?*'

'*Sì,*' Polly agreed, her throat tightening. 'This—is good.'

Dorotea beckoned to Julie, and they both disappeared into the night nursery, leaving Polly alone with her child. Leaning back, eyes half closed, she listened to the storm retreating over the hills. Just the act of holding Charlie quietly seemed to offer a kind of peace amid the turmoil of emotions that assailed her.

Whatever Sandro might feel about her, she told herself, whatever darkness there might be inside him, his love for Charlie was unqualified and beyond doubt, and she could cling to that. Because even if her husband never smiled at her again—never touched her—their son remained an indissoluble link between them.

She was suddenly aware she was no longer alone, and, glancing round, saw Sandro standing in the doorway, watching her, his mouth hard, the dark brows drawn together.

She wanted to speak, but what could she say? Tell him that as long as they were together, nothing else mattered? But they were not together, and how could they ever be, when there was so much to divide them?

Unless you came to me now, she thought, her heart in her eyes as she looked back at him. Unless you held us—your wife, and your child. And if you would promise to try and love me a little as you love him. Then I wouldn't care about anything else.

Surely—*surely* he could feel the yearning in her, the unassuaged and aching need, and show her a little mercy—couldn't he?

But just as her lips pleadingly framed his name, he turned away and left as silently as he'd appeared.

And Polly sat where she was, forcing back the tears that were bitter in her throat, because she could not allow Charlie to wake and find her crying.

She spent a restless, unhappy night, and woke late the following morning, to the sunlight and an incongruously flawless sky.

'*Buongiorno, madame.*' Rafaella appeared with coffee as if on signal. 'It is so beautiful today with no storm.' She beamed at Polly. 'The *marchese* asks if you will honour him by joining him at breakfast. And wishes you to know that Signor Molena will be there also.'

'Molena?' Polly queried, feeling the name should mean something.

'His *signore*'s *avoccato*,' Rafaella explained.

'Oh,' Polly said in a hollow voice, recalling that terrible afternoon at her mother's house. 'The lawyer. I—I remember.'

'*Sì*, the lawyer.' Rafaella said the word with care, and smiled again. 'Today, *vossignoria* is to meet with my grandfather,' she added with real excitement. 'His excellency has said so.'

Polly stared at her. 'Your grandfather?' she said slowly. 'Are you serious?'

'*Certamente, madame.*' The girl paused. 'Also the *contessa* goes with you,' she added more hesitantly.

'I see.' Polly digested that apprehensively, not understanding at all. 'Is she—well enough?'

She had questioned Teodoro haltingly about the *contessa*'s condition the previous evening, and been told that the doctor had paid her a lengthy visit, and administered a sedative. Also that a nurse would be coming to spend the night, and that a transfer to a private clinic the next day was also being considered.

Polly, wincing inwardly, had given him a quiet word of thanks.

But if the *contessa* was well enough to go out, maybe a less rigorous solution would be found, she thought.

She popped into the nursery on her way downstairs to kiss Charlie good morning, and wished she could have lingered there forever.

When she finally reached the door of the *sala da pranzo*, she had to force herself to open the door and go in.

'Good morning, *cara*,' Sandro rose politely. 'You remember Alberto, of course.'

'It is a pleasure to see you again, *marchesa*.' Signor Molena bowed politely, and she murmured something in reply.

Why was he there? she wondered as she helped herself to a slice of cold ham she would never eat, and poured some coffee. Had he been summoned to tell her that her brief, ill-starred marriage was over?

She sat pushing the meat round her plate, while the two men talked quietly, their faces slightly troubled.

But the coffee put heart into her, and when Sandro said abruptly, 'If you have finished breakfast, Paola, we will go,' she was able to rise to her feet with a semblance of composure.

There were two cars parked in front of the house, and Polly saw that the *contessa* was being helped into the second of them by a brisk-looking woman in a white uniform.

The older woman looked bent and ill, and for an instant Polly quailed. Then she felt her arm taken firmly, and Sandro was guiding her towards the leading car.

She hung back, looking up into his face, searching in vain for some sign of softening.

'Sandro,' she whispered. 'Please—we don't have to do this.'

'Yes,' he said quietly, 'we do, *cara mia*.'

'But it's none of my business—I see that now. And I'm sorry—so sorry to have interfered.'

'It is too late to draw back,' he told her harshly. 'Only the truth will do for my cousin, and for you, it seems. This is what you wanted, and this is what you will get. So, *andiamo*. Let's go.'

She sat rigidly beside him in the back of the car, her hands clenched together, as Signor Molena took his place beside the chauffeur, and the cars began to move forward.

And above the whisper of tyres on gravel, she could hear a small voice in her head repeating 'Too late' over and over again, and she was afraid.

CHAPTER TWELVE

THE dusty road in front of them climbed steeply and endlessly. They had passed through several tiny villages where the main streets were passable by only one vehicle at a time, but all signs of habitation were now behind them.

Polly had gone down to the town and visited the marina several times, but this was the first time she had been driven up into the mountains behind Comadora, and she was too tense to take real stock of her surroundings.

After the rain, the air was clear, and the creamy stone of the jagged crags, heavily veined in shades of grey and green, seemed close enough to touch. It was a landscape of scrub and thorn, stabbed in places with the darkness of cedars. Above it a solitary bird wheeled, watchful and predatory.

She found she was shivering slightly, and broke the silence. 'Is this the road to Sorrento?'

'One of them.' He did not look at her, and she could see his hand was clenched on his thigh.

I've made him do this, she thought bleakly. Made him confront whatever demons are waiting in this desolate place, and he'll never forgive me.

They had been travelling for about ten more minutes when the chauffeur began to slow down. The car rounded a sharp bend, and Polly gasped soundlessly as she saw that immediately beyond it the ground fell away, and she was looking down into a deep gorge with a glimmer of water far below.

They pulled over to the rough verge on the opposite side of the narrow road, and stopped.

Sandro turned to Polly, his face expressionless. 'Come,' he said, 'if you wish to see.'

After the fuss she'd made, she thought wretchedly, she could hardly tell him it was the last thing she wanted, so she followed him out into the sunlight. In spite of the heat, she felt cold.

Sandro's face was rigid, the slash of the scar prominent against

161

his dark skin. Alberto Molena came to his side, talking softly, encouragingly, and eventually he nodded curtly and they crossed the road together, and stood looking down into the depths below.

She did not go with them. Her eyes had detected a flash further along the road, as if the sunlight was being reflected back from glass. She could see a smudge of colour too, and guessed this was the shrine that Sandro had mentioned.

There was nothing unique about it. Polly knew that they were seen all over the Mediterranean where bad accidents had occurred. But none of the others had carried any meaning for her.

Slowly, almost reluctantly, she went to face one of her own demons. Bianca had indeed been a beautiful girl, her face heart-shaped, and her eyes dark and dreaming. The only jarring note was struck by a set, almost hard look about the mouth, but Polly supposed she could not be blamed for that.

Knowing the man you love feels nothing for you in return can do that to you, she thought sadly.

Also in the elaborate frame was a small plaster figure of a saint, with an unlit votive light in front of it, and a vase of slightly wilted flowers.

She heard a step, and, glancing round, saw the *contessa* approaching, leaning heavily on a cane.

'Get away from here.' The older woman's voice was harsh, almost metallic. 'You are not fit to breathe the same air that she did.'

She turned and stared malevolently at Sandro, standing motionless on the edge of the drop, only yards away. Polly's heart missed a beat, and she was just about to cry a warning when they were joined by the nurse, who took the *contessa*'s arm gently but firmly, murmuring to her in a soothing tone.

Polly crossed the road and stood at Sandro's side. She said in a low voice, 'Coming here may have been a bad idea. I think your cousin's getting agitated.'

'She has been here many times before,' he said stonily. 'Unlike myself.'

She looked at him, shocked. 'Is this the first time—since the crash?'

'The first, and I hope the only time. We came here solely to meet Giacomo Raboni, so that you could see what happened at this place through his eyes.' Sandro paused. 'He speaks little

English, but Alberto will translate for you—if you can trust his accuracy,' he added with a touch of bitterness.

'Yes,' she said, 'of course I can.'

She looked down. Just below the edge, the ground, littered with rocks and boulders of all sizes, sloped steeply away for about a hundred yards before reaching a kind of rim, beyond which it disappeared into infinity.

The kind of drop, she thought, that nightmares were made of, and shuddered.

She said, 'Will Signor Raboni be long? I'd like to get away from here.'

'It has always been a bad place,' Sandro told her quietly. 'But it is part of the truth which is so important to you.' He paused. 'And you will not be detained here much longer. Giacomo is coming now.'

She heard a rattle of stones behind her and turned. A man was coming down the hill, half walking, half sliding, an elderly dog scrabbling beside him.

Giacomo Raboni was of medium height, and stout, wearing ancient flannel trousers, a collarless shirt and a cap pulled on over curling white hair. He had a mouth that looked as if it preferred to smile. But for now, his expression was faintly grim.

He gave the *contessa* a measuring look, then turned his head and spat with great accuracy, just missing the dog. Then he turned shrewd dark eyes on Polly, telling her without words that she wasn't the subject of his whole-hearted approbation either.

He took Sandro's offered hand and shook it warmly. He said gruffly, 'You should not be here, *excellenza*. Why not let the dead girl sleep?'

Sandro's voice was harsh. 'Because, my old friend, she still poisons my life as she did when she was alive.' He paused. 'You agreed to keep silent to protect the living, and spare them more grief. But my father can no longer be hurt by what you saw, and the Contessa Barsoli has tried to use your silence to damage me, and my marriage, so she is no longer worthy of my consideration.'

He threw back his head. 'But my wife is a different matter, so it is time to speak, if you please, and tell her what happened here. And slowly, so that Signor Molena can tell her what is said.'

Giacomo Raboni gave a reluctant nod. He said, 'I had been on the hill that day, looking at my goats. A neighbour had told me that two of them seemed sick. As I came down the track, I heard the sound of a car. As it came round the corner, I recognised it as the car which belonged to the Signore Alessandro. But it was being driven strangely, swerving from side to side, and I could see why. There was a passenger beside him—a girl, but not in the passenger seat, you understand. She was leaning towards him—clinging to him, it seemed.'

He stared at the brink, frowning. 'At first I thought it was love play between them, and that they were fools, bringing their games to such a dangerous road. Then I realised that the *marchese* was not embracing her, but struggling, trying to push her away, and control the car too.'

He turned his head and looked steadily at Polly. 'At that moment, *vossignoria*, I knew that your husband was fighting for his life. Because she was not reaching for him, but trying to grab the wheel. I think, also, she went for his eyes, because he flung up an arm to defend himself, and in that instant she turned the car towards the edge of the cliff.'

'Oh, God,' Polly said numbly. 'Oh, no.'

'As it went over, I heard her scream something. Then there was the sound of the crash, and I ran.

'I saw that the car had hit a rock, but glanced off it and continued down. It had reached the brink, but there it ran into a dead tree so it could go no further.

'But the *marchese* had somehow been thrown clear. I climbed down to him and realised he was badly injured. There was much blood and his pulse was weak.'

He paused. 'I realised too that the girl was still in the vehicle, and that the engine was running. The tree was a spindly thing, old and brittle, with shallow roots. It could not hold the car for much longer, so the *signorina* was inches from death.

'I went down to her, careful not to fall myself. The driver's door was open, and she was lying across the seat. She too was terribly injured, but I reached in to her, tried to take her hands to pull her free before the tree gave way.

'I spoke to her—called her Signorina Bianca, but she seemed barely conscious, and it was plain she did not know who I was. In her pain, she looked at me with eyes that saw nothing, and whispered something.

'She thought she was speaking to the *marchese*—that he was

with her still, and she repeated the same words she had used before.'

His own voice was hushed with the horror of it. 'She said, "If I cannot have you then no one will." And with her last movement, she put her foot on the accelerator and sent the car over the edge.'

Polly stood rigidly, her hands pressed to her mouth. Then the *contessa*'s hoarse voice broke the silence. 'You're lying,' she accused, her face twisted. 'The *marchese* has paid you to say these terrible things.'

He drew himself up with immense dignity. 'The *marchese* has paid me with nothing but his regard. All this I would have said at the inquiry, but he knew the distress it would give his father, who loved the Signorina Bianca and was already a sick man. For his sake and no other, we allowed it to become an accident. And, for the honour of the Valessi, I have kept my silence until now.'

His voice became deeper, more resonant. 'But I, Giacomo Raboni, I tell you that the Signorina Bianca tried to murder the Signore Alessandro. And I saw it all.'

There was a terrible keening noise from the *contessa*, who had sunk to her knees in the dust.

'No,' she was moaning. 'It cannot be true. Not my angel—my beautiful dove. She never harmed anyone—or anything in her life.'

'No,' Sandro said, harshly. 'That is the real lie. There were stories about her—rumours of cruelty from the moment she came to Comadora. A dog that belonged to one of the grooms tied up in the sun and left to die without water or food because it left paw-marks on her skirt. The pony my father bought for her which threw her, and mysteriously broke its leg in its stall soon after.

'And the convent school she attended. Did you know that the superior asked my father to remove her? Or how much he had to give to the chapel-restoration fund for her to be permitted to remain? He insisted of course that the nuns were mistaken.'

He shook his head. 'All I knew was that she'd repelled me from the first. And nothing my father could have said or done would have persuaded me to make her my wife.'

The *contessa* was weeping noisily. 'It cannot be true. She would never have harmed you. In spite of your cruelty and indifference, she loved you. You know that.'

He said grimly, 'I knew that she was obsessed by me. And that she was determined to become the Marchesa Valessi. Between you, you forced me away from my family home, and drove a wedge between my father and myself. Unforgivable things were done at your instigation.'

'No,' she moaned. 'No, Alessandro.'

Polly said softly, 'Sandro—she's in real pain. No more, please.'

He looked at her sombrely, then went reluctantly to the *contessa*, and lifted her to her feet. He said more gently, 'Just the same, I would have spared you this knowledge, as I did my father, if you had not started your insidious campaign against my wife— the whispers at the party you organised with such kindness, the rumours among the staff, all stemming from you.

'But Paola emerged triumphantly from each trap you set for her. How that must have galled you. But it is all over now. There are no more secrets, unless you choose to keep from Emilio what you have heard today. Can you imagine what a feast he would make of it—what the headlines would say about your beloved Bianca?'

A shudder went through her. She looked up at him, her face suddenly a hundred years old. 'I shall say nothing,' she told him dully. 'All I can ask, Alessandro, is a little kindness.'

'There is the house on Capri,' he said. 'You have always liked it there. Alberto will examine your financial circumstances and make suitable arrangements for your comfort. Now he will escort you back to Comadora.'

She nodded with difficulty, then took his hand and kissed it.

Polly watched Signor Molena offer his arm, and lead her back to the car. Saw it turn carefully, then go back towards Comadora.

Leaving her, she thought, to travel alone with Sandro. She stole a glance at him, and saw that he was staring down at the crash site again, his eyes hooded, his face like a mask.

He said quietly, 'There is nothing there. No sign that anything ever happened.'

Only that scar, she thought. The one you will carry forever.

She wanted to go to him. To take his face in her hands, and kiss the harshness from his mouth. To offer him the healing warmth of her body.

But she didn't dare.

I made him face this, she thought. I made him remember the unthinkable—the grotesque. The fear and the pain. And how can he ever forgive that? How can he ever forgive me?

She swallowed. 'Sandro—shall we go home?'

'Home?' he queried ironically. 'You mean that huge empty house I visit sometimes, that stopped being home after the death of my mother?'

'But it could be again,' she said. 'It has to be—for Charlie.'

His sigh was small and bitter. 'Yes,' he said. 'At least I have my son.'

He walked away to where Giacomo Raboni waited. They spoke quietly for a moment or two, then embraced swiftly, and the old man, whistling to his dog, went back the way he had come.

On the journey home they sat, each in their separate corners, the silence between them total.

At last Polly could bear it no longer. She said, 'Is the chauffeur's glass partition soundproof?'

'Yes,' he said. 'Completely.'

She hesitated. 'Then may—may I ask you something?'

'If you wish.' His tone was not encouraging.

'What was Bianca doing in your car that day?'

'You imagine I invited her for a drive?' he asked bleakly. 'I had just had a bad interview with my father—one of the worst. He had done something I could not forgive, and I needed quickly to put it right. Bianca must have been listening at the door as she often did, because when I went out to the car she was there in the passenger seat, waiting for me.

'I told her to get out—that I had no time for her little power games—but she refused. I had no time to argue, and to put her bodily out of the car would have been distasteful, so I had to let her stay. Although I warned her that I was not returning, and she would have to make her own way back to Comadora alone.

'She began bragging to me almost at once about her power over my father. Said that I could run away, but in the end he would make me marry her or strip me of my inheritance. Leave me with an empty title. Then she became amorous—said she would give me pleasure in ways I had never had before. She even described some of them,' he added, his mouth curling in contempt.

'I was fool enough to let her see my disgust, and she began to get angry in a way I had never seen before. She began to talk about you—said filthy, obscene things, becoming more and more hysterical. Finally she was screaming at me that I belonged to her. That she would kill both of us rather than lose me to another girl. That was when she began trying to seize the wheel.

'Even then I did not realise she was serious, may God forgive me. I thought she was just being—Bianca. The one that only I seemed to see.'

He shook his head. 'I was shouting back at her—telling her I was going to throw her out of the car if she didn't stop.' His mouth tightened. 'That was when she attacked me with her nails, as Giacomo said. And the rest you know.'

Polly said in a small voice, 'Do you think she was mad?'

He shrugged. 'I have asked myself that a thousand times. If so, she hid it well with everyone but me.'

'Yes.' Polly swallowed. She said with a touch of desperation, 'Sandro, I'm so sorry—for everything.'

'There is no need,' he said. 'The *contessa* had nursed her delusions for too long, and it was time the truth was told. So do not blame yourself.'

He sounded kind but remote, and her heart sank.

But she mustered a smile. 'Thank you. That's generous.'

'Is it?' he asked, an odd note in his voice. 'But then, Paola, you ask for so little.'

And there was silence again.

Back at the *palazzo*, there was an air of shock that evening. The *contessa* had gone by private ambulance for a few days' rest at a clinic, and it was apparent that she would not be returning.

Alberto Molena stayed for dinner, and, although conversation was general over the meal, it was clear there were pressing matters to be discussed. So Polly was not surprised when courteous excuses were made over coffee, and the two men retired to Sandro's study, and remained closeted there.

Polly listened to music for a while in an effort to calm herself, then went upstairs to her room and sat by the window. She had plenty to think about. Questions that still remained unanswered, but which could be more complex than she'd believed.

Sandro had been on his way back to Sorrento when the accident had happened, she thought. And he'd spoken of some 'unforgivable' action of his father. What had the old *marchese* done to prompt such a reaction? she asked herself.

And why was Sandro coming to her, if he intended to end their affair? It made no sense. Especially as Bianca was clearly convinced that their relationship was still a threat to her, and Sandro had not denied it during their fatal quarrel.

The man who had visited her, scaring her with his oblique threats and offering her money to leave—who had sent him? Was it really Sandro, as she'd always believed? For the past three years, she'd looked on it as the agonising proof of his cruel betrayal. Now, suddenly, that certainty was shaken to its foundations.

I have to know, she thought. I have to put the last missing pieces in place—even if I don't get the answers I want, and all my worst fears are confirmed. But I can't just barge in, asking questions.

Somehow, she knew, she had to bridge the distance between them. And there was one sure way to do that, she thought, warm colour rising to her face.

How did they manage these things in the old days? she wondered, sending the huge bed a speculative look. Did the then *marchese* announce over dinner that he would be visiting his wife later? Or did the *marchesa* send a note to her husband, requesting the pleasure of his company in bed? Or was there simply a look— a smile—any of the covert signals that lovers had always used?

Whatever, she didn't think any of that would work in her own situation. Maybe the direct approach would be best.

She went into the dressing room, and retrieved the black lace nightgown from her jacket pocket, before taking a long scented bath.

A shadow over moonlight, he'd once called it, she thought, looking at herself in the mirror, and the most blatant evidence of her wishes that she could ask for.

She put on a satin robe in case she encountered a lurking servant, and made her way, barefoot, to his room.

She drew a deep, steadying breath, then knocked swiftly and went in. Sandro was there. He was in bed. And he was alone.

In fact he was propped up by pillows, frowning over a sheaf of papers he was reading. He glanced up at her entrance, his expression changing to total astonishment.

'Paola? What is it? Is there something wrong?'

She'd planned what to say, but the words were sliding round in her brain. 'It's Charlie,' she blurted out at last.

He sat up. 'Is he ill?' he demanded, his voice sharpening in alarm.

'No,' she said. 'As far as I know, he's fast asleep. But he's lonely. He was so happy when the twins were here, and he really needs children near his own age around him.'

She swallowed, her fingers nervously playing with the sash of her robe. She said, 'You said I never asked for anything. So—I was thinking—maybe he should have brothers and sisters.'

She stole a glance at him under her lashes, hoping for some reaction, but she was disappointed. Sandro's face was expressionless.

'Indeed?' he said politely, after a pause. 'So what do you suggest—adoption, or some scientific trick in a laboratory?'

She hadn't expected that either. 'No, of course not.' She made a small helpless gesture. 'I thought that you—that I...'

She ran out of words, so she slipped off the robe and let it drop to the floor, allowing him to assimilate the full effect of the cobweb of lace that was the only covering for her nakedness.

He looked at her very slowly, his hooded gaze travelling over her from head to foot.

He said quietly, 'Are you really so desperate for another child? Then take that thing off and come here.'

She'd thought he would get out of bed, and come to her. That he'd tear the gown from her with his own hands as he'd once suggested.

But she obeyed him, quickly, almost nervously sliding under the sheet he'd turned back for her. Knowing with a kind of sick certainty that this was not going according to any plan of hers.

He pushed the papers to the floor and turned to her, the topaz eyes sombre as he looked down at her.

Once he kisses me, she thought desperately, it will be all right. I can make it all right...

But Sandro did not kiss her. His hands slid down her body in an almost perfunctory caress, then moved under her flanks, lifting her towards him. She was already aroused, wildly receptive to even the prospect of his possession, so there was no physical barrier to his invasion of her body, which was wordless, clinical and immediate.

And as she lay beneath him, stunned, it was apparent that it was also going to be over very quickly. He cried out once, harshly, and she felt the scalding heat of his climax. Then he rolled away from her and lay, his chest heaving as he recovered his breath, one arm across his eyes.

When he spoke his voice was muffled. 'I hope I have performed my duties as stud satisfactorily, *marchesa*. I trust, also, that your wish for conception will be granted, as I would not wish to undergo this experience a second time.'

'Is that—that all you have to say to me?' The husky words were forced from her dry throat. Her bewildered, unsatisfied body was aching for the fulfillment he had never before denied her. Burning for him to *love* her.

'No,' he said, '*cara mia*.' He made the endearment sound like an insult. 'I could think of much more, but you would not wish to hear it, believe me. And now perhaps you will leave me to sleep.'

She was dying inside, but somehow she managed to reach her robe, and huddle it round her before she fled.

Too late, she thought, her heart thudding, as she almost fell into her own room and slammed the door shut behind her. He had told her it was too late as they left the house that morning. But she hadn't understood. Or had she just been deliberately blind and deaf?

Now comprehension had finally dawned, and with it a heartbreak that threatened to destroy her utterly. And she pressed herself against the unyielding hardness of the heavy door, and let the fierce agony of tears have their way with her.

CHAPTER THIRTEEN

POLLY got into the rear of the limousine, placing the bouquet of flowers she'd been given on the seat beside her, then leaned forward to wave a smiling farewell to the women who'd thronged out of the restaurant to see her depart.

As the car threaded its way through the narrow streets crowded with tourists, she leaned back and closed her eyes, kicking off her high-heeled sandals and wriggling her toes, the nails enamelled in an elegant pale pink to match her fingers.

Teresa had advised her well, she thought, looking down at the deep blue of her silk suit. Whatever else might be wrong with her life, at least she dressed well.

Today she had been the guest of honour at a charity luncheon in aid of a local children's home, and she'd made a small speech at the end of it in her increasingly fluent Italian, and been warmly applauded.

She took lessons several times a week with a retired schoolmaster, who lived with his plump, cheerful wife in a small white-painted villa on the edge of town. Usually they sat under an awning on the patio, and when work was finished the *signora* would serve coffee with tiny almond *biscotti*, often accompanied by a glass of her home-made *limoncello*.

The first time it had been offered, Polly had felt wrenched in half, remembering with vivid poignancy how Sandro had once teased her about making the delicious citrus liqueur for him. But she had smiled gallantly, and praised it extravagantly, to the delight of her hostess.

But then smiling radiantly, and behaving with grace and modesty, were all part of the public persona she was establishing. A façade behind which she could hide the lonely, heartsick girl that she was in reality.

It was almost three weeks since her humiliated flight from Sandro's bedroom. And it had taken every ounce of courage she

172

possessed to face him the next day, instead of staying in her room, pleading a headache.

And when they had finally met, she was able, somehow, to match his cool politeness with her own. She had even found herself painfully wondering what had happened to the nightgown she'd left on the floor, but she did not mention the subject.

Which was how it still was, she thought, her mouth twisting. Nothing was ever mentioned. She and Sandro were like satellites, pursuing their separate orbits round the small, beloved moon that was Charlie.

By mutual, if tacit, consent, they were never alone together. She went down to the swimming pool with their son only in the mornings, when she knew Sandro would be working in his study, or out. And she was thankful that he respected her privacy. The thought of being caught by him in a bikini, or any other form of undress, made her shrivel inside.

And in the afternoons, after siesta, she remained in the shade of the terrace so that he could have Charlie to himself.

The little boy could swim like a fish now, and he was also learning, under his father's supervision, to ride the pony that was kept at one of the farms.

Although Sandro was not always at Comadora. She was kept abreast of his schedule by Signora Corboni, who was not nearly as dour as she looked, and who presented her with a printed list of his engagements each week, including the occasions when he would be away from the *palazzo*. Polly knew this was only so that she could make the appropriate domestic arrangements, and not because Sandro wished her to keep track of him. And she could not help noticing painfully that two of these absences had been spent in Rome.

But with each day that passed, she found she was learning more and more about her new life, and becoming absorbed into the established routine at the *palazzo*.

For instance, she had soon discovered that Sandro had far more than a hotel chain and the family's banking and corporate interests to occupy him. The Valessi estate owned acres of olive and citrus orchards, together with vineyards, and even a small quarry. In addition, the farms produced enough fruit and vegetables to supply most of the local tourist facilities.

When Sandro was at home, many of the lunches at the *palazzo* were working affairs, where she was expected to act as hostess, and, although she did not understand all that was being discussed, she picked up enough to take an intelligent interest. And invariably she was rewarded by a brief, formal word of thanks from Sandro as their guests departed.

She knew that was probably just for the sake of appearances, but it was a crumb of comfort to be cherished, all the same.

On the downside, there'd been a few moments of nightmare embarrassment the previous week when she'd felt obliged to seek him out and tell him that there would be no baby after all.

Sandro had been at his desk, making notes in the margin of some report, and his pen had stilled momentarily. Then he'd said with remote courtesy, 'My regrets for your disappointment,' and returned to his report.

And she had turned and left the study, and gone to talk to the cook. Because life went on, and people had to be fed and welcomed, even if she felt she was breaking up emotionally.

So, she told herself with bitter self-mockery as the car turned onto the long hill that led up to the *palazzo*, I shall become known for my good works—and Charlie, poor babe, will remain an only child.

Hardly enough to fill her days, she thought with a stifled sigh. While she could not even bear to contemplate the long, restless, driven nights that were already her torment.

She knew that most of the people who saw her in her chauffeur-driven car and designer clothes thought that she had nothing else in her life to wish for.

Only Polly knew that the Valessi family now had another closely guarded secret—her total estrangement from the only man she had ever loved.

On arrival at the *palazzo* she went straight up to her room, where Rafaella was waiting for her. She took Polly's flowers to place in water, and waited for her to change out of the suit, so she could restore it to its usual pristine condition.

Polly took a quick shower and changed into a jade-green halter-necked sun-dress, which was cool and decorous at the same time. Then she collected her sunblock, and the book she was reading, and made her way towards the stairs and her intended destination of the terrace.

She was halfway down the wide sweep, when she heard a man's

voice in the entrance hall below, and hesitated, finding herself oddly reluctant to proceed any further. For one thing, this was not the usual time of day for visitors, she told herself. For another— there was something disturbingly familiar about the visitor's smooth tone, as if he was someone she should recognise.

Moving cautiously to the balustrade, she leaned over and looked down.

She saw him at once, talking to Teodoro. A tall, well-dressed man with a smile that seemed to have been painted on his thin mouth. As he spoke he was hunching his shoulders, spreading his hands to emphasise a point, and always that smile—quite unforgettable and still with the power to scare her even three years on.

She would have known him anywhere, she thought. It was the man who'd told her to leave Sorrento—and who'd offered her Sandro's pay-off. And who was now here at the *palazzo*.

Suddenly her stomach was churning, and she lifted a hand to her mouth to stifle her startled cry of recognition. And as she did so the bottle of sunblock fell, and rolled down the stairs.

Both men turned and looked up at her, so her planned retreat was impossible. Cursing her clumsiness, she made herself walk down the rest of the stairs, moving slowly and gracefully, steadying her breathing with an effort. Teodoro had retrieved her sunblock, and returned it to her with a respectful bow. Polly thanked him mechanically, knowing that the other man's flat dark eyes were devouring her.

'So,' he said in English. 'The charming Signorina Fairfax. Or should I say—the Marchesa Valessi? An honour I had not anticipated.' The smile widened. 'Your ladies' luncheon was expected to last longer, I think.'

The significance of that was not lost on her. I'm not supposed to be here, she thought, stiffening.

She turned to Teodoro. 'Does this person have business here?' she asked in Italian, with an assumption of coolness.

'*Sì, vossignoria.* He had an appointment with the *marchese*, but his *excellency* has not yet returned from his own lunch engagement.'

'You do not ask why I am here,' the other man intervened mockingly. 'But perhaps, *marchesa*, you already suspect the nature of my business with your husband. After all, it would not be the first time.'

Polly lifted her chin. 'My husband sees a great many people, I do not question his business with them—or his choice of associate.'

Teodoro was regarding her round-eyed, having never heard his mistress speak so dismissively to a visitor before.

She looked stonily back at him. 'Please show the *marchese*'s—guest to the *salotto*.'

'I already know my way,' he said. 'But I thank you for your graciousness.' He paused. 'Would a cold drink be possible?'

Polly said, 'Will you see to it, *per favore*, Teodoro?' She walked away, her head high, but she was quaking inside, and a block of ice seemed to have settled in the pit of her stomach.

The terrace was altogether too accessible from the *salotto*, she realised, so she walked down into the gardens, finding a secluded stone bench under a flowering hedge, and sinking onto it.

So it was true after all, she thought with desolation, her hands clasping the edge of the bench so tightly that her knuckles turned white. He had been working for Sandro after all, and any lingering hopes that she might have misread the situation were stone dead.

And now he had returned, which could only mean that Sandro had decided to put an end, once and for all, to the tragic farce their marriage had become. And with unbelievable cruelty, he'd summoned his stooge, all over again, to conduct the negotiations and offer her a final settlement.

Go away and keep quiet, would be the ultimatum once more, as it had been three years ago.

But this time there was Charlie to put into the equation, and the kind of deal she might be offered made her feel sick with fear.

He would stay in Italy, of course, because this was a battle she could not fight without weapons. All she could hope for was to be allowed to spend time with him on some regular basis. Surely Sandro would permit that, and not send her off into some kind of limbo of isolation and misery.

The *contessa*, she knew, was now installed in the house on Capri, with a nurse-companion. Was similar accommodation being planned for her somewhere? They said, she thought numbly, that Ischia was very beautiful...

She heard someone moaning, and realised that the low, desperate sound was coming from her own lips.

Had Sandro decided it was time for her to be finally dismissed from his life when she'd told him that she was not pregnant by that brief, soulless coupling a few weeks earlier?

But what difference did it make? she asked herself, wrapping her arms round her shivering body. Even if she was expecting another child, it would only win her a temporary reprieve at best.

She rose, and began to pace up and down the flagged walk, suddenly unable to keep still. Needing to do something—anything—while her raging, unhappy mind tried to find its focus. A way forward into a future that was no future at all.

But she would not wait meekly to be told, she thought with sudden determination. If it killed her, she would take matters into her own hands and leave with some kind of dignity.

And she would take nothing from him except the right to see Charlie. That, surely, he could not deny her...

The *salotto* was empty when she returned to the *palazzo*, and Teodoro was just coming from the direction of Sandro's study, having presumably delivered the unwelcome guest to his host.

He gave her a wary look, and she couldn't blame him. She'd behaved with an outstanding lack of hospitality, and she probably looked like a madwoman.

She laid a detaining hand on his sleeve. 'Teodoro, so silly of me. I've forgotten the name of my husband's visitor.'

His expression changed to astonishment. 'It is Signor Ginaldi, *vossignoria*. The *avvocato* from Salerno.'

'Of course,' she said. '*Grazie.*'

A lawyer, she thought. Why hadn't she guessed? Sandro was bound to have more than one. There was Alberto Molena, the acceptable, trustworthy face of the law, and, in the shadows, this other to do his dirty work.

She forced a smile. 'Will you be good enough to tell me when he's gone? I—I need to talk to the *marchese*.'

'Of course, *vossignoria*.' He paused. 'And a package came for you earlier, which I have placed in your living room.'

A package, Polly thought. She wasn't expecting to receive anything. And surely it couldn't be divorce papers already? Wasn't there some minimum time for a marriage to exist before it could be legally dissolved? Maybe this was another point for Sandro to consult his shady lawyer about—whether the process could be hurried on in some way.

She closed the living-room door, and stood looking round her.

My room, she thought, her throat tightening. Created specially for me. But why—when he must have already known I would not be staying? Why pretend that he cared—even this much?

The package was lying on a side-table, a large padded envelope addressed to her in her mother's handwriting. Polly picked it up, frowning a little, weighing it in her hand. This was the first direct communication she'd received from Mrs Fairfax since she'd arrived in Italy.

She'd written to both her parents, of course, and she telephoned several times a week, but conversation with her mother was still faintly stilted, and confined to strictly neutral subjects.

Oh, God, she thought, wincing. What would her mother say when she came back without Charlie? Her father had said only last week that she seemed to be recovering from her depression, but this latest blow was bound to have a profound effect on her.

And what consolation can I possibly offer? she wondered.

She sat down and opened the envelope. A sheet of folded notepaper fell out, followed by another package, wrapped in plastic and heavily taped.

Her mother had written,

Dearest Polly,

This is not an easy thing for me to tell you, but it has to be done. After you came back from Italy three years ago, these letters began arriving, sent on by the travel company you used to work for.

I realised, of course, that they must be from *him*, and I opened the first ones and read them. My excuse was that I saw how unhappy he'd made you, and I didn't want him to cause more misery and disruption in your life. But that wasn't all of it. It was obvious that he wanted you to come back, and I knew I couldn't bear to part with you or the baby you were expecting. I told myself that I had a right to see my grandchild born. That he'd had his chance, and blown it, as people say these days.

The letters continued coming for months. I meant to burn them because you seemed to have accepted the situation and settled down. And I didn't want your father to find out about them either, because I knew he'd say I must hand them over.

When your husband came here, one of the first things he asked was why he'd never received a reply to any of them. I tried to tell him that we hadn't received any letters, but I can't be a very good liar because he guessed immediately. He was terribly angry, and very bitter, but I begged him not to tell you, because I was afraid you would never forgive me. And he eventually agreed he would say nothing to you if I didn't fight him for Charlie. It was the hardest thing I've ever had to do, but I see now I deserved it.

Some of the letters were heartbreaking, Polly, and I had to stop reading them, but I had no right, even so, to keep them from you. There were things in them that you needed to know. And maybe you still do, because I can tell from your voice that you're not as happy as you make out.

While we were in Cornwall I told your father everything, and he was very shocked. He said I had to make things right between you both, and that is what I'm trying to do now.

He has forgiven me, bless him, and I hope so much, darling, that you'll feel able to do the same one day. And your husband too, perhaps.

Darling, I'm so truly sorry.

Your loving mother.

Polly snatched up the packet and began to tear it open, her carefully manicured nails snapping as she wrestled with the tape, until she reached the bundle of airmail envelopes inside.

About five of them had been opened, in all, but each of the letters had been carefully inscribed by her mother with the date it had been received.

The first one began abruptly,

Paola,

I have to tell you that I am in hospital in Naples. I have been in a bad car crash, and will have to remain here for several more weeks. There is an English nurse working here on an exchange, and she is writing this for me, because I can do very little for myself, except lie here and think. And my thoughts are not happy. I have known for some time that you have left Sorrento, and no one will tell me where you have gone. But the company you worked for has said it will forward this to you, so I can only hope it will reach you.

Forgive me for not writing before, my dearest love, but when I first recovered consciousness I could remember little of what had happened. However my memory has slowly returned, and with it came you, my blessed girl.

The specialists also feared that I had damaged my back so severely that I might never be able to walk again, and I knew I could not keep you to your promise of marriage if I was to spend the rest of my life in a wheelchair.

I know now that I shall make a full recovery, but it will take time, which would pass more quickly if you were with me. Please write or call me, and come to me soon.

Your Alessandro.

'Oh, dear God,' Polly whispered. She slid off the sofa onto her knees, the flimsy blue envelopes cascading round her.

The next one was in his own shaky handwriting.

My darling, why have I not heard from you? If it is the money that my father gave you to leave, I promise it does not matter to me. I know how ruthless he can be, and how confused and miserable he must have made you. It was the last thing he told me before the accident, and we quarrelled terribly. I swore to him that if he had truly forced you to leave, I would never see him or speak to him again. And that I would find you wherever you had gone, and make you my wife.

In the letters that followed he told her his real identity, and all about Bianca, and the accident, holding nothing back, she discovered with incredulity. He wrote,

It has been decided that for the sake of the family name, none of this should be made public. Also my father is very sick, and any more shocks could kill him. He has asked me to forgive him for sending you away, and we are better friends than we were. I hope you can forgive him too, as he accepts now that I shall always love you, and is ready to welcome you as a daughter.

He ended, 'My dear love, this silence from you is more than I can bear.'

'Sandro,' Polly whispered, tears pouring down her face. 'Oh, *Sandro.*'

She tore open more envelopes, scanning the increasingly desperate words.

'My face was torn by a piece of rock,' he told her at one point. 'The doctors say I should have plastic surgery, but I know that if you were only here to kiss me, I would be healed.'

And later:

I think of you night and day, my sweet one, and pray for you to come back to me, but God doesn't seem to hear me. If you no longer want me, be merciful and tell me so. With each day that passes, it becomes more difficult to hope.

And eventually the desperation faded, and the anger and bitterness began. And the reproaches.

I see now that you never loved me. That my father was right when he said that you had found out somehow who I was, and decided to make money from your knowledge. You should have held out for a better price, Paola. The lovely body you gave me was worth far more than that pittance.

And at last:

My father has died, may God give him peace, and I am now the Marquis Valessi. I am also enough of a fool to still want you. Even now, if you came to me, I would take you, although not as my wife. And if the thought of my scarring revolts you, you can always close your eyes, and think of the financial rewards.
But I shall not ask again.

'Yet you did,' Polly wept aloud, rocking backwards and forwards on her knees. 'In spite of everything, you came to find me. Oh, God, if I'd known—if I'd only known...'

She suddenly heard the unwelcome sound of the door opening. She looked round, her eyes blurred with tears, and saw Sandro in the doorway, staring at her, his lips parted in shock.

If she'd been humiliated the other night, it seemed nothing to what she felt now. She'd intended to walk out of the *palazzo*, and his life, with her head high, commanding his grudging respect if nothing else.

But, at this terrible moment, Polly knew exactly what she looked like. Because she did not cry prettily. Her face would be blubbered with tears, her nose running and her damp hair plastered to her forehead. And when she sobbed out loud, her mouth looked like a frog's.

'What the hell are you doing here?' She choked on the words.

'Teodoro said you were asking for me.' There was no harshness in his voice, or arrogance. He sounded uncertain—bewildered.

'But I was coming to you, not you to me.' She glared at him, and actually hiccuped as she did so. 'So will you please get out?'

But instead, he walked towards her. Sank to his knees beside her, his hands framing her wet, snuffling, desperate face.

'Paola,' he said gently. 'What is it?'

She tried to think of a lie, but somehow, with his eyes looking tenderly and gravely into hers, only the truth would do.

'You loved me,' she burst out, her voice breaking. She gestured wildly at the scattered letters. 'You really loved me, and I never knew,' she ended on a little wail.

'I loved you the first moment I saw you.' He produced an exquisite linen square, and began to dry her white, unhappy face. 'You know that.' As he moved he heard the rustle of paper under his knee, and glanced down. His brows snapped together. 'Where did you get these?' he demanded abruptly.

'My mother sent them. She wanted me to know how you'd really felt after I left. And that you hadn't sent me away—only it's too late—too late.' And she began to sob again.

'*Mi amore,*' he said softly. '*Mi adorata.* What are you talking about?'

'You're going to send me away,' Polly said wildly. 'You're going to ask that man to tell me—to get rid of me. I—I saw him earlier, waiting for you. Waiting for his orders. But from you, this time, not your father.'

She tried to swallow. 'And I'll go—really. I won't make a fuss, I promise—except that I'm doing that already, I suppose, but you weren't meant to see me like this, so it doesn't count.'

'Paola,' he said, cutting through her confused ramblings. 'My beloved, my angel. How can I send you away? It would cut the heart out of my body.'

'But I saw him,' she gulped. 'The lawyer—your lawyer, who threatened me and tried to pay me that money. And you think I took it.' She began to grope for the appropriate letter. 'But I didn't.'

'I know you did not,' he said quietly, capturing her hands and holding them in both of his. 'As he has just been persuaded to admit. He deceived my father, and he deceived me. And he has never been my lawyer. He is simply a creature of the *contessa*'s that my father used once as an intermediary. You need never think of him again.'

'But what happened to the money?' She stared at him.

'I believe that he and the *contessa* divided it between them,' he said drily. 'Alberto has found unexplained funds deposited to her credit around that time.'

'The *contessa* a thief?' Polly took his handkerchief and blew her nose. 'Surely not.'

He shrugged. 'For years, Teodoro has suspected her of—er—creative accountancy with the *palazzo*'s finances. But forget her too,' he added firmly. 'And tell me why you have been crying.'

She bent her head. 'Because you were alone and in pain all those months, and I didn't know.'

'How could you,' he said, 'when you did not get my letters?' He paused. 'Would you have come to me if you had known?'

'Yes,' she said, and tried to smile. 'Even if I'd had to walk all the way over broken glass.'

He said softly, 'My sweet, my beautiful girl.'

She kept staring at the floor. 'That's not true,' she said gruffly. 'When I cry I look like a frog.'

'Do you?' There was the breath of a smile in his voice. He bent and kissed her lightly and tenderly on the lips. 'Then now you are a princess again. And I will try very hard to give you no more cause for grief.'

He got lithely to his feet, pulling her up with him, then seated himself on the sofa with her on his knee, held close in his arms.

He looked deeply into her eyes. 'Paola, is it true? Do you love me?'

'I never stopped,' she admitted shakily. 'Although God knows I tried.'

'I cannot blame you for that,' Sandro said ruefully. 'I tried hard myself, but it was impossible. And I knew that despite anything you might do, I was condemned to love you always, until death, and beyond. So, at last, I came to find you.'

She smoothed the collar of his shirt, not looking at him directly. 'But what about your mistress in Rome? Your vile cousin Emilio told me about her.'

'That was over a long time ago,' he said, adding grimly, 'As Emilio well knows.' He hesitated. 'But she was not the only one, *cara*. See, I confess everything, but it was a time when I thought you were lost to me forever. My father had just died, and my life was hell. But all it taught me was that you were my only love, and always would be.'

She looked up into the dark face, her eyes questioning. 'Then why—*why*—that other night...?'

He was silent for a moment, then he said slowly, 'Because I was angry, and I wanted you very badly. That is a dangerous combination in a man, *cara mia*.

'When I saw you standing there, I thought paradise was mine at last. I looked at you, longing for you to tell me that you loved me—or at least that you desired me. One kiss—a touch of your hand—and I would have been yours.

'But you spoke only of Carlino—his happiness, his need for a playmate, as if that mattered more, somehow, than you being in my arms, a woman with her man.

'It was as if my being exonerated of Bianca's death had convinced you that I was a suitable candidate for fatherhood again. I felt as if I was some tame stud, to be used only when required. And that my needs and emotions were immaterial.

'And frankly I found that unbearable—an insult to my manhood, and everything I felt for you. But I was also scared that anger might get the better of me, and I would lose all control and treat you in a way we could both regret for the rest of our lives.

'So I told myself, *Bene*—if that is all she wants, it is all she shall have. Until afterwards, when I saw your wounded eyes.' He drew her closer repentantly. 'I was afraid that I had hurt you too much—driven you away forever.'

'But I'd been scared too,' she whispered. 'In case you rejected me. I knew how much you loved Charlie, and thought he might prove a link between us. A way to approach you.'

'And do you know why I love him so?' Sandro asked quietly. 'Because he reminds me of you, when we first met—so innocent, so trusting, so unstinting in affection. And he wanted to be with me, even though I was being shunned by you.'

Polly sighed. 'And I thought you only wanted him. That I was just here on sufferance.'

His mouth twisted. 'More suffering than sufferance, I think, *bella mia*. Living with you has been heaven and hell. Heaven to hear the sound of your voice, see your smile, breathe, sometimes, the fragrance of your skin—your hair.

'But hell to be aware of all these things, and yet be denied the right to hold you in my arms at night.

'I should have told you. I came back early from that trip principally because I could not bear to be apart from you another day.'

'I dared not believe you,' she said. 'I couldn't risk having my heart broken a second time.'

He said softly, 'So, are you prepared to take that risk now, *carissima*? To be my wife, and face whatever our lives bring at my side?'

'Yes.' She smiled into his eyes. 'I'm ready to do that, *caro mio*. My dear love.'

He carried her in his arms out of the room, and up the broad sweep of the staircase.

'So much for public decorum,' she teased breathlessly.

'At least you are still wearing your clothes.' His answering grin was as mischievous as a boy's.

But when they were alone and the door was not merely closed but locked, Polly saw the stark hunger in his eyes, and knew a fleeting moment of fear, in case he demanded more than she had the power to give.

Then his hands descended on her bare shoulders, and her body exploded wildly in the sheer shock of recognition. And of overwhelming, aching need.

He bent his head, and his lips parted hers deeply and sensuously. His arms tightened round her, crushing her breasts fiercely against his hard chest.

When the long kiss ended, they were both breathless. Then he reached for her again. They undressed each other, swiftly, almost frantically, tearing at buttons and zips, ripping recalcitrant fabric away. And the years of separation faded into oblivion as Polly lay naked in his arms at last in the sunlit warmth of the afternoon.

Their mouths feverishly explored the familiarity of flesh and bone, seeking unforgotten pleasures, reviving the shuddering sweetness of touch, their voices whispering—urging.

His tongue was liquid fire against her taut nipples, his fingers like silk as they found the molten, eager core of her and lingered, creating their own exquisite torment.

'Do you remember?' he murmured against her lips. 'The things you once said to me?'

'I've forgotten nothing.' Her voice was a husky purr.

'Then say them now.' He whispered, as his body slid into hers with one powerful thrust. He was not gentle, but she did not wish him to be so. His claim on her was as total as her surrender to him, and she gloried in it, her body arching against him, drawing him ever more deeply into the moist heat of her. Closing round the pulsating length of him, and making him groan with pleasure. And all the time, her lips whispered against his skin, until time ceased to exist, and her voice splintered hoarsely into rapture. Speech was impossible, overtaken by her incoherent, delirious cries of delight.

And, as he came in his turn, Sandro cried out her name as if it had been dragged from the very depths of his being.

Afterwards, they lay wrapped together, sated and languid. 'Am I forgiven?' he whispered.

'For the other night?' She stretched herself against him bone-lessly, smiling against his shoulder. 'Far too early to tell, *excellenza*.'

'*Dio mio*. You have other penances in mind?'

'Enough to last for the rest of our lives.' Polly sighed luxuriously. 'And only an hour ago, I thought I would never be happy again.'

'I always hoped, *mi adorata*,' Sandro said drowsily. 'Even when it seemed all hope was gone.'

'Now we have something better than hope,' she told him gently. 'We have each other. Forever.' And she pressed her lips tenderly to his scarred cheek.

THE ITALIAN'S MARRIAGE DEMAND

by

Diana Hamilton

Diana Hamilton is a true romantic and fell in love with her husband at first sight. They still live in the fairytale Tudor house where they raised their three children. Now the idyll is shared with eight rescued cats and a puppy. But, despite an often chaotic life-style, ever since she learned to read and write Diana has had her nose in a book – either reading or writing one – and plans to go on doing just that for a very long time to come.

CHAPTER ONE

'WELL, thanks a bunch!' Sophie directed a ferocious hiss at the tail-lights of the lorry which had drenched her and the antiquated pram with a breath-snatching spray of icy rainwater. Frustration and growing anxiety tightened her delicate jawline. If she didn't get across this wretched road in the next few minutes she was going to be late getting to the address in Finsbury Circus.

Last night, in response to her frantic phone call, when Tim had agreed to give her a roof over her head just until she'd got herself sorted out, he'd stressed that he would only have a half-hour window in his lunchbreak to let her into his flat. Already there was a scant fifteen minutes of that time remaining.

Sophie's temperature rose another few hectic degrees. If Nanny Hopkins's landlord hadn't been late turning up to collect the key and the final week's rent she would have made it to Tim's flat with time to spare. But now—

Poised to take advantage of any gap in the traffic, she took a deep breath and made herself remember that dear old lady's firm stricture when things, as they usually did for her, went drastically wrong to 'look on the bright side, child. You'll always find one'.

Nanny Hopkins's little homilies had always been predictable, but were almost always dead right. So

Sophie made a conscious effort to relax her tense shoulders and remind herself that things weren't all bad. At least her sleeping seven-month-old son and their possessions were dry beneath the capacious hood and apron of the ancient contraption that would have caused passers-by to cast superior stares in her direction if scurrying through the murk and rain of the gloomy late-January day hadn't preoccupied them.

And if Tim had to give up on her—mindful of his hopes of promotion to manager of the travel agency—then she could always find a modest café where she and her baby would be warm and dry, and nurse a cup of tea until Tim was due to return in the evening. No problem—well, not a huge one. The great thing was she and her son had somewhere to stay while she looked for employment and she wouldn't have to go cap in hand to Social Services.

Hopes of spotting a break in the constant stream of traffic were now fading to non-existence. She would have to trudge further down the street and hope providence would provide a pedestrian crossing. Fuming at the enforced lengthening of her journey when minutes were ticking by, Sophie tightened her grip on the push bar and heaved the unwieldy pram around to face the new direction—and found progress blocked by an unquestionably solid lamp-post.

Compressing her lush pink lips, she struggled to make the necessary reverse-press-on-manoeuvre, slipped backwards off the edge of the kerb in haste and landed in the gutter in a miserable, undignified heap, with the screech of brakes in her ears and the bumper of a sleek silver car just a fraction of an inch from her shock-whitened face.

She could have been killed, as well as being homeless and as near-as-dammit destitute! Then what would have happened to her darling baby? A huge hot sob filled her throat. It didn't bear thinking about! Why was she such an idiot? As a mother and provider she would give herself nil out of ten—and that was being overly generous.

Ettore Severini swung the hired silver Mercedes into the traffic heading out of Threadneedle Street and into Bishopsgate with decisive panache. Business meetings for today had been completed as satisfactorily as expected. As always.

He had the afternoon free, apart from looking through some paperwork. Then two more days here in London, on one of his regular visits—two days packed with more scheduled meetings—then back to Florence, back to base. To an early spring. Probably a false spring. But no matter. To be out of the seemingly perpetual gloom of this rain-soaked, cloud-oppressed city would be a relief.

Five days of intense negotiations, business dinners, board meetings and sessions of stamping his authority around the London headquarters of the Severini family bank had failed to give him the expected surge of satisfaction of work well done. Signally and strangely failed today.

He felt...not tired—he was never tired; his stamina was legendary—what? Empty? As if an elusive something was missing in his gold-plated life. A frown pulled level ebony brows down, narrowing his coolly brilliant dark eyes. He despised negative introspection. Refused to waste time indulging in the stuff!

Madonna diavola! Didn't he have everything a guy could ask for? Thirty-six years old, with his health and strength, wealth beyond the dreams of avarice and, since his father's death four years ago, the undisputed driving force behind his family's long-established merchant bank. He had even—to his wry amusement—been recently described in one of the more sober broadsheets as a financial genius. Plus, he had his pick of beautiful women—when he could be bothered to take up their overt invitations—and a fiancée who was happy to turn a blind eye and was as laid-back as he was about setting the date for what would be a purely dynastic marriage.

A lifestyle any red-blooded male would envy. So what the hell could be missing?

Not one single thing!

Back at the Severini London apartment he would shower, open a bottle of Brunello di Montalcino, listen to music—Verdi? Yes, definitely—and let the rich red wine transport him back to Tuscany, to cypress shadows banding hot white roads, the cool green reaches of the Apennines, olive groves, the drowsy hum of bees in the wild herbs. The odd, discontent that had no name would be entirely banished.

His strong yet finely made hands relaxed on the wheel. The traffic was horrendous. The wipers rhythmically handled the murky drizzle, and the greasy spray thrown up by other vehicles. It would depress anyone who let it.

Another depressing sight was a few dozen yards

ahead—one of the unfortunates. A bag-lady bunched up in some sort of raincoat, an old woolly hat pulled down over her head, struggling with an ancient pram that undoubtedly held her meagre possessions. He supposed it was a 'her'. It looked too short and round to be a guy.

Traffic was moving at a steady, if frustrating ten miles an hour. Drawing almost level with the tussle on the pavement, Ettore stamped on the brakes as the disreputable figure toppled backward, landing in an ungainly heap just beneath the sleek silver bonnet.

Cursing through suddenly colourless flattened lips, Ettore exited the car in one driven movement, oblivious of the traffic, the blaring of horns. Had he hit the pathetic creature? He didn't think so. He would have felt the impact. Nevertheless...

Long, rapid strides propelled him around the front of the car. She was still sitting where she'd landed, in the gutter with all the other discarded rubbish, her back towards him, head downbent. A lock of long, rain-darkened blonde hair escaped the sodden woollen hat. Definitely female.

As he reached out a hand to gently touch the back of her hunched shoulder he demanded, 'Are you hurt?' and she shot to her feet as if a bomb had exploded beneath her, lurching forward towards the stranded pram.

A small crowd of onlookers had gathered, but, seeing the victim on her feet and shooting forward with energy, lost interest, remembered the now driving rain and drifted away.

'Wait.' If he was right and the woman was one of the city's homeless—and appearances suggested that was the case—then the least he could do was offer her the price of a good meal and a bed for the night. Make sure she was okay. 'You've had a shock.'

Both hands firmly on her shoulders, he swung her round, mentally calculating how much sterling he had in his wallet. A couple of hundred or so. Adequate compensation?

His faint frown developed into a full-blown black scowl as her pale-as-skimmed-milk face lifted to his. His heart gave an almighty, totally sickening thump. *Dio mio!*

His voice was an icy bite when he finally got out, 'Sophie Lang, by all that's unholy! Down and out in the gutter, where you belong!'

Ettore regretted the scathing words as soon as they'd spilled out between grindingly clenched teeth. Insulting the wretched woman was both undignified and a waste of breath. And what did that instinctive, ill-considered outburst say about him? That he still cared that the lovely, caring, warm and incredibly sexy woman who had bewitched and beguiled him had turned out to be a scheming little thief?

Of course he didn't care! How could he? He'd sliced her out of his heart and his head with surgical precision, well over a year ago. Written the whole unsavoury business off as valuable experience.

Sophie couldn't have said a word if her life had depended on it. A moment ago a hand on her shoulder, a voice saying something, had galvanised her out of the immobility of shock. But now every scrap of energy had drained right out of her again, leaving her as limp as a lump of over-boiled cabbage.

Him! Here in London! The very last man she

wanted to see, to have to admit back into a mind that had finally wiped him from her memory banks. As savagely handsome as ever, with raindrops sparkling against that superbly cut, soft as silk night-black hair and a mouth that promised and delivered heaven on earth—a mouth to die for. Expensively classy tailoring clothed his honed, blow-your-mind-sexy six-foot physique with fluid Italian elegance, and the impressively beautiful package was toughened by the reluctantly remembered quality of intimidating detachment that could be turned on at will.

She could barely breathe beneath that now dismissive stare, her face flaming with fiery colour then immediately whitening.

Her wide grey eyes looked haunted, Ettore noted dispassionately, ringed by dark circles and entirely dominating her ashen features. Her soft unpainted mouth was quivering. The shock of a near accident? Or something else? She was obviously unharmed.

Uttering a curse beneath his breath, Ettore told himself that the way she looked was of no possible interest to him. If she was down and out, maybe even recently released from prison—not all her victims would be as generous as he had been—then she only had herself to blame.

With that common sense thought in mind, he was turning away when a rageful squawk issued from the depths of the unspeakably dreadful pram. His brows lowering, he watched as Sophie leant over and extracted a soft shawl-wrapped bundle and cradled it against her heart. The tender, loving expression that suffused her features momentarily recaptured the inner beauty that had once so entranced him. But then she had impressed him by treating Flavia's twins not only firmly but as if they were the most precious and special children to walk the earth.

An excellent nanny. Reluctantly, he couldn't fault her on that. And working through a highly respected UK agency, which meant that she was still successfully duping everyone around her, which in turn brought on his terse, 'Surely your present employers can afford to supply your charge with a more up-to-date conveyance? It looks as if it was found on a skip.'

He rocked back on his heels, his hands thrust deep into the pockets of his fine cashmere overcoat, one ebony brow raised. The tightly swaddled child was settled now, blowing burbling bubbles into the side of her neck.

He watched Sophie's cute triangular face pinken, the dark, blonde-tipped lashes veiling her eyes as she countered woodenly, 'I no longer work. As a nanny. A fact I'm sure you're perfectly aware of, *signor*.' The stress on the formal mode of address was slight but unmistakeable. 'Torry is my son.'

And yours, she mentally added. Nothing would induce her to say the words aloud. Wild horses wouldn't drag them from her!

'And now—' she made an economical movement towards the pram, tension pulling a line between her eyes '—I have to go. I'm already very late.'

'Where to?'

A mean wind was gusting now, and the rain was falling more heavily, blowing horizontally. Her face was thinner than he remembered it. Pale. On the island her skin had glowed with health, with the touch of the sun, and she'd had a charming band of light freckles across the narrow bridge of her neat nose. A nose that wrinkled when she laughed and sometimes even when she simply smiled.

She had smiled a lot. Her unfeigned, uncomplicated *joie de vivre* had been the first thing to draw him into her web. With hindsight he accepted that her warmth and lightness of spirit had been some of the tools in her impressive armoury. That armoury had to be five-star-rated, he conceded bitterly, to have bamboozled a cynically sophisticated hardnosed banker, turning a life that had been planned with mathematical precision on its head.

She was ignoring him, bending over the pram, doing her best to shield the wriggling child from the rain while folding back the waterproof apron.

Irritated with her lack of response to a perfectly reasonable question, and even more irritated with himself for caring one way or another, he loomed over her. 'Well?'

Why couldn't he just go away? Sophie felt like screaming. Seeing him again was turning her into a mental wreck. She'd forced herself to forget. Wipe out the memory of those magical weeks on the island, of the way they had been, the way she'd loved him and fooled herself into believing he'd loved her. And the aftermath. A nightmare filled with humiliation, pain and cringe-making disgrace. His willingness to believe she was a thief, his icy indifference to her flustered denial, the way he'd made very sure she never worked as a nanny again.

'Finsbury Circus,' she muttered, stiff-jawed. If she answered his question—although he had no business

asking it in the first place—then he just might remove his unwanted presence and she could get a real
move on. She sagged defeatedly.

No use hurrying. By the time she got there Tim
would have left. He wouldn't want to be late back
for work, not while promotion was in the offing. And
the taxi crammed with the rest of her gear wasn't
due to arrive until early evening—at Tim's suggestion. Apparently there were stairs, lots of them, and
she'd need a hand getting the bulkier stuff to his
second-floor flat.

'I'll drive you. It's no distance.' Not a suggestion.
More of a tersely delivered command.

'No.' She'd walk until her feet dropped off rather
than accept a lift from him.

'Don't be an idiot,' he gritted with deep impatience. 'You're soaking wet and on your own admission you're incapable of keeping your appointment
under your own steam.'

He already had her arm in an unbreakable grip,
steering her reluctant frame towards the illegally
parked silver car. He had the passenger door open.
The leather seat looked inviting. The interior was
blessedly warm and dry. But there was the lingering
fragrance of the aftershave he favoured. It was too—
too intimate. He wouldn't feel it, of course. He
deeply despised her. He wouldn't demean his exalted
person by feeling a resurgence of that wild craving
that had catapulted them into a passionate affair, en-
slaving her utterly. But, hatefully, she did. She
couldn't bear it!

Her insides in a knot, Sophie dug her heels in. 'My
pram! I can't just leave it—it's got all my stuff—'

'I'll deal with it. Stop wasting my time and yours. Just get in.'

It was delivered in the authoritative tone of a man who called all the shots. Sophie fulminated as Torry stiffened in her arms. They could stand out here in this vile weather arguing the toss all day, and she had her baby's welfare to think about. That came streets ahead of her need for total independence as far as Ettore Severini was concerned.

Flags of bright colour flashed across the delicate arch of her cheekbones as she reluctantly capitulated, obeying his bitten instruction to 'belt yourself and the child in' as he strode over to the pram and pushed it across the glistening pavement towards a charity shop.

It took only seconds, and a generous donation, to offload the hideous thing and extract soft woolly blankets, a furry blue teddy bear and assorted bulging carriers from the cavernous depths. Ettore didn't know why he was bothering. Not for the sake of that sly, thieving minx, that was for sure!

He was bothering for the sake of the poor, innocent kid. Yes, of course. Pleased with that solution to his admittedly bizarre behaviour, he dumped the contents of the pram on the rear seat and slid behind the wheel. No wife of his would be forced to venture out in such weather, pushing a child around in something that might have been in fashion when Queen Victoria was on the throne.

His teeth set. Perhaps they couldn't afford anything better?

'Address?' he gritted, firing the engine.

Absorbing her snippily delivered reply, he eased

out into the traffic. She was wearing no wedding ring. Single mother? She must have gone straight from his bed into another's! His insides gave an angry twist.

The baby gurgled. Blew a loud raspberry. A swift sideways glance revealed plump arms vigorously waving, the woolly bonnet thing riding high on his head revealed a mass of glossy dark curls. Curls as dark and shiny as his big brown eyes. Cute kid! Pity the poor thing was landed with a promiscuous thief for a mother.

Peering at the digital clock on the dashboard, Sophie reckoned they might make it. Just. Concentrate on that, she drilled firmly into her head, willing herself to stop mourning over the fact that she looked such an awful fright. Like a bloated whale!

The pile of her possessions—baby stuff that now cluttered up the hallway of Nanny Hopkins's kindly neighbour, waiting for collection—would have to be shoehorned into the taxi as it was, without adding a binbag full of her own clothing. Spare space in the pram had been taken up with Torry's essentials—nappies, changes of clothing, bottles of formula that only needed heating, packets of rusks—so she'd had no option but to wear everything she owned, covering up with the voluminous old raincoat Nanny Hopkins used for tending her beloved back garden in poor weather.

So, okay, she looked absolutely dreadful. It couldn't matter less, could it?

'So what's this appointment? Business or personal?' Ettore asked, simply for something to say to break through the taut wall of silence that was blistering his eardrums. Not because he was interested. No way. He'd taken it on himself to get her kid out of the vile weather and he'd prefer the short journey to be a little less uncomfortable.

'Personal.' Nervous tension made her voice thin and squeaky.

Ettore's gaze slid in her direction. His brow lowered. She looked ill. Pale. Her face was thinner than it should be, with perspiration glistening on her forehead and short upper lip. Yet her body was undeniably overweight, the former fantastic curves and delectable indentations lost in bloated shapelessness.

'And?' he bit out. Too harshly? What in the name of all that was sacred was the matter with him? He didn't give a toss about her personal arrangements! Indicating, he swung the car into a relatively traffic-free street, slowing, searching for the number she'd given.

He heard her sigh. Then, in an irritated rush, 'I'm moving in with a friend. He's only got a limited amount of time to hang around to let me in.' She pushed the words at him—anything to get him off her case. 'He might already have given up on me.'

But he hadn't. Sophie's heart gave a huge jerk of relief as Tim bounded down the short flight of steps that led to the street door of the tall terraced house as Ettore braked to a halt outside the looked-for address.

Exiting as Sophie all but scrambled out of the car, clinging onto her wide-awake and wide-eyed son, Ettore reached for the stuff he'd bundled onto the back seat. Was this the baby's father? She'd said she was moving in with him. Had he belatedly accepted his responsibilities? For the kid's sake, he'd feel easier if he believed that.

Eyes narrowed, he watched the guy. He didn't look the dependable type. Tall and gangly, blond hair all over the place, pale blue eyes, as fair as Sophie was. Not likely to be the baby's father. His temperature rose. How many guys did she run through? Not that he cared, of course. Just thanked heaven for the lucky escape he'd had.

Her new guy was talking quickly, pressing something into Sophie's free hand, jerking his head back towards the house. Then, after dropping a swift kiss on her upturned cheek, he was off, heading down the street, uncoordinated long legs covering the pavement at speed, his unbelted trench coat ballooning out behind him.

Sorted. She and her kid would be out of the rain in seconds. So why wasn't he feeling comfortable with that? Wide shoulders lifted in a minimal shrug beneath the smooth cashmere before he wrote the aberration off as inconsequential and strode towards her. 'Everything all right?'

She mumbled something inaudible, willing him to go away, leave her alone. She hated the way he made her pulses leap, the way she loathed him for what he'd turned out to be, for what he'd done to her, yet couldn't stop herself remembering the heat of his passion, the hauntingly vivid memories she'd thought she'd blocked out for ever. She mounted the steps at what she hoped was a dignified pace, the backs of her knees prickling because she knew he was following.

Opening the back door onto a narrow barren hallway, she stepped inside and said, with ultra-politeness, 'Thank you for the lift.' She didn't look at him. Her mouth ran dry. She just couldn't! She just indicated the blankets and carriers he was holding. 'Leave them here. I'll come down and collect them later.' And turned for the stairs.

Torry was starting to grizzle. She held him closer to her over-padded body. She didn't want him drawing attention to himself. Ettore was no fool. She didn't want her baby's physical characteristics to start wheels turning in that clever Severini brain!

She heard him following. Still following! He had no right—she didn't want him near her or her baby. He had forfeited any rights he had in that context when he'd branded her as a thief and made sure she would never be employed as a nanny again!

Recognising the waves of heat banging inside her brain as incipient hysteria, she dragged in a deep, albeit shaky breath and tried to cool it. Pointless to throw a hissy fit over something as mundane as mere politeness.

His inherent good manners had impressed her on first meeting him at his sister and brother-in-law's timelessly elegant home in Florence. He'd treated her, the stop-gap nanny, only there while the permanent holder of that plum position had been recovering from a broken leg, as if she were a valued guest. So, even though he had her marked as a common thief, that inbred politeness wouldn't allow him to walk away and see her carry the bulky belongings up two flights of stairs.

Even so—she bit down hard on the soft flesh of

her lower lip as her wobbly fingers inserted the key in the lock of the door plainly marked with Tim's name—he was so close now. His nearness was practically blistering her skin. Could he sense how her pulse rate scampered? Her breath was coming in shallow gasps, all the old primitive responses well and truly triggered, assailing her body every which way there was! It was loathsome and horribly demeaning to accept that her body still reacted to him when she hated him with both her head and her heart.

'Thank you.' And how she managed even those two thin, bitten-off words she would never know. She was wound up to the point of explosion. She'd meant no more to this privileged, exalted being than a furtive holiday fling.

Her world had fallen apart when that unsavoury, deeply humiliating fact had hit her right between the eyes. That he'd believed the word of that upper-class, superior snob Cinzia di Barsini above her flustered rebuttal had left her feeling bitterly hurt, rejected and broken-hearted. The fact that he'd gone on to deny her the career she loved had added deep resentment to the mix.

The door opened directly onto the living area. Typical bachelor pad, the only concession to creature comforts was a vast leather-covered sofa in front of a state-of-the-art flatscreen TV, and a low side table sporting a couple of empty beer cans. How Ettore, used to discreet luxury and priceless antiques, a feather-bedded existence, would view the drab featureless walls, the piles of old motoring magazines stuffed in one corner of the low-ceilinged attic room, was a given.

'Goodbye.' Sticking to formality was the only way she could handle this. She half turned towards him, watching as he placed her belongings on the sofa. But dignity was difficult to maintain when Torry had grabbed her woolly hat with one determined little fist and was dragging it down over her eyes, and she was horribly sure that her disintegrating ponytail would be sticking out at the back.

Ettore's dark eyes were on her now. Pitying? Sophie's chin came up as she fought for cool.

'You've been—' a struggle to get the words out '—very kind.' Nosy, more like. Wondering to what depths the thieving little slapper who had briefly spiced up the tedium of a duty visit to the island had sunk! Willing her thumping heart to settle down, she turned to practicalities. 'Did you ask when it would be convenient for me to collect my pram?'

If the charity shop wouldn't store it beyond today it would mean another trek in the rain, toting Torry. Though the arrogant brute wouldn't have thought of that, would he?

One dark brow lifted, and the beautiful mouth quirked at one corner. If she'd been feeling generous Sophie might have attributed it to slight amusement.

She wasn't. The suspicion that he was presenting her with a very superior sneer was doubly confirmed when he stated, 'You don't. I donated it to the charity.' Plus a generous cheque for any trouble they might have in getting it into the nearest skip. But, to spare any lingering sensibilities she might still possess, he held his tongue on that slice of information.

Ettore slid a hand into his breast pocket, the movement stilling as Sophie finally lost it.

'How dare you?' Grey eyes glistened with tears of rage. 'You had no right to give my property away! It had sentimental value!' Her chest heaved with a hot mixture of anger and anguish as she vividly recalled the day when Nanny Hopkins had proudly wheeled the pram down the street. She'd acquired it through an acquaintance who worked for a titled old lady who resided in Belgravia. It had been in the attic for decades, and Lady Gore-Blenchley had been only too pleased to learn that it would be going to a good home.

'Just think of the aristocratic little boys and girls who've taken their daily airings in it.' Nanny Hopkins had beamed, pleased as punch. 'They don't make them like this any more. This is quality. See how beautifully sprung it is! Give me an hour and it will come up like new. It will be perfect for when your precious little baby arrives.'

Heavily pregnant, Sophie had had her doubts. But she wouldn't have let them show for all the tea in China.

The gentle elderly lady had been her rock for all of her twenty-four years. After she'd been dismissed from her post when Sophie's father had remarried after her own mother's early death Nanny had kept in touch, writing long, upbeat letters, sending small gifts, caring about her former charge. It had been Nanny Hopkins who had taken her in when she'd returned from Italy. Jobless, pregnant and homeless.

And now her dear old friend was gone. Felled by a massive stroke. And this uncaring—uncaring brute—

Tears spilling, she faced him, recent grief making

her chest feel as if it must burst. 'Nothing matters to you unless it comes gold-plated with a breathtaking price tag. Not even other people's feelings!' She heaved back a throat-tearing sob. 'Just get out of my sight! Right out! Just go!'

His face paling beneath the olive tones of his skin, Ettore's eyes narrowed to slits of glittering jet as his proud head came up. No one spoke to him that way. No one!

One searing glance of withering contempt, then, his wallet extracted, he flipped notes onto the floor at her feet. His barely accented voice was terse as he instructed, 'Get your child something more suited to this century.' And he stalked out, washing his hands of the creature for the second time in his life.

CHAPTER TWO

IT WAS no use kidding himself he was listening to Verdi's *Aida*. He had to face up to the irritating fact that almost literally running into Sophie Lang had ruined any hopes of a well-earned relaxing couple of hours before he got down to dealing with the waiting raft of paperwork.

So, hissing impatiently through his strong white teeth, Ettore jettisoned the whole idea and jack-knifed to his feet, abandoning the leather-covered padded lounger and switching off the sound system.

Unsettled, and hating the unprecedented state of affairs—he always knew what he was at, didn't he? Well, didn't he?—he paced over the honey-blonde polished hardwood floor to the sheet of toughened glass that comprised one wall of the penthouse suite's spacious living area. He stared out over city lights shrouded in the misty gloom of late-afternoon, bunching his fists into the pockets of the casual sweats he'd dragged on after he'd showered.

Edgy. Something continually nagging at the back of his mind. Couldn't access it. His ebony brows met in a frown of sheer aggravation. And then he had it.

Guilty conscience!

Which was a bit rich, considering Sophie Lang didn't possess anything remotely like a conscience, he half humorously conceded. But finally pinpointing the source of his edginess made him feel a whole load better—back in control of his head.

He'd been too incensed by the way she'd lashed out at him over the business of that wretched pram to assess the situation calmly. And, come to think of it, her whole attitude during their enforced and regrettable reunion had been confrontational when, from his standpoint, she should have been, if not embarrassed by and apologetic for her past sneak-thief activities, because that was obviously beyond her, then at least suitably and quietly humble.

But for all her lippiness there was no denying she'd been genuinely distressed over the loss of that awful old pram. Sentimental value, as she'd so forcefully told him. If he'd had any inkling of that he wouldn't have offloaded the thing. He'd genuinely thought she would be happy to see the back of the ancient monstrosity and more than grateful to use his cash to buy something more attuned to the needs of a modern mother and her baby.

A mistake, obviously. And an even worse one had been the way he'd tossed that money at her feet with what he now conceded was uncalled-for dismissive arrogance. She'd made him lose his temper, forget the code of manners that had been instilled in him since birth.

That couldn't be remedied, but the other error could. An impatient glance at his gold Rolex showed it was just gone five-thirty. The charity shop might stay open until six. It was worth a try.

Salve his conscience and she'd be out of his head again. No problem. In the aftermath of that dreadful night well over a year ago he'd coldly put her to the back of his mind under the mental heading of Bitter Experience and moved on—right on.

Within seconds he'd shouldered his way into a soft-as-butter black leather jacket, collected his car keys and exited the apartment. The lift carried him smoothly down to the parking area.

He made his destination just as a boot-faced woman was about to lock the shop door. The effortless charm of his smile gained him entry, plus an immediate relaxing of the woman's features into an incongruously girlish simper. The writing of another healthy cheque made out to the charity gained him the promise that the ancient pram would be delivered to the given address first thing in the morning.

Back in the car, waiting his opportunity to ease out into the traffic, Ettore brooded over the ongoing and utterly annoying reality that something was still bugging him.

Still!

But what? Something he didn't want to face?

Ebony brows flared with mounting exasperation. He owed the dishonest little baggage nothing further. Hadn't he picked her up out of the gutter, transported her, her child and her belongings to where she wanted to go? Reclaimed the old pram at inconvenience to himself?

In fact his future wife, the wronged Cinzia di Barsini, would consider his time and energy spent on Sophie Lang's behalf to be way beyond what was necessary or wise. The guy Sophie Lang had moved in with could look out for her. His own conscience was clear. She'd get her precious pram back and that should be the end of the matter.

But it wasn't.

Then the answer to what was still needling at the back of his mind hit him with a force that took his breath away, pumped his heart into overdrive.

Mentally venting a string of curses, he swung the powerful car out into traffic, heading in the direction of Finsbury Circus.

Sophie Lang had one highly pertinent question to answer. And he'd get it if he had to drag it out of her!

'I don't like to dash off and leave you.' Tim Dunmore patted a breast pocket to make sure his wallet was present and correct. 'But Rocko would kill me if I missed his stag night.'

'No worries!' Sophie gave him a warmly affectionate smile. 'You've been really great. I'll never be able to thank you enough for taking us in.'

Her best friend Tina's big brother, whom she hadn't seen for a couple of years, since Tina's wedding to her Canadian boyfriend, had walked into the wine bar where she'd been working one day and had got the whole sorry story from her. She'd been three months pregnant at the time, lodging with Nanny Hopkins, dismissed by the agency and blacklisted for being accused of dishonesty, her protestations of innocence brusquely brushed aside.

Just like Nanny Hopkins, Tim had believed her implicitly, and had written his mobile number on the back of a business card, making her promise to get in touch if she ever needed anything—cash for stuff for the kid when it came, a part-time job at his place of work if he could swing it, a place to crash.

Despite not forseeing any eventuality that would have her asking him for anything, Sophie had kept the card, and when her whole world had crashed around her head she'd been so glad she had.

Nanny Hopkins had seemed as invincible as ever, willingly babysitting Torry while Sophie worked shifts at the local supermarket to support them, so as not to be a drain on the elderly lady's slender resources. Then she had gone. The massive stroke had been so sudden, so shocking.

Grief-stricken, in the middle of making funeral arrangements, she'd been handed the news that as Nanny Hopkins's name had been on the rent book Sophie was to vacate the property in double-quick time. House prices were rocketing. A swift up-grade job and the landlord could sell at a whale of a profit.

Because she'd had Torry to think of she'd swallowed her pride and phoned her stepmother. But the request for somewhere to stay while she got herself sorted had met with a blasé, 'Don't look to me to get you out of a mess of your own making. You should get the kid adopted, for both your sakes. Besides, I'm cultivating a well-heeled widower—no kids of his own, thank heaven—and you and a squawling brat would rather cramp my style. You could try Tiffany, but I don't hold out any hope. She's doing brilliantly, of course, sharing a nice address with two of her model colleagues...'

And on and on, rubbing in her beautiful daughter's breathtaking success on the catwalk against her ordinary stepdaughter's abject failure in every department.

Utterly dispirited, Sophie had cut her stepmother

off in mid-flow. Stacia had never had any time for her. The moment she'd walked in as Sophie's father's new wife she'd dismissed Nanny Hopkins and done all she could to belittle her, pushing her own daughter Tiffany to the fore. Tiffany was so much prettier, so much brighter...

Then she'd remembered Tim's offer of help if she ever needed it.

'I'll always be grateful,' she repeated sincerely now, as Tim grinned down at her.

'No probs! You and Tina were practically joined at the hip when you were kids, so I guess I'm an honorary brother. Anyway, better make tracks.' He headed for the door. 'Don't wait up. Oh, yes.' He turned in the open doorway. 'Tina said she'd call you after she'd had lunch. There's a five-hour time difference, so you should be hearing from her any time now.' And he was gone, leaving Sophie smiling at the space where he had been.

Tim Dunmore was such a dear. Taking her and Torry in, finishing work early so that he could rush back and carry the bulkier of her possessions that the taxi had delivered up the two flights of stairs, finding the bits of the cot and erecting it so that she could put Torry down as soon as he'd been fed...

In fact the Dunmores and Nanny Hopkins had been the nearest thing to a loving family she'd had since her mother had died so tragically young. Tina, her best friend since primary school, had made sure she was invited to spend most of her school holidays with them.

Stacia had been glad to be rid of her, and although she was sure her father must have loved her in his

own undemonstrative way, he had been too busy
making the money the new wife he was besotted with
wanted to spend to show it. He'd worked himself into
an early grave trying to keep up with Stacia's demands—which had been like trying to plug a dam
with a single piece of straw, because when he'd died
he'd been virtually bankrupt.

Swallowing the lump in her throat, she staunchly
told herself to forget the past. She could do nothing
to change it. The friends she did have were good
people, worth their weight in gold, more than making
up for the bad. Like Etorre Severini.

But she wasn't going to think about him, was she?
Her run-in with him today had been unfortunate, but
it didn't mean she had to let him inside her head
again—did it?

She had Tina's phone call to look forward to, and
as Tina's parents were over there on an extended
visit she might get to have a few words with them,
too. Thankfully they had all respected her decision
to stay silent on the subject of Torry's father. And in
the meantime she had the evening paper to look
through in her quest for paid employment.

A live-in position as housekeeper to someone who
wouldn't object to a child would be ideal. But whoever employed her long-term would ask for references, and the agency that had blacklisted her most
certainly wouldn't supply them. The best she could
hope for would be something part-time, badly paid
and menial. She would never earn enough to pay for
proper child care, she thought on a wave of deep
despair, and she couldn't sponge off Tim for more
than a week or two.

Consciously relegating such unnerving thoughts to the back of her mind, to be taken out and examined later, Sophie checked Torry, peacefully asleep in his blue-painted cot at the side of the narrow bed in Tim's spare room, and had just settled down to scan the Situations Vacant columns when someone knocked on the outer door of the flat. Imperiously.

Someone looking for Tim? Leaving the paper open on the table, she brushed a lock of long blonde hair back from her face and padded barefoot to the door. Immediately she did her best to shut it again, but her strength in no way matched Ettore's as he effortlessly resisted her attempts and walked right in.

Her face flaming with fiery colour, Sophie placed a hand on her breast, where her heart was beating so furiously she couldn't get her breath, her eyes widening painfully as she watched him walk to the centre of the room and then swing abruptly round to face her.

He dominated the space, seeming to charge the very air with electric currents of raw primal energy that touched every nerve-ending, making them fizz. He'd had this effect on her since she'd first set eyes on him. The sexual vibes were intensely shocking. Once the chemistry had overwhelmed her into believing they were meant for each other. She had welcomed it—now she just didn't need it!

'What do you want?' The words came out like the challenge they were, the effect somewhat spoiled by the breathless delivery.

Borderline insolence was the only way to describe the arrogant way he held his unfairly handsome head and the set of those wide shoulders. The soft leather

jacket virtually screamed expense and a top-flight designer label, topping what looked like a pair of jog-
gers, and feet encased in a pair of worn trainers.

Only the mega-confident, super-wealthy, with a
long line of illustrious ancestors behind them, could
get away with that sort of sartorial mix-and-match,
was her self-admittedly inconsequential thought as
she watched those intelligent eyes narrow to slivers
of glittering jet.

Violently ignoring the hateful physical awareness
that had never failed to mount a massive full-frontal
attack whenever he was near her, she forcefully reminded herself of what a lying, heartless super-snob
he really was, and pushed out firmly, 'We have nothing to say to each other.'

The phone rang.

'Answer it.' Ettore's dark head tipped towards the
intrusive wall-mounted instrument when Sophie
seemed set to ignore it. He watched as mutiny simmered in her clear grey eyes only to give way to
sudden compliance as she took the few paces necessary to reach for the receiver.

Watching her, he expelled his breath slowly. He'd
been wrong about her being overweight. Narrow-
legged well-worn jeans and a shrunken woolly
jumper revealed a body that was as delectably vo-
luptuous as he remembered it—the waist tantalisingly tiny in between bountifully luscious breasts and
the tempting curves and the feminine flare of her
hips.

Lust surged. He didn't want it. He could pick and
choose among some of the world's most glamorous
women, should he feel inclined—which he didn't—

so why did this devious little baggage make him feel as horny as an adolescent when his sex-drive had been non-existent ever since her true colours had been revealed?

His mouth dried. He swallowed harshly and made himself concentrate on his reason for being here at all. And it had nothing to do with remembering how her warm, seductive flesh had felt beneath his shaping hands before he'd had exactly what she was pushed under his nose.

It had to do with timing, with genes. Her huge eyes were a soft smudgy grey, overlaid with shimmeringly clear crystal, and her long hair was a fascinating silvery blonde. From what he'd seen of the guy she was now shacked up with, he, too, was as blond as they came. So he was highly unlikely to be the father of her baby. And unless she was in the habit of flitting in and out of men's beds...

Only the delayed realisation that the caller was likely to be Tina, and that her friend would only worry needlessly if she didn't pick up, had Sophie obeying an order she'd had every stubborn intention of ignoring.

But it was impossible to carry on an uninhibited conversation under the cold stare of six feet of supremely self-assured intimidating male. And when Tina said, 'You've had a really rotten time of it. Stacia wouldn't give you the time of day, that goes without saying, but couldn't Torry's father—whoever he is—do something to help?' Sophie pushed in hastily.

'Look, I can't talk right now. I'll phone you back.'

She replaced the receiver and, turning slowly, willed her face to stop glowing like a boiled lobster.

She couldn't have regaled her friend with the information that her baby son was far better off with no father at all rather than one who was a first-class snob, a liar, and a silver-tongued seducer of fanciable members of what he probably regarded as the underclass—not when he was standing like a brooding Nemesis right under her nose, listening to every word she said.

And Ettore Severini must never know that he'd sired a son. Given what she now knew of his character, he'd probably flatly deny any responsibility because—let's face it—he'd already earmarked a classy bride to be the mother of his children. But she couldn't face even the remotest risk that he might want custody of her beautiful baby. Because if he did, he would make damn sure he got it. And where would that leave his child's far from aristocratic, cash-strapped and, in his jaundiced view, sticky-fingered mother?

Nowhere.

'Where are they?' The question emerged with the velocity of a bullet.

Sophie, swallowing sickly, parried, 'Who? What?'

'Your son and your lover.'

'Tim is not my lover,' Sophie stated, tight-lipped. He had no right to question her, but since he looked as if he would stay exactly where he was until he got an answer she preferred to keep his attention on her friend's brother and right away from her baby. 'He's a very good friend and, not that it's any of your business, he is out for the evening.'

'Right.' An ebony brow was slightly elevated in a gesture intended to convey that he wasn't buying the just-good-friends bit. Not that she cared one way or the other. His opinion of her was rock bottom, so it couldn't go any lower.

Shaking inside, her legs feeling like chewed string, she walked to the door and held it open. 'Please leave. You must have had a reason for coming here, but whatever it is I'm not interested.'

Being with him again brought too many memories back, most of them so beautiful they were full of pain because they were founded on cynically expert seduction techniques. He'd shown himself for exactly what he was on that last evening. And she didn't want to remember that, either.

'No?'

Sophie whitened. She didn't know how a simple two-letter word could sound like the direst threat. But it did. Her stomach jumped.

Horribly aware of those narrowed jet eyes on her, she quivered. The soles of her bare feet were cringing on the strip of cold lino, and a howling draught was gusting up the stairs like a force ten gale, but she stood her ground, willing him to leave.

He didn't. He simply strode over and closed the door decisively behind her, then asked with a smooth urbanity that chilled her to the bone, 'So, exactly how old is he?'

A hot surge of adrenalin made her want to run like the wind, set her heart knocking against her ribs. She'd been absolutely dreading this ever since he'd found her in the gutter. Had been hoping and praying that the ultra-wealthy, sophisticated, smooth-as-oil banker would have about as much interest in a small baby as he would in a passing ant.

Still clinging to that very slight hope, she lifted her chin and snipped out, 'Twenty-eight.'

Madre di Dio! She was pushing her luck here! Ettore held onto his speedily dwindling patience and pointed out, 'I'm not remotely interested in learning anything about the man you've just moved in with. How old is your baby?'

Sophie felt her already shaky knees weaken even further. The bitten-out question was a glaring sign-post to the way his mind was working. She clamped her teeth together, tightening her lips, saying nothing.

Ettore, the calculations he'd already made at the forefront of his mind, queried smoothly, 'Seven months?'

Sophie's heart felt like a cold, heavy stone. This was turning into a nightmare. Her mouth ran dry as she lifted her eyes to his, trying to formulate something telling that would leave him in no doubt that she and her baby were off-limits as far as he and his delving questions were concerned.

But Ettore got in first, his voice as chilling as the dark glint in his eyes. 'You told me you were protected and I took you at your word. I may have been as misguided in that as in everything else. Reckless must be your middle name.'

Hatefully, and predictably, Sophie felt her face flame. He already believed she was reckless enough to steal a highly valuable piece of jewellery from under his fiancée's nose. But reckless enough to have unprotected sex and lie about it?

She had been taking the contraceptive pill, but

sometimes—probably owing to what had happened on the island, the world-toppling event of finding the love of her life and believing that he felt exactly the same, caring for the twins—sometimes she'd plain forgotten.

And the fiery state of her face would be telling him more than she wanted him to know.

Dark eyes glittering, his spectacular bone structure hardening, he spelt out, 'You may have been enjoying the rampant sex I know you're so hooked on with some guy before I arrived at the villa. My brother-in-law's gardener also has dark eyes and hair. It's certainly a consideration. But perhaps you can enlighten me? Or don't you know who the father is?'

His jaw tightened forcefully and Sophie paled at the insulting opinion of her morals. She couldn't have spoken a word if her life had depended on it, and felt mortally sick.

'You are obviously not going to enlighten me,' he asserted coldly. And then, astonishing her, turned on his heels and paced towards the door.

He was leaving! He had no further interest in Torry—in whether the baby was his or someone else's! A dry sob of relief swelled in her chest. Her fear that he might guess Torry was his son and insist that custody was rightfully his, take her baby from her to be brought up in the style that befitted his father's illustrious bloodlines, had been unfounded and foolish.

But no sooner had the relief allowed her to uncurl her tightly fisted fingers than her misconception was dealt a savage blow.

Ettore Severini turned one last time, the door already partly open. 'I mean to have the truth. I suggest you sleep on it. If, tomorrow, you still refuse to answer then I will find all the evidence I need. A simple DNA test will do it.'

Halfway down the dreary flight of stairs Ettore was already speaking on his mobile. In the past the bank had had occasion to use the services of a discreet and highly efficient firm of private investigators. Reaching his car, he ended the call. Someone would be here within minutes. Someone would watch. And if she tried to do a runner with her child—his child?—she would be followed and her whereabouts dutifully reported.

His eyes narrowed with lethal anger as he slid behind the steering wheel. If the dark-eyed, dark-haired child was his, and the increasing tug of gut instinct told him he was, then she would discover that there was nowhere to hide.

CHAPTER THREE

NO YOUNG lady, with or without a babe in arms, had been observed leaving the premises. That was the information Ettore received as he strode through the crisp morning towards Finsbury Circus, preferring to use up a fraction of his restless energy rather than sit behind the wheel of his hired car as it crept through the appalling rush hour traffic.

As Sophie Lang's present address came into view Ettore ended his call, together with the agent's assignment, and the unremarkable car parked on the opposite side of the street pulled discreetly away. He slotted the mobile into an inside pocket of his suit jacket, uninterested in the further signing off information that a tall fair-haired young man had taken delivery of a big black pram as he'd been hurrying out of the premises at just before nine this morning, taking off at speed a few moments later.

That her latest lover had already left for work, running late, by the sound of it—because of a night of steamy sex with Sophie?—was neither here nor there, and the hard hot knot that twisted in his gut was not down to jealousy. Of course not. Most definitely not. Just completely understandable anger that his maybe-baby faced a childhood under the doubtful care of a numberless succession of 'uncles' and a mother with no morals worth mentioning.

If the child was his.

And swift as a knife the astounding thought that he wanted the child to be his slashed into his mind, rooting his feet into the pavement for shell-shocked seconds. Until the momentary aberration passed and he was able to haul himself smartly together, grit his teeth and mount the steps with his honed jaw at a determined angle.

One way or another, he was going to find out.

Have a nice nap, my own precious darling,' Sophie breathed as she laid the sleepy infant down in his cot, gently tucking the soft-as-down covers around him as the thick lashes that framed his huge brown eyes finally drifted closed.

Quietly leaving the tiny bedroom, she stood still for a moment, drawing in a deep breath, still miraculously holding herself together. Just about.

Torry's bellows for his breakfast had broken into her restless dreams at just before five-thirty. So the entirely pleasurable business of feeding him, bath-time, and the gentle playtime that was always so special had kept the demons at bay.

Now they were marching back, all teeth and claws, terrifying her!

She was going to have to tell Ettore Severini, she acknowledged with a lurch of her stomach, confess that Torry was his son. Apart from packing their bags and taking off—destination unknown—she couldn't see a way out of it.

He was already deeply suspicious, and if she tried to lie about it he would insist on having that DNA test and get to the truth. And that would hand him further evidence of what he saw as her deceitful character—another nasty label to pin on her. Yet another label he could use should he—heaven help her!—decide to go for custody.

So she would have to tell him and hope to goodness he would see sense, see that publicly acknowledging his son would do his relationship with his wife no good at all. From what she remembered of his then fiancée's cold black eyes, her beautiful but frigid features, she didn't have a forgiving bone in her body.

She felt physically sick. Remembering. She didn't want to remember, and pressed cold fingertips to her burning temples to try to block it all out again. But it didn't work, and the scenes that had led to what happened on that last dreadful night replayed remorselessly through her cringing mind like an endlessly recurring nightmare.

She and the four-year-old Valenti twins, Matteo and Amalia, had returned from the island the day before—Ettore having left the day before that, to attend what he had announced was an unexpected and urgent business meeting. On the mainland Signor Valenti had met the private launch—to the delight of his children, who hadn't seen Mama or Papa for four whole weeks.

As the company helicopter had taken off for Florence Signor Valenti had sighed. 'Such a summer! No escape this year for my wife and I from the heat of the city—too many pressing business meetings and entertainings. Poor Flavia complains of being wilted, and she is pining to see her children again. She would be here with us now, but she is deep in the arrangements for her birthday party.'

Sophie did her best to look really sympathetic, but she knew she wasn't. If the Valentis hadn't had to do without their annual escape to their villa on the island then Ettore, Flavia's brother, wouldn't have been pressed into dropping by to make sure the temporary nanny was coping.

And they wouldn't have found each other, fallen passionately in love, made each other so blissfully happy. And now the island idyll was over, and in a day or two she'd be returning to England—because the children's permanent nanny was fully recovered and waiting for her charges in the elegant house in the Oltrano district on the other side of the Arno where, traditionally, the prosperous ruling families resided.

But it wasn't really over—not by a long chalk! Ettore hadn't proposed, not in so many words, but every tingling instinct told her that he knew they were meant to be together for all time. Hadn't he, on his last night on the island, promised to escort her back to London, hinting that they had much to discuss?

Back in Florence, on Sophie's final day, Flavia warmly pressed her to join the lavish birthday celebrations planned for that evening. Already the overnighting guests had started to arrive—prominent among them the spectacularly glamorous Cinzia di Barsini, travelling with her obsequious, mousy personal maid.

'You are no longer employed as a nanny—until you leave us in the morning you are our valued guest. Please don't disappoint me!'

Faced with such a warm invitation from her

charming erstwhile employer, Sophie could only agree, though her natural inclination would have led her to keep well out of the way rather than spend the evening among a crowd of ultra-sophisticated strangers.

And only the absolute conviction that Ettore would be attending his sister's birthday celebrations had her scrabbling through the suitcase she'd just packed, ready for her early-morning departure, looking for something vaguely suitable to wear.

She hadn't seen him since he'd left the island, but she wouldn't let herself get uptight about that. He was a busy man. But a man of his word. She trusted him without reservation. So he'd be here this evening, if not earlier, and he'd been adamant about returning to London with her, making plans for their future.

The party was in full swing when Sophie ventured to join it. Still no sign of Ettore. She was doing her level best not to be anxious at his continued non-appearance.

The large salon, with its tall, elegantly proportioned windows, walls of soft dusky rose, immense gilt-framed mirrors and glittering chandeliers was alive with the buzz of the great and the good at play. The women in their designer gowns, jewels in their beautifully styled hair, made her feel as out of place as a big sticky bun on a dish of hand-made Belgian chocolates.

She'd thought the light cream-coloured cotton dress with its full knee-length skirt and fitted bodice would pass muster. But it didn't. It was hopelessly old-fashioned and bargain basement, and she would have crept back to her room if Flavia hadn't taken her arm and insisted on introducing her to the nearest knot of guests, taking a glass of champagne from one of the smoothly circulating waiters and pressing it into her hand.

It was on the tip of her tongue to come straight out with it and ask her hostess if Ettore was expected when she saw him.

In the arched doorway. Talking to the glamorous Cinzia di Barsini. Her heart swooped and soared on a rollercoaster of relief, and she hated herself for allowing, even for the smallest moment, those utterly unworthy anxieties to creep in. How could she have allowed herself to wonder if he wasn't going to show up before her flight in the morning, if he had no intention of seeing her again? He loved her, and what they'd shared had been special for both of them—it hadn't been a brief holiday fling!

Love melted her bones, made her clear grey eyes limpid. He was so indescribably beautiful. He wore his cream dinner jacket and narrow dark trousers with elegant urbanity and, unsmiling, the perfection of his features took her breath away. And he was hers! Unbelievable, but wonderfully, gloriously true!

Moving slightly away from the group she was with, she willed him to look up and see her. And as if she'd shouted the command at pitched volume his stunning eyes lifted from the coldly beautiful features of the woman who was engaging him in seemingly deadly serious conversation, found hers and held for a moment, cranking up the already fluttery feeling in the base of her tummy and setting her heart racing, exactly replicating the sensations that had turned her near-naked body to quivering jelly when he'd appeared in the isolated cove on that warm, starlit Italian evening just as she'd been emerging from the gentle swell of the water.

Then his attention was recaptured by something Cinzia said, by the tender, slightly tremulous smile she gave him, the touch of her long white fingers on the sleeve of his jacket.

Sophie sipped her champagne, stupefyingly happy. He would join her when that woman had stopped bending his ear. He was far too well-mannered to brush her aside.

As Flavia performed that task for him, swooping across the floor to place both hands on her brother's shoulders and stand on tiptoe to flutter kisses, continental-fashion, Sophie's lush lips curved in a gooey smile as her beloved Ettore extracted a long, slim jeweller's box from an inner breast pocket and put it in his sister's hands. His birthday gift.

She was contentedly watching the happy tableau, mooning over him, because mooning with a besotted grin on her face felt as natural as breathing, when Cinzia di Barsini slid up to her with the sinuous silence of a snake. The analogy was heightened by the black sequinned gown that clung everywhere it touched, and that was everywhere, and the cold black eyes glittering with venom.

A huff of breath disguised the emergence of a giggle at her own fanciful notions, but all thoughts of giggling or smiling ever again fled when Cinzia drawled patronisingly, 'Might I make a suggestion? Make yourself scarce. Seeing the hired help gawping at my fiancé only causes embarrassment for everyone concerned. You've got the hots for him and it is so uncool. I know he spent three weeks on the island with you and the twins—purely in a supervisory capacity, dear Flavia being naturally unsure of your capabilities.'

A slight understanding lift of the elegant shoulders accompanied the statement. 'And, knowing him, Ettore probably flirted a little to relieve the tedium. It is in the nature of the Italian male to do so. It would mean absolutely nothing. So do us all a favour, especially Ettore, and forget it—whatever 'it' is. He has already said he almost gave the party a miss because he knew you'd be hanging around him like a lovesick calf, just as you did on the island, boring the socks off him, but he knew he and I had some serious work to put in on the last-minute plans for our upcoming wedding.'

As the Italian woman had glided away Sophie had felt physically sick. She could still remember the feeling—remember how she'd shuddered with cold and nausea as Cinzia had rejoined Flavia, who had been admiring the emerald-studded bracelet her brother had fastened round her wrist, touching Ettore's arm, saying something. Something urgent, judging by the look on her face, and the swift frown that had momentarily darkened his fantastic face.

Turning, they had left the room together, and Sophie had sunk onto a small gilded chair because her shaking legs had given up on her. So he wasn't even going to speak to her. He'd be too busy being up close and private with his bride-to-be, discussing wedding plans. She had hardly been able to take it in.

Had all that passion been false, everything he'd said a lie? His seduction merely an exercise in boredom relief? It had truly been almost impossible to believe. And yet the Barsini woman wouldn't have claimed to be his fiancée, on the point of celebrating their marriage, if it weren't the truth. What would she gain by telling lies that could so easily be disproved?

People had begun to look at her. An unfashionably plump creature in a cheap dress, perched on a gilded chair and looking as if her world had fallen apart.

Which it had.

Summoning all her will-power, she'd got to her feet and walked over to where Flavia was still turning her wrist this way and that, admiring her brother's gift. She'd had to make sure. Cinzia might have been lying. She hadn't been able to imagine why, but stranger things had happened.

'It's so lovely,' she'd said, her voice sounding thin in her ears, meaning the bracelet.

'*Si*. Ettore has always spoiled me!' Flavia gave her lovely smile, and Sophie took her courage in both hands and did her best to look relaxed as she replied.

'Then he's bound to spoil Cinzia, too. I hear they're betrothed.' Privately she'd thought the verb sounded really old-fashioned, but she had been unable to say the words 'engaged to be married' because they would have choked her. She tacked on as a breathy afterthought, 'She is very beautiful.'

Flavia's smile faded. 'Beauty is only skin deep. However, many advantages will come from a union which was our late father's dearest wish.' Then she brightened, 'Come, shall we mingle? I will introduce you to—'

'I'm sorry...' Sophie pushed out on a whisper. Stupid to have pinned her hopes on Flavia flatly denying the engagement. There was a strange roaring sound in her ears and the floor seemed to shift beneath her feet. 'You'll have to excuse me. Migraine.'

'Oh, my dear!' Flavia was full of concern. 'What can I do? Shall I call the housekeeper? You are very pale! Do you have something you can take?'

'I just need to lie down. Please don't worry.' She felt such a fraud, but a migraine was the only excuse she could think of to save her the agony of trying to talk to people and pretend she wasn't howling and screaming inside. 'By morning I'll be fine,' she promised, trying to look as if she meant it, knowing it would be a long time before she felt anything like fine again.

And with a final wobbly smile she made it from the crowded room, noting the Barsini woman's personal maid creeping down the stairs in the deserted great hall, wearing an odd look of triumph on her narrow, sallow face.

Ignoring the other woman's simpering, *'Buona sera, signorina,'* because she couldn't trust herself to speak to anyone without bursting into floods of tears, Sophie headed for a distant side door that led to the rear courtyard garden, found a stone bench and sat there, letting the warm scented darkness wrap itself around her.

She had some serious thinking to do, plus a whole lot of growing up.

How pathetically green she'd been to believe a

word he'd said! He was a highly sophisticated creature, scion of a world-respected banking family, fabulously wealthy, charismatic, and stunning to look
at. Why would he consider tying himself to a nobody
who had only one thing going for her—a shaming
willingness to jump into bed with him?

The truth made her cringe and hurt like hell, but
she'd just have to take it, wouldn't she? She could
run Ettore to earth, spill out her pain and anger, but
that would only make her look even more of a gullible fool. She wasn't the first woman to be swept
off her feet and into the bed of an unprincipled
charmer, and she wouldn't be the last.

How long she sat there, with the moonlight touching a statue of Pan, making it glimmer palely through
the surrounding dark foliage, she would never know.
All she did know, as she used the service stairs to
silently creep up to her room in the nursery quarters,
was that she might have lost her heart but she still
had her dignity.

And if—and it was a big if—Ettore did seek her
out before her departure she would rise to the occasion. No tears or passionate recriminations. Just a
throwaway comment that, provided he let her know
the date of his wedding, she would send them a nice
little toaster. With ribbons on.

But he wouldn't seek her out, she acknowledged
as she got ready for bed. It was late now, and although no sounds from the main reception areas
could penetrate into the peaceful atmosphere of the
nursery rooms she guessed the party would be over.
And Ettore, the pressing last-minute plans for his
forthcoming wedding having been sorted out with his

future wife, would have scarpered—no room in his head for the no-account temporary member of staff he'd amused himself with as an antidote to the tedium of being stuck on the family's small private island, where the pace of life was slower than the crawl of a geriatric snail.

She had to accept it, acknowledge that she'd been used by a master charmer, try to put the pain of it behind her and somehow get on with the rest of her life.

Gulping down a sob, she opened her case and stuffed the cream dress in any old how.

She would never see him again. Loving him had become her whole world, and in spite of what she'd been told this evening she couldn't just turn it off. She turned to the bed, hating the knowledge that she was going to spend the night crying her eyes out, and then gasped with alarm as the door to her bedroom was flung open.

Silence—just the dying echo of her own shocked gasp for air. And Cinzia di Barsini, framed in the doorway, the sequins that spangled on her black gown glinting as cruelly as her coal-dark eyes. Then, from behind her, Ettore shouldered into the room. His jacket had been discarded and his cream silk shirt was open at the neck, revealing the oiled satin of his bronzed skin—the skin that had been her delight.

But his face was pale, the fabulous bone structure clenched tight beneath the skin, and his eyes were bleak. The sensual mouth that was capable of giving mind-shattering ecstasy was drawn into a tight line as his beautiful, aristocratic fiancée swept an imperious hand towards Sophie's battered suitcase.

'Open it! It will be there. If not, then search every inch of this room.'

'What do you think you're doing?' At a huge disadvantage in one of the ancient T-shirts she usually wore to bed, her sun-streaked blonde hair all over the place, Sophie knew her question had emerged sounding like the bleating of a frightened child rather than the voice of a justifiably outraged adult.

Cinzia ignored her, advancing on the suitcase and prodding it with the pointy toe of an expensive shoe, and Ettore said tightly, 'Accusations have been made.'

Half turning, he beckoned, and Cinzia's personal maid sidled in, her eyes shifty. Sophie's stomach lurched. She had no idea what was going on, but whatever it was she didn't like it.

Her eyes full of bewildered appeal, she demanded unsteadily, 'What accusations, Ettore?'

'That you have stolen from me!' Cinzia said with utter contempt. 'Filomena, repeat what you saw, so there can be no mistake.'

The staccato burst of Italian was impossible to follow. Sophie could only understand if the delivery was clear and relatively slow. Besides, how could she concentrate when her head was spinning with the shaming accusation? She gave a whimper of distress, tightly banded pain wrapping around her chest as, probably to set the record straight, Ettore translated heavily.

'Filomena claims to have seen you coming from Cinzia's room a couple of hours ago. When she asked, thinking you'd been looking for her mistress, you refused to give an answer.'

'I haven't been near her room,' Sophie denied hotly. 'I don't even know which one she's using!' Her legs threatened to give way beneath her. 'I haven't stolen anything!'

Ettore carried on tautly, as if her outburst hadn't happened, 'Cinzia had left her jewel case open on her dressing table. On retiring she discovered that a highly valuable item was missing.' He glanced at the woman she had learned he was to marry as if for confirmation. 'A diamond choker?' Receiving Cinzia's tight-lipped nod of assent, he sighed heavily and intoned, 'She rang for Filomena, to ask if she moved it, and was told how you'd been seen leaving the room while everyone was occupied at the party.'

'I haven't taken anything!' Sophie wailed, at her wits' end, humiliation piling on humiliation with alarming speed. 'How could you believe I have?' she demanded.

How could he? Even though he'd deceived her, used her, surely after those long nights of shared passion, when he'd made her believe that heaven itself could hold no greater happiness, after the laughter they'd shared as they'd played with the children, the lazy picnics, the late-night intimate suppers for two, he had grown to know her well enough to know she was at least honest?

The frown line between his eyes increased as, taking matters into her own hands, Filomena bent down to open the suitcase. Sophie surged forward to stop the invasion of her privacy. Ettore's hand stayed her.

The touch of his strong, beautifully crafted fingers on the bare flesh of her arm filled her throat with raw emotion, and she was sure compassion lurked at the back of his fine eyes as he murmured thickly, 'I apologise for this. There is nothing to fear. I promise.'

But there was. Sophie knew it in her bones. Bones that were shaking, unfortunately adding to the impression of guilt. She'd been set up. By the maid? By Cinzia herself? It seemed totally ridiculous, but she knew it was a fact when Filomena gave a screech of triumph and jerked to her feet, her outstretched hand displaying the jewel.

After that, she was too deep in shock to say another word in her own defence, not even when Ettore asked harshly, 'Well?'

Her eyes wide in the pallor of her face, her mouth quivering uncontrollably, Sophie fought against the hot tide of rising nausea. Her eyes were a mute appeal for time to pull herself together, get her head around this latest horror.

She knew he was believing the evidence of his own eyes, and this coming on top of learning he was about to be married, had taken her love and tossed it aside as if it had no more value than a used bus ticket, was the final incapacitating blow to a brain that was already too traumatised to function.

'So. Nothing to say.' Ettore gave her one long, unreadable look, turned on his heels and walked out, his head high, his shoulders rigid.

His future wife had taken the key from the inside of the door. 'I will make sure you are released when the driver arrives to take you to the airport in the morning. Be thankful that I'm not in the mood for pressing charges. It would give me pleasure to know you were behind bars, but I have my wedding to think of, and that is all the pleasure I need at this moment.'

Sophie swallowed the lump in her throat, wondering wildly if, after all, she and Torry should make a run for it. Find somewhere to hide out until he shrugged those impressive shoulders, gave up looking for them, and returned to Italy. And his wife.

The resurgence, in such vivid and painful detail, of the memories she'd shoved to the back of her mind was making her lose all sense of proportion, she decided, and made herself summon all that remained of her common sense. Running out into the street with nowhere to go would be the worst thing she could do for her baby.

She had to tough it out, she assured herself as she went to the window overlooking the street, hoping against hope that he'd changed his mind and wouldn't bother to show up. What would a wealthy Italian banker and his aristocratic wife want with his bastard son? Or the adverse publicity of a custody battle?

Torry was her much loved child. Surely he would see it would be a crime to separate him from his mother.

But he would say she wasn't fit to rear his child to manhood. And all the reasons he could summon up to back that premise made her feel decidedly queasy. Her insides jumping with nerves, she changed her mind and wished he'd arrive so they could get the threatened interview over. Only then could she begin to try to find a solution to her present unenviable homeless and near penniless situation.

And then she saw him, approaching the street door with an intimidating, purposeful stride. Her heart lurched, and on impulse she opened the flat door and shot down the stairs to meet him. She knew she was being irrational in wanting to keep him at as much distance as possible from her innocently sleeping son, and in her haste to reach the door, to keep him on the steps before he could enter, she collided with a large solid object and went sprawling on the floor.

Deploring the complete lack of security attached to the house, Ettore mounted the steps and swung open the front door. Biting back a caustic comment at the sight of the mother of his maybe-child sitting on the dusty floor for no sensible reason he could fathom, he swept his eyes over her pink-flushed features, the tangle of long silky blonde hair, noting the way her wide eyes swept incredulously between him and the dreadful old pram.

He extended a hand, determinedly hardening his heart, scorning the way its tendency to turn mushy at her surely manufactured air of vulnerability.

Ignoring that seemingly imperious hand gesture, Sophie scrambled to her feet. She didn't need his help.

But she couldn't help wondering, even softening. 'You got my pram back for me?'

He dipped his dark head in terse agreement. How well he remembered that look—all wide-eyed innocence, clear and direct, with the underlying sparkle of warmth and wonderment. All the act of a seasoned con-artist. It was the reminder he needed.

'Not personally,' he disclaimed coolly, disregarding his last-minute dash to the charity shop, the shelling out of a further hefty donation. 'I wouldn't be seen dead pushing that heap of old iron through the streets. But you appeared to be unaccountably attached to the thing. I merely arranged to have it returned to you.'

Sophie stared at him, wide-eyed. He had done her a real kindness. It might have been in tune with the man she'd fallen head over heels in love with, but it didn't gel with the man he had eventually shown himself to be. Shamelessly cheating on his fiancée, seducing and deceiving the hired help, hinting at happy-ever-after and all that stuff, then believing anyone's word over hers and branding her a thief. Not forgetting the way he'd contacted the agency and made sure she never worked on her chosen career path again.

But... 'Thank you,' she uttered sincerely. That much at least was due to him, though his mean, moody and arrogant stance told her he didn't rate the concession.

Cold eyes pinned her to the spot, and Sophie shivered in the arctic blast, wrapping her arms around her body to hold herself together.

Crunch time.

She knew it.

Even prepared for it, she still felt a tide of nausea rise within her as he stated chillingly, 'You have something to tell me.'

CHAPTER FOUR

SOPHIE was only too aware that she had to be giving an award-winning impression of a fish out of water as the words that could seal Torry's fate hovered on the tip of her tongue—only to be convulsively swallowed back again. And, equally demoralising, she felt her knees weaken treacherously beneath her, felt what colour she did have leach out of her skin beneath the hard challenge of those glittering dark eyes.

He looked as cold and unapproachable as the far side of the moon, and the prospect of actually saying the words that would give him rights over her precious baby was scaring her silly. She lowered her own eyes to the floor and gave a huge shudder of reaction when his tension-riven voice arrowed at her downbent head.

'Upstairs. We can't talk in this benighted hole.'

That restored the loss of her vocal chords quicker than any surgical procedure. 'Of course we can,' she yelped, panic stricken. 'It won't take more than two seconds flat!'

She didn't want him anywhere near her baby. He might demand to take a good long look at the fruit of his loins. And no one seeing the little charmer could fail to fall in love with him. Not even a hard-hearted brute like Ettore Severini.

Not giving him the chance to argue the toss, she made herself spit it out, not letting herself wimp out.

'Torry is your son. But, listen, I promise to make no demands of any kind on you. No one but I—and now you—knows who his father is, and never will. Your wife need never know—there's no reason for her to be upset. You can forget about both of us.'

'Where is he? In the flat?'

Taking in the feverish glitter of those dark eyes, the faint flush of colour now washing the fascinating arch of his prominent cheekbones, Sophie knew he hadn't taken in a word she'd said beyond the stunning fact that he was a father. And where else would he think her baby was? Put out with the garbage? What kind of mother did he think she was?

No, don't answer that, she informed her whirling brain as anxiety formed an acid ball in her tummy, increasing a thousandfold when he brushed past her, heading for the stairs, taking them two at a time.

Her throat convulsing, Sophie gathered her shocked wits and sped after him, her eyes transfixed by the rigid determination of his broad back. His actions weren't those of a man who would shrug his shoulders and walk away, dismissing the existence of an illegitimate son—even though he'd just been handed the opportunity to do so on a plate.

But then he hadn't taken in her statement that she'd make no demands on him, that the identity of Torry's father would remain their secret, she hastily rationalised as he pushed the door to Tim's flat fully open and walked on through.

A frantic spurt of activity brought her to his side as he reached the centre of the unprepossessing living area. Her instinctive restraining hand on his arm had him dealing her a clenched brow look that was as savage as a physical assault. Sophie tried not to flinch and struggled to get her breath back as he shrugged her hand aside. But he was a reasonable man, surely? Once she'd grabbed his full attention and reinforced her earlier statement—no demands, a secret kept—he'd—

'So where is he?' He denied her the opportunity to say anything, striding to the inner door that led to the two tiny bedrooms.

He was impossible! Big, domineering—something else! Perhaps he'd listen to her when he'd sated his curiosity. That was her self-admitted feeble thought as she resigned herself to leading the way to the box-like room Tim had allowed her to use.

Opening the door with deliberate care, because she'd discovered the hinges protested gratingly if not treated with the utmost respect, Sophie stood aside and allowed Ettore to enter, her breath snagging in her throat and her heart beating as if it had gone crazy.

Would one look at his sleeping son satisfy him? Alarmingly, she didn't think so. He was not easily satisfied, was he? Her face reddened as she shamingly recalled how insatiable he'd been on the island—insatiable for sex, she reminded herself hollowly, not for her as a loved individual, just for sex with the nearest halfway presentable willing woman.

One look at his son would never be enough, instinct now told her. And the look was long, lingering—as if he was absorbing every detail of the tiny features, the soft sleep-flushed skin and the mop of silky black hair.

At last he turned, and the tenderness tinged with

something that looked suspiciously like pride she was sure she had fleetingly glimpsed was replaced by tough aggression as he told her, 'We need to talk.'

'Of course.' Her spine rigid, Sophie led the way back to the living area. 'And maybe this time you'll listen.'

She refused to be intimidated by his anger, refused to sit when he gestured towards the leather-covered three-seater.

'As I said—'

'I know what you said.' He brusquely cut her off. 'No demands. Secrets. Do you imagine for one fluff-brained moment that I would be ashamed to acknowledge my own son? Blood of my blood! That I would wash my hands of him and leave him to be brought up fatherless, relying on his mother's latest lover for a roof of sorts over his head, the bread in his mouth?' His own mouth was hard with bitter condemnation. 'Dragged up with no real security, with no moral principles to guide him!'

'How dare you say that?' Sophie shot at him with fierce outrage. Her fisted hands knuckled firmly on her curvy hips. 'Hypocrite! How many moral principles did you have when you seduced me, vowed you loved me, and all the time you were engaged to marry someone else?'

Huge grey eyes sparked with an angry flare of triumph as she noted his immediate discomfiture, the way the long dark sweep of his lashes lowered to hide his expressive eyes. A muscle jerked at the side of his hard, blue-black shadowed jaw, and Sophie suddenly felt compassion swell like a big soft ball inside her heart.

She didn't know why, but she really hated to see him at a disadvantage—even though she knew he deserved everything she'd thrown at him. Had she thrown enough to get him off her case? The possibility should be filling her with elation, but all she felt was a weird emptiness.

Ettore Severini was not a man to be routed so easily, and his slightly accented voice was cool and smooth as he commented, 'It is pointless to rake over past sins when we need to concentrate on the present and the future of our son.'

He saw the lush pout of her mouth quiver, then tighten, and his heart gave a savage jerk as he remembered how that mouth had felt beneath his, how incredibly responsive she'd been. He'd been blown away.

Agreeing to his sister's plea that he drop in on the family's secluded holiday home—'Just for forty-eight hours to check that Sophie's coping. I'm sure she is. During the weeks she's been with us she's been perfect in every respect. Call me clucky if you like, but it would set my mind at rest.'

In the event forty-eight hours had stretched to three weeks.

Arriving on the island that first evening, he'd been deeply troubled. The future of his personal life had suddenly seemed so achingly empty.

The long-standing arrangement he had with Cinzia di Barsini, only child of his father's friend and one-time business colleague, negotiated primarily by both sets of parents, had always seemed acceptable—entirely normal.

In the elevated circles he moved in marriage was

regarded as a merger, with family name, social standing and wealth the accepted currency. Marrying for the ephemeral emotion named love was for lesser beings—people who did not carry the responsibility of huge estates, business and banking empires on their shoulders.

Consolidating wealth and status was a set-in-concrete duty that must be followed. That was the tenet that had been drummed into him almost from birth. And sensibly accepted.

But recently something inside him had started to rebel, to question. Could there be something more than the empty union that lay somewhere in his future?

Cinzia had always been honest, a trusted friend. 'We're not madly in love with each other—but that sort of romantic candyfloss is for airheads. We value and respect each other, and that, for intelligent adults, has to be a more lasting basis for a meaningful relationship. We will marry when you decide you want an heir. And I will give you heirs,' she had told him, when the death of his father had had her family pressing for their marriage.

Her smooth cool hand had briefly touched his, her smile—as it always was for him—had been pure sweetness and light. 'Unlike Papa, I understand that your loss means a mountain of more work for you. We can wait a little while longer. I'm in no hurry to settle down, and as your future bride I will remain untouched—that goes without saying.' She had primmed her mouth fastidiously. 'If you have certain needs, in the meantime, I do insist the way you satisfy them is not brought to my attention.'

At the time he hadn't seen the lack of what people called love as a problem. In the upper stratum of society such an arrangement was entirely acceptable. Dynastic marriages worked well far more often than not. And no eyebrows were raised when a man took a mistress. Besides, his life was full, intensely satisfying. Work filled most of his waking hours, and the women who filled the remaining corners—though not as many as he'd been credited with—knew the score.

When he finally said goodbye to his bachelor freedom he would gain a beautiful, wealthy, ultra-sophisticated wife to give him an heir and run his household elegantly, to act as a brilliant hostess. Could any man ask for more?

But in the weeks preceding his agreement to check on Flavia's children and the temporary nanny doubts had tormented him—until he'd reached a decision to break his engagement. There had to be more than such emptiness, such shallowness.

His father would turn in his grave, and his mother, now permanently living with a paid companion in a lavish Venice apartment, would disapprove. But he couldn't live his life the way they wanted him to, hidebound by rules that he now saw as positively medieval. For the first time in his life he wanted to find what poets called love—if it existed. And as Cinzia's emotions had never been engaged the di Barsini family would look around for another suitable merger. No one would suffer from his decision.

He would tell her of his decision to break the engagement when he returned to Florence. In person. Giving her the option of letting it be known that it was she who'd had second thoughts and called it off, saving the pride that was so important to her.

It was at that point in his deliberations that he had announced his arrival to the resident cook/housekeeper, had checked on his sleeping niece and nephew and, still edgy, wandered down to the moon-lit cove—to be struck by a shaft of primeval lust such as he'd never experienced before.

He'd watched the temporary nanny slowly emerge from the glassy water, moonlight silvering her luscious body, clad in the tiniest triangles of fabric, her arms above and behind her head, thrusting her ripe breasts into tempting prominence as she rung sea-water from her long blonde hair.

And in the days that had followed, as he'd grown to know her—or thought he had, he now amended—lust had rapidly blossomed into love. Such love as he'd never expected to experience or even believed possible.

Everything about her had delighted and fascinated him. She was like no other woman he had ever met in his social or business circles. She was warm and funny, generous with the unforced love she lavished on Flavia's children, and completely natural, with no hint of the artifice that seemed the stock in trade of most of the women he came into contact with.

She didn't flirt, he doubted that she would know how, but reciprocal desire had simmered in the depths of her huge smoky-grey eyes, and he had been stingingly aware of her heightened flush, the rush of her indrawn breath if they happened to touch.

Making love had been so natural, so right. It had had the inevitability of night following day. And her generosity, her willing response, had blown his mind, enslaved him utterly.

She hadn't been a virgin. He'd accepted that. This was the twenty-first century, after all. As an Italian male he would have preferred to be the first with this woman he'd already decided he could never be parted from, but he'd prided himself on being pretty laid-back about it. And he'd believed her when, after that magical first time, she'd confided that she had never believed it could be like that. So wonderful, so earth-shattering.

Looking at her now—all silky blonde hair, limpid eyes, kissable lips and soft womanly curves—a surge of anger so savage it threatened to send him into orbit brought a red mist in front of his eyes. He dragged a long breath through pinched nostrils as he controlled it. It wasn't directed at her, not primarily, but at himself—for acting like a lovestruck loon, allowing her to pull the wool so thoroughly over his eyes, blinding him to what she really was.

A promiscuous thief.

Barely sparing her a further glance—in his present mood he couldn't bear to look at her—he pointed out, 'I had hoped never to have to see you again, but, that being said, we have to put the past behind us and concentrate on our son. Please sit.'

Flooded with self-loathing for ever believing this monster was the best human being ever to draw breath, for naively believing that such a sophisticated, filthy rich hunk could have any long-term interest in an ordinary nobody like her, Sophie capitulated with bad grace and sat down stiffly onto one end of the long leather sofa. She watched him fold his lean and magnificent length into the opposite end. As far away as possible. Which was fine by her!

Despite the defiance that speared from her eyes Sophie paled, her insides churning nauseously. Were her worst fears about to be confirmed? What had he meant when he'd stated that he had no intention of leaving his son with a no-good, sticky-fingered scrubber like her? Or words to that effect!

It was on the tip of her tongue to burst out with accusations of her own. She wasn't a thief. She'd been set up. But accusing his wife—and that sly maid of hers—wouldn't bring any bonus. It would cause mischief—and what was the point of that? Besides, he probably wouldn't believe her in a million years.

Putting him straight on what really mattered, in a voice that aimed for cool determination but merely achieved an anguished croak, she said, 'I suppose I can understand your not wanting to wash your hands of Torry—if I try hard enough,' she amended, to let him know that, knowing what a love-rat he was, she'd expected the complete opposite. 'And I promise you can see him whenever you like—to make sure he's being brought up properly,' she added, with an injection of heavy sarcasm, still stinging from his opinion that she would make a rotten mother. 'Think about it. Publicly acknowledging him would only hurt and humiliate your wife.'

Or wouldn't he care about that either? A prescient shiver juddered its icy way down her spine. And her lush mouth dropped open when he came back smoothly. 'No problem. I don't have a wife.'

Watching the shock register on Sophie's gorgeous features, Ettore wondered how Cinzia would take the news of his newly discovered son. Would she stick with the arrangement he'd coldly and pragmatically agreed to re-enter on the morning after his fantasy woman had shown herself to be a common thief, proving that falling in so-called love was for the birds? Or would she walk away from it? A mental shrug confirmed that as neither of them had emotions invested in their future marriage it didn't matter a damn either way.

The only thing that mattered—would ever matter—was his son. His son. Already showing distinct signs of developing the distinctive Severini features, as he had noted with a fierce stab of pride.

'I won't accept vague visiting rights,' he uttered emphatically. 'Who knows when you might take it into your head to shack up with some other guy, leaving no forwarding address?'

Flaming at that jaundiced view of her lack of morals, Sophie opened her mouth on a vehement protest, but Ettore's hand sliced her to mutinous silence.

'Unfortunately I can't do what I want—what I without doubt could do—and that is gain sole custody of my son. A child needs his mother.'

At that concession Sophie's rock-bottom spirits lifted. Only to plummet down to the sickening depths again as he spelt out with a lethal bite, 'But my son also needs his father. Especially so when his mother appears to have no means of support and, if past records are anything to go on, may be again tempted to resort to theft if her sexual favours don't gather the expected financial rewards.'

Which was what, surely, had happened in

Florence. That was the self-justifying thought that occupied the ensuing stunned silence.

How many times on the island that had become, for him, the earthly embodiment of heaven, had he fantasised over the day when he would be free to lavish on her everything her heart could possibly desire? The mind-deluding plans he'd made—after formally breaking his engagement to Cinzia he would escort his sweet Sophie back to the UK and ask her to be his wife, cover her with kisses and priceless jewels, make his precious darling his for all time.

Some remnant of duty—surviving the enchantment that had turned a tough, analytical business brain to candyfloss—had made him keep his plans to himself until the break with Cinzia had been made. So, with no pay-off in sight that she could see, that witch in an angel's skin had taken the opportunity to lift a valuable piece of jewellery. Her idea of payment due for services rendered!

From being momentarily turned to stone by his hateful low opinion of her Sophie felt anger rage through her with the strength of an out-of-control forest fire. On her lap her small hands clenched into fists and her words hissed through gritted teeth. 'I've never stolen anything in my life! So don't you dare say I have!' Her heart beat heavily against her chestbone in blistering outrage. 'And as you're not married to—to that ghastly woman, I can tell you that she must have planted whatever it was in my case. Or she told that maid of hers to do it!'

Ettore appraised her with unreadable dark-as-night eyes, drawling with cutting sarcasm, 'And why would she do that?'

'Because she's off her rocker!' Sophie, rigid as a broomhandle, shot right back.

Ignoring that off-the-wall scenario, he said smoothly, 'You didn't deny the attempted theft.' He could swear his heart had stopped beating while he'd waited for some believable explanation for the presence of the missing jewel tucked away in her luggage. 'Your final silence was an admission of guilt.'

It would have looked like that, Sophie admitted with weary hindsight, feeling like a pricked balloon. Eyes lowered, she mumbled, 'I was hurting—speechless. It was like a nightmare.' She didn't want to bring it all up, she never wanted to have to think about that traumatic period in her life again, but she had to stand her corner. 'I believed you were the love of my life. And all the time you were lying. All the time you were on the brink of marriage. I only found out that night.' The anguish of that dark memory tightened her voice as she spelled it out. 'I was having trouble trying to come to terms with that. And when you lot barged into my room and accused me of being a thief—well, like I said, my denials might have sounded half-hearted—because I was knocked speechless.'

So put that in your pipe and smoke it, you two-timing, lying rat! was her unspoken bitter thought, smartly switched off as a frustrated bellow from the bedroom invaded her ears.

Torry. A tender smile warmed her features as she rose to go to him on legs that weren't as steady as she would have liked.

Watching her go, his eyes annoyingly fixed on the sway of her jeans-clad nicely rounded behind, Ettore drew his dark brows into a frowning line. So that was how it must have happened. His sister or brother-in-law must have casually mentioned his long-standing engagement. Certainly not Cinzia, because at that time he'd already told her of his change of plan, confessing he'd fallen fathoms deep in love with Sophie.

It hadn't gone as smoothly as he'd expected on the night of Flavia's birthday party. Cinzia had demanded so much of his time to 'talk things through', sounding so reasonable when she'd pointed out that their forthcoming wedding—some time in the future of his choosing—would still be so right, that marrying the hired help would be the biggest mistake of his life. Could he see her entertaining his business associates, arranging glittering functions, holding her own with their set? If he had the hots for her, then by all means he should discreetly get it out of his system, but he mustn't throw away the eminently suitable union of their two great families and all the accruing social and financial benefits.

Cinzia had been right, he'd bitterly acknowledged the next day. Reason went out of the window when a guy was in the throes of a passionate love affair with the wrong woman. So the long-standing engagement had been back on.

Learning of his engagement would have led Sophie to believe that her affair with him had no future. Not bothering to wait and ask him to confirm or deny it, she'd followed her sly, greedy instincts and lifted a piece of valuable jewellery. And now she had the bare-faced cheek to accuse Cinzia of planting it!

He could hear her moving about in the poky kitchen he'd glimpsed off the living area, her voice warm and soothing as she talked to her son.

His son!

On his feet in a nanosecond, Ettore let his long stride carry him through to a kitchen that was the size of a cupboard. She held the wriggling child high on one shoulder while she juggled with a pan and a bottle of baby milk. Ettore's brows crashed down.

Two strong hands fastened around his son's squirming little body as he lifted him into his own arms, ignoring Sophie's disgruntled, 'Hey! What do you think you're doing!' concentrating instead on the way the child's big dark eyes widened as they fixed on his.

Ettore smiled. Torry smiled right back, showing a single white tooth, and reached out chubby hands to grab his father's hair. Ettore grinned unstoppably. He felt almost light-headed with emotion.

'Why didn't you tell me when you knew you were pregnant with my child?' he demanded thickly.

Resisting the possessive instinct to snatch her baby right back again, Sophie got on with what she was doing, her cheeks pink with scorn as she pushed out, 'When I finally realised, as far as I knew you were already married. You wouldn't have wanted to know. That kind of bombshell wouldn't have gone down well with your high-quality new wife! I was perfectly capable of coping alone!'

What she had against Cinzia, Ettore neither knew nor cared. The only time they'd had anything to do with each other had been when Sophie had been shown to be a thief. Resentment at having been found out? Probably. He dismissed the subject, concentrating instead on the outflowing of paternal love for the tiny child he held against his heart.

'But you're not coping, are you?' he pointed out as she assembled the baby bottle. Her hands were unsteady, he noted, without a jot of sympathy.

'I am so.' She kept her voice carefully level, afraid of Torry picking up antagonistic vibes. Sliding the bottle onto what passed for a breakfast bar, she settled herself on the solitary plastic-topped stool and held out her arms for the baby—who, annoyingly, seemed to have taken to the tall dark stranger.

Necessity overcoming his reluctance to hand his child back to such an unfit mother, Ettore obliged, gently placing the firm, warm little body on Sophie's lap. He could have strangled himself for the powerful onslaught of animal lust as the back of one of his hands inadvertently brushed against the underside of one perfectly formed, bountiful breast.

Furious with himself, he paced sharply back until the claustrophobic confines of the space that only an estate agent could have named 'kitchen' brought him in contact with an ancient gas cooker. His hands thrust deep into the pockets of his Savile Row trousers, he enquired with an acid bite, 'So, how do you propose supporting my son? And I warn you, relying on hand-outs from a string of dubious lovers won't cut it.'

Flushed, hot and bothered, Sophie overlooked that highly insulting warning. Someone should have warned her that the brush of his hand against her breast would still be lethal, turning her insides into quivering jelly, shafting wicked sensation directly to the core of her being, making her poor heart pound. He'd been so close as he'd leant over her, the warm tangy male scent of him a powerful aphrodisiac. She gulped thickly, hoping he wasn't noticing the way the almost painfully tight peaks of her breasts were thrusting against her woolly sweater as the last of Torry's milk disappeared into his eager mouth.

What was it about this man? her mind berated. He was, to use a word Nanny Hopkins would have chosen, a cad—and yet just to look at him sent rampant hormones raging all through her stupid body!

In her late teens she'd believed herself in love with Jake. Meeting him at a friend's party, she'd thought he was the cat's whiskers. Disenchantment had only set in when she'd learned that his idea of commitment extended no further than choosing which socks to wear. The only time they'd made love it had had no effect on her, had only made her wonder if this— a painful handful of seconds—was what all the fuss was about.

So what made Ettore Severini so very different? She knew he was a lying creep, yet still—

As Torry made a lunge for the bottle she'd forgotten she was holding she smartly made her mind abandon that line of questioning and got out, as coolly as she could, 'I'm job-hunting, if you must know.'

And into the beat of chilling silence that followed that slice of information her resentment flared and unstoppably spilled out. 'Though, entirely down to you, I'll have to accept something really low paid. But I'll manage—see if I don't!'

'*Basta!*' An impatient hand sliced through the

three feet of space that lay between them. Dark-as-night eyes glittered at her. 'Enough of this pointless waffle. Do you expect me to believe you could earn enough to provide decent accommodation, regular reliable childcare and meet the day-to-day living expenses of you and a child in a city as high cost as this? Get real. If the aim of your spiel about "managing" and "coping" was to disguise your intentions of living off some guy in return for bedroom favours, you've failed abysmally. I will not allow my child to have anything to do with such a sordid situation.'

Sophie's blood turned to ice. Tears of sheer fright spangled in her eyes. He was going to take her baby from her. Everything he'd said pointed that way. She clutched Torry more closely to her. Following Nanny Hopkins's death, and the loss of the little home they'd shared, she had believed that things couldn't get worse.

Wrong.

She was staring at her very worst nightmare. Her eyes flooded.

Ettore smothered a groan. He guessed that turning on the waterworks was a well-honed act, expertly choreographed to make a guy feel a heel. Dismissing the humiliating fact that just for a few moments it had actually worked, that portraying helpless female vulnerability had made him instinctively want to back-pedal, cut the tough male stuff, find a tissue and wipe her eyes, he bit out, 'You have two choices. You and my son return to Italy with me, where you will be provided with a luxurious villa and my son will grow to manhood with every possible advantage—and that includes his father as a permanent fixture. Or you refuse and face a court battle. Which I will win.'

His dark eyes fixed her with arrogant intent. 'Do as I want and you will have a life of luxury and you will keep your son. Go against me and you will lose him. Oh, the court might grant you occasional visiting rights, but with your track record I wouldn't bank on it.' His wide sensual mouth hardened. 'Your choice.'

CHAPTER FIVE

IT HAD been no choice at all.

He had called all the shots. Either option on offer meant that Ettore would have his son. Sophie had no doubt at all that with his financial clout and high-status family background, not to mention his own forceful personality and the list of the sins she'd been landed with, which he could produce at will, he would win the most fiercely fought custody battle.

The third option that had wildly occurred to her, to tell him to go right ahead and take her to court, and then take Torry and do a runner, had been reluctantly dismissed as being plain selfish, not to mention downright stupid. He would have tracked her down. And in the meantime what sort of life would Torry have had on the run? And when he found them—as, given his limitless resources, he surely would—he'd have another big black mark to hold against her.

So she had given in for the sake of her son. Had meekly allowed them to be torn away from London and transported—in the sort of style and luxury that made her eyes goggle—around the major capitals of Europe for a full month, conscious that Ettore was dead set on keeping them—Torry especially—where he could see them for all but the few hours it took him to conduct his no-doubt extremely important business.

He had an ego the size of a barrage balloon, she had decided, not for the first time, and it suited him to have the cowed little woman trudging along in his kingly wake. Her sense of self-worth had gone underground, and the only murmur of dissent coming from her mostly held tongue had issued when on their first stopover—Paris for five days—she'd been presented with the nanny he'd hired for Torry.

'Torry doesn't need a nanny! I can look after him myself,' she'd muttered on a fierce undertone, as Nanny had taken herself off to the adjacent hotel suite to unpack and settle in. She'd had nothing against the highly referenced, plain, obviously competent and kindly Minette personally, but she refused to be sidelined.

But he'd come back at her in the smoothly detached tone he'd used to her ever since she'd agreed to return to Italy with him. 'It is expected. For a son of mine not to have the best, highly trained professional care available would raise eyebrows. That aside, I personally demand the best for him.'

So what did that make her? Fourth rate? The bottom of the heap? Incensed, and still in that furious undertone, she'd ripped back at him, 'Not only am I his mother, I'm a highly trained nanny, too! Or I was until you made it impossible for me to work in that field again! Or had you forgotten?'

His insulting response had been to look through her, turn on the heels of his hand-made shoes and walk out of her suite and back to his.

So here they were at last, at his luxuriously spacious villa deep in the unspoiled Tuscan countryside, having collected enough baggage to break several dozen camels' backs.

Clothing and toys for Torry, which his father had picked out with loving enthusiasm, and enough designer gear to clothe a dozen catwalk models for a year for her. Plus newly shaped hair, wildly expensive make-up and perfumes. Not that he'd had much of a hand in that, apart from paying the horrendous bills. He'd hired personal shoppers—definitely hands-off where she was concerned. The desire to please, pamper and spoil her wasn't taking up a millimetre of space in his mind; the need to ensure that the mother of his son didn't disgrace the family name by any hint of second-hand shabbiness was to the forefront.

A sigh dredging through her, Sophie turned from her contemplation of the Tuscan night sky, spangled with stars, slowly letting the drapes fall back to close out the cool March night.

The long evening yawned ahead. What to do? Silly question. The same as on each of the other week's worth of evenings since they'd arrived at the luxurious hill villa and Ettore had taken off somewhere unspecified. Sit in this elegant drawing room trying to read until it was time to take herself off to bed.

She felt like a spare part. Useless.

There was a housekeeper, a cook, a daily maid of all work, and a brace of gardeners to tend the beautiful grounds. She didn't have to lift a finger. The only real stand she'd made was to insist that she and she alone cared for her baby while he was awake, and took him in his brand-new buggy for his twice-daily airings.

If this was to be the norm there would have to be changes, she vowed, her small chin at a defiant angle. So much for Ettore's pious spoutings on the subject of his son needing both his parents—he'd taken off at speed as soon as he'd ushered them over the threshold!

Possessive, or what? Torry was his son, and unfortunately she came with the package. So he'd shut them away out of sight where no one who hadn't been thoroughly vetted could have anything to do with his child—especially not all those imaginary lovers he'd lined up for her in his warped, highly inventive imagination!

Close to spitting bricks, Sophie felt her mood suddenly change. Did she really want Ettore as a close part of her son's life? Around most of the time? It would be unbearable. Around him she felt... Felt what?

But that didn't bear thinking about either, because she'd be lying to herself if she pretended she didn't know exactly what she felt around him. Sheer animal lust. Crazy. She was disgusted with herself. She no longer loved him—of course she didn't—and she didn't trust him an inch! So why did her wretched body come alive so vibrantly when he was around?

Resolutely she pushed him out of her mind, picked up the thriller she'd been trying to read for the last few evenings and opened it. From the position of the bookmark it seemed she'd got to page thirty, but she couldn't remember a single word.

Ettore drove between the tall cypresses that bordered the drive up to the villa feeling all wired up, as if a high-voltage electric current was fizzing through his bloodstream. He couldn't understand it. He should be feeling relaxed. The tough part was over.

Winning Mama over when it came to a surprise grandson had been a doddle. She couldn't wait to see him, hold him—and what sort of name was Torry? A contraction of Ettore, obviously!

The darling newest addition to the Severini family must be brought to Venice at once, for a proper christening. The Barsini family would politely turn a blind eye to his lapse, and Cinzia would accept the child, she was sure. The advantages of the forthcoming union were too great to be jeopardised over one little slip.

As for the baby's mother—she didn't want details of his affair, too tiresome—she couldn't stay indefinitely at his country villa, of course. A small apartment in Florence, perhaps? An allowance? Wasn't that how men conducted these things? And had he heard the gossip? Signor di Barsini had been involved in some catastrophic investments. Though she didn't believe a word of it…

As always, Ettore had allowed his adored mother's prattle to wash over him. He had heard no such rumour. He'd check it out. Marriage to Cinzia was now out of the question, but he'd help if he could, if it was needed.

He would do what he had to do and, as always, Mama would eventually accept it and claim it had been her idea in the first place. Dropping a kiss on her powdery cheek, he had presented her with his gift of her favourite perfume and taken her to lunch.

His sister had been a different matter. The newest

member of the family presented no problem, but the child's mother *was* a problem.

'I really took to her,' Flavia had said. 'Wonderful with the children, such fun—they both adored her. But she knew when to be firm. We all respected her, and I got really fond of her in the few months she was with us. I felt physically sick when she turned out to be a thief—it showed what a poor judge of character I was. You too, if you went far enough to get her pregnant. Do you really think you can handle that?'

He could handle anything. Ettore mentally reinforced that statement of fact as he garaged his car. Even the knowledge that in order to make his son legitimate he would have to marry a common little thief who would give her body to any man she thought she could get something out of.

His stomach twisted in an angry knot. If she'd had a little more patience on that fateful night she would have learned that, his formal breaking with Cinzia over, he would walk barefoot to the ends of the world for her, that he adored her, was begging her to be his wife. He would have married her without knowing what she really was and suffered a devastating blow when he'd found out that she viewed him as nothing more than a meal ticket.

His jaw tightened. He'd got over it, hadn't he?

This way would be better, he assured himself as he let himself in by the main door and made his presence known to his housekeeper. Sophie Lang had already fallen from the pedestal he'd put her on with a resounding crash.

Knowing what she was, he wouldn't be in any

position to suffer a future knock-out blow, and he would keep a strict eye on her to make sure she didn't stray, was never even tempted to. They'd be good in bed. He'd make it so good she'd never think of looking at another man. And this time his emotions wouldn't be involved. Been there, done that, learned the lesson.

Loyal to her fingertips, his housekeeper hadn't raised an eyebrow when he'd arrived with his surprise entourage a week ago. His son, his son's English mother and a French nanny. And now she blandly informed him, when asked, that Miss Lang was in the first-floor salon with the tray of tea she'd just had delivered.

Cinzia had taken his news just as expected, given the cold pride that was the dominant part of her character. And he congratulated himself as he took the stairs up to the nursery suite, complacently putting his wired-up feeling down to the prospect of seeing his son again after a whole week away.

He'd been feeling bad about letting Cinzia down after such a long engagement. Especially when the last time they'd dined together, prior to his departure for his London branch, she'd remarked idly, 'I suppose we should think about naming the day. Not that I'm pushing you, of course. No rush as far as I'm concerned. We both accept that our marriage will be a financial and highly successful social arrangement—it's not as though we can't wait to get our hands on each other, or anything so crass.' She'd given the tinkling laugh that was beginning to irritate him more each time he heard it. 'But Papa's getting a touch impatient. So give it some thought while you're away.'

Anxious to formally tie the Barsini and Severini fortunes together. Ettore could easily understand that. Cinzia's father wasn't getting any younger. Naturally he would be pushing for their union.

Remembering his mother's mention of gossip about the di Barsini financial difficulties, when he'd seen Cinzia he'd probed gently, 'Mama says there are rumours that your father is in financial difficulties. Tell me, is there any truth in them?'

Her denial had been immediate and emphatic, but his conscience had been pricking him when he'd then broken the news of his son's existence to his about-to-be-dumped fiancée.

He'd been immediately salved by her, 'If you think I'd marry you and share my home with your bastard, you must be mad! I'd be a laughing stock!'

That that scenario had never been on his agenda was something he hadn't bothered to mention. He had just endured her ongoing shrill outrage because it was the least he could do in the circumstances.

'And even if you keep your bastard hidden away somewhere in Italy the secret's bound to get out. People will snigger behind my back. I refuse to be put in that position! You should have washed your hands of it. Got it adopted or something. Or left the mother to get on with it. Discretion—we agreed, remember? Not siring bastards all over the place and flaunting them! So until you get it out of our lives, consider the engagement off! I'll reconsider when you've sent them both packing to the other side of the earth!'

'My son stays with me,' he'd imparted formally, appalled by this shrewish side of her he'd never seen before. He'd put it down to shock, gently pointing out that the cold-blooded arrangement they'd entered into had been a monumental mistake, that brainwashing offspring into following outdated ideas of family duty should be classified as a mortal sin. 'You are a beautiful woman, Cinzia. One day you will find someone you can love. I wasn't that man, but one day you will find him, and he will truly love you. You deserve more than a union of financial and social convenience.'

Putting aside the memory of that final interview, he lost track of the time he spent gazing down at his sleeping son, the self-admittedly fatuous grin on his face to be replaced by a slashing frown when, on calling in on Nanny in the adjacent room, he learned that *bébé* Torry now had another tooth and had begun to crawl.

Milestones in his son's life—and missed. A short week ago he'd got around—admittedly at speed—by shuffling on his bottom and chortling. Now he could crawl!

Madonna diavola, he would not miss any more!

Getting to the first-floor salon took him only a matter of rigid-shouldered seconds, with the tension inside him building to massive proportions.

If his son's mother had truly been the angel she'd so cleverly hoodwinked him into believing she was then there would have been no problem. She would have been everything he'd wanted and more—much more.

Hot hatred for the fact that she was the opposite

of the angel he had so besottedly once believed her to be made his brain hurt and his heart clench. Cool it, he commanded the unwanted physical reaction to an emotion he'd confidently believed over and long forgotten.

The course he had set himself to follow was the right one. For his son. He'd accepted the idea of a loveless marriage with Cinzia—with a few mental kicks—for outmoded dynastic reasons. He could take a loveless marriage to his son's mother in his stride, and make sure the flaws in her character, which were huge, didn't get to gape any wider.

Marginally calmed by that slice of common sense, he pushed the door open and walked in.

And his heart stopped beating. Then raced on. A rosy flush had stolen over her entrancing features at his entry, the huge grey eyes widening, her long throat convulsing as she swallowed back what he took to be a gasp of surprise. Such a delicate throat...the purity of its lines revealed by the deep V neckline of the dress she was wearing. Something soft and silky of a deep misty blue that made all that long blonde hair look like spun platinum.

A surge of lust as powerful as the one that had so comprehensively shattered him on that distant beach on that distant night had him fighting for control over the tempestuous, treacherous torrent. So his voice, when he finally got the words out, didn't emerge as he'd intended—smooth and cool as polished ebony—but on a harsh rasp that made his statement, even to his own ears, seem almost obscene.

'I've decided to marry you. It's the only way you

get a life of luxury and I get my son. Fall in line and we both get what we want.'

The moment the insensitively put statement of intent was out Ettore suffered an acutely sharp attack of conscience and self-loathing—a condition so new to him it took his breath away.

Her face turned the colour of skimmed milk and the book she'd been holding dropped to her lap as her fingertips flew up to cover her mouth, and he wished the unfeeling words unsaid.

She was the mother of his child, and despite past sins she deserved better than a proposal that had come out like a threat. A good, loving mother, as he'd been at pains to note. It now hit him that she was vulnerable too, transported against her will away from everything and everyone she knew. She would be on the defensive, and persuading her to do the right and sensible thing for their son's sake would take gentle coaxing.

Sophie gulped around the painful constriction in her throat and shoved out a rather wobbly 'no', sickeningly aware that there had been a time when she would have crawled over hot coals to accept his proposal of marriage, no matter how coldly put.

But not like this. She didn't want an empty life of pampered, idle luxury. She wanted love. And trust. And that was not on offer—never had been as far as he was concerned, she acknowledged wearily, wrapping her arms around her slender body to hold herself together.

'I could have put that better,' he acknowledged gently, taking the paces necessary to bring him to where she sat, as if turned to stone.

He took both her hands within his and pulled her unresisting body to her feet. The warmth of her, the perfume she was wearing, filled him with sudden raw need. He had been without a woman for far too long. In fact he'd lost interest in the opposite sex since this amoral little temptress had revealed her true colours, he calculated with unpleasant surprise.

Ettore clamped his jaw, denying the insistent throb of desire that bade him take those lush soft lips and kiss her senseless, and managed, with a smoothness that belied his ragged thoughts, 'I'm not asking for a knee-jerk response. If we marry, our son will have a stable family life. He will be legitimate—not my mistress's bastard.'

Sophie dragged her hands from his. This close to his magnificent body she was horribly tempted to agree to anything he said. But... 'Who said anything about my being your mistress?' she shot at him, delicate colour flooding her cheeks, making her huge eyes sparkle.

Two unthinking steps away from him had her sprawling back in the chair so recently vacated. The breath escaped her lungs on a shaky gust. If he thought that housing her beneath his roof, doling out the food she ate and the clothes on her back, gave him any rights at all over her body then he'd have to think again. Her weak body might crave him but self-preservation firmly reminded her that she could easily fall in love with him all over again. And that would lead to even more heartbreak and misery.

A beat of silence as he stuffed his hands into the pockets of the superbly cut trousers of his immaculate dark business suit. His wilfully passionate mouth had a wryly sardonic twist as he rocked slightly back on his heels and pointed out in a tone of unarguable reason, 'Between us we have made a beautiful child. You and he are under my protection. We will be living together, in my home. Whether we avoid each other like the plague or spend every opportunity writhing between the sheets is of no consequence. People will draw their own conclusions—that you are my kept woman, my mistress. And they will brand our son a bastard. Is that what you want for him?'

Hating the stark truth of that, Sophie squirmed. 'Then let me take Torry back to England,' she shot at him. 'Avoid unpleasant gossip. No one I know would be so outdated and downright hypocritical as to hold the fact that my baby was born out of wedlock against him! You can visit him whenever you like, and there won't be a snob in sight to turn a hair!'

'Not an option,' he uttered brutally, his patience fast dwindling—because he wanted to kiss her into compliance. His whole body burned and tautened with the need to stamp her with his ownership, to know again the shattering ecstasy of having her soft, all-woman, wildly responsive body beneath his.

She was the mother of his child; ergo she was his woman, warts and all! Quelling the unworthy desire, he forced himself to find and hold onto a reasonable tone. 'Put the welfare of our son first and think about my proposal. No immediate hurry. Just weigh up the advantages. And in the meantime—' the sudden grin that lit up his unforgettably handsome features made her shudder with the usual devastating reaction '—I suggest we start getting to know each other. Very thoroughly.'

CHAPTER SIX

'STARTING now?'

One winged ebony brow was urbanely elevated, and a slow smile curved his sinfully beautiful male mouth as long fingers unknotted the pale grey silk tie from the collar of his pristine white shirt with deft deliberation.

A heart that had picked up the wild speed of sheer panic rendered Sophie speechless. So she couldn't coolly announce, *Forget it. I'm tired and going to bed*, as she would have liked. She would have got up and walked from the room if she'd thought her legs had a snowflake's chance in hell of holding her upright—but she knew they hadn't.

His stunning eyes, sliding languorously from the crown of her smooth blonde head to the toes of her extravagantly expensive shoes, mesmerised her. Told her he'd meant 'getting to know each other' in the carnal sense.

Gulping shakily, Sophie felt her breasts peak with almost painful anticipation and surge against the fine silk of her dress. The way he was undoing the top buttons of his shirt was nothing short of downright erotic. Any moment now he would casually dispose of the suit jacket that clothed his honed, blow-your-mind-sexy physique with such fluid elegance.

She squirmed. Her breath shortened. Her tummy tightened on a spiral of renewed panic—and something else she was too ashamed to identify. If he moved towards her and—heaven forbid—touched her, she'd be utterly lost. His to take his pleasure on. And she would give it back with interest, just as she'd mindlessly done before. She was too honest to kid herself otherwise. Where he was concerned she had as much self-discipline as a lump of putty.

But having sex without deep emotional commitment would make her hate herself. Having sex without the cement of love would never be for her.

That the sex with him had been truly almost unbelievably wonderful once was undeniable. When she'd loved him so. She had no argument with that. But then she'd believed him to be the most fabulous creature ever created. Endlessly considerate, utterly charming, warm and passionate. Loving. Addictively sexy. All an act, a perfectly honed exercise in effortless seduction.

Now she knew him for what he really was: coldly autocratic, unfeeling, distrustful, all held together with a thread of cruelty. She loathed him. She absolutely did!

Yet, perversely, she still wanted him like crazy!

The jacket removed, he smiled that very male smile. Sophie pulled a ragged breath into her already hopelessly shaky lungs. The wide shoulders beneath the fine cotton white shirt owed not a thing to any top-of-the-range tailor's discreet padding.

As she already knew. Because she knew every inch of that lithe, sexy body. As he knew every inch of hers. Inches he was now reappraising with avid intensity.

Dazed grey eyes followed the slow sweep of his

much darker gaze, and her throat went dry as fiery heat pooled between her thighs. She knew he was reading all the signs she was incapable of hiding.

Cursing the unwanted rush of hormones that invaded her helpless body whenever he was around, she had to force herself to stay sane, hovering between savage disappointment and a bone-weakening rush of relief when he hooked the discarded suit jacket over one shoulder and drawled, 'On consideration, it's late. We'll leave it until the morning.' And sauntered out.

Another glorious Tuscan spring morning. Sophie crawled out of bed, her limbs feeling as if they belonged to someone else, her head throbbing, eyelids gritty.

A largely sleepless night. Tossing. Turning. His harshly delivered, unbelievably awful proposal of marriage running rings in her weary brain.

Marry him? As if she would!

She could see where he was coming from. Of course she could. She wasn't completely stupid. If he was married to her, the new found son he was so unexpectedly possessive of would bear his name. Every facet of her child's upbringing would be his to direct exactly as he felt fit, with her own wishes deemed of no account whatsoever—as witness the hiring of Nanny. And that little cruel charade he'd staged last night had been to make sure he could still turn her on if he wanted to. He wouldn't want a wife who gave him a slap in the eye whenever he could be bothered to go to her bed!

So—bingo! Got her! Got a willing body to use

whenever he felt like it, an addict of what he could do to her. Keep her compliant and clingy, all the time cynically despising her for her weakness, for her supposed many faults—while he got exactly what he wanted.

Her stomach rolled as she wondered wildly how she could handle the coming day, then guilty conscience dealt a hammer blow. Grabbing her aqua satin robe, she cursed herself for letting him monopolise her thoughts. This was the first time ever she hadn't leapt from bed at Torry's first wakening holler.

Barc feet cringing on the cold marble floor tiles, she flew to the nursery, one door down the corridor from her suite, to find she was redundant. She could have stayed in bed all day and everything would have proceeded like clockwork.

Ettore was sprawled out in the nursing chair, the sunlight streaming in through the partly opened window making his tousled hair gleam like a raven's wing. Tousled because Torry, bouncing on his knee, was grabbing handfuls and squealing, happy as a sandboy, and the unwanted, resented French nanny was tidying up his discarded night things and breakfast pots in the background, radiating an aura of kindly, comfortable, quiet efficiency.

Surplus to requirements. A spare part. Not needed.

The energy that had brought her sprinting into the room drained from Sophie's body in a sickening flood. Would she ever be able to assert herself in the face of this totally dominant male who always got exactly what he wanted?

The answer was given when he finally noticed her

presence and remarked blandly, 'Get dressed. We'll take Torry for an airing. We'll take a picnic breakfast with us. Main door in twenty minutes.' Dismissing her entirely, he gave his undivided, doting attention back to the bouncing baby, who seemed as besotted with the father as the father was with the son.

On automatic pilot, and utterly miserable, Sophie returned to her room and showered and dressed, in classy cream-coloured linen pants and a tawny silk knit short-sleeved top which clung like a lover's touch to every curve of her bountiful breasts.

Awful! Her cheeks flamed with disgust—not with the classy top but with her body. She dragged it off and stuffed it back in a drawer. After her undisguised physical response the night before he would be bound to think she was flaunting herself, begging for his attention! She couldn't help the shape of her body, could she? But at least she could disguise it.

The puppy fat that had brought forth uncomplimentary, cringe-making remarks and unkind jokes from her stepmother and stepsister during her unenviable teenage years had mostly melted away, but it had left her with still too much bounty both north and south of her gratifyingly tiny waist.

Fingers flying through the contents of the spacious hanging cupboard, she found what she was looking for. A slate-grey silk shirt. Meant to be worn, so the personal shopper had informed her in Paris—or had it been Milan?—with the sleeves rolled up, casually unbuttoned to cleavage level, tucked into the white silk harem pants that languished amongst all the other stuff in the crammed cupboard, and with a scarlet silk scarf knotted round her waist.

She left the shirt hanging loose, hopefully disguising the difference between north, south and middle, buttoned the cuffs at the wrist, buttoned the front firmly up to her throat. Worn thus, it did nothing for her. Good!

A smear of moisturiser was her only make-up; her hair she scooped back and scalp-tinglingly tied with a length of ribbon. The pressing need for self-assertion firmly lodged in her brain now, Sophie strode purposefully down the broad sweeping staircase into the huge, airy entrance hall.

There was no point in simply feeling miserable at the situation she found herself in, or giving up. She had to be firm, fight her own corner, let Ettore Severini know he couldn't call all the shots.

Only to find herself going weak at the knees and definitely breathless when she saw him on the sunlit sweep of gravel in front of the beautiful house. Designer casuals clothed his powerful frame with smooth sophistication, and the warm spring sunlight threw those hard cheekbones, the aristocratic blade of his nose and the beautiful mouth that was now set in a slightly mocking line, into heartstopping prominence. He had never looked more handsome.

One brown hand held the bar of Torry's pushchair; the other, extended in her direction, offered a compact wicker picnic hamper.

Hauling herself together, doing her utmost to avoid those compelling dark eyes, Sophie ignored the hamper and fastened both slender hands on the pushchair. Bag-carrier she would not be—not while he took charge of her precious baby!

Setting off at a breathless pace down the long cypress-shaded drive, the tot-sized filmy parasol fluttering, shading Torry from the beat of the sun, Sophie headed off across a sweeping expanse of emerald-green grass.

'This is the way we normally come.' She tossed a belated explanation for her manic behaviour over her shoulder. Ettore was following, doubtless frowning his displeasure over the graceless way she was wearing the designer clothes that must have cost him a bomb.

Let him! She didn't care what he thought—just as long as he didn't get it into his too-handsome head that she was making an effort with her appearance for him! She couldn't afford to give him any encouragement in the seduction department—not when he was too darn difficult to resist!

And she had taken charge, hadn't she? It should have made her feel good. But it didn't. A huge lump of heavy hopelessness was lodged in her chest. Only she wasn't going to think of why that should be.

Her apparently rock-solid antagonism crumbled away as they reached the spot that was her all-time favourite, discovered on Torry's daily airings.

A flight of shallow stone steps led down to idyllic perfumed seclusion, an intimate circle of grass bordered by the flowers of quince, pink and white, and smoky lavender-tinted lilac bushes, all underplanted with dusky, sweet-scented violets. Tuscan spring in all its jewelled glory, working its insidious magic.

Gently negotiating the buggy down the steps, pointedly ignoring Ettore's immediate offer of assistance, she headed for the comfy wooden bench seat beneath an arbour of white jasmine.

Parking the buggy, she bent to lift Torry high into her arms, drinking in the sweetly soft baby scent of him, the touch of his velvety skin against her face. He began to wriggle. She knew he recognised where they were and, obliging, she put him down on the short smooth grass and watched him excitedly crawl away in ever-increasing circles. She savoured the brief moment as peaceful contentment filled her, honestly admitting that her baby would never have known this kind of freedom, the benison of clean country air, back in Tim's London flat. At least as far as Torry's wellbeing was concerned she'd done the right thing, and as for herself—well, she'd have to cope somehow.

But there was a very unsettling sensation deep in her stomach as Ettore's long tanned fingers fastened around her arm and he drew her down beside him on the wooden bench. Her pulses jumped at his nearness. Even seated a few inches away, as he fondly watched his son's blue romper-clad rump bobbing about in the dappled sunlight, she could feel his body heat. It was decidedly unnerving.

If he was going to broach the subject of marriage again she would gather Torry and walk away, leaving him in no doubt that she would never agree in a month of Sundays. But he didn't. A soft smile curving that mouth to die for, he asked gently, 'Why Torry? It's not a name I've come across before.'

From the flash of bright colour that flooded her cheeks at his lazily couched question Ettore knew he had hit a raw spot. Good. His aim was to get to know what made her the woman she was. If she was to be his wife—and she was; for his son's sake he would entertain no doubt on that score—then he had to delve deep into her psyche. He knew very little about her background except that she'd lost her mother at a very young age. He'd been too besotted, too involved with the immediacy of earth-shattering physical attraction on the island, to have any spare time for sharing personal confidences.

He slid his arm across the back of the seat behind her and saw her tense. He wasn't going to touch her, but wryly admitted that he wanted to. His fingers were itching to remove the scrap of ribbon that held her glorious hair starkly back from her face, to drift through the luxurious silkiness. Whatever her failings, criminal activities amongst them, he couldn't deny their sexual chemistry.

Once it had made a besotted fool of him, but this time round he had his brain in gear. He would call all the shots. He simply needed to know what had made her into the kind of woman she was. Having the salient facts—maybe even rooting out mitigating circumstances—would make having her in his life easier. Getting rid of her completely wasn't an option. Not while Torry needed both parents.

Firmly resisting the impulse to touch her—he could control animal lust when he wanted to, couldn't he?—he reminded himself that last night he'd decided to take his time over prising information out of her. Go at it like a bull at a gate and she'd clam up, and he would never learn her secrets. Finding out what made her what she was more important than assuaging a sexual itch.

Besides, from the signals she'd displayed last night—the flush of colour across her delicate cheekbones, the shortening of her breath, the give-away peaking of those luscious breasts—he was confident that he could take her any time he wanted, persuade her that great sex, unlimited luxury, was a fair exchange for giving him what he really wanted. Parental rights over his son.

Pushing away the uncomfortable feeling that care for his son, flesh of his flesh, was a laudable emotion but his means of making it happen were undoubtedly questionable, he reminded her softly of his question. 'Well?'

Sophie gulped, her throat convulsing. Impossible not to tell the truth—it took a very nimble mind to come up with a really convincing lie just like that— so she got out woodenly, 'I named him for his father. Shortened to Torry. Okay?'

Very okay—despite that final note of embarrassed defiance. He'd known it already. He'd have been to-tally stupid not to make the connection. At least she'd answered him honestly. Something warm curled around his heart, much to his surprise. Probably down to the fact that despite erroneously writing him off as a bottomless source of goodies all that time ago, and helping herself to Cinzia's prop-erty, she hadn't forgotten him completely—not if she'd named their baby for him, he supposed.

There were more questions—one in particular was puzzling him—but they could wait. Withdrawing his arm, determined to get her to relax, he opened the hamper, withdrew a silver-plated Thermos, poured hot coffee into a bone china mug and handed it to her.

'Help yourself to what you want.' Ettore shifted

along the bench and placed the open hamper between them. 'While I prevent our son from eating the violets. He has a very inquisitive nature, yes?'

The warmth of his smile solidified the breath in her lungs. Her throat convulsed. When he turned on the charm she had about as much backbone as a jellyfish! Acidly wondering what he was up to, she watched him lope across the lawn towards Torry, who was now trying to eat his sunhat. Guessing that bully-boy tactics weren't going to work had he decided to turn on the charm? Charm her into agreeing to be his wife and then, that accomplished, reveal his true nature by showing how much he despised her— or what he trenchantly believed she was—ignoring her until he felt the urge for a female to share his bed?

Well, it wouldn't work! Once a cheat, always a cheat. Had Cinzia, the woman he'd been engaged to, had supposedly loved, found out somehow that he'd been unfaithful and called the wedding off? She didn't suppose she would ever know. But there was no way she would tie herself into such a demeaning union, with a serial womaniser to boot, she vowed, her eyes fixed on him. He'd scooped Torry up into his arms and was now tickling his fat little tummy to chortles of baby laughter.

Drat him for all that wretched charisma! Torry obviously adored him—Torry, who hadn't come into contact with adult males in his short life, had viewed Tim with wide-eyed wariness, clinging to her like a limpet when he, their temporary rescuer, had offered to hold him while she had attempted, one-handed, to fill his plastic baby bath with warm water.

Unlike before, at the start of their passionate affair, she now knew that Ettore's effortless charm, the warm smiles and gentle words, delivered in that spine-tingling, lightly accented voice, were just a well-polished technique to be turned on at will to get what he wanted. So she was immune. Wasn't she?

Of course she was. Ignoring the sigh that seemed to swell up from the soles of her feet, Sophie gave her belated attention to the contents of the hamper. Her stomach growled as she selected a slice of focaccia filled with creamy soft cheese and salami wrapped in a linen napkin and bit into it hungrily. No point in behaving like a Victorian maiden who had lost the love of her life and was going gracefully into a decline! She had his number, and she wouldn't let herself be seduced, cajoled or charmed into again believing that they could have a worthwhile relationship.

No way!

She had absentmindedly started on the luscious purple grapes when Ettore fastened his sleepy son into his buggy, adjusted the parasol and gently wheeled him into the shade cast by a blowsily blossoming white lilac. Sophie was sure the heady perfume must have narcotic qualities, she felt so relaxed and at ease, even able to give a soft, contented smile when Ettore sat beside her.

His mesmeric dark eyes were teasing as he noted the greatly depleted contents of the hamper and commented, 'I hate skinny women who pick at two lettuce leaves and half a radish. I'm glad to see you're not a member of the great dieting army!'

'Even if I get really fat?' Sophie handed him a

linen-wrapped portion of focaccia, not minding the banter. Not now she'd worked out where he was coming from. Besides, always being on the defensive got to be exhausting.

'Not fat. I can think of a better description.' His eyes gleamed wickedly beneath dense dark lashes. 'Delectable, delicious, desirable.'

Sophie closed her eyes and leant back. She wasn't impressed by that old flannel! Desirable? More like a useful commodity to be used if he was in the mood and more sophisticated social equals weren't immediately available! She was getting the hang of being cynical, she decided, amused, at least where Ettore Severini was concerned.

He had once desired her—stuck on that island with no other prey in sight—and look where that had got her! But she'd do it all again, suffer the excruciating pain and humiliation he'd dealt her, because the end result had been her beautiful baby son, whom she loved more than life itself.

A sudden chilly breeze gusted, moulding her shirt to her breasts, and the intimate touch of his lips on her softly parted mouth was like a bolt of lightning, sending electric currents through her bloodstream, making her feel giddy and disorientated.

Hands raised to push him away even while her treacherous mouth clung greedily to his, and she was only brought back to her addled senses by a grumbly whimper from the buggy.

'What was that for?' she demanded crossly, deeply annoyed by the feverish hunger she couldn't in all honesty hide from herself.

Jumping to her feet, she found her legs disgracefully unsteady. She knew her face was scarlet, and wanted to hit him for immediately standing up with her, too close, making her far too aware of the hard, muscular strength of his lean body, and for saying, with a curl of seduction, 'You had cream cheese on your top lip. I couldn't resist. I'm still hungry.' The sinful gleam in his dark eyes told her exactly what he was hungry for, torturing her.

'Then finish the fruit!' she snapped, forgetting to be cool and laid back in the turmoil he'd just created. 'I'm taking Torry inside.'

'Of course.' He fell in step beside her, thrust the hamper at her and lifted the buggy up the steps, striding up them as if his burden weighed no more than a feather, leaving her scurrying to catch up. 'The Tramontano blows straight from the frigid alps. A Tuscan early spring is like a beautiful woman. She blows hot; she blows cold.' A dark brow quirked. 'Just as you do, *cara mia*. You show bad temper because you don't like yourself for enjoying my kiss. I wonder why that is?'

About to offer a vehement denial, Sophie bit the words back. He'd know she was lying, so why bother? He couldn't have failed to notice how her whole body had leapt to life as he'd deepened that tasting of her lips to full-blooded plunder.

'It is a puzzle. Once you panted for my kisses—in the most flattering and delightful way—and very much more, if my memory serves. Now you like to pretend your panting-for-me days are over and throw—what is the current phrase?—a hissy fit if I come near you. It is a riddle I mean to solve.'

Given her dubious track record, he'd imagined that

she'd leap with unseemly haste at his offer of marriage and the pampered lifestyle that went with it. He'd spoken lightly, teasingly, about solving that particular riddle, but he'd never been more serious. The enigma was actually bugging him.

As the villa came into sight Sophie breathed a sigh of relief. Escape! Surely he could find something to do other than follow her and Torry around all day. She was far too susceptible where his all-too-male animal magnetism was concerned.

Her distinctly perturbed mind was further soothed when, reaching the main hall, he took the hamper from her and imparted, 'Paperwork and phone calls will occupy me for the rest of the day.' But her mental processes were sent haywire again when he tacked on smoothly, 'We will eat out this evening—the local trattoria—so wear something casual. It is time you got to know something of the area. It is not good for you to be confined to the grounds.'

To hide her dismay Sophie busied herself extracting the sleepy infant from the buggy. An intimate dinner was a definite no-no. It would remind her too forcibly of those late suppers they'd eaten beneath the stars on the island—and, more to the point, of what had followed.

Coming up with the only get-out she could think of, she veiled her eyes. 'I couldn't possibly. I have a baby, remember?' And, if he still didn't get it, she raised her head and looked him straight in the eye, pushing home the duties of parenthood. 'I have a baby alarm in my room should he wake and need changing—or want a drink.'

'So does Nanny. Have a baby alarm.'

Those fascinating eyes were lit with gentle amusement and his voice softened as he—unforgivably, in Sophie's tremulous opinion—drifted the backs of his lean fingers across her pinkened cheeks.

'That is why she was hired, *cara*. Not to take all care of your child from you, but to allow you to spend the quality time with him, which you both need, while she looks after the more boring side of things—laundry duties, clearing up, babysitting and so on. So that as his mother you are content and not deprived of any outside interests or freedoms.'

His hand dropped back to his side, leaving Sophie feeling weirdly bereft, and open-mouthed at the worrying thought that he actually meant what he said, that he hadn't—as she had initially believed—installed Nanny Minette to distance her from her baby.

Don't be nice to me! she shouted inside her head. Please don't!

And she lacked the spare thought capacity to object when he told her, 'Be ready at eight-thirty,' turned on his heels and strolled away, the angle of his dark head and the set of his wide shoulders displaying the supreme confidence of the alpha male.

CHAPTER SEVEN

SURPRISING herself, Sophie found her mood was quite definitely upbeat, despite the uncomfortable situation she found herself in. Changed and ready, she headed for the nursery and looked in on her sleeping son. Tucked up in the fancy cot Ettore had provided he looked adorable, one tiny hand curved around the fluffy blue teddy that went everywhere with him. Her heart blossomed with love.

Her voice low, she stated, 'He should sleep right through, and we shouldn't be away for long, Minette.'

It was the first time she'd addressed the Nanny by her forename, not being sure whether it was the done thing in a household belonging to a member of the boot-lickable Severini family, and not caring either, because it sounded more friendly. Now that Ettore had actually promised that the Frenchwoman hadn't been expressly hired to form a solid wall between her baby and herself, she found herself relieved to be able to like her.

Minette turned from the blue and cream painted hanging cupboard, folding the minuscule garments destined for the fitted shelves, her homely face beaming. 'All will be well, *madame*. Just relax and enjoy your evening. And may I say how nice you look? I can recognise a Paris designer label when I see one!'

Actually, the soft suede honey-coloured skirt suit

106

carried a top-flight Italian label, but Sophie wouldn't have hurt the older woman's feelings by disabusing her for the world. So she simply smiled her wide, infectious smile, said thank you, and drifted out of the nursery on kitten heels, trailing subtle fragrance.

Getting ready for an evening that promised the torment of being with a man she loathed and lusted after in equal measure, a man who could turn her on and swipe through her defences with one flicker of a disgracefully long eyelash, a man she also had the inclination to hit with a brick, she'd had a monumental and enlightening change of direction.

Her personal situation needn't be all bad, not if she really worked on it. Ettore might have shown himself to be the sort of man she despised—the sort of man who would seduce his social inferior, speaking of eternal love and all that stuff while being on the brink of marriage to a blue-blooded, filthy rich and beautiful snob—but he hadn't actually married the vile Cinzia di Barsini. He was a free man now. Not engaged to anyone else, as far as she knew, and for some reason that seemed to make things easier.

Besides, a man who could take the tiny son he hadn't known he had straight to his heart, treat him like a little prince, take his parental duties so seriously that he was prepared to marry a socially inferior, penniless, promiscuous little sneak thief to give him the stability he deemed necessary to his wellbeing—never mind the spiteful tittle-tattle that would be bound to surface—couldn't be all bad. So surely, having at least some redeeming features, he would be open to persuasion.

All she had to do was convince him of her integrity. There was nothing she could do about her social or financial status, but she had never stolen a thing in her life—and as for being promiscuous, it was so off the mark it was laughable.

All she had to do was convince him and he would have to respect her as a poor but honest peasant and scrub his crazy idea of trying to persuade her to marry him! That idea had surely been born out of a total lack of respect for her feelings, because being the dregs—in his mind at least—he thought he could make her do whatever suited him.

Marriage would be a disaster. As his wife she would easily find herself believing she was falling in love again—she was silly enough where he was concerned—and her life would be utterly miserable because he had never loved her and never would.

Absorbed in her thoughts, she cannoned straight into him as he waited at the foot of the stairs, his arms going round her in instinctive chivalrous support.

'You smell of heady summer flowers—nice.' His voice was smooth as honey and his arms tightened as his dark head lowered to hers, his taut, proud cheekbones sinking into the soft fall of her silky hair.

With a helpless gasp Sophie felt the length of her body melt with programmed willingness into his. Full breasts peaked urgently against the hard span of his black cashmere covered chest, and the immediate and insistent throbbing between her thighs made her knees go weak, the spicy masculinity of the cologne he used, the underlying unique male scent of him, intoxicating her senses.

He was working his old magic, the potent magic

that made her incapable of reasoned resistance. Helplessly she wriggled closer, heat coiling through her as, unbidden by the mush that passed for her brain, her hands slid up to his broad shoulders and then around his neck, her face lifted expectantly to his.

This was the very last thing she wanted to happen, but how could she deny it? She was as lost as she'd been when he'd walked towards her on that moonlit beach, his face intent on her, drinking in every water-spangled curve and indentation of her near-naked body as he'd scooped up her towel and gently enfolded her—

'Breath back?' Gently he put her away from him. His long mouth curved sardonically. 'Next time look where you're going. I could have been a brick wall. Shall we go?'

The feeling of loss as he stepped away from her was so intense it made her shudder. Lowering her head, so that her hair fell forward to hide a face that was violently daubed with Humiliation Red, Sophie allowed him to tuck a hand beneath her elbow and lead her out to where his car was waiting.

Without any input from her brain she had acted like a sex-mad trollop. She couldn't have made her needs any clearer if she'd been wearing a T-shirt emblazoned with the legend 'I Want To Have Sex With You' across her far too ample chest! And the shaming fact that Ettore hadn't been similarly affected with a similar rush of hormones made her cringe with even more humiliation.

Pushing her aside with a mocking remark about

brick walls when he couldn't have failed to notice how she'd been behaving. Asking for it!

The very real fear that, through sex, he could make her an addict, make her agree to marry him just so she could share his bed whenever he beckoned, was now firmly and finally knocked on the head. She must have been out of her mind when she'd believed that scenario.

He'd house her, feed her and clothe her for the sake of their son. He'd even grit his teeth and marry her for the sake of appearances. But he wouldn't touch the likes of her with a bargepole!

Even more reason to make him believe in her integrity, respect her—a task, she admitted dourly, that was even more difficult after that shameful display.

As the headlights of the powerful car raked through the dusky evening air and they descended to the village Sophie did her utmost to return to being upbeat.

To convince him that she had been wronged. That he'd been acting shamefully when he'd pretended to be madly in love with her just to get her to go to bed with him, all the time knowing he was about to be married to someone else. Force him to see that she wasn't a thief, that she'd been set up. Give him a really guilty conscience and he'd just have to agree to her way out of this mess.

If he continued to flatly refuse to let her set up a home for herself and Torry back in England, then a simple little cottage with a piece of land in this area would do just as well.

He could contribute to Torry's upkeep if he really wanted to, see him at weekends and have him to stay with him for part of the holidays when he got to school age. And she would be self-sufficient, grow all their fruit and vegetables, keep chickens—

'What are you thinking?'

Sophie blinked. His question had startled her. They were parked in a narrow street outside a stone building. She hadn't even realised he'd stopped the car. Still struggling to extricate herself from cosy, rose-tinted upbeat plans for the future and haul herself back into the far from comfortable present, she answered without thinking, 'Eggs.'

The sound of his entirely natural rumble of laughter made her tummy curl with pleasure. It had been such a long, achingly empty time since they'd laughed together, but she bit down hard on her lower lip to stop her instinctive answering grin. He wasn't aware of it, but this evening was going to be serious—deadly serious.

'Hungry, obviously. Good.' Ettore exited the car at the speed of light, sternly denying the temptation to put his hands on her shoulders, pull her round to face him and kiss her until neither of them knew what day it was.

Back at the house it had taken every last ounce of his will-power not to take advantage of that melting, enticing, mind-blowingly sexy little body, pressing and squirming against his, not to sweep her up in his arms and into his bed.

He had gone beyond trying to deny the imperative sexual chemistry that existed between them so he deserved a medal for forbearance, for seeing a picture larger than immediate and fantastic self-gratification. *Madonna diavola!* He had to get inside her head, understand what made her what she was, before he could set about her moral reclamation and even think about making love to her, tying her to him as his wife and creating a proper family for his son.

Back in control—well, as much in control as he'd ever be around this little witch—he opened the passenger door and helped her out, carefully keeping physical contact to a minimum as he guided her over the cobbles towards the welcoming lights of the trattoria.

'The food's basic, but superbly cooked. We are early, but later you will be able to meet some of the locals.'

Which was not what Sophie wanted to do—not at this moment in time. She wanted to talk to Ettore, really talk to him, make him see her side of the story.

Ettore was greeted by the rotund proprietor, Beppe, as if he was a valued and favourite relative, while his even more rotund wife beamed from behind a bead curtain that, so far as Sophie could see, led into the kitchen region.

Gaudy hand-painted cupboards flanked an enormous hearth where an untidy log fire flared and fluttered, and Beppe led them over the stone floor to a plain wooden table decorated with a fat candle in a stout terracotta holder.

'Comfortable?' Ettore enquired, his dark eyes level, his smile slight and studiously polite as he moved the candle nearer to the edge of the table, so that there was nothing for her to hide behind.

Was this the way it was going to be? Courteously polite provided she did exactly as she was told? Fell meekly in line with his plans?

'Not very.' She answered his question unhesitatingly, seizing the opportunity to put her oar in and muddy his cold, placid waters, and watched him raise a quizzical brow, leaning back in his seat as Beppe brought a carafe of wine and two glasses to the table.

Alone again, after an animated discussion of vintages, Ettore filled both glasses and levelled at her, 'Why's that, I wonder? You'd have preferred some place glitzy and upmarket?'

Sophie's heart jumped. This was exactly the opening she needed. She took it, her huge grey eyes snapping as she told him forcibly, 'You don't know me at all, do you? Not really.' She lifted one hand, indicating the warm, welcoming and relaxing room, with its quirky cupboards, the herbs hanging from rafters, ancient family photographs in faded velvet frames and dim, sentimental paintings crowded on every inch of wall space. 'This suits me fine. It's down-to-earth, honest—and so am I! I'm not smart or sophisticated—take me to a glittering banquet and I'd spill dinner down my frock!' Her cheeks were burning, peony-pink. She was getting too darn hot, seated so near the fire. Struggling out of her suit jacket, she draped it haphazardly over the back of her seat and got out with a vehemence she couldn't prevent, 'And I'm not a thief and I don't sleep around!'

And I'm a Dutchman! Ettore parried inwardly, but his mouth was quirking at her heated diatribe. She'd be a wow at any function, glittering or otherwise. Utterly gorgeous, eyes like deep pools—sometimes charcoal, sometimes silver—and lips like plump rosebuds, just asking to be kissed. What red-blooded male would be able to keep his eyes, or his hands, for that matter, off those fantastic breasts, temptingly revealed by the ribbed silk cream-coloured sleeveless sweater she was wearing beneath the discarded jacket.

'Don't laugh at me!' she spat like a ruffled kitten as Beppe approached with a chunky earthenware plate of antipasta.

Ettore's lurking smile widened to a grin as he watched the temptation to toss her glass of wine in his face cross her expressive features, an impulse only kept in check, he guessed, by the arrival of olives, tiny vegetable tarts and grilled prawns.

Her dander was up, and this time, instead of being incensed that she should dare to be snippy with him, he found himself enjoying it. Though push her too far and anything might happen! Amazing himself, he found that prospect exhilarating.

With difficulty he straightened his features, but his voice was thickly roughened as he suggested, 'Shall we eat?'

Sophie picked up a plump olive, then put it down again, her heart thumping against her ribs. Unless he got up and walked out she had a captive audience, and she wasn't going to pass up the opportunity.

Folding her arms across her chest, she stated, 'You said we should get to know each other. As I've already told you, you know nothing about me.'

'Right.' Ettore bit into a delicious tartlet. Time to jump in himself, start on that journey he'd promised himself—the journey that would take him inside her head. Time to get serious and stop lusting over her abundant, if superficial physical attributes, pandering to his libido. A libido that had been strangely passive since the night he'd discovered what Sophie Lang really was.

Ettore's sensual mouth flattened. 'Let's start with this. On more that one occasion you've accused me—wrongly, I believe—of ensuring you never worked as a nanny again. I've been wondering why. Because you fell pregnant? Not an even-handed accusation, surely, when you told me you were protected? Which seems to suggest that the larger blame lay with you. Besides, who would employ you as a nanny when you have a small child of your own?'

As a defence, his holier-than-thou attitude stank! Sophie gave him a fulminating glare, selected a prawn and took her time peeling it, her eyes clouding as she remembered what had happened. Her voice held bite as she informed him, 'Immediately after I returned from Italy I was told I'd been sacked from the agency. A serious complaint had been made. By you and that woman you were going to marry—who else? I'd stolen from a guest of my employer. I could expect no references and should think myself lucky that I wasn't being prosecuted.'

Sophie took a long, shuddering intake of breath. It had been a truly terrible time. Ettore had broken her heart, she'd been branded a thief and humiliated. All she'd wanted to do was throw herself back into the career she loved and try to forget she'd ever met him.

'I hadn't stolen anything,' she snapped, her voice brittle with the pain of it all. 'You'd lost me my job and any chance of working in that area again. It really rankled! At the time I didn't know I was pregnant. Luckily there were people who believed in me—unlike you! Nanny Hopkins took me in while I looked for work. A guy took me on at that wine bar, satisfied with a couple of character references—from Nanny Hopkins and my friend Tina's father, who's a GP. So, no thanks to you, I survived!' Her chin came up and the sparky-eyed glare she lanced at him would have shrivelled a lesser man.

She'd peeled a mound of prawns but they lay untouched in a heap amidst the discarded shells, Ettore noted with the part of his mind that wasn't working overtime.

There was no doubt as to the truth of what she was saying. She'd been blacklisted. For the first time since that dreadful night his mind returned willingly to the sombre aftermath. He had been hurting, sick with the betrayal of his love, but he'd insisted on a conference of everyone who knew what had happened: Flavia, Cinzia and Filomena.

His heart beating like a lead pendulum, he'd ordered that the unfortunate episode should go no further. The diamond trinket had been returned; nothing had been lost. Except the dream—more fitting for a green adolescent than an intelligent adult male—of spending the rest of his life with the only woman he had ever loved. Plus a large chunk of his self-respect, he'd added sourly to himself. Even so, he hadn't wanted to see her punished.

Flavia, her eyes moist, had whispered, 'I wouldn't have believed a word of this if you hadn't caught her red-handed. Of course I won't let it go any further.'

Cinzia, a small smile on her scarlet lips, had said nothing. It had been left to Filomena to raise the obvious.

'Shouldn't the agency she works through be informed? She might steal from future employers.'

He had wondered how to make them understand—without sounding like a total wimp—that put out of work Sophie might well resort to darker ways of gathering ill-gotten gains—prostitution even. His blood had thundered in his ears at the hateful images his tormented mind threw up, but it had been Cinzia who had scotched the idea.

'You heard what Signor Severini said. Not a word of this unpleasant episode will go any further. I forbid you to speak of it again.'

His sister Flavia wouldn't have contacted the agency, and Filomena would have been too conscious of the consequences to go against the orders of her mistress to do any such thing. Which left Cinzia—Cinzia, who had stated that she had no intention of pressing charges. At the time such magnanimity had seemed out of character, and now he wondered why.

But it was too early to share his suspicions. He hadn't gained a reputation for hard-headed financial dealings by jumping in without gathering all the relevant information.

Leaning back in his seat while Beppe presented them with a dish of baked sea bass, Ettore studied Sophie's set features, her soft mouth set in a stubborn line. She must have had a tough time coping with the unexpected pregnancy, finding work, earning enough to support herself and save for the coming baby.

Dio! Regardless of the way evidence of theft had so clearly pointed, and her telling silence, she'd been carrying his child and he hadn't given her any support. So he'd been bitter at that time, but that was no excuse! He should have had someone check up on her movements on her return to England. That way he would eventually have learned of the pregnancy! Offered practical help, insisted she return to Italy with him, ensured she had the best possible care while they waited for the birth.

To her credit, she hadn't had an abortion—his hot blood ran cold at the very thought. She had struggled on, alone…

Okay, so he didn't much like himself right now, but regrets were useless. He battened them down with cool efficiency. The future and how it affected his son was all that mattered. And only by getting to know everything about her could it be guaranteed to run smoothly, with no more unpleasant surprises.

Dividing the fish, he passed her a plate. 'How did you manage? You mentioned a nanny—Hopkins?'

Sophie nodded, her mouth still signalling mutiny. She picked up her fork and wished she could attack him with the sharp-pronged instrument instead of the fish! The too-handsome, too-wealthy, too-darned-confident creature had just ignored what she'd said about his having her blacklisted! As if it didn't matter!

She wasn't a violent person, but Ettore Severini brought out the very worst in her. To combat that demeaning trait, she said with ultra-coolness, 'She invited me to share her home and was wonderful. About everything. Always cheerful, seeing silver linings behind every cloud.'

'You had known her a long time?' Ettore topped

up her wine glass. She wasn't eating, but she'd drained her glass as if it had been water. No matter. The alcohol might loosen her tongue.

With a sigh, Sophie lowered her fork and the untasted morsel of fish. It would be a relief to get off the subject of her supposed theft—he obviously found it beneath his dignity to even mention his part in blowing the whistle, never mind look even slightly ashamed for having done so. Because nothing would convince him she hadn't helped herself to that vile woman's diamonds. A relief to talk about someone who had always believed the best of her.

'She was engaged after I was born. My mother had always been frail, apparently. She died when I was three, so I have no clear memory of her. I think Dad always blamed himself for getting her pregnant and me for being born.' She took a swallow of wine to ease her parched throat. It had a subtle hint of strawberries underlying the heady grape, and a fragrance that reminded her of a flower she couldn't quite place. Her mouth curved in a soft smile.

'And?' Ettore prompted, wondering if the refill had been altogether wise. But at least it had got her talking freely.

'Nanny Hopkins was with me until I was seven. Like a mother. Then Dad married Stacia, a divorcee. She had a daughter, Tiffany, and, as she never failed to point out, Tiffany was everything I wasn't. Pretty, graceful, bright.' Her voice wobbled. 'That didn't matter because Nanny Hopkins loved me. Then a few weeks later Stacia dismissed her. Waste of good money, she said—though she didn't mind wasting more than Dad could afford on expensive clothes for her and Tiffany, or caterers for the fancy dinner parties she was always giving.'

She dragged in a long breath, as if regretting having said too much. 'Will you just listen to me?' Her wonderful smile flashed. 'Whining! I had a happy childhood, really. And of course Dad loved me—he just wasn't very good at showing it. Besides, my best friend Tina's family had me to stay with them for school holidays, and we had great times. And Nanny never forgot me. She was always sending letters and little gifts—I was lucky!'

Her smile wavered around the edges and anger tightened Ettore's facial muscles. Lucky? To lose her mother so young? To be made to feel partially responsible for that untimely death? To be brutally deprived of the obviously kindly woman who had taken her place? Not to mention having a stepmother from hell.

He could read between the lines as well as anyone. No expensive clothes for Sophie. Old ones worn until she was bursting out of them? And what young child drew invidious comparisons? Tiffany's supposed superiority in every department must have been rammed down her innocent young throat!

Cool it, he told himself, ignoring the dish of roast vegetables Beppe had slid onto the table as completely as he ignored the impulse to reach across the table and take her small hands in his. This delving was supposed to be forensic, not a haywire mixture of anger, compassion and—and guilt?

'So you moved in with her and worked in a wine bar,' he stated smoothly. 'And Torry was born. Then what?'

Any minute now he was going to lash out at her for what he saw as her irresponsibility in not letting him know he was a father. She could see it coming! But she'd already explained about not wanting to upset the apple cart. She'd thought he'd married that vile woman!

She shrugged. She was beginning to get a thumping headache. And she was sure she wasn't thinking straight, because this was more like an inquisition than a concise statement of her innocence. And why he was interested in where she'd lived, how she'd earned a living of sorts, when he should be concentrating on making a huge apology for his own behaviour, she couldn't imagine. Too much wine. Shouldn't have touched it!

Her tongue felt thick, but she spoke out, aiming to close the subject and get on to what really mattered. 'I got a part-time job at the supermarket round the corner. We managed okay. Then—then she died. It was sudden. The house was rented. Torry and I had to go—' Her voice dried up and her eyes filled with tears. 'I miss her.'

Dio! He saw it all now. Understood why she'd moved in with that blond guy. Without thinking, his mind absorbed with just how she must have felt— grieving for her old friend, suddenly homeless, hopeless, with a young child to care for—he ground out, 'So you moved in with a boyfriend?'

About to add that he perfectly understood why she had taken that step, he found the words forced back, bunching like a lump of solid rock in his chest, as her tearful face iced over and she pushed back her chair and tottered with more haste than dignity across the floor and out through the door.

CHAPTER EIGHT

DROPPING enough euros to cover the cost of their meal plus a generous tip down on the table, Ettore swiftly gathered up Sophie's abandoned jacket and followed, giving himself a mental kick. He hated to see her so hurt. Hated it! His own fault entirely for blurting out like that.

Long strides propelled him over the cobbles. Sophie was leaning against the car, the picture of dejection, head downbent. Gently he draped her jacket over her slender shoulders, opened the passenger door and murmured, 'In you get. The spring nights are cold.'

Obeying—because what other option did she have?—she slumped in her seat, her eyelids drifting down in abject misery as he closed the door at her side and walked round the car to settle himself behind the wheel.

This evening had been a total, utter disaster. She'd intended to convince him once and for all that she was innocent of all charges against her, but he'd discounted whatever she'd managed to say, as if comment of any kind was beneath him, staunchly believing he'd been right to immediately contact the agency she worked through to get her blacklisted because he was certain, beyond any possible doubt, that she was the low sort of creature who would stoop to stealing from a guest in his sister's home.

What earthly hope did she have of making him believe something he didn't want to believe? Why waste her breath in trying?

She felt his head turn towards her and kept her eyes firmly closed. But when he said, 'I'm sorry. I didn't mean to sound censorious about your moving in with that guy,' she batted them open.

Alcohol-fuelled anger stiffened her spine at that patronising excuse for an apology. He had a low opinion of her and he was sticking to it, marking her down as the type of woman who would live off a man in return for sexual favours. Was that why he believed she would jump at his offer of marriage?

Her hands twisted together in her lap as she stared ahead into the dark, starlit Tuscan night. Her words slightly slurred, she came right back. 'Why should you? Sound censorious, I mean. You of all people must understand what it's like to grab what's on offer—you're damn good at it, as I remember!'

'Meaning?' His voice was quiet, level and deadly.

'You really need me to spell it out?' Unfazed by the coldly simmering silence now coming from the driver's seat, Sophie let her voice drip with scorn. 'You think everyone's like you! See something tempting, something easy, and you take it!'

'You are now accusing me of stealing other people's property?' Ettore answered her statement with a quellingly dry bite.

'Worse. You steal hearts—and then—then stamp on them!'

The moment the words were out Sophie was utterly appalled. Fingertips flew to her overheated aching forehead.

He'd know now—wouldn't he just? Know she'd meant it when she'd said she loved him, that she hadn't been playing his game of Casual Holiday Fling! That her silly girlish heart had been well and truly mangled.

Add that to the way her stupid body had so recently and obviously responded to his touch—his merest look!—and he'd know she was still hopelessly in love with him, a real pushover. Know he could twist her round his smallest finger, make her agree to marry him—anything at all as long as she could be with him—and she would never be able to escape him and make a peaceful life for herself and Torry at a safe distance!

Cursing herself for swilling the wine that had led to her telling indiscretion, she cried thinly, 'Take me back!' And wished she'd never been born as she registered the final humiliation, the unstoppable flow of scalding tears that flooded her eyes, soaked her cheeks and dripped off the end of her chin.

His lean face taut, Ettore fired the ignition and pulled away from the cobbled forecourt, all his suspicions reinforced. He glanced at Sophie with narrowed eyes. Frowning darkly, he depressed the accelerator and headed for the hills at speed.

He hated to see her cry! It tore him apart. He and Cinzia between them had done her a terrible wrong. Cinzia actively. He passively.

He had been shocked and savagely hurt by the evidence presented to him, by Sophie's seemingly guilty silence, but now he was sure it had stemmed from a shock as great as his had been.

But that was no excuse! *Madonna diavola*—he should be shot!

When he thought of what she must have gone through he wanted to punch holes in stone walls. Leaving Flavia's home under a terrible cloud, and then, thanks to Cinzia—who else?—being brutally thrown out of work. Later discovering she was pregnant with his child and being unable to come to him for help because she believed he was a recently married man. A lesser woman would have approached him anyway, demanding support, careless of the size of the spanner she threw in the works!

Instead she had coped bravely on her own, bringing their son up in humble circumstances until fate had dealt her another terrible blow with the death of her old friend. So she'd moved in with that blond guy? So what?

So it gave him a sourness in his stomach. But looked at dispassionately, from her viewpoint, what else was the poor kid to do? Suddenly homeless, and out of work because of the death of her old nanny, who'd cared for their beautiful son while she scraped a living at some menial job, she wouldn't have had a wide choice of options—not with a baby to care for. So what right had he to mentally name her *putana*?

Amends would have to be made.

Tomorrow he would take his suspicions—now burning holes in his brain—and confront Cinzia, get the truth out of her. Then he would do what he could to redress his appalling behaviour.

A muffled sob at his side brought his head jerking round. *Dio!* Sitting rigidly to attention, Sophie had her knuckles tightly pressed against her mouth—the classic gesture of someone scared witless.

He immediately slowed to what he considered a snail's pace. He knew these narrow hill roads like the back of his hand, but she didn't. He knew he never took risks, but she didn't. His heart contracted. He'd just earned himself another black mark to add to all the rest! He couldn't wait to get the whole mess sorted out. Get his facts straight. At no level would he consider acting without having everything cut and dried, at his fingertips. And only then would he feel free to move heaven and earth to try to make amends.

'We are almost home,' he assured her gently, taking the final tight bend at a commendable creeping crawl and progressing up the long drive at a hearse-like pace. But if he'd hoped to impress her with his consideration he wasn't doing too well, he recognised, as another muffled sob made him loathe himself.

Home? If only! Sophie swallowed another sob, despising her weakness. This lovely house, set in the beautiful Tuscan countryside, would never be her home—unless she agreed to his cold-hearted offer of marriage.

Yet, still loving him, as she now had to bitterly acknowledge that she did, how could she in all sanity accept such a life sentence? Unfortunately, by refusing to lay herself open to a lifetime of hurts, humiliations and hopeless yearnings, she would be depriving her precious child of everything the son of a Severini could expect. The very best of everything. It was a dilemma that was sending her hysterical!

As the car pulled to a sedate halt in front of the

main door Sophie scrambled out. She tried to steady her wobbling legs by taking a deep breath and telling herself that money and privilege wasn't everything.

'Let me help you.' The kindness of his tone made her want to start crying again, and the supportive arm he slipped around her waist made her want to turn to him, bury her head against the warmth and strength of his broad chest and sob out all her misery.

Telling herself she was made of sterner stuff, Sophie clamped her jaws together and concentrated on walking in a relatively straight line as they approached the main door. Desperately she tried to ignore the warmth of his arm as he held her, the strength of the hand that was pressed to the side of her tiny waist, and didn't really succeed because her heart was thumping like a steamhammer and something wicked was unfurling right at the heart of her.

The door opened easily under his hand and they were in the warmly lit main hall. Sophie had the presence of mind to mumble, 'Thanks. I can manage.'

He obviously didn't think much of that declaration, and Sophie found herself swept up into his arms and carried swiftly up the broad staircase, her heart pattering like crazy as she drank in the fascinating and familiar scent of him, the potent power of his shattering masculinity.

By the time he thrust open the door to her room she was melting all over, Sophie registered with a not entirely unpleasant shock. Dazedly she wondered if he was receiving the messages sent by arms that had somehow wound lovingly around his neck, by a body that was positively snuggling into his, and how she would be able to resist if he decided to act on the information he was receiving.

Her breath shortening, the whole of her body on fire, it took a few moments for her fuddled brain to process the information that her resistance, or probable lack of it, was not about to be tested.

Sliding her down to her feet, Ettore took a smart backward pace, his voice tight and dismissive as he advised, 'Take a shower. As you barely ate a thing, and drank rather too much wine, I will ask someone to bring sandwiches and black coffee.' And he left, closing the door firmly behind him, leaving her to mentally castigate herself for entertaining the ridiculous thought that he still felt any of the old sexual magic that had drawn them together back on the island.

That he had never loved her was in no doubt. Lying about eternal devotion was the oldest trick in the book, aimed to ensure she returned willingly to his bed time after eager time.

But now he didn't even desire her.

A sobering thought. And one she shouldn't need reminding of after plenty of past evidence.

Summoning all her reserves of common sense, she tartly told herself to hold onto that thought and never let herself forget it again—because it strengthened her conviction that marriage was completely out of the question.

A cold shower enabled her to regain the senses that had gone missing when she'd been held so close in his arms.

Slipping into one of the filmy silk nightdresses she had acquired during her travels through Europe, she wrapped her hair in a turban-tied towel, then tossed it aside impatiently. Her hair could dry on its own.

Out of the *en suite* bathroom, she registered that someone had deposited a tray of coffee and a plate bearing a couple of small crusty rolls stuffed with a variety of fillings on the low table next to the comfy brocade-covered armchair to one side of the massive bed.

Her stomach lurched. Hot coffee she could handle—but food?

'Eat.'

Ettore's voice startled her, bringing her head round. He stood near the door, in shadows not touched by the soft glow from the shaded lamp next to the bed. Covered by confusion, her hard-won composure flying out through the walls, Sophie could only stare. Drink in that impressive physique, the hard planes of his devastating features, the glint of those dark eyes that seemed welded to hers. Her own eyes misted with the sting of more despised tears.

If she wept again, he would be lost. Ettore knew it, and struggled to regain the resolve that earlier had allowed him to set her down on her feet and walk away with honour, when every atom of his being had been crying out for the ecstatically intimate melding of his hard boy to the soft, yielding femininity of hers.

Watching her, watching the warm colour flood her lovely face, the glow from the lamp caress the enticingly lush contours tantalisingly glimpsed through the thin, lovingly clinging silk of the ivory-coloured nightdress she was wearing, he felt his body harden. That she wasn't immune to him made her even more tempting. His throat thickened. *Dio!* Didn't he have any integrity? Until his suspicions were confirmed Sophie was strictly off limits, and even then the air would have to be cleared before their relationship—if they were ever to have something truly worthwhile—could move forward.

His chest expanded on a harsh, painfully indrawn breath. She might physically respond to him—a hormone thing—but the perfect gift of her love was no longer his. After his less than understanding treatment of her since he'd found her in London she would hate him. And he couldn't blame her.

She moved. Just a little. Edging nearer to the support of the armchair. Silky fabric moved with her body, clinging to the shape of her thighs, to the slight feminine curve of her tummy.

Ettore began to sweat.

He shouldn't be here. With her like this. It was more than flesh and blood could stand! Unconsciously, his hands fisted.

What had possessed him to prepare the tray himself? His self-righteous excuse had been a disinclination to disturb the staff he had given leave to take the evening off. But all the time what he'd really wanted was to be with her, make sure she wasn't still upset. Look at her, touch her. Want to be with her...

He moved. Helplessly drawn towards her. Glistening silver-grey eyes lifted to his. Shallow breathing. Dark eyes lowered to the rapid rise and fall of her chest, her beautiful breasts straining against the sheer cradling silk.

His throat thickened. His heart hammered.

'Sophie?'

Was that a question? Was this him? Was this the self-confident alpha male who up until this moment had inhabited the skin of Ettore Severini? Or was he now a humble supplicant, a worshipper at the feet of an angel, struck low and inarticulate beneath the force of what he was feeling for this woman?

Her lush lips parted, trembled, as if she were seeking to make some kind of response. Her small bare feet shifted on the thick carpet. His awareness of her, of how he craved her, shook him to the depths of his being, and as suddenly as it had been stripped from him the power was back.

A touch was all it took. Just one. Just the palm of his hand on the satin-smooth skin of a warm naked shoulder. And then he was reaching for her.

With a tiny gasp she came willingly, melting against him as his hands curved round the enticing flare of her hips and pulled her into the hard ache of his manhood.

All thoughts of resistance, of self-preservation, and every scrap of pride disappeared in the flicker of an eyelash as his mouth invaded hers. He did desire her! For some reason his past actions, his seeming indifference, had appeared to deny it, but now the walls were down. The old magic was back with a vengeance, a force stronger than both of them combined.

Blind emotion claimed her as her mouth answered his raw passion. Greedy fingers curved into the luxurious thickness of his dark-as-night silky hair as the heat of his arousal, hard against the yielding softness of her tummy, turned her into a delirious wreck.

He tore his mouth from hers, only to bury it in the

deep cleft between her swollen and unbearably sen-
sitised breasts, and Sophie's pulses leapt with elec-
trifying sensation. Her head flung back as long fingers pushed down the narrow straps, peeling the
fabric from the twin pink-tipped engorged globes.

Another swift movement and her nightdress
pooled at her feet. With a smothered, wickedly sexy
groan Ettore held her slightly away from him, his
hooded eyes magnetic, holding her in thrall, as they
very thoroughly slid like a caress over her unashamed nakedness.

'I burn for you, my Sophie,' he breathed on a
driven undertone. 'Come to me.'

The part of her brain that would have had her telling him to get lost, that she had no intention of being
conned a second time, had closed down. No one at
home. The veiling of her starry eyes with the sweep
of thick lashes and the smallest dip of her blonde
head was drugged acquiescence—all he needed to
enclose his arms around her and carry her to the waiting bed.

He stood above her, his tanned fingers intent on
hauling the black cashmere sweater off his magnificent torso, and Sophie could only stare and quiver
with the fierce heat of desire as her needy eyes re-
discovered every all-male inch of the body she had
once known better than her own.

He had lied to her, deceived her, treated her as if
she were contaminated. But she was his woman. She
had borne his child. He would never know it, but she
would love him always, warts and all. This one last
night with him would be all she would ever have or

ask for. More than that—marriage, even rights over her body on a casual basis—would destroy her.

That for him this would be a natural slaking of the lust of a highly sexed male animal was something she wasn't about to start worrying about.

She was his woman. And this just had to be fate. That was her last coherent thought as he lowered his superb naked length beside her. And reached for her.

CHAPTER NINE

SOPHIE stirred. Thick, blonde-tipped lashes lifted just enough to tell her that early sunlight was streaming through the partly open louvres. She smiled blissfully, eyelids drifting closed again, a surge of almost uncontainable joy making her body glow as she reached for him.

Empty space where he had lain when they'd finally fallen asleep, wrapped closely in each other's arms.

A sharp stab of frightening insecurity was quickly stamped on. She would not go there! Never again would she torment herself by looking for dark motives, Sophie vowed staunchly as she stretched her sated body with luxurious abandon.

So he'd woken early, slipped back to his own room, gone out for a walk, gone fishing—so what? It didn't signify anything. She might be his mistress, sort of—as of last night—and if he still wanted it she would soon be his wife, but she wasn't his keeper. He didn't have to clear every move he made with her before he made it.

Last night had altered everything. She had to give what they did have a chance and stop thinking of the downside. And not just for Torry's sake either, but for her own—loving him, how could she be whole and happy without him?—and for Ettore's sake, too.

He needed his son, needed to know his child was happy and beautifully cared for, had all the advantages he could give him. They could marry and be happy. A happy family. The three of them. It might

134

take her considerable time and the expenditure of a
great deal of patient forbearance to get him to believe
she wasn't what he thought she was—the evidence
against her was stacked high; she had to admit that—
but she'd get there in the end.

Last night had shown her that it could be done.
Their lovemaking had been so wildly emotional at
first. It hadn't been just about sex, because if it had
been she would have known it and woken this morning feeling besmirched, hating herself, instead of
feeling gloriously confident in the future they could
have together.

It had been as if two eager souls had found each
other again after being lost in dark limbo, clinging
to each other, almost sobbing with raw passion. The
second time it had transcended mere ecstasy. Slow,
tenderly explorative, divinely special, two souls
home, dissolving into each other.

So even if his head told him she was a worthless
little tramp, his body and maybe even his heart already told another story. On a basic physical level
he needed her just as much as she needed him, and
with love on her side and his eventual and necessary
recognition of her innocence they would stay the distance.

Her breathy sigh of pleasure at the rightness of her
newly found confidence was swallowed as a knock
on the door heralded the arrival of the housekeeper
with a large cup of coffee on a silver tray.

'It is the good morning,' she announced in her
careful English, and Sophie beamed and hauled herself up against the pillows, clutching the sheet over
her naked breasts. 'Spring has come to stay with us.'
She placed the tray on the bedside table, diplomati-
cally disregarding the rumpled silky nightdress so
unceremoniously dropped the night before. 'Signor

Severini left half an hour ago and asked me to tell you that he has business in Firenze for one, maybe two days. As the morning is so good I will bring breakfast to you out in the courtyard. Yes?'

'Thank you.' It was as much as Sophie could do to get the pleasantry out, to smile and reach over to cradle the coffee cup in suddenly unsteady hands. Despite her good intentions doubts flooded back. She hated them, but they insisted on creeping in, spoiling things.

Why hadn't he woken her to say goodbye, explain where he was going and why, instead of leaving a message with his housekeeper? It would only have taken a moment or two out of his busy day. Didn't she rate that much consideration? Had she seen what she wanted to see last night instead of what was really there?

Hold it there! she grouched at herself as the housekeeper left the room. Just stop it! She was asking too much of him, too soon. He had already committed to their son, and to her as his son's mother because she was needed by Torry. It would take a lot longer for him to commit to her as a person in her own right, to her as a wife who was much more than an extra piece of luggage, dragged about because she was needed on the journey of their son's life.

But she had time on her side. That was her sensible thought as she finished her coffee and slid out of bed. It was a beautiful day and she was early enough to bath and dress Torry. The three of them could breakfast together in the courtyard, where the fountain played and tubs of narcissi perfumed the air—Minette would like that—and when Torry took his afternoon nap she could continue her now-and-then Italian lessons with the housekeeper—because if she was going to make her life here she would need to speak as fluently as the natives.

As Ettore drove out of Florence his heart kicked in his chest. It had been just as he'd begun to strongly suspect. Cornered, Cinzia had told him all he needed to know. Sophie had been set up, just as she'd so often protested.

And he hadn't listened! Faced with the 'evidence' he'd been shattered. His long-standing friendship and respect for Cinzia had taken precedence over anything else, and he hadn't listened. He had been fond of Cinzia—he'd never loved her, but had trusted and respected her. He would never in a million years have believed her capable of such duplicity.

Cursing his closed mind, the initial shock and deep hurt that had self-protectively turned into the stiff-necked pride that had allowed him to believe the worst of his wronged Sophie, he stood on the accelerator. He needed to be with her, to start trying to put things right.

Would Sophie give him a second chance? She might have enjoyed making love with him, but could she ever fall in love with him again after the way he had behaved?

Despite the car's efficient air-conditioning system he began to sweat and, realising he might be stopped by the traffic cops, causing further unendurable delay, he slowed down and tried to fix his mind on something other than his gorgeous, wronged Sophie.

Suspicions, having taken root when it had become obvious that someone had gone against his instruction that the theft should not be reported back to the agency, had grown into certainty. But he'd needed to check. He worked with facts, always had, not on assumptions. And early this morning he'd set out to find them. He had the clout.

Calling in a favour that had given him access to confidential material, he'd verified those suspicions.

On the day of Flavia's ill-fated birthday party Cinzia's father had already been in worrying financial difficulties, so—as she had this lunchtime savagely verified—when he'd taken her aside to gently break the news that their marriage of convenience wouldn't happen, because he'd finally and deeply fallen in love with Sophie, Cinzia had known she had to do something drastic to keep her future marriage to a bottomless money pot on track.

Instructing Filomena to plant the diamond choker in Sophie's luggage and making the subsequent 'discovery' had done the trick. It had been pure spite that had led her to contact the agency. The way she had for the very first time pressed for the actual marriage to take place soon, when up until then she had been as laid-back about taking the plunge as he had been, now made sense.

The di Barsini family were now on the financial rocks. Her earlier denials had been defensive lies. Her father's final ill-advised last throw of the dice— a high-risk investment with borrowed capital—had lost him everything, threatening the imminent public disclosure of bankruptcy. Little wonder Cinzia had finally decided to bite the bullet and press for marriage and an end to their long engagement.

The interview with her today over a lunch neither had eaten had been deeply unpleasant. How he could ever have gone along with the outdated idea of a sterile dynastic marriage with such a creature gave him goosebumps. It might have seemed a sensible tradition at one time, but now it turned his stomach.

Refusing to dwell on the past when the future was

so very important, Ettore swiftly turned his mind to trying to figure out how he could persuade Sophie to forgive him, to try and love him again as she once had done. As he loved her.

The late-afternoon heat was cooling towards a deep amethyst evening as Sophie wandered back to the villa barefoot, over grass studded with fragrant narcissi and the bruised purple buds of wild irises.

Torry was sound asleep in the nursery, tired after another day of new scents and sounds and the exciting discovery that he could almost, with his mother's hands firmly around his round little body, stand on his own two feet.

She would have to change out of the worn old jeans and collarless cambric shirt—of pre-makeover vintage—and make herself respectable. Trig herself up in one of her many elegant little designer dresses for eating her solitary dinner at one end of the vast dining table in the *sala da pranzo* and try to stop willing Ettore to come home. Now. This evening. Not make her wait until tomorrow!

Home to her.

Her stomach flipped, just as if she'd been in a lift that had whooshed her skywards at supersonic speed and dropped her back to earth just as swiftly. She wanted him so badly it made her breathless and giddy just thinking of him and what they could, in time, have together—provided she had the faith and forbearance to change his opinion of her morals.

Reaching the cool interior of the great hall, she paused to let her breathing return to normal. She was wondering if she would ever manage it, when her body still sang from last night's passion, when the housekeeper emerged from the now gathering shadows that led to the staff quarters.

'You had a phone call, *signorina*. English man. The name Tim. You are to contact him. There is some urgency, I think. You have his number? I didn't think to ask.'

'Yes, of course. I'll phone from my room.' A smile. No hint of the sudden sweep of guilt that made her feel really awful. She'd phoned, as promised, on her arrival here, but not since, and she'd said she would. She'd had too much on her mind to remember her promise.

Her room felt over-warm and airless. She left the door open and flung open the windows, gratefully breathing in the cooler breeze before hunting in her purse for the card Tim had given her all that time ago. Clutching it, she sank down on the bed, curled her legs beneath her and punched in his number.

'You okay?' he asked gruffly, as soon as she gave her name. 'I haven't heard a dicky-bird since the day you arrived. You promised to phone again in a couple of days. For all I knew he could have locked you away and lost the key. And Tina's going spare. She blames me for letting that guy drag you and the kid away. Is he treating you okay? From what I saw of him when he collected you and your stuff he looked pretty formidable.'

'We're just fine, and Ettore dotes on Torry. He even—' her face went pink with sheer happiness '—wants me to marry him, and I'm going to tell him I will,' Sophie assured him, her soft mouth curving. 'So tell Tina not to worry. I'll phone her myself and put her mind at rest. I'm sorry,' she breathed, guilt striking again. 'I should have got round to contacting you both before now.'

'So you should be sorry!' Tim came back, trying to sound stern and big-brotherly and failing. 'I'm glad things are working out, if that's what you want, but the olds and Tina have been giving me a hard time. I should have been looking after you and the kid, and they hold me personally responsible for letting some strange guy as good as abduct you!'

Swallowing a giggle—it wasn't funny, and it was good to know that there were people who really cared enough to worry about her, and she hated to think that Tim had been put through the wringer—Sophie said contritely, 'Don't feel like that, Tim. He is my baby's father—what else could I have done in the circumstances? I'll make it right for you, I promise.'

A movement in the open doorway caught her peripheral vision and she swung around, the receiver clamped to her ear, her huge eyes suddenly glitteringly bright.

Ettore! Home at last! She wasn't going to have to endure another night and day before she saw him again!

An ecstatic smile on her face, she turned back to the phone and quickly, quietly, ended the call, promising to contact Tina and rapidly jotting down her old friend's Canadian number before turning back to the man who was the one and only, the love of her life.

But empty space greeted her.

Considerately leaving her in peace to finish her phone call, he'd probably gone to look in on his sleeping son. She'd go and find him and this evening—maybe after dinner, maybe out on the terrace in the moonlight, because she wanted the occasion to be special—she would tell him she would marry him.

She felt indescribably happy. Everything, eventually, would be all right. She just knew it. They were in for the long haul, a lifetime together—plenty of time to convince him she wasn't a thieving little slapper! She was sure, after his tenderness last night, she was already on the way to achieving it.

She was deliberating over whether to change swiftly out of her old grunge and get into one of the exquisite dresses he had provided her with and make herself look a bit more attractive, or to run and find him, like right at this moment, when the phone rang.

After only a moment's hesitation she snatched it up and gave the number in muddled Italian, her breath catching when her *bête noir* said with sugary venom, 'Cinzia di Barsini here. I just wondered if you're proud of yourself. Right now I imagine you are. It is what you would call a red letter day for you, yes? By using the oldest trick in the book you've managed to break up an engaged couple who were made for each other.'

Sickened by the poisonous tone of the woman she just knew had set her up all that time ago, Sophie was tempted to replace the receiver. But the news that Ettore hadn't been the free man she'd imagined him to be, had actually still been engaged to marry the other woman, had left her bed this morning to drive to Florence to break the engagement off and confess he'd asked his son's mother to marry him, left her stunned into keeping her ear glued to the phone in shattered, sickly, perverse fascination.

'But don't be too pleased with yourself,' the hated voice purred. 'He's only marrying you for the kid's sake—he's got more honour than you could ever dream of. You've trapped him, and he hates that. And he'll end up hating you for it. When we said our goodbyes today he looked as if he already did. I've never seen the poor darling look so hopeless. It's me he's always wanted to marry. And he's ashamed of you—well, who wouldn't be? He won't be faithful—or haven't you figured that out yet? He'll play away. A common little thing like you hasn't got what it takes to satisfy such a highly sexed sophisticated man. The people in our circle won't even pity you—they'll simply laugh at you—'

Sophie slid the receiver home with shaking fingers. Everything that vile woman had said was poisonously hateful.

But sickeningly true.

CHAPTER TEN

ETTORE knotted the plain dark blue tie that added the final sober touch to his charcoal shirt and narrow-fitting black trousers. The reflection that stared back at him from the pier glass was unrelievedly sombre. He looked as if he were about to attend a funeral. That was his painfully wry thought as he went down to dinner.

The funeral of his hopes.

He had never felt less like eating, but the motions had to be gone through. Italians might be famed for their volatile natures, but Severinis never wore their hearts on their sleeves. Hurts must be kept inside. Appearances were to be maintained.

Tonight he had to offer her her freedom.

While he lived he would never forget the moment when every last one of his hopes had died. Not screaming and fighting, but with the dark still silence of helpless inevitability.

His heart had been swollen with love for his enchanting Sophie, the mother of his son, pounding with excited anticipation, with the intoxicating memory of her passion and sweetness of the night before, and he'd gone to her room to begin the process of making amends, of persuading her that he could be worthy of her love.

She'd been curled up on her bed—the scene of the sheer ecstasy he had only ever found with her, of so much wonder. In his absence she'd reverted to the type of clothes she was obviously comfortable with, disdaining designer labels. She'd been speaking to the guy she had moved in with before he'd forced her to leave him.

His already stricken conscience had been left writhing in mortal agony as he'd heard her heartfelt, 'Don't feel like that, Tim. He is my baby's father— what else could I have done in the circumstances? I'll make it right for you, I promise.'

How she aimed to do that propelled a spear of agonising jealousy straight into his heart. But that wasn't the issue. The only issue was the way he had behaved.

He'd had no right to make demands. The circumstances she'd talked about had given her no option but to do as he said. He'd had no right to drag her away from her country, her friends, the man she had moved in with—the man she loved? No right to try to stamp her with his own standards—expensive designer gear, top-of-the-range accessories and make-up—turning her into his idea of how the mother of his son should present herself. And he'd thought the very worst of her, dismissing her protestations of innocence as so much bluster. Even when he'd started to have his suspicions about Cinzia, in his arrogance he hadn't shared them with her.

He'd been piling wrong on unforgivable wrong.

She was already in the dining room. His face set— he refused to let his pain show in his eyes—he greeted her coolly, took his place opposite her, at the far end of a table that could comfortably seat twenty, and shook out his napkin.

Tonight she looked heartbreakingly beautiful. All flags flying. Because she knew it was expected of her? Gone were the comfortable old casuals she would have worn from choice. Dressed now in Milan's finest. Something in silky material in a soft amethyst shade that deepened the colour of her clear grey eyes, left her arms bare and dipped discreetly between those magnificent breasts.

Smartly he diverted his attention to the food that had just been served to him, ignoring the wine. His tongue would not be loosened. By his behaviour, his crass mistrust, he had forfeited any right to speak of his love, to beg for a second chance.

Sophie chewed something she couldn't for the life of her swallow because her throat had closed up. Ettore looked so austere, his strikingly handsome, lean, dark features forbidding. The sombreness of the clothes he was wearing seemed very fitting, perfect for the doomy occasion.

And for that she had to be thankful, she supposed, as tears pricked behind her eyes. If he'd shown the slightest, the very slightest hint that he remembered what they'd shared last night—valued it as something blissfully special—the tiniest hint of warmth, she would have been completely undone, unable to get through what she knew had to come next.

After she'd put the phone down on Cinzia she'd been in a state of shock, all thoughts of finding Ettore vanished. Sitting on the edge of the bed, she'd gradually pulled her tumultuous thoughts into some kind of order.

Ettore was nuts about his son, so he'd gritted his teeth and offered to marry her to legitimise their child. She'd said no. The part of him that craved his high status, beautiful and wealthy fiancée would have been relieved, even though duty told him otherwise.

This morning he must have woken up to horror. He'd betrayed the woman he really wanted as his wife not once, but twice. He'd fled to her side, his sense of honour making him confess, end the engagement, because he had a duty to his son and his son's mother had welcomed him to her bed with huge hunger. It looked like she had changed her mind about marriage.

No wonder he looked as if the light had gone out on his life, Sophie agonised as she took a huge swig of wine to help the obstruction in her mouth down her throat. And it was mostly her fault. Somehow she was going to have to make it right.

As her plate was taken away and another put in its place she leant back in her chair. She couldn't even look at what had been served, much less make another abortive attempt to eat.

Quietly dismissing the maid, Ettore rose to his feet. Six foot plus of sexual dynamite.

'As neither of us appears to be hungry, I suggest we take coffee outside.'

Bereft of speech, Sophie stumbled to her feet, her stomach going into freefall, then recovering itself somewhere back around her throat.

Crunch time. And she would just have to bear it. Because she loved him far more than her life and she wanted him to be happy.

Needed to know he was happy, living the charmed life he and Cinzia had mapped out for themselves, not a life forced on him.

She had to lie as she'd never lied before in the whole of her life. Tell him that last night had meant nothing. She still wouldn't marry him. Swear that she and Torry would melt discreetly away, that he could see the little boy whenever he felt he wanted to, and urge him to assure Cinzia that she, Sophie, would never intrude or make demands of any kind—would be unheard, invisible. If the other woman had been as gutted by the ending of her engagement as she had sounded she could surely be persuaded to overlook his infidelity, regard it as a meaningless fling that would never be repeated.

Coffee was waiting for them. Set out on the table where, this morning, she, Torry and Minette had breakfasted in sunlight. She had been so happy then.

'Won't you sit?'

A lump the size of a house in her throat now, Sophie sat in the chair he was holding out for her with chilling politeness. He had spoken to her, but she knew from the cool distance of his voice, the rigid line of his powerful shoulders, that he had shut her out.

He would be feeling pretty disgusted with himself. Giving in to base animal lust wasn't exactly an admirable trait, one that he could be proud of, but her mistake—forgetting to take her contraceptive pill which, scattily, she'd thought she was only taking to regulate her periods—had meant that he was now looking at a very different future with a very different woman than the one he'd hoped for.

'Are you cold?' The slender hand that lifted the chased silver coffee pot was shaking, Ettore noted with aching sympathy as he sat opposite her. Well out of touching distance. He wasn't sure he could resist reaching out for her if they were closer.

'I'm fine.' She passed his cup, pushing it over the surface of the table. To her own mortification she knew she'd sounded as if she were being strangled. In the dusky light, silvered by starshine, his features were bleak. He looked exactly what he was: a man who had committed himself to stern duty. She could put it off no longer. She had to set him free to be with the woman who'd vowed they were meant for each other. She loved him so and couldn't bear to think she had ruined his life.

She took a shaky breath, willing her heavily beating heart to slow down, her mouth to stop wobbling. Until those two feats were accomplished she wouldn't be able to say her piece and sound determined and practical, glad to cut all ties with him save those of a shared child.

'You don't look it.' She looked on the verge of tears. The aftermath of her earlier conversation with the guy she'd wanted to live with? A fraught conversation that had doubtless reminded her of the life she and the Tim guy had planned together? That she'd made love with him last night wasn't something he'd hold against her. He wasn't into double standards.

Throughout his long engagement to Cinzia di Barsini he'd been free to take a mistress, with his fiancée's tacit agreement, because in their circles such arrangements were totally acceptable. It was a freedom he had, until finding Sophie, availed himself of on only a couple of utterly forgettable occasions.

'I won't keep you long,' he imparted heavily. 'Out

here we are guaranteed privacy. Do say if you're cold. I'll fetch a wrap.' All he craved was the liberty to take her in his arms and warm her body with his, to hold her, care for her, treasure her.

She shook her head, and was gearing herself up to say her piece when he knocked the words right out of her head with a taut, 'You are free to leave as soon as you wish to. I was wrong to insist that you left your homeland. You may take Torry and return to England, if that is your wish. Naturally I insist on reasonable access, and I will support him, and you, financially. However—' His long fingers curled round his cup, the knuckles tightening until they showed white beneath the tanned skin. 'I would like to think of you—and my son—living within reach of the open countryside and clean air. I will make the necessary funds available to facilitate such a move.'

'There's no need to buy me off!' Heat returned to Sophie's cold-as-stone body with a fiery rush. So much for her noble intentions of setting him free to be with his wonderful, socially acceptable Cinzia! He had taken matters into his own hands—decided that his broken engagement was too high a price to pay for his son.

Forgetting that until last night she would have given everything to hear the words he'd just spoken, if only to save herself from the pain of living with a man who would never love her, she struggled to get to her feet—but subsided with a thump as he put in swiftly, 'You are owed, Sophie. There's no question of my buying you off.' And then, despising himself utterly for his shaming weakness he added, 'There is another option. My offer of marriage still stands.'

Sophie felt as if her heart had exploded with pain, her face whitening as she struggled for breath. She'd spent most of the day soppy with happiness, convinced they could have a great life together. Convinced that accepting his one-off proposal of marriage was right for both of them. Living in a silly girlie dream. She had believed he was a free man. But he was not.

She lifted her eyes to his and her mouth trembled. He was putting his future in her hands and she had never loved him more.

Say the word and he'd go through with it. His sense of honour would see to that. It had already made him remind her of that second option. It must have taken a great deal of courage to get the words out.

She couldn't and wouldn't do that to him.

Gaining her feet took a monumental effort. Schooling her voice to an even level took even more, as she managed, 'May I leave the arrangements for our flight with you? Bearing in mind I'd like to leave with Torry as soon as possible.'

CHAPTER ELEVEN

SPRING was at last making a tentative appearance in England, but as yet it hadn't made any noticeable impression on the grey London street where Sophie lived with that blond guy.

Lived with her lover, Ettore growled savagely at himself. Just face it!

The house was depressing, just as he remembered it. Borderline seedy. The sooner Sophie and his son moved into something far more salubrious the better.

The lover would go with them?

Probably.

The thought of the other guy being around his son twenty-four-seven when he, his father, would have to make an appointment to see his own flesh and blood made him want to kick holes in brick walls! But it was what Sophie had chosen—what she wanted.

An iron band of tension tightened around his temples as he thrust back his shoulders and mounted the steps.

A fortnight wasn't a suspiciously short length of time, was it? Of course not. Not like him to be unsure of anything. *Inferno!* He had every right to drop by and see his own son! Two weeks was already too long.

Besides, there was the matter of the financial settlement, her signature on the document in his briefcase. Something his lawyers could have handled, but which he preferred to do himself.

Why? Scrub the excuses he'd come up with: the saving of time, personally making sure she understood the legalities. He ached to see her, that was why. Not that it would show. He wouldn't let it.

His mouth hardened as he thrust open the street door.

And it tightened until he felt his jaw might snap in two as the guy—Tim, she'd called him—clattered down the stairs.

'What do you want?' Tim was the first to break the charged silence, the note of belligerence stark in the musty air.

The kid's father, Tim recognised in minor panic. All perfectly groomed, six-foot-plus of expensive Italian tailoring, harsh won't-give-an-inch features. Rich as Croesus, power-mad.

Remembering the endless ear-bashing he'd got from Tina and his parents when he'd let this bastard drag Sophie and her kid away that first time, he was torn. Should he stay around to make sure it didn't happen again, and then be back late from his lunch-break—not a good idea for a new manager on probation?

He fabricated with breathless speed, off the top of his head, 'If you've come to see Sophie, she's out with the kid. They'll be gone all day. I'll take a message. If you want access in the future, you'd better make an appointment.'

He pulled back his thin shoulders, horribly conscious of the Italian's aura of bred-in-the-bone dominance, his obvious physical superiority, and instinc-

tively aware that this man wouldn't stand idly by
while he received a mouthful of what he would see
as abuse from a mere nobody. He had to force himself to find enough bottle to mumble, 'Why don't you
leave her alone? You've done enough damage. She
won't say what you did, but you've only got to look
at her to know you put her through the wringer.
You've hurt her enough already. So stay clear!'

And he scarpered before the killing look in those
black eyes could be translated into physical action,
congratulating himself that the Italian would now
make tracks, believing Sophie was out with the kid.

The other man had been lying, Ettore decided
without rancour. Where the shabby old pram had
once stood there was now a secondhand-looking
buggy. Tim had been protecting his Sophie. Ettore
understood the feeling. But protecting her from
what?

Sophie had what she wanted, he told himself acidly. She'd had the choice. She'd freely chosen this
gangly chap in his off-the-peg blue suit, blond hair
gelled in place, with his open, honest face, and this
seedy house, over him and the life of luxury he had
told her was hers for the taking. He'd asked himself
why on too many occasions to count, and had shamingly come up with the same answer every time.

She'd once heatedly told him that Tim had believed in her innocence implicitly, no question.
While he had named her thief and liar.

Her choice, though it had hurt like hell and still
did, made sense. He, with his pride, arrogance and
distrust, had forfeited any right to expect her love.

Just punishment. No arguing with that, he reminded himself heavily.

Unused to and despising such negative thoughts, bordering on self-pity, Ettore took the stairs two at a time. When she'd chosen to return to England he'd been too gutted to do anything other than make the arrangements with icy, silent efficiency. Neglecting to tell her of the suspicions that had now been verified by a cornered Cinzia.

Time to put that right. She might not want to see him, but he owed her that much. An apology. Time to let her know of the generous settlement that would enable her and his son to leave this dump and make a decent life.

Then maybe his conscience would lie easy. Though his heart never would.

Sophie put Torry down in his cot, scarcely daring to breathe, and gently covered him with a soft blanket, mentally crossing her fingers. He did, at long last, look as if he might actually fall asleep. Her back and arms ached from carrying him round all morning and most of the night as she tried to comfort her fractious baby.

The poor little darling was teething again, if the angry red smudge on one cheek was anything to go by. She pushed her mussed hair back off her face, and her eyes momentarily lost their now habitual bruised, punished look, her mouth curving in a smile that for once wasn't forced as she watched him fall asleep.

Coffee was the only thought in her head as she

walked with exaggerated, silent care into the tiny kitchen. Hot, black, and very, very strong.

She'd been up with Torry most of the night, rubbing gel into his poor inflamed gums, rocking him against her shoulder, because whenever she put him down he started to cry again and she didn't want Tim's rest to be disturbed. He'd been so good to them, insisting they stay until she'd got their future sorted out.

Tim, bless him, hadn't turned a hair when she and Torry had landed on his doorstep a fortnight ago. She'd had nowhere else to go.

As she cradled the mug of scalding coffee in both hands and ambled into the sitting room she told herself that things were looking up, even if her heart still wept and told her differently.

In another fortnight's time Tim's parents would be returning from their visit to Tina and their son-in-law in Canada, and they were pressing her to make a home temporarily with them, in their bungalow on the outskirts of a tiny picture-postcard Herefordshire village.

'Basil and I talked it over,' Enid Dunmore had stated only a couple of days ago. 'There's a nice guest room that's rarely used, and you've always been like one of the family—you know that, Sophie dear. It will be healthier for you and baby Torry, and besides, you must make sure the father supports you financially. I gather he's wickedly wealthy. So you shouldn't have to worry about making a living for you and the baby. I don't see why he shouldn't buy a property for you—somewhere near to us, where we can help out with babysitting and generally make ourselves useful. Being a single parent can't be easy. So until you can get things sorted out you must stay with us.'

Curling up on the long leather sofa, Sophie sipped the hot brew and pondered Enid's suggestion. Short on family—her stepmother and sister wouldn't shed a tear if she disappeared off the face of the earth tomorrow—it would be nice for Torry to have adoptive grandparents close by. The Dunmores had always been closer to her than her own dysfunctional family. But she would like to work again, when Torry was old enough for nursery school. She wanted to be independent, and not have to rely on handouts from Ettore even if she was entitled.

And she hadn't given a thought to Ettore's offer of financial support. When she thought of him at all—which, despite all her good intentions, she found herself doing a trillion times a day—it was to wonder if his engagement to Cinzia was back on again. If he was happy, with his life going the way he wanted. If his high-status woman had decided to overlook his fall from grace—bedding someone no better than a peasant—and whether he'd passed on the message that she, Sophie, wouldn't make waves, would stay well out of their lives.

When the doorbell rang—long, loud and insistent—she stumbled groggily to her feet, fighting to keep her leaden eyelids open. The slightest sound could wake Torry, and the poor little poppet needed his sleep.

Tim. It had to be. Forgotten something? Forgotten his door key, too, by the sound of it! He'd taken to coming back at lunchtime for a sandwich, instead of piling into the burger bar across the road from where he worked. Checking she was okay, he said. Even though she'd told him she was fine. He'd be late back now…

Flinging the door open, prepared for Tim to rush past her, all gangly legs and arms, and retrieve whatever he'd forgotten, she found herself staring up into that beloved, starkly handsome, starkly unsmiling face. Her clucky smile vanished.

For a moment she held his suddenly frowning gaze and then her stricken eyes fell. So soon. She hadn't expected this. Didn't know if she could handle it.

'If you've come to see Torry—I'm afraid he's asleep,' she gabbled thinly, clutching at the edge of the door as if to bar his entrance. She wanted to see him so badly it frightened her. And she wanted him to disappear, to save her the savage pain of being within touching distance, and that frightened her too, because she wanted to keep him with her always and that couldn't happen.

She wasn't yet strong enough to deal with this, she thought in acute misery as he strode past her into the centre of the room and laid his briefcase on the low coffee table, nudging aside her half-empty coffee mug and last night's newspaper.

'Then I will see him when he wakes.' His mouth was taut. *Inferno!* What had happened to her? Her face was all huge bruised eyes, pale, trembling mouth, and the defeated droop of her head on the slender stalk of her neck gave her the look of a woman who'd been put through hell.

Down to him, so her lover had accused. Nonsense!

She'd chosen freely to return to this dreary place, to live with her callow lover.

A sudden thought turned the blood in his veins to ice. 'Is my son ill?' he demanded harshly. It was the only viable reason he could supply for the utterly beaten way she looked.

A powerful surge of adrenalin flooded his bloodstream. He was already mentally organising his precious son's immediate removal to a private clinic, the attendance of the best paediatrician procurable.

The ensuing wave of bone-shaking relief weakened him when she stated dully, 'Torry's fit and well. He's teething again. That's all. He was awake most of the night, but he's sleeping peacefully now.'

Weakened him, but only for that panic-filled moment. Back in control, he ordered, 'Sit down. Before you fall over,' he added censoriously. Then, with icy cool, 'My business is principally with you.'

Sophie sank onto the sofa. The jelly-like state of her legs gave her no other option. He would see his son before he left, he'd stated, as was his right. When he woke. But after such a restless night Torry might sleep for hours! How would she endure it?

He joined her, the long fingers of his strong, beautifully crafted hands clicking open his slim leather briefcase. Remembering the way those hands had caressed her body made her swallow convulsively, sweat suddenly beading her short upper lip.

Not turning his dark head to her, he extracted a sheet of closely typed, heavy and ornately headed paper. His voice was clipped and formal as he explained, 'This document sets out the terms of your settlement. A lump sum for the purchase of a suitable home, and monthly payments to ensure you and my son want for nothing. It also sets out my rights. To see my son at regular, mutually convenient times, and later, when he reaches school age, to have him spend his holidays with me in Italy. There is much he will need to learn about his heritage. I have already signed in the presence of my lawyer, as you will see...'

His words were drowned out in the thunder of blood in her ears. This was how it was going to have to be. Seeing him at regular intervals, the pain of loving him savagely intensifying every time, and as the years went by watching the growing closeness between father and son, never able to be part of it.

She felt the coolness of the paper against her hands and struggled to pull herself together. She had known how it must be, she thought rawly. Now all she had to do was accept it. Put up with it and stop behaving like a fool.

Welcome to the real world, Sophie Lang!

Glancing down at the document—she supposed she was meant to sign it too—her eyes widened with horror at the size of the lump sum stated. Buy a suitable home? She could buy a couple of palaces with that amount, and still have some left over!

The rest of the type blurred beneath her suddenly hazy eyes.

'I don't need that much—'

Tearing his masochistic gaze from devouring her enchanting profile, Ettore bunched his hands into fists to stop them reaching for her, holding her to his heavily beating heart, keeping her there always, close to him, caring for her, loving her.

'What you do need is a massive dose of common sense,' he got out gruffly, hating to see her so pale and tired, as if all the life had been drained from her. 'You're obviously not taking proper care of yourself. You need to, for my son's sake. You look a wreck.'

The moment the brutal words were out he deeply regretted them. *Madonna diavola!* Her soft mouth was quivering now, those long blonde-tipped lashes fluttering, to keep back the moisture that threatened to spill down her marble-pale cheeks.

Fighting the instinctive need to enfold her in his arms, to comfort her, take back his words, tell her that she would always be heart-wrenchingly beautiful in his eyes, he took his fountain pen from the brief-case, uncapped it and slid it over the table towards her.

'If you will sign? The funds will be immediately available to you. I will need your bank details, of course. And I will have a copy of this document sent to you in a day or two.'

Then he would be out of here. It had been too soon—much too soon. This visit had been a crass mistake. He should have left everything in the hands of his lawyers. He had wanted to see her, had thought of nothing else since the day she had been driven to the airport. He'd thought he could handle it. But he couldn't. For the first time in his life he was up against something he couldn't cope with.

'Of course. Excuse me. Bank details,' she squawked.

Fired by the need to remove herself before she started howling her eyes out, Sophie shot to her feet and headed on unsteady limbs for the relative privacy of the kitchen, ignoring the pen.

Leaning against the sink, she let the tears she'd desperately held back gush. She knuckled her hands against her teeth to stifle the sobs that were building painfully in her throat. Once he had called her beautiful. Now she was a wreck. Well, she knew that, didn't she?

Too many sleepless nights—and only one of them down to a restless teething baby. Long sleepless hours tossing and turning in her brick-hard narrow bed, thinking of Ettore, missing him with every fibre of her body and soul. And she was unable to do more than pick at her food; the strain of trying to keep up a cheerful façade around her baby and Tim was wearing her down.

Vowing to pull herself together, to make herself get on with it and count her many blessings, she scrubbed her eyes with a fistful of kitchen roll and all but leapt out of her skin as that deep, velvety voice demanded, 'Why do you weep? Is Tim—' the name stuck in his craw but he got it out '—ill-treating you? If he is—'

The incisive warning of danger was a definite wake-up call. Turning quickly, her heart racing, she plastered what she hoped would pass for an incredulous smile on her mouth and tried for lightness. 'Of course not! Tim's been absolutely wonderful. He wouldn't ill treat a fly!' And trembled inside because filling the doorway, so gorgeous, so dark, so shiver-makingly brooding, he overpowered her senses. She had to make herself get over this, so she asked. 'And you? Have you got what you wanted? How is Cinzia?'

This was hurting, but she had to know. After that phone conversation with his jilted fiancée she had known that her own hopes of future happiness with this man were pretty well non-existent, so she really hadn't sacrificed anything, had she? 'Has she forgiven you?' she burbled, trying to sound sympathetic and hopeful at the same time.

'You talk in riddles. But on the subject of Cinzia there are things I have to tell you.' He stood aside, an imperious brow lifting. 'Come—this is not a pleasant place to be. I have a belated apology to make.'

About what? was Sophie's hectic question as she took a reluctant step towards him. Even if his moral behaviour had been decidedly iffy, he had been fair. He had offered to marry her, even breaking off with his high-status longstanding fiancée when he'd believed she might change her mind and grab his offer with both hands. And on her second refusal he had made eye-popping sums of money available to her. He'd even given up on his stated intention of being around full time for his son. She had to give him credit for that.

He didn't touch her as she slid past him in the doorway, although every inch of her heatedly wished he would—just one last time. She was like an addict, needing a fix regardless of the danger, she decided, loathing her weakness. He did that to her—always had done. Made her desire him, intoxicating every sense. Her awareness of him was sheer torture. And there were flags of bright colour on her pale cheeks as a brusque hand gesture motioned her to the sofa.

His dramatically handsome features had never looked so grim, and his velvet-smooth voice had never sounded so abrasive as he sat beside her, angled into the corner, and stated, 'From things said—small, unconnected pieces of information—I began to suspect I had misjudged you in the matter of the theft.'

'Well, bully for you!' Her sarcasm was edged with apathy. How she'd once craved to hear those words from him, the smallest inkling that he believed her. But that had been in the past. Now they didn't matter a toss.

Ettore gritted his teeth. He supposed he deserved that. That and much more punishment. He watched her swipe a lock of that glorious blonde hair away from her face and ploughed on, hating what he'd discovered, hating himself even more for ever believing the accusation of theft for a single moment.

'I had to have them confirmed before I spoke to you. I work with facts, not suppositions. You will remember the morning I left you early to drive to Florence?'

Sophie buttoned her lips and flatly refused to answer that! Of course she remembered! How could she forget how stupidly happy she'd been, how sure they could make marriage work? She didn't want to remember, but how the heck was she supposed to forget! She twisted her hands together in her lap and gave him a stubborn glare.

'I'll take that as a yes, shall I?' This was proving to be even more difficult than he'd imagined. 'Faced with what I had been able to put together, Cinzia confessed to having instructed her personal maid to put the diamond choker in your suitcase.'

He owed her this apology, but it would be truncated. Of necessity. He shouldn't have come. He needed out. As in right now. Loving her more than he'd believed possible, it was not a good idea to be here with her alone. It tried his mental and physical control to its outer limits.

It was Tim she wanted. Not him, he reminded himself with stark vehemence.

'I'm deeply sorry for doubting you.' He put the pen back in her hands and edged the document towards her.

She immediately dropped the pen back on the table. Ettore sighed edgily. A heavily voiced minimal apology wasn't good enough. He owed her more than that.

Biting the bullet, he went on flatly, 'My only defence is that, as I said, I always deal with facts—that is the way my mind works. The banker in me, I guess!' His feeble attempt at humour made no impression. He drew in a heavy breath and pressed on. 'When Cinzia first made that accusation I refused to believe a word of it. When the jewel was discovered in your suitcase I still did not want to believe. But it was a fact. I couldn't pretend any differently. And, wrongly, I translated your silence when the proof was revealed as guilt, though now I can understand you were in shock.'

An anger that was as unexpected as it was fierce and swift took hold of her. She recognised it as a form of release from the web of helpless yearning she had been unable to shake off ever since she'd left Tuscany, and accordingly she let rip.

'So a stilted apology for something that was unforgivable makes everything all right, does it?' Sophie snapped, hands gripping her hands, as if she had every intention of breaking all her own fingers. 'I didn't know the wretched woman and she didn't know me—yet she got me thrown out of your sister's home in disgrace, humiliated, and you made sure I was blacklisted by the agency! And you—' Tears of rage glittered in her eyes. 'You still want to marry such a creature, even knowing what she's capable of! Well, I hope you'll be very happy!' And ignominiously she burst into tears.

Then found her clenched hands being gently prised apart, Ettore's long fingers stroking hers. 'Please don't cry.' He sounded hoarse.

'I can if I want to!' she howled, deep in the grip of childish fury. Sick of being a martyr, she yelled, 'She's deranged and spiteful, but she's got a top-notch pedigree and loads of money and mixes in the right circles—that's why you want to marry her! You don't love her, only what she stands for. If you did you wouldn't go around sleeping with the nearest willing female! And I really don't know how I can love such a creep!'

She snapped her mouth shut, her face turning bright crimson as she wished she could claw the revealing words back, and shrivelled in horrified silence as his fingers stilled on hers, then tightened, his voice rough round the edges as he commanded softly, 'Say that again.'

CHAPTER TWELVE

HER face burning with humiliation, Sophie wished the floor would open up and swallow her. What had she gone and said that for? What in heaven's name had possessed her? Too much raw emotion, she supposed, shrivelling up inside.

Those intelligent black eyes of his pierced her. He could see straight through her, and it made her feel so vulnerable and utterly, utterly stupid.

'Just forget it—'

As a response to his command it was totally pathetic, but the best she could think of right now. Somehow she had to put the lid on that line of questioning. Somehow!

Scrambling awkwardly to her feet, she avoided those too clever eyes and babbled, 'You'd like coffee while you're waiting? Or you could go and come back later, when Torry's awake, and—'

'Like an elephant, I never forget.' Two firm hands had moved to her waist, depositing her back on the sofa rather closer to him than she thought she could reasonably be expected to bear. Her heart was beating fast enough to choke her, and she knew her face was still glowing like a red traffic light.

She'd blurted something he couldn't possibly want to know, so why couldn't he brush it aside as she wanted him to? His hands were still clamped around her waist and beneath them her flesh burned and trembled, the old familiar spiral of desire squirming around her pelvis. Like everything else about her, she decided, her instinctive reaction to this one man was pathetic, and there was nothing she could do about it.

She had to say something to explain that verbal slip-up. Anything! Would *Only joking!* do? But her mouth had run dry. Her breath catching, she tried to moisten her lips with the tip of her tongue and risked a look at him between the tumbled, all-over-the-place wild strands of her hair.

He looked as if she'd just struck his face. Hurt, with a definite underlying layer of anger—or was that distaste? Of course, he would find her blurted admission about as welcome as a bad smell!

Back on the magical island, when she had first fallen fathoms-deep in love with him, they'd spoken words of love. He because it had prettied up raging animal lust, had been part of the game he must have played dozens of times in his privileged, sophisticated life. Doubtless he would have reasoned that she was playing the same game and knew the rules. And now her stupid words had alerted him to the fact that she'd meant it, and still loved him despite everything that had happened.

As a sophisticated member of the cream of Italian society he would think she was exactly what she was. An inexperienced fool whose natural habitat was cloud cuckoo land! Oh, why had she opened her big mouth and complicated an already fraught relationship?

'What are you trying to do, Sophie?' His hands dropped away. Was she deliberately trying to hurt him? Reject his offer of love and opt to return to her English lover, then turn round and torment him, talking of love? 'I want an answer,' he stated grittily.

She stole another upward glance, and the 'only joking' quip died in her throat. His beautiful mouth was drawn in a tight line, but the dark pools of his eyes were strangely vulnerable. And dismay claimed her when he pointed out the obvious.

'You chose to leave me and return to your lover. Now you tell me the very thing I've longed to hear! Payback time for past wrongs?'

Longed to hear? As if! Her expressive features clouded. If she tried to get to her feet and walk away he would pin her down again. Compromising, she shuffled to the far end of the sofa and pushed out, 'Tim's not my lover and never has been. He took me in out of the goodness of his heart. Torry and I had nowhere else to go. I've known him since I was about seven years old; he's my best friend's brother. And why on earth would you 'long' to hear me say I loved you? To boost your ego? I don't think it needs it, do you? It's already six times as big as a house.'

Brushing the insult aside, Ettore let his eyes track over her bristling figure, dressed in a thick check shirt and an old pair of jeans. He flinched inside as he recalled how she'd left everything he'd bought her behind at the villa. She'd wanted no reminders of him.

'Then why did you indulge in that long, cosy conversation when you believed me to be absent?' he questioned, his features rawly defined as he recalled the moment when all his hopes had died. 'A conversation that included your protestations that as I was your baby's father you had no choice but to agree to my demands but that you'd make everything all right. For him. Do you know how that made me feel? Two inches tall!'

About to yell *Good!*, Sophie swallowed the word and tipped her head on one side. Everything was beginning to look strangely out of kilter. In view of what she'd learned from his jilted fiancée, nothing made sense. She asked 'Why?'

'Why do you think?' he shot at her with scorn as he got restlessly to his feet.

Pacing the sparsely furnished room, he came to an abrupt halt in front of the window, with its uninspiring view of dustbins. 'I hate reminding myself, but I'd truly given you no option but to dance to my tune. Right from the beginning, still uneasily believing you were light-fingered, I had every intention of marrying you for our son's sake. My own, too,' he confessed raggedly. 'I was still crazy for you. Still in love with you, if I'm going to be completely honest. Though at that time I didn't admit it to myself.'

He stuffed his hands in the pockets of his immaculately tailored trousers and turned his back on her, taking, so it seemed, an inordinate interest in the neighbourhood dustbins. 'That telephone conversation, at least the part I overheard, brought home to me how unfair I was being. I did the only thing I could do. I offered you the choice of marrying me or returning here—to him. Loving you, I wanted—still want—you to be happy.'

Sophie's stomach looped the loop. Pressing her fingertips to her overheated temples, she tried to calm the churning muddle that passed for her mind and heaved herself onto her feet.

Crossing the room to stand directly behind him, wincing at the prospect of talking to that rigid broad back and deciding that she now knew exactly how Alice must have felt when she wandered into Wonderland, she swiftly inserted herself between him and the windowframe.

He didn't step back, away from her, but she did hear the ragged tug of his indrawn breath. She hadn't been hearing things, she staunchly impressed on herself. She had heard him say he loved her. But she didn't understand. It was driving her crazy!

He looked so remote, too. Clearly he wasn't into soul-baring. Typical man! How could he drop such an unexpected bombshell and then, in that superior male fashion, decide that he owed her no further explanation!

'Tim only phoned to find out if I was okay,' she bristled up at his tough-as-rock features. 'I'd promised to keep him up to speed but I forgot. And he was getting a load of hassle from his parents and my best friend—his sister—for allowing me to be what they'd decided was as good as kidnapped! So I was putting his mind at rest, promising to contact his folks and put the record straight, wasn't I?' she demanded fiercely, noting that not by so much as a flicker of an eyelash did he register that he was taking in a word she said. 'And because of a handful of overheard words you decided to give me and Torry our marching orders!'

Ettore took a backward step, putting space between them. Being this close to her was a severe strain on his self-control.

He had told her how he felt, but for all the good it had done he might have been reciting a chunk of the telephone directory. She had said nothing to explain her earlier blurted and—as he now had to deflatedly accept—patently untrue protestation of love. 'I did no such thing. I offered to marry you,' he reminded her tonelessly. 'You chose to turn me down.'

A response at last! But totally frustrating! Sophie wanted to shake him! Stepping closer—he wasn't going to back out of this—her breasts heaving with agitation, she shot out, 'I had no option, did I? I'd just had the lovely Cinzia bending my ear, accusing me of breaking up your beautiful longstanding engagement only that very morning. Pressing home the fact that you and she were the perfect couple but you felt duty-bound to marry me because I'd had your baby!'

She dragged in a heaving breath, horribly aware that she was in danger of losing it altogether—breaking down into a heap of frustrated misery. Because although he'd said he loved her he was obviously uninterested in sorting out the tangled strands of this messy eternal triangle. 'I was obviously standing in the way of your future happiness with your so-perfect life partner, so what else could I do?'

Ettore's brain clicked into gear. His heart took wing. His darling's head was downbent now, and a single silvery tear was trickling down the petal-soft skin of her cheek towards the corner of her lush, tremulous mouth. Taking immediate advantage of her obviously highly emotional state, he gathered her into his arms, one hand driving up to hold her head against his rapidly beating heart.

'Forget Cinzia. Put the wretched woman right out of your mind. You are the only woman I've ever truly loved,' he vowed thickly. 'Believe me.'

Sophie's heart jumped. She wanted to believe him with a desperation that was truly frightening. Wanted to wriggle ever closer to that strong male body, to be held, to be safe.

But the danger that she might be led again on the path to a fool's paradise and end up even more hurt, if that were possible, had her muttering against his perfectly tailored jacket, 'How can I believe that when up until a couple of weeks ago you had been planning to marry her? You've been engaged to the perfect Cinzia since the day you were born!' she exaggerated wildly, attempting to push him away as she became aware of the telltale hardening response of that beautiful male body.

'Virtually,' Ettore agreed with a resigned huff of amusement, and gathered her graceful body close to his again. He would never let her escape him, not while they were both breathing. To post his intentions, he tipped her head back and found her mouth hungrily, and Sophie, all her instincts for self-preservation thrust heedlessly onto the back burner, responded with passionate exuberance, melting into him until, lifting his dark head, he said shakily, 'Now deny that you love me.'

She shook her head, her mouth burning from his kisses, her body aching for more. 'I can't,' she assured him breathily. 'I have loved you since—since the island.'

His dark eyes flared with triumph. 'Me too.' His voice was soft, compellingly so. 'Come, I need to clear your beautiful head of any lingering misconceptions before I take you back to our home in Italy. Because, my only love, whether or not you agree to be my wife, I am never going to let you out of my sight again.' He took both her hands in his and led her to the sofa, releasing fingers that would have clung with a self-deprecating smile. 'If we are touching I will not be responsible for my actions.'

A scenario that set Sophie craving him even more, and her eyes were hazy with her need for him as he stated grimly, 'Don't look at me like that! You will tempt me into forgetting my own name—never mind what I have to say to you.'

'Which is?' Sophie lowered her head demurely, but she was smiling. She had never felt so sure of herself, of her feminine power, as she did at this moment.

Shifting at the other end of the sofa, as if he were experiencing a few anatomical difficulties, Ettore said gruffly, 'You were right. I was betrothed to Cinzia di Barsini when I was barely out of my teens. An arrangement instigated by both sets of parents. Highly advantageous to all parties concerned. The done thing in the circles we moved in. We didn't love each other, but it was a highly suitable match. And neither of us was in the least hurry to set a marriage date.'

His wide shoulders lifted dismissively. Then, his

glittering eyes intent on hers, he vowed, 'Even before I fell in love with you I had decided that on my return to Florence I would terminate the engagement. With honour, I knew it had to be done in person. Regardless of our families' desire, I just knew there had to be more to marriage than the consolidation of two great fortunes. Even so, my falling in love with you—for the first time in my life I understood what love meant—led to a delay in returning to Florence. I told Cinzia that the engagement was off, and confessed I'd found you and that you were my life, on the night of Flavia's party—the first opportunity I had. She tried to talk me out of it—I didn't know at that time that her father was getting into troubled financial waters—and when, finally, I was free, I tried to find you—only to have Flavia tell me that you had gone early to bed because you felt unwell.'

'Cinzia had told me that you and she were shortly to be married,' Sophie put in. 'Your sister confirmed it. I was in shock. I'd never felt so hurt—so betrayed.'

Pale-faced, she shuddered at the memory, and Ettore, good intentions blown in the wind, moved to her side and gathered her in his arms, begging hoarsely, 'Will you ever be able to forgive me for what happened? Will you try? Cinzia did an evil thing. Realising that none of her arguments could sway me, she decided to blacken you in my eyes, brand you a thief. And to my shame I believed the evidence. You were in shock. I had no idea at the time that you'd been told of my engagement. And those two shocks in swift succession had rendered you speechless in your own defence. I am as culpable as she!'

Staunchly resisting the incredibly strong impulse to tell him she would forgive him anything and everything, Sophie got out shakily, 'And you went back to being engaged to her again?'

'Yes.' He looked devastated. 'I was beyond caring!'

He vented what she took to be a blistering oath in his own language.

'As far as I knew at that dreadful time, the woman I'd loved as I'd never loved anyone in my entire life had turned out to be a common thief. She had never loved me, only what she'd thought she could get from me.'

His anguished frown brought his dark brows together. 'Please, my darling, try to understand—I fully intended to return to London when you did and beg you to marry me. I said nothing of this to you, though I ached to do so, believing it was my duty to break off with Cinzia before I made my future intentions to you clear. Therefore I thought—unforgivably— that as I had made no move to give you a pay-off for services rendered on the island, you'd decided to help yourself to what you thought was owed to you. So,' he said with heavy regret, 'I again fell in with everyone's wishes. I was beyond caring about my future. Threw myself into my work to the exclusion of all else. Then I saw you again in London. With our child.'

His thick lashes swept down as he drew in a shuddering breath and Sophie, her heart so full of love it positively ached, raised her hands to run the tips of her fingers over the fascinating planes of his face. 'You frightened me then,' she confessed lovingly. 'I thought you would move heaven and earth to take Torry from me. You still thought I was a thief, and I believed you were responsible for getting me black-listed.'

'That was Cinzia.' He lifted his head and his mouth twisted wryly. 'Against my wishes. And for what it's worth I would never have separated you from our baby. You need each other. But I needed you, too, and threats were the only way I could think of to keep you with me.'

'Don't beat yourself up about it! I'm glad you did.' And to drive her point home she raised her head and touched her lips to his.

His response was masterfully immediate, his mouth devouring hers, his tongue delving with ex-plicit provocation between her lips, setting up a wild conflagration inside her, and it was a long time be-fore Sophie found herself being thrust gently back against the cushions, out of breath and aching for more.

'I'm rapidly losing all control,' Ettore husked, un-der visible strain. 'But when we again make love it's going to be perfect for us.' His firm mouth curved wryly. 'Not in this place, with a hungry baby liable to disturb us at any moment.'

Then, smiling that utterly charismatic smile of his, always to be relied upon to melt every last bone in her body, he softly pushed the tangled strands of her hair away from her face with strong, gentle hands and confided, 'If you remember, I left you at the villa at almost the same time we'd arrived there. I was in haste to end my sterile relationship with Cinzia once and for all, and to tell my mother and my sister that I had a beautiful baby son and intended to marry his beautiful mother.'

Colour slashed over his fabulously sculpted cheekbones as he said tightly, 'Cinzia obviously led you to believe that I had only broken with her on that second time I visited her. Not true. I'd already suspected she was behind the so-called theft for mercenary reasons of her own. I went to confront her. Her father is now facing bankruptcy. It has been coming on for some time, it appears. She was desperate to hold on to me, and my wealth, hence her scheme to blacken your character.'

His eyes intent on her pale features, he grated, 'My suspicions confirmed, I came back to you. Desperate to seek your forgiveness and to ask you again to be my wife, to go down on my knees, if necessary, and beg you to try to love me as I love you. But Cinzia, even though she'd known for some time that our engagement was over, had to put her poison in. I should have expected it. I'd made her confess to her malicious behaviour, and I'd told her exactly what I thought of her. That, together with the bitter knowledge that she would never now happily enjoy the wealth I could provide, must have led her to decide that you, the woman she knew I loved, wouldn't be happy either.'

He swallowed hard, his eyes holding hers. 'You will marry me?'

Suppressing the wicked impulse to say, *Try your very best to persuade me!*, she wrapped her arms around his neck, her heart in her eyes as she breathed,

'Yes, please. Tomorrow. Today. This minute!' and watched sheer joy light his wonderful eyes.

At the same moment they heard Tim's key in the door.

Sophie stilled as her friend clumped into the room, calling out, 'You okay, Soph? I left work early to check—that guy was here—'

He broke off as Ettore rose to his feet, six feet plus of lean, powerful masculinity. For a moment the two men stared at each other. Two splashes of red colour appeared on Tim's winter-pale cheeks and Sophie held her breath, fearing some kind of confrontation in which poor Tim would come off decidedly second best. Then Ettore grinned.

'Thank you for looking after her for me. Sophie's told me how good you've been.' He turned to her, his dark eyes alight. 'Sophie, you have something to tell your friend?'

Liberated from her frozen stance, she leapt to her feet and tucked her hand beneath Ettore's arm, her face radiant. 'We are to be married in—' A questioning look at the man she adored.

'In four weeks,' he supplied. 'I'd like it to be very much sooner, but if the love of my life is to have the wedding she deserves it cannot be arranged much earlier.' He dragged his gaze from his darling's vibrant features and turned again to the younger man. 'We would both be happy if you could attend, as one of Sophie's oldest friends and part of the closest thing she has to a family.'

'And Tina and her husband, if they can manage it. And your parents, of course. They'll be back from Canada by then,' Sophie put in, her euphoria making her babble, and her relief when Tim broke into a huge grin making her feel light-headed.

He shrugged out of his coat and advanced to where they stood, holding out a hand, which Ettore took, returning the younger man's hearty handshake.

'Congrats, and all that!' His blue eyes twinkled at Sophie. 'I seem to have spent the best part of my growing up years looking out for my kid sister and Sophie. Tina's safely married, and now you'll be taking Sophie off my hands! Not to mention getting my folks off my back!'

'In that case,' she put in, beaming from ear to ear, 'you will be happy to give me away!'

'You bet!' He ruffled her hair, grinning. 'It would be an honour. Now, who wants a sandwich? I'm starving. Corned beef? Or corned beef?'

Not waiting for a reply, he made for the kitchen.

Sophie said, 'I'm so happy I could burst! Will you always love me? Tell me how much.'

Ettore gave her an adoring look. 'More than my life, and I have a lifetime to prove it.' He tipped his head on one side. 'Do you hear something?'

'Our son is waking. Come.' She tugged at his hand. 'He has missed you.'

Torry was lying on his back, kicking his legs in the air and gurgling. The moment two doting parents bent over him he bestowed a chortling laugh, and Ettore said proudly, 'He has another tooth!' as if it were the greatest achievement the world had ever seen. He bent to pick him up, hoisting the ecstatic baby in the air and finally bestowing kisses on both chubby cheeks before putting him in Sophie's arms, enfolding them both in his own, and vowing, 'My family—I am the luckiest man in the universe!'

Four weeks later

It had been a perfect wedding. Handing Sophie, still in her wedding finery, into the car, for the drive back to their villa, Ettore carefully tucked what seemed like acres of creamy wild silk around her dainty feet and told her huskily, 'You are so beautiful I can't take my eyes off you!'

He brushed the short filmy veil away from her face and kissed her lingeringly, and Sophie felt her breasts tighten beneath her close-fitting bodice. She placed her hands on his wide, impeccably clad shoulders and murmured breathlessly, 'If you don't stop kissing me we will both disgrace ourselves in public!' and earned herself a wry grin of total understanding as his hands slid from her tiny waist, where they'd been creating havoc, and he drew himself upright.

Driving away at last, to cheers, laughter and the good wishes of the assembled guests, Sophie spared a special backward glance to where Torry, clad in a miniature sailor suit and looking completely adorable, was waving his chubby arms haphazardly in the air, firmly held by his doting grandmother.

'You were right. He won't miss us, just for this one special night,' she admitted, devouring Ettore's startlingly handsome profile.

'Of course. Aren't I always?' He spared her one of his slashing grins. 'Everyone adores him, and Minette will make sure he doesn't get too spoiled or over-excited, and tomorrow she and our son will be driven home to us and our family life will begin.' A tanned hand rested briefly on her knee as he assured her, 'I'm looking forward to that more than I can tell you. And next week the four of us will travel to my villa in the hills behind Amalfi for a summer-long honeymoon. Where Minette will take charge of Torry when we want to be alone. But tonight, my darling, is for the two of us. I need you all to myself.'

Suffused with pleasure and mounting anticipation, Sophie relaxed back in the comfort of the leather upholstery. They would be completely alone. Indeed, all the staff had attended the wedding and would be travelling back in convoy with their baby and his nanny tomorrow.

This night was just for the two of them.

Blissfully, her mind wandered back over the past four weeks. It had been hectic.

Flavia had welcomed her with hugs and kisses. 'I'm so glad that horrid misunderstanding has been cleared up. Oh, that dreadful, evil woman—I could cheerfully strangle her! I knew why the engagement had been arranged, but I never liked the idea. She would have made him miserable. But now we will talk of her no more—just concentrate on how happy you will make Ettore. I have never seen him look happier than he is now—I can tell you, since you left us in those terrible circumstances he turned into a workaholic with such a bleak face!'

Flavia and her husband had insisted that she be married from their home in Florence—insisted, too, that the English contingent stayed there over the wedding period.

Roberto make such a statement, a confession of such destructive deceit, unless he wanted—needed—to clear his conscience?

And if what he said was true… Horror swept through Luc's mind, unlocking a sealed compartment of memories, letting loose the ghosts of intense hurt and fury, images of the damning photos that had driven him to cut Skye Sumner out of his life. Roberto having sex with her, the raspberry birthmark on her thigh, the long blonde hair streaming across the pillow, the distinctive bracelet—three circles of white, rose and yellow-gold—around her wrist.

Her face—the incredibly appealing face with joy always sparkling in vivid blue eyes, the sexy full-lipped mouth that had so many different smiles, the fascinating dimples that came and went—had been hidden by Roberto's head, bent low as though he was whispering something in her ear, but Luc had not doubted it was Skye. The hair, the long lissome legs, the birthmark, the bracelet…

Apart from which, Roberto had backed up the evidence, admitting to a *playboy dalliance* with her, belligerently stating he'd seen Skye first, and why shouldn't he have her when she was willing?

Willing to laugh with Roberto, flirt with him… Luc had dismissed it as just light-hearted fun between them, glad that Skye had felt comfortable with at least one member of his family. He'd actually felt grateful to his brother…until the photos had blasted him into a different reality.

Blinded by the unbearable images, he'd seen no reason to suspect a set-up, no reason to accept Skye's wild denials, no reason to believe her explanation that